"Miss Navaez, I'd like to have a word with you after the others are gone."

Filled with anticipation, Missie waited impatiently for the office to empty. When the door finally closed, she hurried toward Matthew Blaine, longing for the feel of his arms around her, his mouth on hers—

Instead he remained seated, his face a blank.

"Missie, I'm sorry about last night. It won't happen again."

She stood frozen, hearing him out. "It won't work out for us. Dammit, I've been thinking about it all day; the way you stepped right back into your job; your book; this—this damned women's rights business. I've done you a disservice—"

A disservice? He had killed something inside her, that was all!

"Not at all, Matthew," she said in a brittle voice. "You forget, I'm a widow, an emancipated woman. I consider my moral behavior—or lack thereof—my own responsibility. Thank you for a pleasant interlude."

"Missie, you realize this doesn't affect your job. I hope we can continue to see each other on a friendly basis—"

"Of course!" Her smile was too hard, too brilliant. "And I shall not even ask for overtime. That would put me in an entirely different category, wouldn't it?"

Books by
Aola Vandergriff

Wyndspelle
Wyndspelle's Child
The Bell Tower of Wyndspelle
The House of the Dancing Dead
Sisters of Sorrow
Daughters of the Southwind
Daughters of the Wild Country
Daughters of the Far Islands
Daughters of the Opal Skies
Daughters of the Misty Isles
Daughters of the Shining City

Published by
WARNER BOOKS

Daughters of the Shining City

Aola Vandergriff

WARNER BOOKS

A Warner Communications Company

WARNER BOOKS EDITION

Copyright © 1982 by Aola Vandergriff
All rights reserved.

Cover art by Elaine Duillo

Warner Books, Inc.,
75 Rockefeller Plaza,
New York, N.Y. 10019

 A Warner Communications Company

Printed in the United States of America

First Printing: October, 1982

10 9 8 7 6 5 4 3 2 1

For
Justin Allen Blickenstaff,
A Survivor

SAN FRANCISCO

Chapter 1

Moonlight through the barred windows of the cell made patterns on the bare floor, and on the face of young Missie Narvaéz. She sat upright, her thin shoulders rigid as she considered her plight.

She was in trouble, just as her Aunt Em had predicted. She had no idea what was in store for her, and there was no one to turn to for help. She hadn't dared mention the well-known Courtney name. And her job at the *Examiner* was too tenuous to ask for aid there. A girl who emptied wastebaskets, wrote squibs, and corrected the grammar of male reporters was expendable. The famous William Randolph Hearst didn't even know her, and her immediate superior, new on the job, had a low opinion of working women. She could imagine the disdain in his sardonic face if he had to come to her rescue. He would consider his opinion justified.

Forget him! The day that began so beautifully was ruined. Here she was locked into a cell with a thief, a prostitute, and a drunken old Indian woman. Still, she had no one to blame for what had happened but herself.

Elizabeth Anspaugh, the leader of their march, had made it very clear: Women deserved a measure of independence, the right to vote, to enter certain occupations, to hold office. Women in the east were already fighting for those rights. San Francisco, in this year of 1890, was behind the times. Today, this was to be remedied. They would parade down Market Street with their signs and placards. There would be resistance, jeering, perhaps even violence.

But they must comport themselves in a ladylike manner at all times. Any deviation from good conduct would be ammunition for the antisuffrage factions. This must be fully understood.

Missie Narvaéz had not behaved like a lady.

She managed to withstand the leering, the catcalls, the occasional rotten tomato and egg. The march moved in orderly lines down Market Street, the drivers of horse-drawn vehicles pulling to the side to watch. People gaped from passing cable cars. Women shoppers turned their faces away in seeming revulsion.

Missie wanted to shout, "We're doing this for you!" But she held her tongue. She must be a lady—

Then suddenly they turned into a side street. It was lined with men of the working class. Missie felt her face redden under their stares. The silence was broken as one of them shouted, his voice carrying clearly.

"Bet they's wearin' britches under them skirts! Let's see? Whadda you say?"

The men surged forward and Missie felt rough hands on her body. For an instant, she was taken back in time, back to Australia and her runaway marriage to Arthur Melvin, swagman, thief, sadistic, brutal to his immature bride.

She lifted her sign, which read, aptly, *Down with male domination*, and struck her attacker.

And now she was here, in this cell. And even her fellow

prisoners did not agree with her, except for the Indian woman, too inebriated to talk coherently. The blowsy creature jailed for thieving had been sent out to steal by her ne'er-do-well spouse. "Man's the boss, honey. Allus has been, allus will be. No sense buttin' yer head agin a stone wall."

The prostitute, imprisoned, not for her trade, but for rolling a customer, was even more explicit. "Man only wants one thing. Shut up, lay down, an'—"

Missie shut the coarse words from her ears. They brought back the ghost of Arthur Melvin.

What was wrong with her, she wondered miserably. She should have been happy in Australia, living on Opal Station with her mother and father, her beloved aunt and uncle, Tamsen and Dan Tallant; her sisters, Ramona and Luka.

Instead, she had been a prickly loner, wishing her days away, making a disastrous marriage in her early teens.

When her Aunt Em and her husband, Duke Courtney, left Melbourne, coming to the States, she had come with them, planning to go to school, to become a famous writer. The school, chosen by Aunt Em, was a small girls' seminary, more intent on teaching Mrs. John Sherwood's Manners and Social Usages than dispensing useful information. Again, Missie had rebelled, leaving before graduation, taking an unfulfilling job at the newspaper against her aunt's better judgment.

Even her book, the book about Aunt Tamsen's life, written in secret, an outpouring of her heart, was in limbo. She'd sent it to New York. Though it had not been actually rejected, and was still in the publisher's hands, she'd received a cautious letter.

The book was well written, colorful, exciting, but the publisher was uncertain as to how it would be received by the public. Even in this year of 1890, the tale of a woman who began as a dancer in a cantina, then went on to become the madam of a famous San Francisco house, was a questionable topic. If she would allow them to publish her novel under a man's name—

She had sent an immediate answer. The answer had been no.

The book would probably return before long. It was possible she'd made another stubborn mistake. As Aunt Em said, she was always cutting off her nose to spite her face.

It was a man's world, after all.

She was so tired! Yet she couldn't bring herself to lie down on the soiled cot, imagining it to be populated with all kinds of creepy crawly things. The thieving woman slept, hands folded on her chest, virtuous at having obeyed her husband's demands. The prostitute sprawled in an abandoned position, probably glad to have one night's respite from her work. In a corner, the Indian woman snored, twitching in an occasional alcoholic dream.

Finally, Missie's head nodded forward, and she fell into a half-sleep, only to jerk erect at the sound of a familiar voice.

"Goddamnit," Duke Courtney bawled in the distance, "I know she's here! To hell with Narváez! Try Courtney, Melvin! There it is! Melissa McLeod. She used her mother's maiden name. Sure I'm sure! Tiny little thing, blond, big blue eyes, skinny—"

Skinny!

Missie's mouth tightened, then she smiled. The way he described her wasn't important. It was enough that he was here. He'd be furious, but she felt a sudden sense of release.

"I want her out of there," the distant voice continued. "Now! I don't give a goddamn whether it's legal or not! I'll wake up the mayor if I have to! Hell, I'll send to Sacramento for the governor—"

A few minutes later, the cell door clicked open. Missie was led to a large room where Duke Courtney was busily signing papers. He ignored her, handing over a wad of bills to the desk sergeant.

"That ought to cover it, take care of the sonofabitch she

hit, and shut up any nosy reporters who might tie this up with the Courtney name. Think you can handle it?''

The sergeant thought he could.

Duke Courtney took Missie's arm and maneuvered her out the door and into a waiting carriage. Taking the reins, he drove for some time without speaking. Then he said, ''I reckon you know Em's fit to be tied!''

''She—knows, then?''

''Hell, yes, she knows! When you didn't show up for supper, she went all to pieces. I've had ten men out looking for you. Someone saw a girl answering your description picked up after that damned march, hauled off to the pokey. Em's going to be mad as hell—''

''I'm sorry, Uncle Duke. So sorry—''

''You're sorry!'' He looked at her gloomily. ''I have to live with her! Now, don't get me wrong, Missie, I love that woman, but you got yourself into this mess, and I'm not going to stand up for you. Not this time.''

He closed his lips tightly, and it was clear he intended to do no more talking. Missie settled back against the seat, feeling small, lost, and forlorn. Em, gentle and feminine, cherished her husband, her home, her social position. And she would fight like a tigress to protect her status. She had no idea that Missie knew of her past, or that it had been incorporated into the book on Tamsen's life. The avoidance of a confrontation if it appeared in print had eased some of Missie's pain at the book's rejection.

Now it looked as if there would be a confrontation, anyway. It might have been better if Duke Courtney had left her where she was—in jail.

Chapter 2

Duke Courtney had gauged his wife's disposition accurately. Lying in her pastel room, a cold cloth over her forehead, Em awaited her husband's return. In addition to being angry, she was frightened. For Duke's sake, she told herself. Not her own.

When they returned to San Francisco a few years earlier, she'd been so afraid; afraid someone would recognize her as the wife of Senator Alden, who had committed suicide following a run on the banks; afraid that someone would remember her as the sister of Tamsen Tallant, operator of the notorious establishment known as Madam Franklin's Parlor for Gentlemen.

San Francisco was a city of shifting population, however, and more than thirty years had lapsed. No one had connected the beautiful, well-groomed lady with her past.

Only Duke knew of those terrible days. Only Duke knew of her even more dreadful secret; that her oldest daughter,

Martha, now happily married and living on a sheep station in Australia, was never Alden's daughter, but a child of rape—

Emmeline Courtney had built a new life, here in her ornate mansion on Nob Hill; a life that made her the social equal of her neighbors, the Stanfords, the Crockers, the Floods. Duke's international business dealings were much admired. Em had a secret desire to see him enter the political arena. And why not? From the rough-hewn man she'd married, he'd become distinguished, wealthy, respected—

And young Missie Narvaéz could spoil it all! A curious newsman looking into the family background would move the Courtneys from the society page to the front page! Especially that Hearst, with his scandal sheet!

Em moaned, twisting her head on a satin pillow. The little maid who hovered nearby rushed to her.

"Your head is worse, Mum? Perhaps a cup of tea?"

Em waved a limp hand. "Please. I'd like to be alone."

The door closed behind the solicitous woman, and Em sat up, flinging the damp cloth to the floor. She was so angry! Missie, in jail! Bringing the child here had been a mistake! Except for Martha, she'd had no problems with her own children! Cammie and Vickie were settled housewives, young Scott off at Berkeley and doing well in his studies.

This was Arab's fault! She frowned, thinking of her sister Arabella Narvaéz, now in England. Arab, after the birth of Luka—a strange girl—utterly ignored the existence of her two older daughters. Tamsen actually reared Ramona and Missie.

Maybe that's where the girl got some of her wild ways—from Tamsen.

Em shook her head, wearily. She mustn't blame Tamsen. When the three McLeod sisters were orphaned, it was Tamsen who helped them survive. Tam, despite her lurid past, was always the strong one. Arab was a bit spoiled and self-centered; Em herself needed someone to lean upon.

She shouldn't have taken the responsibility of bringing

Arab's daughter here. And, seeing the way things were going, she should have contacted Arab sooner. Only last week she had written a letter stating her concern at Missie's interest in suffragette activities—

The memory of that letter reminded her of another. She rose, taking it from a drawer, and reread it. Martha was sending Petra to her; Petra, Martha's child, her own granddaughter. Em had been thrilled at the prospect, but now she wondered. Perhaps the girl was a problem to her parents, and they were shifting that problem to her—

She wouldn't think about that! She couldn't bear to think about that! Not now—

The sound of wheels on the gravel drive below sent her scurrying for a blue satin robe. Belting it around her still slim waist, she headed determinedly for the stairs. Her husband's red face, the drooping figure of her niece, told her what she'd dreaded: that Missie had been the girl someone saw carted off to jail.

Em, on the stairs, her graying blond hair aureoled by a gaslight on the landing, looked like an avenging angel to Missie. Missie stood silent as she descended, dismissed Duke with a few terse words, and led the girl into the kitchen. A pot of coffee stood waiting on the stove. Em didn't speak as she poured two cups, then seated herself opposite Missie.

"What do you have to say for yourself, young lady?"

Missie flinched at her tone. "Only that I'm sorry to have caused so much trouble."

"Sorry enough to stop behaving like a—a common woman? To stop exhibiting yourself in the streets? To quit that—that yellow sheet you're working for?"

"It isn't a yellow sheet—"

"I'd like to know what it is, then," Em scoffed. "Lurid headlines! Scandals! We do not subscribe to it!"

"You like the *Chronicle*'s society pages," Missie pointed out. "Uncle Duke likes their editorials, their reporting of the weather. The *Examiner* tells what's going on among the people in the streets, like—"

"Like a member of a prominent family going to jail!" Em's voice was jerky. "Is that what you mean? Dear God! I have never been so ashamed! But you haven't answered me! I'm giving you a choice. Either behave yourself, or I will send you to England, to your mother. Petra is coming to stay with me. I will not have you being a bad example—"

"I will not be a bad example," Missie said dully. "I promise you. Now, if I may be excused—"

Leaving her aunt at the table, she went upstairs. There, she methodically packed the few things she intended to take with her. It was time to seek out her own roof, to become an independent woman living alone. The Courtneys would be horrified, seeing her as a scarlet woman, but it couldn't be helped.

Something Em had said stayed in her mind. A member of a prominent family going to jail? She would never write that, of course, but what about a girl—a reporter, defending herself from attack on a public street? Laws that sent the girl to prison, while her attacker went scot-free?

Taking out her notebook, she began: *The moon through the bars casts a shadow on the floor, giving enough light so that I can see the prostitute across the way—*

She wrote on, re-creating the scene, the sights, the reek of urine and antiseptic, the sour odor of wine and vomitus, the soiled beds; a prostitute and a thief who accepted a male-dominated world without question.

Finished, she reread it. It was good, and should appeal to Mr. Hearst—if it ever reached his desk. The word was that Hearst was occupying himself with plans for buying another paper, and new people were being brought in. Her own senior she'd met only two days before; a strikingly handsome young man with a firm jaw and dark, unruly hair, named Matthew Blaine. He'd been decidedly cool, and someone whispered that he didn't like women in the offices, considering home and family as the only suitable career for a female.

Missie signed the article with the name that appeared on the police blotter, the name she'd chosen as signature to her poor, doomed book. There would be no link to the Courtneys. Only to a woman on her own.

When she slept, she dreamed that, like Nellie Bly, a reporter for Pulitzer publications, she was flying around the world, trying to best the record of Phileas Fogg in the novel by Jules Verne. At every point, aboard ship, sampan, ricksha, train, or burro, she was confronted by Matthew Blaine's frowning face.

"A woman's place is in the home."

Behind the masculine voice sounded Aunt Em's, like an echo, saying the same thing.

She woke long before Em and Duke, still tired, but with much to do. Taking the cable car, she made her way to the offices of the *Examiner,* where she read all the advertisements for rooms to let. One by one, the staff arrived. Missie greeted them with the easy, sexless camaraderie she'd developed to cover the fact that she was a woman in a predominately male world. She was engaged in conversation with several reporters when she glanced up to meet Matthew Blaine's disapproving eyes.

Excusing herself, she followed him to his desk, blushing because he looked as he appeared in her dream. Wordless, she handed him her notebook. He scanned her article with a mingling of surprise and distaste.

"It's good," he admitted, "though I do not agree with its suffragette slant." He looked at her curiously, noting the mass of blond hair pinned high, the ringlets escaping over delicately shaped ears, the slender figure.

"Can this article be verified?"

"It can be checked at the police station."

"Who is this Melissa McLeod?"

"Me—I. It is my pen name."

"You spent the night in jail?" There was incredulity in his tone. Missie stiffened.

"I did. It—it's all there. If you will show it to Mr. Hearst—"

Shrugging, he took the folder into William Randolph Hearst's office. Missie hastened to her other duties. There were baskets to be emptied, articles to be carried to the typesetters, who lifted the leaden type into place with their inch-long fingernails. Within an hour, she was called to Blaine's desk, heart fluttering as he lifted dark eyes to hers.

"We're going to use it," he said tersely.

Missie had a difficult time swallowing her excitement. The dreadful events of yesterday had brought her first real break. Her excitement faded as Matthew Blaine lifted a quelling hand.

"As I said, I do not agree with suffragette activities. Do not bombard me with further articles of this type. I might add, I do not approve of working women. I do not know if there is need—"

"I must support myself," Missie lied. "I live alone."

"Then much depends upon your conduct here. I would suggest you refrain from fraternizing with the male employees. We need no problems of that sort here at the paper."

Missie spun away from the desk, her face crimson. The nerve of him! The nerve!

She wished she had the sign she was carrying yesterday! She'd used its rough edge on the wrong man!

Chapter 3

That day, Missie left work as soon as she could get away. She looked at apartments, one room after another, rejecting them all. One was out of reach of her budget, another filled with cockroaches. A third involved a long walk that would be miserable in the rainy season. Finally she took the Sacramento Street cable car, walking the three blocks east to Van Ness. Here, too, the accommodation was unsuitable. It seemed to be a house of men. She looked at her list, and walked one more block to Polk. Here, she found what she was looking for.

The two small rooms—with a water closet and copper tub, were situated above a bakery. Missie introduced herself to the baker's wife, a German woman who eyed her suspiciously. She'd been thinking of renting to a family, not to a lone girl. Exactly what was Miss Narvaéz's occupation?

Missie blushed, her mind racing. She knew exactly what the woman was thinking, and she must convince her of her respectability. Reporter? Writer? She had a notion neither would do. She looked down at her ink-stained hands.

"It isn't Miss," she said firmly, "it's Mrs. I'm a widow." At least that part was true. "And I teach." She held her hands as evidence, and the woman's face softened.

"I am sorry," she said in her heavy accent, "but one cannot be too careful. I am happy to have you as a tenant. Please call on me if you have needs. I am Frau Schmitt."

After the woman lumbered down the rickety stairs, Missie stood for a long time, studying the rooms. They were small, shabbily and sparsely furnished, but they were clean. The scent of fresh baked bread rose from below, reminding her that Em and Duke would be waiting supper, frantic once again, wondering what trouble she'd got herself into now. She must go. Tomorrow, she would return with her few possessions.

Downstairs on the street, she surveyed it with new eyes. Polk Street was lined with bakeries and delicatessens. The music of pianos tinkled from the swinging doors of saloons. It was bazaarlike, a place of color and humanity, a place for a new beginning, a new name, a place for a writer.

She could hardly wait until tomorrow.

Duke and Em were as concerned as she'd expected. Duke met her at the door with a vast sigh of relief. "Hell, I thought you were in jail again," he said, his laughter booming. Em hurried from the dining room, her pretty brow creased.

"Missie! We've been so worried." She flushed, then said, "I'm sorry I was cross with you last night. Can you forgive an old woman?"

She was sincere, her cornflower blue eyes tender and pleading. For a space, Missie felt the pull of a warm, loving household; a home where she was safe and cared for, a sheltered little pool in the turbulent river of life. Then she remembered Polk Street. There, she would be in midstream. That was where she belonged, not here.

She hugged Em back, and waited until the meal's end to mention her news.

Duke and Em took it badly. Em was certain she'd shirked her responsibilities to her sister's middle daughter; certain that Missie had chosen to move in a moment of hurt and anger brought on by Em's attitude the previous night. She wept, and Duke was upset.

Every argument was brought into play. Arab and Juan Narvaéz would never approve of Missie's move. Nice young ladies did not live alone. Such conduct could only lead to disaster.

"You and my mother and Aunt Tamsen were on your own when you were younger than I am," Missie said quietly.

Em's startled eyes met Duke's. To her knowledge, the past of the McLeod girls had never been discussed with the children. Was it possible Missie knew—?

Of course not. But all Em's arguments trailed off feebly, her authority fading.

They reached a compromise. Missie was to remain in the Courtney mansion for one more week, during which Duke would have her little apartment papered and painted. And she was to take the furnishings from her room in the Courtney home. Em was planning to have it done over for Petra, anyway.

With mingled feelings of love and irritation at their smothering, Missie agreed. She went to work the next day with a light step, knowing her freedom lay ahead of her.

Her article was set up for this evening's edition. She snatched the first copy off the press, the ink still wet, reading it avidly. There it was, her new name—Melissa McLeod.

"Miss Narvaéz?"

It was Matthew Blaine, his dark eyes stormy and unreadable. Missie thrust the paper behind her, but not quickly enough.

"Perhaps I should say, 'Miss McLeod.' Are you pleased with your story?"

"It reads well." Missie's tone was defensive, her cheeks burning.

"Then perhaps you'll look into this. Hearst seems to think it needs a woman's touch." He handed her a slip of paper. It contained only a few facts. *Coleen Evans, aged thirty, slays husband following beating.*

"She's in jail," Blaine added. "Try to get an interview. Do you have a press card?"

She shook her head, mutely.

"Then get one." He turned on his heel and walked away. It was evident that he didn't approve of the assignment, but had been ordered to pass it on. Missie felt a flush of victory. The assignment had been earned! She'd managed on her own merits!

She felt less assured when she was shown into a cell, very like the one in which she'd spent a night. There was one difference. Coleen Evans had it all to herself, since she had performed a major crime.

The woman may have been thirty, but it would have been difficult to prove. Her rust-colored hair was streaked with gray, her features battered beyond resemblance to anything human. Her nose had been broken, no attempt made to repair it. Her eyes were slits that looked out through purpling bruises, her mouth puffed and swollen.

At Missie's involuntary exclamation of sympathy, tears rolled from the slitted eyes.

"I didn't go to do it," the woman whimpered. "Wouldn'ta done it, if he hadn't been hittin' the kids."

With a few gentle questions, Missie learned that there were four children, all of them sent to the hospital after their mother had shot their father to death. She learned also that the beatings were not of recent vintage, but had been a continuing thing, over a period of years.

"Dear God," she whispered, "why didn't you divorce him?"

The devastated features registered surprise and shock. "Divorce is wrong," the woman said stiffly. "I couldn'ta done that! Besides, it woulda left me an' the kids with nothin'."

She stretched out a pleading hand. "Lissen, would you check on my kids for me? Tell 'em I didn't go to hurt their pa? Tell 'em I—I love 'em?"

"Of course I will," Missie promised, blinking the tears from her own eyes. "Of course I will."

She left the jail and went directly to the hospital. The children, three girls ranging from seven to four, and a two-year-old boy, were in not much better care than their mother. The nurses knew their history. They had all been in before. They had survived then, and would do so again.

It was too late to return to the paper. Heartsick, Missie went home to the mansion on Nob Hill. That night, she had no appetite, but excused herself and went to her room to stare at a blank page of paper.

She remembered a teen-aged girl, beaten and mauled by a sadistic husband, coveted by his half-senile father. She remembered a girl left without food or fuel, bearing a stillborn child in the Outback while that husband and his father were off to do robbery. She remembered burying that child—

She remembered her life with Arthur Melvin.

Taking up her pen, she began to write, writing of Coleen Evans, a woman who had lived with terror for years, who had watched her children suffer unimaginable tortures. She wrote of a woman who had no skills, no recourse in the law, whose moral nature shuddered at the thought of divorce—but who had not balked at murder.

The population must awake to the problems of Coleen Evans and her kind. No longer must a man be considered supreme. Women must be allowed to vote, to legislate, in order to make a better world. They must learn skills in order to support themselves.

Every word blurred before Missie's eyes. Each sentence was punctuated with a tear. And when she'd done, it was better than anything she'd ever written.

In the morning, she took it straight to Matthew Blaine's desk, awaiting his reaction with trepidation. He read it slowly. "You are to report," he said, "not to editorialize. No matter. It will have to be rewritten, anyway. Larry?" He called across the room, and a male reporter came forward. "Do a rewrite on this. Cut the opinion, and add the latest facts."

Missie was trembling with anger. "I don't understand!"

"Rules of reporting," he said. "Better learn them. Besides, there's more to the story." He stood and headed for Hearst's office, talking back over his shoulder. "Last night, Coleen Evans slit her wrists. She's dead."

Dead! Missie thought of the woman's pleading words. "Would you check on my kids for me—tell 'em I didn't go to hurt their pa—tell 'em I love 'em."

"But—the children," she stammered.

"Are probably a helluva lot better off, all things considered," he answered. "And if you're going to be a reporter, you've got to have the guts to take this kind of thing." The door to the office slammed behind him.

Missie's hands clenched into fists. Matthew Blaine was a cold, horrible man! She hated him! Hated him! After a few moments, she forced herself to relax. He was probably right, but that didn't make his words any more palatable.

She left the desk and went to where the man called Larry sat editing the article that had poured directly from her heart.

"I want you to show me," she said, "what I did wrong."

Larry Hiller was essentially a kind man. Reared by a doting mother and a bevy of sisters, he had an empathy for, and an understanding of women. He'd watched the progress of the small, intense girl and taken a kind of pride in it. He was happy to help her in any way he could.

He went over the article, line by line. "You must show the need for reform in a way that the reader sees it for himself, rather than telling him. This way—do you see?"

Missie saw. She also saw Matthew Blaine glowering at

them as they talked, his dark eyes smoky with anger. She remembered his remarks about fraternizing with the male employees, not wanting any problems.

Her jaw set. She intended to learn the trade, and since it was a man's world, she must learn it from a man. She did not intend to let Matthew Blaine stop her!

But looking at Larry Hiller, with his gentle blue eyes, his thinning sandy hair, she wished that his hair was black and rumpled, and that his expression held a touch of fire.

Chapter 4

Coleen Evans's funeral was on a Sunday. Missie was going to attend, then decided against it. The poor troubled woman was beyond any help now. It was her children who needed comforting. And not, she thought, looking down at her black skirt and sacque, almost a uniform at the office, by a woman who looked like a funeral, herself.

She put on a gentian blue frock that brought out the color of her eyes, the frilled yoke and leg-of-mutton sleeves becoming to her slight figure. Loosening her hair from its usual severe style, she donned a small blue bonnet that perched at the back of her head, her blond locks swirling softly beneath it.

After a critical glance in the mirror, she took up her purchases—three dolls, and a stuffed toy for the smallest one, and set off on the cable car, her brow creased with worry.

What would become of the children?

The nurse at the desk had an answer for her. A normally sour, competent woman, she spared a rare smile. A gentleman had been kind enough to institute a search for surviving relatives. A cousin of Mrs. Evans had been found. She and her husband lived on a small farm near Yreka and were childless. They would collect the children as soon as the funeral was over.

"I think I'd ought to warn you," the nurse called after Missie as she went down the hall. "Those kids have been bawling all morning."

Nervously, Missie entered the room where four small beds were set side by side. Four battered faces, swollen with tears, lifted at her approach, the younger ones shrinking away like frightened mice.

"It's all right," the older girl informed them. "It's just our lady." She eyed Missie curiously. "You been to the fun'ral?"

Missie shook her head. "I'm sure your mama had a lot of friends there. I thought maybe she'd rather I visit you."

"I want my daddy," the four-year-old wailed, "where's my daddy?"

Missie was speechless. The man had beaten them and their mother to a bloody pulp, and they missed him! What should she say?

"Shut up, Kay-Kay," the older girl ordered. She turned to Missie. "They told us about Mama, but not what happened to Daddy. Is he—?"

Missie bit her lower lip to keep it from quivering. "He's— with your mother."

"Dead? I figured he was. Mama shot him with a gun."

"I got blood on my hand," the second child said solemnly. "Somebody washed it." She held up a hand as evidence.

Missie turned away quickly, lifting the parcels she'd placed on a chair. "I've brought you something to play with—"

The two-year-old snatched at his stuffed animal and hugged it tightly. The girls were more reticent. After an instant of doubt, as if they could not believe the dolls were theirs to keep, they cuddled them close. Little Kay-Kay breathed a sigh of delight.

"I ain't never going to hit you," she promised her doll. "Not with anything."

For a time their plight was forgotten as the girls inspected their gifts. Beneath the long, lace-trimmed baby dress each doll wore was a cloth body, jointed at appropriate spots. The bisque heads looked amazingly lifelike, as did the dimpled bisque hands and feet. Caught up in their enjoyment, Missie began to relax.

"Lady?"

It was the older girl again, her bruised eyes questioning. "Lady, do people still fight in Heaven?"

Again, Missie was at a loss for an answer. How could God forgive a child-beater! A woman who allowed her children to be beaten—until she was driven to kill him?

"I'm sure they don't. In Heaven, everything is—peaceful."

"That's good." The child sank back against her pillows, her battered mouth curved in a smile of relief. Missie knew that she was worried about her mother and father being together, carrying their battle to a celestial plane. She was glad when the little boy held his arms to her, wanting to be picked up, sung to.

At the feel of the warm little body cuddling into the curves of her own, she felt a maternal yearning that was almost pain, thinking of her own baby. If he had lived—

If he had lived, he would also be the child of Arthur Melvin, a living memory of a time of horror.

There was a rocking chair in the room and she sat, the words of a lullaby coming back to her. She sang until the baby slept, and continued as the older children closed drowsy eyes. Poor battered little creatures, physically beaten, emotionally exhausted. Her heart welled with love—and pity.

Matthew Blaine, coming upon the scene with his arms stacked with packages, stopped dead still in the open doorway. It was hard to believe the sweet-voiced creature before him was the tense young lady who worked at the *Examiner*.

The way she was holding the little one—perhaps he had misjudged her.

In the meantime, he felt like a fool, standing here with his three music boxes and a bag of blocks. Maybe he could sneak away, hide out until she was gone—

It was too late. Her eyes had widened in surprise and recognition. He stepped inside, feeling like a bull in a china closet, as if he had intruded on a tender scene.

"Kids all right?" he whispered awkwardly.

"They're fine, Mr. Blaine. And something wonderful has happened. Someone found some relatives. They're taking them all."

He tried to look surprised. "That's good."

"I hope so." A shadow of worry darkened Missie's eyes. "I hope they're not going into a place like they came from. What if these people mistreat them, too?"

"They won't," he said hastily. "They're nice folks. They—," he stopped suddenly, knowing he'd given himself away, his ears reddening. At her smile of gratitude, he waved a deprecating hand as if to erase his deed. "It's part of the job. The readers will want to know the end of the story. That's all."

Missie looked meaningfully at the gifts he carried. "Is it?"

"Hell, yes," he growled. "Hey, look, somebody just woke up!"

One by one the older girls awoke. Soon the baby was sitting on the floor, happily playing with his blocks. The music boxes, imported from Germany each held a different melody, and were all going simultaneously to the sound of giggling little girls. In the middle of the melee, the O'Briens arrived. Coleen Evans's cousin and her husband were plump, smiling people, both with rusty hair and freckles, like enough to be brother and sister. The children took to them immediately, and it was clear the feeling was mutual. Missie and Matthew Blaine left them to get acquainted.

"I like them," Missie sighed. "If Coleen Evans had only given the children to them sooner—"

"Some people love their children," Blaine pointed out. "She was trying to hold her family together."

"She could have divorced that man! They would have helped her!"

"Some people do not believe in divorce."

"You think she did the right thing, staying with that—that maniac?" Missie glared at him.

"We don't know all the circumstances, Miss Narvaéz—McLeod, whatever the hell you call yourself!" He was glaring back, his black brows knitted in a frown. "I've been a reporter long enough to know that all you women aren't lily white! I've seen mothers who beat their kids, deserted them, run off with other men—or figured they wanted some kind of damn fool career! That's why you suffragettes make me sick, encouraging that kind of thing."

"We only want our rights," Missie said hotly. Then her voice softened. Matthew Blaine wasn't arguing for the sake of arguing. His eyes were sincere, and he was entitled to his beliefs. "I'm sorry," she said with a painful smile. "I didn't mean to judge—"

His anger disappeared. For a moment, he looked young, like a sheepish boy. "I'm sorry, too. Maybe if we didn't talk about Coleen Evans, divorce, or suffrage, we might get along, do you think?"

Missie laughed. "Maybe—"

"Let's give it a try! I have my surrey, and I'd planned to drive around a little, take the air. Would you be kind enough to accompany me, ma'am?"

Missie faltered. She knew nothing at all about Matthew Blaine, except that he didn't care much for women and that he had a terrible temper. Aunt Em would definitely not approve. Then she thought of the Evans children, how he had gone out of his way to ensure they had a home. And after all, she would not be a member of the Courtney household much longer, but a woman on her own making her own decisions.

"I'd like that," she said.

The drive was a delight. At first, it consisted mostly of shop-talk, since the newspaper was their common interest. Did Missie know that Hearst had some long-range plans in mind? He was looking into the possibility of purchasing a New York paper—and the rumor was that he planned to send a member of his staff to check things out at that end.

"Is there a chance that you might go?"

Matt frowned, his worries returning. He'd heard his name was mentioned, and it would be a feather in his cap. But, with his present problems, it would be difficult.

"I suppose so," he said reluctantly.

"I envy you." Missie's voice was wistful. "I wish I were the one."

Blaine wanted to tell her that she hadn't a chance in hell. Hearst wasn't about to send a woman to do a man's job. Instead, he changed the subject, encouraging her to talk about herself, interested in what she had to say.

Carefully avoiding the skeletons in the family closet, she told him of her beautiful red-haired mother, Arabella; of her father, Juan Narváez, reared to be a Spanish grandee, giving up his heritage to marry his American wife. They were in England now with Aunt Tamsen and her husband, Dan Tallant. She spoke so lovingly and wistfully of Tamsen Tallant that Blaine wondered.

"Why are you here, in San Francisco? Why did you leave your family?"

She couldn't tell him that she'd left to escape memories almost too terrible to bear. Or that she'd come to live with an aunt who was married to Duke Courtney. The Courtney name was well known, and she'd already told him she had to earn her own living.

"I wanted to go to school," she said evasively. "There

was nothing where I lived then, in the Australian Outback. My parents went to England later.''

Australia? So that was the slight accent he'd detected. He looked at her with new eyes as she talked of Opal Station, where she'd spent her earlier years; set in its little valley, forested slopes rising to become scrub and mallee. She talked of the goanna lizards, their ugly little relatives called stumpy-tails; of birds that soared in flights of glowing color. There were kangaroos, pretty-faced wallabies; a settlement of aborigines near the ranch. She told of a family of aborigines who had become her friends, their powers which seemed almost magical.

"If a man has a pain—that is not a pain—in his upper right arm, he knows his oldest brother is ill. At the wrist, it is his youngest, the others in between. The left arm stands for his sisters, and here," she placed her hand over her heart, "the father. Of course, the father's brothers are also their fathers, the mother's sisters, their mothers.''

"It sounds confusing.''

"Not really.''

"Are they ever wrong in their predictions?''

"No.''

He shook his head at her positive note, smiling. It was clear she had loved the people, another facet of her odd contradictory nature. And he had been enthralled with her description, the use of color in her words, the hallmark of a writer.

He would not tell her so. He had no use for a woman in any career or profession, and he did not intend to encourage this girl in that direction. Someway, she'd managed to get past his guard, and he was more attracted to her than was wise. It was time to turn back.

He maneuvered the horse, reversing direction. "If you will give me your address, I'll see you to your home," he said in a distant tone.

Missie looked at him, puzzled. In the last moment, something between them seemed wrong. And she could not give the Courtney address. She gave him the one on Polk. She would look in on the job of renovating, then take the cable car home.

He pulled up before the bakery and came to assist her to alight. As she left the surrey, her long gown caught something that lay beneath the seat. It fell to the ground, and Blaine hastily scooped it up, putting it in his pocket.

"Something I was taking to the Evans children," he said hastily. "I must have dropped it."

Missie thanked him for the pleasant day, and climbed the stairs to her rooms, wondering over the incident. She had seen the fallen object clearly. It was a tiny stuffed rabbit, one ear fallen over an eye, the other missing. It had once been white, but it was soiled and dingy as if it had been much loved by a child.

He had brought a gift for each of the Evans children. Those gifts had been wrapped and new. Why had he lied?

With a sense of misery, she realized she just might have spent the afternoon with a married man.

Chapter 5

The following day, at the *Examiner*, the pleasant drive of Sunday might never have occurred. There had been a shooting on Bush, near Montgomery, an affair of the heart. A runaway had occurred in front of St. Francis Church, careening through a wedding party. The young bride had been trampled, and was not expected to live. A boatload of Chinese, illegal aliens due to the exclusionary acts, had attempted to land up the coast. Preparations to blow up Shag Rock, a navigation hazard in the harbor, were under way. Bubonic plague in Chinatown. A fire—

Matthew Blaine was tense, overworked, shouting orders, sending reporters to designated areas. There were not enough men to go around, and Missie waited hopefully for an assignment. It did not come. Instead, she was put to handling the telephone—one of the few in San Francisco, taking notes, correcting copy as it came in.

It's what I get, she thought grimly, for trying to make friends with the boss. And though she'd learned from Larry

Hiller that Matthew Blaine was indeed a bachelor, the information didn't help anything but her conscience. Evidently his brief show of friendship had been a one-time thing.

On Wednesday night, Missie moved into her rooms on Polk Street. The larger room served for living space, kitchen, and dining. The smaller held her bed, a small chair, and her own white writing desk, stationed under a window that looked out into the gardens of the old mansions along Van Ness. Looking covetously down into the gardens—her gardens, she thought complacently, she dreamed for a long time before opening the day's mail that Duke delivered along with the furniture.

There were two letters, one from Aunt Tamsen, another from the publisher in New York. Dear God, not her manuscript back—just a letter!

Superstitiously, she opened Tamsen's first, reading it with interest. It told of her sister Luka's coming wedding. Ramona, and now Luka. They both had someone. Blinking back tears, Missie read the letter twice, then turned to the second, her mouth falling open as a railway ticket dropped from the envelope.

We still hold your book under consideration, it read, *and would be pleased if you would journey to consult with us. A draft is enclosed to cover any additional expense.*

They were considering her book, in spite of her negative answer! The book on which she had collected notes since she was a child. She'd drawn the truths of the past from her beloved Dusty, now dead and buried on Australian soil—and Nell, the bawdy old ex-madam, who'd helped Tamsen and her sisters survive. Nell, and Dusty, almost-grandparents.

Her eyes welled and she sank to the chair before the desk, blond head on her arms. She'd promised Dusty she'd become a writer one day—and she would! Please God, she would!

Finally she sat back and wiped her streaming face. Her chance had come. She had written a monument to the people she loved most—especially Aunt Tamsen. Now she had her big chance. And if her dream came true, it would make all the horrors of her girlhood worth having lived through.

Now there were things to do. She must see what clothes she had that were suited to New York. And she must devise a way to tell Aunt Em and Uncle Duke she would be away—without revealing her secret. She must try to get a leave of absence at the paper—again without telling her reasons. This could so easily fall through!

She suddenly had a vision of Matthew Blaine, driven to the edge by the pressure of this week. Today had been as chaotic as ever. He'd worked in his shirt sleeves, poring over stories, skipping lunch. She couldn't just walk out when he was short-handed. And there were still boxes to sort here in the apartment. A day or two's delay would make no difference.

She would not leave until Monday.

Thursday morning she went to work, almost unable to contain her excitement. If her eyes were too bright, if her cheeks glowed, they went unnoticed.

Matthew Blaine, his desk covered with paperwork, seemed to ignore her. It was only once, when Larry Hiller teased her, holding her hand overlong, that Blaine lifted his head to scowl at her laughter.

She shivered, wondering if a leave of absence would even be considered. With all the confusion, it might be just as well to talk to him on Saturday—

The situation with Em and Duke proved to be easier. Missie dropped by on Friday night, after work, to find the household in an uproar. Em's granddaughter, Petra, had arrived. And at the same time Duke had business in Los Angeles that would require a stay of a few weeks. Em and Petra would accompany him.

"I feel so guilty leaving you here alone," Em said hastily. "Do you suppose you could—?"

"We're very busy at the paper. I couldn't possibly get away," Missie lied. "Besides, I'm looking forward to quiet evenings in my new rooms."

Em pressed a list of friends' names upon her, friends who could be notified in an emergency, and Missie left, making her way back to Polk Street, relieved that one problem had been resolved. Perhaps she could return before they even missed her. She was grateful to Petra. Her coming would divert Em's mind from Missie's activities.

A strange girl, Petra. Beautiful, in spite of her rustic Australian dress, she was so shy she'd hardly said a word. Aunt Em, Missie thought wryly, hadn't given her much chance! But it was more than shyness. The girl looked different, with her ivory yellow complexion, tilted eyes, a blue black cast to her hair. She certainly didn't resemble any of the family. She seemed—almost Oriental.

Petra was forgotten as Missie turned to her remaining problem, that of telling Matthew Blaine she needed a leave of absence. She had a notion he wouldn't take too kindly to the idea, especially since she planned to keep her reason to herself.

The next morning Missie steeled herself to approach his desk. She had no idea that Blaine had just returned from speaking with Hearst. Hearst had told him to forget any notion of going to New York on his behalf. He might just decide to handle the job himself. Though the journey would have posed a problem for Blaine, it was still a let-down when he learned the trip was off.

Now, he had to get back to business at hand. He did not look up, but pored over the papers before him, his brows drawn together in a scowl. Even frowning, he was shockingly handsome, she thought with a tremor.

"Mr. Blaine, there is something I need to discuss—"

An arrogant hand erased her presence. "Not now," he muttered. "I'm busy as hell!"

Cheeks crimson at his rebuff, she backed away, returning to her work with a fury. If he didn't talk to her today, he could just figure out how to replace her Monday, when he found out she was gone!

Larry Hiller caught up with her as the workday ended. "I was just wondering, Missie, do you ever go out? I was thinking, maybe tonight we could—"

"Are you finished, Hiller?" Matthew Blaine's commanding voice sounded behind them. "Go on, if you're through. Missie, you wanted to talk to me. If you'll stick around until I handle one last problem, I'll be with you."

The unfortunate Larry found himself outside the door. Missie waited quietly while Matthew returned to his work. In a few minutes he was done.

"I'm sick of this damned office," he said finally. "I imagine you are, too. Any objection to talking over dinner at the Baldwin?" An odd expression passed over his face and he added, like a reluctant afterthought, "And perhaps the theater afterward?"

Missie was speechless for a space, then she looked down at her slightly dusty skirt, her ink-stained hands. "I'm not exactly dressed for it."

"Neither am I," he grinned. "But all reporters are eccentric, aren't they?"

Missie's heart sang. He had included her in his statement. A reporter? She felt wonderful!

The wonderful feeling continued as they talked together over a delightful meal. Later, she could not even remember what they discussed, only the shadows and planes of his sensitive features in the lamplight; the way his rare smile softened his somber eyes. They had finished dessert when she recalled what she must tell him. She pleated her napkin, reluctant to break the spell, then sought a pause in the conversation.

"As I said this morning," she began, "there's something I want to discuss—"

"If we talk now, we'll miss the first act. Perhaps when I take you home—" He stood, and extended his arm. Missie had no choice but to follow.

The show was enchanting, a melodrama in which the

audience joined with enthusiasm, the gentlemen stamping and whistling, ladies giving little cries of alarm or approval. Missie booed the villain so roundly that Matthew laughed and leaned toward her. "I forgot you were a suffragette," he whispered. "No violence, please!"

Missie settled back, blushing, until the next dramatic scene.

Between the acts, a curtain closed for a scene change. Three pert girls appeared, singing a slightly naughty song to fill the interim. A blond, a brunette, and a redhead. Missie smiled, thinking of her red-haired mother who had sung and danced on stage, of blond Em who, too, had done a stint; of lovely Aunt Tamsen who performed in a bawdy house. It was some time before she became aware of a change in Matthew Blaine. The arm touching hers had grown rigid. She turned to face him.

Dear God!

Blaine's face was set in an expression of anger, his eyes like looking into the fires of hell. He seemed on the verge of doing murder! Missie followed his gaze to the stage, then returned to his awful face.

"Matthew?" she whispered, touching his hand. "Are you ill?"

As though her touch had galvanized him into action, he turned, stumbling across her feet, oblivious to the muttering of the crowd behind him. Reaching the side aisle, he made his way down it and through a door that led backstage.

He had gone to kill someone! She knew it! What could she do? Stand up and shout a warning to the girls onstage? It was clear that one of them had precipitated his anger! Oh, Matthew! Matthew!

It seemed that she cringed in mindless terror for an eternity. In fact, it was only a few minutes until his return. His face was dead white and he looked exhausted, but he excused himself as he moved along the crowded aisle to sit beside her.

"I'm sorry I left so suddenly. I thought I saw someone I knew. But I was wrong. It was someone else."

Missie shivered, thanking God that it was a mistake. Matthew Blaine had left his seat with murder in mind. It was over now. He was himself again. But the pleasure had gone out of the evening.

Blaine knew it, too. Taking a roundabout way to Polk Street, he pulled into a secluded area and apologized. It had been rude of him, leaving her sitting without an escort while he searched for—an old acquaintance. "That's all I can say," he finished helplessly. "It is too long and involved to really explain."

"It doesn't matter," Missie said dully, plucking at her skirt. "It's over now. I'll admit I was frightened. You looked—"

"Don't ever be afraid of me, Missie. As I said, it was a misunderstanding. Am I forgiven?"

"Of course. And it has been a wonderful evening. But I still have to tell you—" she faltered; his eyes were dark and intense in the glow of a streetlamp. It was difficult, now that she had his attention.

"I must tell you," she said weakly. "I'm leaving for New York on Monday."

There was a harsh sound as he drew in his breath, a moment of silence. When he spoke, his voice was cold, remote.

"You are an ambitious little woman, aren't you?"

"Why, yes, I suppose so." She was startled. What was he getting at?

"I knew it when you started cozying up to Hiller," he said bitterly. "He's been pushing to throw some stories your way. And now you're traveling with the boss! Smart lady! Always start at the top!"

"I don't know what you're talking about—"

"Don't you? Isn't it a coincidence that Hearst is making a quick trip to New York, too?"

"Mister Blaine!" Missie's face was splashed with angry red. "You've said quite enough!"

"Perhaps I have! Maybe it's action you prefer! Well, dammit, you'll get it!" His arms went around her and he pulled her to him, roughly, bruising her arms as his mouth sought hers.

Missie cowered under the violence of an attack that took her back in time. She was no longer in San Francisco. She was in a lost valley in the Australian Outback, trapped in a little shack in a duffing yard—a spot where stolen cattle were brought to be rebranded. The arms that surrounded her were those of Arthur Melvin, former cow cocky at the family station; Arthur Melvin, who wooed her with poetry, marrying her to spite her Aunt Tamsen; Arthur Melvin, who tore her gown from her body and made vicious, punishing love to her—under his senile father's grinning eyes.

Involuntarily, Missie reacted as she had to any man's touch since that terrible time, kicking, scratching, in a frenzy to be free. Then sanity slowly returned and she felt a melting inside. For a moment she yearned toward him in an aching surrender.

Her softening was misinterpreted. Blaine's eyes were bleak as he pushed her away.

"In case you're interested, I don't want you," he said brutally. "I've had enough of cold, scheming women in my life! I'm going to take you home."

The drive was accomplished in silence. When they reached the address on Polk Street, Blaine made no move to assist her from the carriage. Holding her skirts, she climbed down, clinging to the side for a moment as she looked up at him.

"You said what you had to say," she said in a small frozen voice. "Now you're going to hear me out. I am going to New York on personal business. I plan to return. You can give me a leave of absence, or not, as you wish. As far as I'm concerned, you can go to hell!"

She turned, stumbling a little; then, lifting her skirts, she ran to the narrow dark stairs that led up to her rooms. In the shelter of her own surroundings, she burst into tears. Finally, she scrubbed them angrily away. Let Matthew Blaine think of her what he would! No man was ever going to hurt her again! Wait until her book was a best seller! That would show him!

Even then, she thought bitterly, he'd probably think she'd slept with her publisher!

Chapter 6

Stuyvesant Ellsworth Brown, the most junior member of the publishing firm of Brown, Halpert and Brown, paced the floor of his well-appointed office. He looked at the clock. It was now five minutes until ten, when his lady author was due to arrive. If his father were correct in his assumption, the woman—an old war-horse, for certain—would come steaming in an hour late, looking like a frump, then try to steamroller him with impossible demands.

His father was probably right, he thought glumly. And he'd meant what he said when he advised him he'd better not fail on this one. It was the most important assignment he'd had to date, and he'd read the book. It was just spicy enough to blow the lid off the market and, hopefully, written with enough taste to keep it from being banned in Boston.

Halpert and the elder Brown had first been shocked, then titillated, just as he had been. If young Stuyvesant—Stew, as he was known to his friends—could pull this off, talk the lady into using a man's name instead of her own, settle on a small advance, they'd be moving into one of the new tall buildings that were going up in Manhattan.

In spite of the backslapping and flattery they'd handed him along with the job, he knew why he'd got it. Nobody else had the courage to face a female dragon. In his position as son of the senior partner—he didn't have the guts to turn it down.

Two minutes until ten. He walked to the window and looked down. The streets were filled with scurrying people. A horse-drawn streetcar paused and let a few passengers off. He could see nothing that looked like a boxcar in a dress. Sighing, he turned back to his desk, fumbling with a pencil as he watched the seconds tick by.

At exactly ten o'clock, his secretary opened the door. A thin, frenetic woman, she'd been chosen for her acid tongue and her ability to protect the inner sanctum from budding authors. At the moment, she wore a look of surprise.

"Mrs. McLeod is here for her ten o'clock appointment."

He braced himself. "Thank you. Send her in."

The next moment he was on his feet, his chair nearly tipping as he moved. The pencil fell from his fingers and rolled under his desk as he gaped at the vision in the doorway.

"You—you are Mrs. McLeod?"

Missie inclined her head gravely, looking at him with gentian blue eyes that held an innocent, wistful expression. Good God, she was small enough to put in his pocket! And this girl had written a book that was—fast, to say the least!

"Come in," he said, too heartily. "Come in! Please sit down."

She complied. Safe behind his desk, he put his palms together. "Well," he said a little foolishly. "Well!" Sadly, he realized he'd lost his advantage. He'd planned to handle the deal smoothly, sharply, put the author on the defensive, play at being the publishing tycoon. And here he was, babbling like an idiot!

"I didn't expect you to be so young," he blurted.

"Time will remedy that," she smiled. "Now, about my book—?"

"Ah, yes, the book." Again, he bogged down, wondering how this girl could possibly have written some of its steamy scenes. "We—we like it. But there are some terms—"

Within the hour, he was hopelessly, irrevocably lost. The girl dug in her heels and stubbornly refused to adopt a masculine nom de plume. "It is a story about women, for women," she said. "Wouldn't they wish to know a woman wrote it?"

Her words made sense. He capitulated, though he knew he would regret it later. His father, he thought drearily, would be mad as hell. "Now," he said with more determination, "about the advance and royalties—"

The senior Brown had given him a low figure and a high one. "Start at the bottom," he'd ordered. "Don't let her get the upper hand. It's a first book, she wants to publish it. We hold all the cards. Just keep the advantage, boy. Always remember that. Keep the leverage." Hypnotized by a pair of blue eyes, Stuyvesant Brown, in his nervous state, named the high figure first.

"I should have thought it would be more," the young lady said, hesitantly. "Perhaps if I went elsewhere—"

"No—no need for that! I'm sure we can work out something satisfactory to us both!"

God, she was lovely when she smiled!

Finally they met in mutual agreement and a temporary contract was drawn up and signed, the signatures of the senior members of the firm being required to legalize it. Mrs. McLeod was to return on the morrow.

Stuyvesant Brown saw his latest author to the door. He was completely undone, unable to believe he had met all the girl's demands—including the use of a woman's name on the binding. It would take the rest of the day to straighten things out with his elders. There was even a chance that he wouldn't be working here when she returned.

"Mrs. McLeod," he stammered, "since you are new to the city—I wonder if I might escort you to dinner tonight, perhaps the theater afterward. Miss Ada Rehan is performing in *The Taming of the Shrew*—"

"How kind of you," she breathed. "I would love it, Mr. Brown!"

"Please call me Stew," he said, relinquishing her hand reluctantly.

Then she was gone. He had only the address of her hotel on a piece of paper—and another paper, that was damned likely to get him fired.

Indeed, that was the first recommendation when the contract was presented to the senior Brown and Edwin Halpert. "I don't know where the hell you got your brains," the elder Brown shouted. "Must have been from your mother! Did the old bitch hold a gun to your head? That," he pointed a shaking finger at the contract, "is the goddamndest thing I ever saw!"

"Watch your blood pressure, Charles," the elegant Halpert said mildly. "We do want the book. We impressed that upon the boy. Don't be too hard on him."

"'Hard on him'!" Charles Brown was breathing heavily. "'Hard on him'! I'm going to demote him so far down he'll be in the basement! I'll tell that woman he had no authority to make a deal!"

The advantage, Stuyvesant thought. Leverage! Give it back to the old man! What have I got to lose?

"Mrs. McLeod will not accept less than the terms set down," he said coolly. "But I will. You do not need to fire me or demote me. I am tendering my resignation as of now. I've had an offer from another firm—"

"Who the hell—?"

"I do not intend to tell you until I'm on their payroll. Let's say it's a—friendly competitor."

Charles Brown drew a deep breath and composed his features in an expression of loving resignation. "Forget it, boy. This—this contract just came as a surprise. I should have handled the old biddy myself. I know you tried.''

"I certainly did. I even have to take her to dinner and the theater tonight, as part of the deal.''

His father slapped him on the back. "That's my boy! But let me tell you, I wouldn't be in your shoes for a hundred-dollar bill! But watch out, boy!'' He laughed suggestively. "A woman who'd write a book like hers might be after more than dinner and a show!''

Stew Brown stepped out of the office, smiling. His father had taught him well. He'd now used leverage and it worked—except in the case of a small blond writer with devastating blue eyes. And right now, he had a date with the most beautiful girl in the world. More than dinner and a show? He only wished it would happen that way!

The evening that followed was like a fairy tale to Missie. Stuyvesant, though only passably nice-looking with his pale skin and brown hair, appeared distinguished in his evening clothes. He was also known to most of the diners in the sumptuous room with its gilt decor and velvet chairs. It was gratifying to be introduced as "Our newest writer—with a book we'll all be talking about.''

If he looked at her all moony-eyed, it was something that could be borne. She let him hold her hand, and when he caressed her shoulder with rather clammy fingers, she did not demur.

She had guessed, today, that his was not the final say-so; that the two elder partners would have to be convinced of the contract's terms. But it certainly didn't hurt to have the younger Brown on her side tomorrow. She smiled at his stories, and lowered her eyes at proper moments, allowing him to see the length of her lashes against her cheek.

I'm flirting, she thought. I'm actually flirting with a strange man! She remembered Matthew Blaine's insinuations, that she would use her sex to further her ambitions. If she had the name, she thought angrily, she might as well have the game!

Following dinner, they moved on to the playhouse. A series of velvet drapes parted majestically; the last, of silken gauze, carried Missie directly into the setting. She watched, enthralled, as Miss Ada Rehan performed magnificently. The play was unlike anything Missie had ever seen. She was caught up in the character of Kate, a liberated woman if there ever was one! At the finale, she was walking in a dream.

Stuyvesant Brown returned her to her hotel, enchanted by her reaction to what had always seemed commonplace to him. "I'm free, after your appointment tomorrow," he said softly. "Perhaps I could show you the sights? Is there anything in particular you would like to see?"

Missie's answer was prompt, her eyes brightening as she clasped her hands in ecstasy. "Oh, yes," she breathed. "I'd like to see Newspaper Row! Oh, thank you!"

He was so startled that he let her turn and leave him before he could utter a word. Morosely, he returned to his carriage. Then his face brightened. There was always tomorrow.

Chapter 7

The senior partners gathered to view their new author the next morning. It was too late to remedy the damage the firm had been done, but they might as well learn what they had to deal with.

The poised young woman who appeared was as much a shock to them as she had been to Stuyvesant Brown on the previous day. The father cast a suspicious look at the boy, wondering if this were some kind of jest. Seeing that it was not, he hastened to hold a chair, seating the pretty Mrs. McLeod.

"I only wish I had been free last night. I would have escorted you to dinner myself. We could have discussed your further writings. I always say that a relationship between an editor and a writer is the most rewarding—"

"Indeed," Halpert interrupted in his dry, whispery voice. "Indeed. In fact, I should be happy to show the young lady our city today. As we drive, we can talk about distribution. There are landmarks that—"

"I have the situation well in hand," Stuyvesant Brown said, almost gleefully, "having already suggested such a course last night. We're leaving as soon as the contract is in order."

The two old gentlemen signed their names and watched as their newest author left the office on Stew Brown's arm. "I knew I should have handled that," the elder Brown said wistfully. "But you remember the last one."

"She," said Mr. Halpert, "would be hard to forget."

As Stuyvesant Brown manuevered his carriage along the crowded streets, he questioned his pretty companion. Last night, she'd only talked about her manuscript, mentioning that she'd lived in Hawaii and Australia to explain her knowledge of local color. At first Stew Brown had been bemused. Now he was utterly infatuated. He wanted to know all about her life before she met him.

As she talked, she mentioned her aunt, Tamsen, her uncle, Dan Tallant; her mother, Arabella, and father, Juan Narvaéz. She'd been inspired by an old friend named Dusty, with the help of another friend, Nell—

Good God!

Stuyvesant nearly ran over a pedestrian. He turned to her, his eyes bulging.

"You mean the characters in your book are real people?"

"Why, yes, I thought you knew—"

"Did you read that contract you signed? You took responsibility for the content of the book? They could sue the hell out of you!"

She laughed. "You don't understand. It's a story of how strong they were, a compliment. They'll be proud—"

But would they? In her pleasure at having her manuscript accepted, she had pushed the thought of their possible displeasure to the back of her mind. To her, the story was beautiful: three orphaned sisters surviving against all odds.

True, there were sordid spots in those early years: Tamsen working in the Magoffinville Cantina; Missie's mother carried into a life of slavery from which she escaped to become a singer and dancer; Em raped by Tamsen's enemies, bearing a child along the trail. The San Francisco fire, Tamsen as madam of a bawdy house, Em's marriage to Senator Donald Alden, his suicide—Alaska, Hawaii—Australia, and now England—

The past must be used to make her point: Tamsen's strengths had carried them all to their present success and happiness. Her indomitable spirit ran through the story like a scarlet thread, holding the lives of Arab and Em together. The background had to be there to give truth to her book.

But there was Aunt Em, so nervous about her social position. Would she see the story as damaging her reputation? Missie wished Em were in England with the others. Then she might be able to view the book in its proper perspective, see it as a panoramic overview of all their lives.

I can't stop it now, Missie told herself. I've signed to have it published. And she knew that she wouldn't stop it if she could. It was too important. And she'd made a promise to herself and to Dusty Wotherspoon, a beloved alcoholic little gentleman who had always been there on the fringes of their lives; seeing, observing, hurting for them, happy for them, heroic in his own way.

She was silent for a long time, unaware that Stuyvesant studied her face. He could see an occasional flicker of doubt, replaced by determination. He hoped to God she knew what she was doing. Finally, he pulled to the edge of a crowded street, so many men moving busily along it that Missie was reminded of an ant colony in Australia. Here, the hills were tall buildings.

"There you are." She followed his waving hand and gasped with delight. Newspaper Row! She read the signs avidly: The *Tribune Bulletin*! The *New York Journal* sandwiched in between the *Tribune* and the *Sun*. The day's headlines were painted on the windows above the foyer. She read them avidly, thinking of the confusion that would be going on inside; confusion that would resolve itself into a miracle to be read by all who wished—

"May I ask what your interest is in—this?" Stew Brown broke into her reverie, gesturing toward the newspaper offices.

"It's my job," she said. "I work for the *San Francisco Examiner*. I am a reporter."

She was full of surprises. Except for nurses, laundresses, boardinghouse operators, and the like, there were still few working women in New York. Those few were like his secretary, aging, sour. He could not imagine this girl in a position where she must rub shoulders with insensitive men, especially the brash fellows of the press.

"Perhaps you will retire now," he said uneasily, "and write full time. The proceeds from your book should—"

She shook her head and laughed. "I couldn't. I intend to support myself. I need a regular salary."

"Then come here!" His voice was eager. "I know the editor of the *Sun*. I can put in a word for you—"

Come here? To New York? She thought of William Randolph Hearst, of his plans to eventually own a paper in this city. He might already be concluding some arrangement. And he would hire her in a minute! Her bright smile faded as she remembered Matthew Blaine's accusations. Such a course would only prove what he suspected, that she would do anything to advance herself. She'd told him she was returning, and she intended to do it. She didn't want to stay in this anthill of a city.

"I can't," she said evasively. "There are reasons."

The younger Brown looked disappointed, but he pointed to a sign on the ground floor of the Journal Building. "That is Hain's Restaurant. It is usually very crowded, but if you'd like some coffee—"

It would be filled with reporters, milling, talking over their stories. It would be fun to sit there for a while, listening. But she sensed her companion was reluctant to share her company.

"I don't think so," she said. "Let's just drive on. What do you think I should see?"

Before the day's end, she was dizzy with awesome sights. She'd thought San Francisco to be a large city, but was amazed at the teeming metropolis that spread before her. It was conceived that its population would reach 3.4 million in the next ten years.

They drove through narrow streets crowded with immigrants: Italian, Jewish, Irish. There were pushcarts on every corner selling flowers, bagels, thick syrupy lemonade. Peddlers of clothing wore a dozen hats, one piled atop another. Shawled women pawed through used merchandise, often struggling for possession of something that seemed a bargain.

It was a scene of poverty, of color—and of life.

Someday, thought Missie, I will write about this, too.

Skyscrapers, slums—Roebling's Brooklyn Bridge, 1,600 feet long, the greatest engineering work of the age. Watching Mrs. McLeod's sparkling eyes, her avid interest, her laughing nervousness as they crossed the bridge that had been so commonplace to him, Stew Brown thought of the girls he knew.

Wealthy, sheltered, graduates of elite finishing schools, they talked of nothing but feminine interests. Would any of them be filled with questions about steel cables, and how a suspension bridge was constructed?

He saved the grandest landmark for the last. The 151-foot copper statue on a concrete pedestal at the entrance to New York Harbor. Called *Liberty Enlightening the World*, it represented Liberty breaking free of the shackles of tyranny. One hand held a torch high. Its light was the lodestar to immigrants approaching their new country.

Missie's eyes filled with tears, thinking of those newcomers with their hopes and dreams. In a way, her own people had been immigrants, drawn to the new west. There was an almost poignant beauty in the meaning of this Lady with the

Lamp, and the fact that it was a woman holding the beacon high.

Stuyvesant Brown, seeing those tears, wasn't too sure what brought them on. They made him uncomfortable. What the hell, it was only a statue. He'd grown accustomed to it in the four years since it was unveiled. He'd brought girls here before, but none of them had cried.

He wanted to put his arms around her, to comfort her. In fact he was at the point of doing just that when she raised swimming eyes to him and smiled through her tears.

"Writers are eccentric, you know."

He supposed they were. Thank God, he was in the business end, dealing in dollars and cents.

Dusk was falling over the harbor, the figure of the Lady purpling with shadows, her lamp sending out its glow. It was time to leave.

They had dinner in a small Italian restaurant with red-checked cloths, more intimate than the elegant dining hall of the previous night. Tonight, Stuyvesant Brown did most of the talking. Missie was quiet, trying to absorb as much atmosphere as possible. Tomorrow, she would leave all this. She would be going home.

Returning her to her hotel, her escort was in a quandary. He'd never been west. He saw San Francisco as a wild city, peopled with gold miners and stray Indians. A place of constant danger in which the young lady could disappear from him forever.

It was too soon to declare himself, but he must!

Helping her from the carriage, he dared to take both her hands in his, looking down into her startled eyes with adoration.

"I can't let you go like this," he said passionately. "Forgive me if I seem—importune on short acquaintance, but you are different from anyone I've ever known. I have something to ask of you—something very important to me! I know this isn't the proper time or place, but I have come to care for you—"

Dear God! In another minute he would be on his knees in the street! Missie had no idea—

She pulled her hands free, interrupting. "I can't stay here. I—I have responsibilities at home. There are reasons—"

"Then I demand to know them. I can think of nothing that could stand between us. You say you are a widow—"

Missie was at a loss for words. She couldn't say that she was returning because of a man—a man with dark eyes that could be soft and deep or blaze with anger; a man whose black hair was always rumpled, falling over his forehead in an attractive way; a man who had accused her of unspeakable behavior.

She closed her eyes, seeing Matthew Blaine as he had been with the Evans children: gentle, tender. With that vision came a solution to her problem.

Opening her eyes, she smiled at Stuyvesant Brown. "Actually, there are four reasons. They range from seven to two, in age. Three daughters and a little boy. And they're all such darlings. I'm sure you understand."

Somehow the embarrassed young man managed to get through the ordeal of a polite farewell. Driving home to the mansion he shared with his parents, there was only one small thought to light his gloom.

He'd learned to use leverage, through this experience. From this point on, he'd see that his father, not he, would handle female authors. And he hoped to God those ladies would all be aggressive, dominating, overbearing boxcars in dowdy dresses!

Chapter 8

Missie's arrival in San Francisco was not accomplished with the dignity of a returning author. She was exhausted. Her face was smudged, her gown black with cinders, a hole in the skirt where it was ignited by a flying ember.

The trip had been long and tedious. On the journey east, she'd been enthralled at new and different scenery: mountains, deserts, flowing rivers, spreading prairies, vistas of green. Children had emerged from shacks along the route, waving to the passengers. Missie had waved back. But on the return trip, all she wanted was to get home.

The little apartment above the bakery was just as she had left it. A warm smell of baking bread drifted upward, making it homelike as she scrubbed her small body in the copper bath, washing her hair until it was gold again. Frau Schmitt appeared at the door with sweet rolls and a fresh pot of coffee, a welcome-home gift.

Missie was bursting to share her good fortune with her book. If there were only someone—anyone she could tell!

But the stocky little German woman would never understand her excitement, never in a million years.

She would tell no one, not until she held a finished copy in her hand. Still, she worried so about its effect on the Courtneys that she felt a compulsion to call, to see if they had returned. As she took the cable car, she hoped, guiltily, that they had not. It would be hard to face them, knowing what she knew—and they might have discovered she was away. She must think up an excuse for her absence, playing it by ear.

The great house was ablaze with light, and she reluctantly put her hand to the knocker on its ornate door.

No one knew she had been gone. Duke, Em, and Petra had returned several days earlier, but had not had time to check on Missie's welfare. Em was delighted to see her niece. She was planning a dinner in Petra's honor. She hoped Missie would attend. She would invite someone for her. Perhaps that nice Guilford Linstock—

Missie turned down the invitation as gracefully as she could. She often took work home to do at night, and she was very busy at the moment. Besides, one of Em's social occasions was a bit rich for a working girl.

Em seized upon her statement. Missie did not have to work. She and Duke would be most pleased to have her live with them, taking a daughter's place. Oh, and she had a short letter from Arab with most exciting news! She hurried upstairs to get it, her petticoats rustling like satiny leaves.

Missie was left alone with Petra. "Are—are you happy in California?" she asked in an attempt at conversation.

"Oh, yes." The girl stared at her clasped hands.

She didn't look happy! She looked absolutely miserable, despite the fact that she was now clad in what Em considered appropriate, ladylike dress. Even in these garments, she still managed to look—alien.

"Missie?" Petra looked up at her with a new determination that must have been painful to the shy girl. "There is something I've been wondering about. I don't know who else to ask—"

"I may not know the answer," Missie smiled, "but ask away."

"What is wrong with being Chinese?"

Missie was startled. "Why do you ask that?"

"Grandfather told Grandmother that she must invite a Mr. Wang, one of his importers, and his son. She—it made her very unhappy."

Missie laughed. "Don't let it bother you. Aunt Em's—prejudiced against anything that isn't a Courtney. The Chinese, when they were first brought here, came as workers, and she can't forget it. Neither can a lot of other people. We've got all kinds of exclusionary and restrictive laws on bringing them in and the way they have to live. It's a shame—"

Petra's eyes were on her slippers. "I always believed that all people were—human."

"I do, too," Missie liked the timid girl. "Aunt Em seems to be a snob, but she isn't, really."

"Thank you. It—bothered me." Petra's smile was radiant, transforming her rather exotic looks into real beauty. And Em had returned.

The letter she carried was very brief. It only stated that Luka's wedding had been held at home, due to an unforeseen event. Missie's older sister, Ramona, had given birth to a fourth child—a little girl, named Denise, after Denis, her Scottish father. She was a perfect child, the image of her grandmother, Arab, with red hair and a temper to match.

It was wonderful news. Missie left the house, her feet winged as she approached the cable car. Her odd conversation with Petra was forgotten in her happiness for her sisters, Luka and Ramona. It wasn't until she reached the apartment that she felt the loneliness of being a woman on her own. Then her worries shifted to the *Examiner* and Matthew Blaine. Did she still have a job? It was unlikely. Her anger had dimmed a little, pushed into the background by her success in New

York. But she had a notion few people had ever told Matthew Blaine to go to hell.

She was going to have to tackle that problem in the morning.

When Missie walked into the offices of the *Examiner*, she was immediately surrounded by a crowd of reporters, welcoming her, teasing her for skipping out without notice.

"This place makes me sick, too," one grinned. "But, hell, I never thought about taking off to the other side of the country. The beach, maybe—or Kelly's Bar."

"I worked in New York once," another chimed in. "Couldn't give me the place! Eats little girls like you for breakfast!"

"I was afraid you weren't coming back," Larry Hiller said, his blue eyes pleased. "Blaine said it was a leave of absence—"

"He did?" Missie felt like jumping for joy. "I mean, it was. There was a—a family emergency." Maybe that was stretching the truth a little, but there might be an emergency when the book came out!

Surrounded as she was, she didn't see Matthew Blaine look up from his work or the expression of relief that passed over his features when he saw her. He promptly lowered his eyes again.

"Hiller, come take a look at this! You ended a goddamn sentence with a preposition. Folkes, take a run over to City Hall. Mayor's got some kind of statement on the street situation. Carrington—"

He paused, seeming to see Missie for the first time. "You're back. Good. This is ready to go to press." He handed her a sheaf of papers. "Then I want you to go over these. Don't know why these jackasses can't spell!"

It was not a welcome, but she still had her job. He evidently intended that their angry parting be ignored, forgotten. She smiled to herself, wondering what Matthew Blaine would think if he knew he had a famous writer emptying wastebaskets, fetching, and carrying.

At least, she thought wryly, it keeps me humble.

At the end of the day, she was exhausted. Larry Hiller was concerned for her, seeing blue shadows of fatigue beneath her eyes.

"Blaine hadn't ought to work you so hard, first day back," he grumbled.

Missie smiled, grateful for his sympathy, but somehow resenting it at the same time. If she'd been a man, he would have thought nothing of it.

"Let me help you with that." He took hold of a wire basket she was carrying, but she refused to let it go. They looked at each other across the basket of waste paper, at an impasse.

"I've missed you," Larry Hiller said quietly.

"And I have missed you," she lied, to be polite.

"You shouldn't be working like a man," he jerked out. "You need a man to take care of you. I've been thinking about it for a long time. Missie—"

"—is trying to do her job," a cool voice said from behind him. "I suggest you get on with yours." Matthew Blaine, his shirt collar unbuttoned, his tie loosened, stood behind them, hands on lean hips. Hiller flushed and moved to his desk.

"As for you," Blaine said to Missie, "I'd like you to stay for a few minutes after work. We need to settle a few things about your leave."

Missie looked angrily at his retreating back. He'd saved her from an embarrassing situation, but he was so high-handed she could not thank him for it. And she had a strong hunch he planned to tell her she was fired. Well, wasn't that what she'd expected? Maybe she'd just quit, throw his damn job back in his face! Tell him she was an author and didn't need it! Then she'd go apply at the *Bulletin*, the *Call*, the *Chronicle*—

Grimly, she remained at her work, the minutes ticking

away. Hiller lingered for a time, then sensing Blaine's eyes on him, left the building.

"Missie—"

She jumped at the soft sound of her name, looking up from her papers and into Matthew Blaine's eyes. She saw no anger there, just an honest, searching expression. He had come to her.

Pulling a straight-backed chair to him, he straddled it, arms folded across the back. "Missie, I want to apologize. Your reasons for going to New York are none of my business—"

"They are not."

"Just as my reasons for feeling as I do about working women are none of yours. Am I right?"

Missie nodded reluctantly.

"If I try to explain my—my boorishness that last night, why I jumped to ridiculous conclusions, we'd probably just wind up in another argument. And I don't want that. I just want to ask you to forget it, and forgive me. Do you think you can?"

She studied him. It was clear he was sincere. A part of her wanted to make him pay for his accusations. He'd clearly implied she was a woman of loose morals. Another part longed for a return to the tenuous rapport they'd reached before their quarrel. Her mouth softened, wanting to smile, and he thrust out his hand.

"Friends?"

"Friends."

He grinned in relief, and put a tentative finger to her cheek. She felt as though the mark of it would show, emblazoned there forever.

"I've been working late, nights, but I ought to have it all wound up by Thursday. We could have dinner—if you're free."

"Free as a bird," she laughed. Then she left him, almost flying on the wings of euphoria.

A bird, that was what she reminded him of. Perhaps a

finch? No, a hummingbird. A delicate little creature that seemed to always flutter just beyond his reach. If he could catch her, she would be still and frightened, her heart palpitating beneath his palm until she was soothed and tamed—

"Chrissake!" He was so startled at his imaginings that he said it aloud to the empty room. He had no business even noticing the girl. He was not free to do so, and never would be. His offer of dinner was only by way of apology for that last time, a fact he had to make sure she fully understood.

Still, when he bent to his work, his mind whirred with the sound of hummingbird wings, and he could swear there was a scent of flowers in the room.

Chapter 9

The following Thursday, Missie dressed carefully for her evening with Matthew. It was very warm and she chose a muslin gown of yellow, carrying a fringed amber shawl. San Francisco weather was unpredictable. It was possible the wind might change, bringing in chill mist from the sea. It was well to be prepared. Frau Schmitt exclaimed over her appearance as she came downstairs. Missie knew the German woman would be peering from behind the draperies that hid the bakery windows as they drove away.

The weather held. This night, they went to a small place on the wharf, dining at rustic tables under the stars, feasting on chowder, followed by steaming platters of abalone. Their conversation was easy, almost merry, over the sound of the sea and a distant concertina.

"I have a confession to make," Blaine said rather sheepishly. "You seem to have developed a readership—"

It appeared that, shortly after she left for New York, Miss Elizabeth Anspaugh, suffragette, had appeared at the *Examin-*

er offices with several other—ah—militant ladies. Her purpose was to praise the newspaper for the wonderful article by the young girl who had been jailed following their demonstration. Certain the *Examiner* was sympathetic to the cause, she'd presented Blaine with an enormous stack of suffragette literature.

Missie could not suppress a giggle. Miss Anspaugh was a formidable lady with an erect back and bosoms that preceded the rest of her most alarmingly. She also had a booming, authoritative voice that brooked no disagreement with her views.

"What did you say to her?"

" 'Say'? She didn't give me a chance to say anything! I just listened!" He drew his mouth down in mock dismay. "Scared the hell out of me!"

Now her laughter rang out in earnest. His joined her, after the briefest delay, and he ran his fingers through his hair. "Somehow, before I could get rid of her, I said we'd do some articles on women. That's where you come in. Can you do it? No suffragette stuff—"

"The shop girls? The seamstresses, laundresses, women in the slum areas, the Chinese—"

"You got it," he nodded. "Just watch your slant. Remember you've got to please your readers—and me. Don't know how the hell she maneuvered me into this."

"She bullied you," Missie said demurely. "Just as you're trying to bully me."

He grinned. "Something like that. Now, let's stop talking shop. We're going to be friends, remember? Any topics in mind?"

"You," Missie said. "Last time I did all the talking. Tell me about you."

Did she imagine the shadow that crossed his face in the flickering candlelight? A slight hesitation before he began?

There wasn't much to tell. He'd grown up in California in a mining camp. His father died of injuries received in an accident. He'd gone back east, where his mother was at the time. There he had attended school, worked for a while at a newspaper in Philadelphia, another in Boston, then—returned here. He could think of nothing that would interest a young lady as widely traveled as she.

With a few deft questions, she encouraged him to talk about his boyhood. He'd been born somewhere above Sacramento. He talked of the mountainous country with its purple shadows and singing streams, of fishing in those streams when he was small, diving to search for gold nuggets in his teens.

"Did you find them?"

He did. He told of diving in a deep pool, the rocks shifting beneath his feet in the stream bed, trapping him; how he'd held his breath, struggling to escape—until his father rescued him.

It was clear his father had been the dominant figure in his life. His mother was barely mentioned in the tales he told of his childhood.

Possibly his mother was responsible for Blaine's opinionated attitude toward women. Or, more likely, it was the father's fault. Missie visualized an outdoor type of man, masculine and domineering, passing on his prejudices to a little boy— just as Arthur Melvin's father had handed down a heritage of cruelty and criminal cunning—

She hated the elder Blaine for a moment, then righted her thoughts. She didn't know the whole story. It didn't matter. It was enough that he had saved his son's life—that Matthew Blaine sat across the table from her now, smiling and comfortable in her presence.

It was a long time since Blaine had been at ease with a woman. The evening was so pleasant that he forgot its original purpose; a means of apology for that other disastrous night. The mists had finally begun to settle, and he wrapped the fringed shawl firmly about her shoulders, not knowing that she trembled beneath his touch. He was only aware of his own feeling; the yearning of a virile man toward a woman. It was a sensation he hadn't had for a long time, and it filled him with consternation and determination to avoid Missie's company from now on.

Yet, when they stood on Polk Street before the little bakery, gaslights blurred and haloed, their reflection puddled in the damp streets, he could not restrain himself.

"Why don't we do this again next Thursday—if you are free?"

The weeks fell into a pattern. At the office, Matthew was as terse and businesslike as ever. On their Thursday outings, he was a different man. Though there was always a barrier that precluded more than friendly interchange, he was boyish, laughing, relaxed in a way he was with no one else.

Even Frau Schmitt, meeting him when he came for Missie, was impressed. "He is a fine man," she whispered to Missie. "If you wish to have him to Sunday dinner in your rooms, Herr Schmitt and I do not object." She beamed coyly. "In Chermany, we say that the vay to a man's heart—"

Missie was shocked at her suggestion. To entertain a man, alone in her apartment? It wasn't done! Still, as she moved through her rooms at night, she imagined Matthew sitting on the sofa, pipe in hand. Or the two of them standing at the window, looking out at the night-dark gardens of the mansions on Van Ness.

He certainly had no romantic interest in her. And she'd vowed to remain single the rest of her days. Even if a man proposed to her—a man whose proposal she'd consider—she would refuse him. A man wanted a virginal bride, not one who had been used, abused, degraded as she had been.

There was no point in dwelling on such things. They were merely friends. Perhaps friendly enemies would be a better word, since they must keep their conversation free of topics on which they disagreed.

Still, there was no reason to confine their dates to Thursday evening. She could not invite him to dinner, but it would be nice to attend the Sunday musicals at the park. She might find a way to suggest it—

His weekends were usually tied up, he told her. The day of Coleen Evans's funeral was an exception. He'd made special arrangements to—to handle his other affairs. Actually, Thursday was his only evening free. But if it was difficult for her—

Missie hastened to tell him it was not. But she couldn't help wondering at it. Did he take work home from the office. Or, was there, perhaps another woman. If there was, why didn't he just come out and say so? It made her feel like a—a back street mistress!

She blushed and he looked at her, amused. "What's in your imaginative little head, young lady? Share the joke?"

"It's nothing," she lied. "Just a story one of the reporters told today."

His jaw set. "That's what I mean! Women have no business working with men! It breeds a disrespect—"

She held up a hand in a signal that said they were getting on shaky conversational ground, and he frowned. "Sorry, but I intend to have a talk with the boys."

"You will do no such thing," she said with determination. "I can take care of myself, and I intend to!"

He had to grin. He was beginning to think that she could.

At the *Examiner,* a boy was hired to empty wastebaskets and do the running. Missie had moved up a rung of the ladder. She interviewed shop girls, laundresses, piece workers, and handed Matthew Blaine her first article.

—Mary Jones worked eighteen hours today. Once a pretty girl, she is too thin, her eyes dim from stitching at men's collars; her shoulders bent.

She must support a tubercular mother, whose cough sounds constantly from a pallet in the corner of an unfurnished room. She has three children, all small and undernourished. Their father walked out on his responsibilities long ago.

On the table is a partial loaf of stale bread, a few

parings of moldy cheese. The pantry shelves are empty.
Water must be carried from a tap on the street, and there
is no man to carry it.

   The welfare of a family rests on the shoulders of Mary
Jones.

There followed a listing of Mary Jones's occupation, wage, and a comprehensive breakdown of her expenses, including the price of a pound of cheese, a loaf of day-old bread. There was nothing left for clothing, blankets, fuel—or medicine for the ailing woman.

The article ended with a plea for justice. Fathers must be forced to accept responsibility for their families, employers to pay a living wage.

"Goddamnit, I can't print this thing!" Blaine growled. "It isn't reporting! I told you, no personal opinion!"

"Then strike out the last paragraph," Missie suggested.

It was done, and she was pleased. The story made its point.

Her next article created more furor. It was the story of a young prostitute, sent out to earn money for her man. He wore expensive tailored suits and smoked cigars, while she walked the streets in a thin, frayed gown, sidling up to likely looking men; often beaten, misused—

"Where the hell did you get this story?"

"I talked to the girl. She told me."

"I will not have you getting mixed up with that kind of trash. Good God! Do you know what could happen?"

Nothing worse than had already happened to her, she thought wearily. She lifted her chin. "I am a reporter, Mr. Blaine. And these are true circumstances. Now, do you want me to write for you? Or shall I go elsewhere?"

"No, dammit!" He stared across his desk, his eyes dark with worry. "But, for God's sake, Missie, be careful."

Her articles began to draw mail, letters to the editor. And more than one of them was signed by Miss Elizabeth Anspaugh.

"I've got to hand it to you," Matthew said one Thursday

night. "You've increased our circulation. But it beats me how you know so much about the seamy side of life in San Francisco."

For a moment she felt an urge to tell him about her upcoming book, then squelched the thought. There would be enough trouble when it appeared. She would wait.

They dined at Cliff House. It was a night of rain and wind, tumultuous waves crashing against the rocks below. When he drove her home, the two of them sheltered in the closed carriage, he had to struggle to keep from taking her hand, drawing her close. Reaching the address on Polk, he watched her run up the stairs, cursing himself for letting her go—and hating himself for letting things reach this point. He was unable to think anymore, always seeing her face between himself and the printed page.

Reaching her apartment, Missie stopped on the darkened landing. Something was wrong! She knew she'd locked the door, but it stood a little ajar.

Her first thought was to go flying down the stairs, to try to catch Matthew before he drove away. Failing that, she would wake Herr Schmitt, have him come back up with her!

Nonsense! She'd insisted she could take care of herself. She must do it.

Missie pushed the door open cautiously, her heart beating so loudly she could hear it, her breath ragged with fear. The rooms were dark. There was no sound of movement. Only her breathing—

And that of someone else.

She held her own breath, to make sure, hearing a rhythmic sound punctuated by small, sobbing gasps. The room was night black, and a shiver of fear touched her spine.

She should have gone for Matthew!

She should have left the gaslights burning, but she was so afraid of fire in this old frame building. There was a candle on the table near the door; some friction matches. If she could only find them—

Reaching down, she pulled off her slippers and stepped inside, expecting a blow—or to be caught up in monstrous arms. Sliding along the wall, she found the table. The first match caught, miraculously, and she lit the candle, holding it high.

There was nothing in the room, only that hoarse rasp of breath. Perhaps it was due to an atmospheric condition, the wind whistling between the window and the sill—

She moved toward the window, frowning. Here the sound was behind her.

She whirled to see a figure on her couch; a small bedraggled figure wet with rain, eyes closed in sleep; face swollen with tears.

Petra! Dear God, Petra!

Chapter 10

Petra Channing had been miserable from the moment she entered her grandmother's home. She knew her awkward-looking woolen clothes were out of place in the California climate; that they were better suited to the sheep station in Australia from which she'd come. That was changed as soon as Em took charge. But nothing could transform the girl within the new gowns her grandmother purchased; a slender girl whose features had an Oriental cast. It was clear Em was disappointed in the result of her expenditures. Petra would always look like—Petra; something a little alien about her.

Though Em was unaware of Petra's origins, Petra herself had no illusions. Her mother, Martha, once a beautiful girl, had become a pragmatic, no-nonsense woman, happily stumping about the station above Adelaide in her gum boots, surrounded by her swarm of children and an adoring husband. No one would have guessed at the terrors of her past.

In her early teens, believing herself to be the daughter of dead Senator Donald Alden, Martha rebelled against Duke

Courtney's fatherly restrictions. After a confrontation, she overheard a conversation between Duke and her mother, learning that she was not Alden's daughter, after all, but a child of rape.

Sent to join Arab and Tamsen, Martha developed an infatuation for Tamsen's husband, Dan Tallant. As a result of that infatuation, she disappeared, stowing away aboard a ship bound for the Far East. She was found by a Chinese bandit, who took her as a concubine.

Petra was not the daughter of Peter Channing, as she believed, but the bastard of the warlord, Feng Wu.

As Petra grew more exotic in appearance as she approached her teens, Martha became fearful. The accidental learning of her own beginnings had been a traumatic experience, almost ruining her life. She did not want Petra emulating her mistakes. The best defense would be the truth.

The time she chose was just before a community gathering. Petra had donned her best gown, and Martha could see traces of an odd, dawning beauty that frightened her.

"Petra, have you noticed that you are—are not quite like your brothers and sisters? Have you ever wondered why?"

Petra's head came up. She had, indeed, thought on it. The Channing children were a variety of complexions, blonds and brunettes, but none had Petra's blue black hair and yellow ivory coloring.

"I want to tell you a story," Martha began. "It goes back to a long time ago, when I was not much older than you."

Her daughter sat immobile as she told the tale. "Do you have any questions?" Martha finished at its end.

"No, Mama."

"But you do know that we love you, your father and I?"

"Yes, Mama."

But love was not enough to ease the pain of her new knowledge. Petra had worshipped Peter Channing. With a few words, Martha had taken away one parent and substituted a sinister unknown Chinese; a warlord named Feng Wu. That

78

Feng Wu was dead made no difference. The horror was that Peter Channing, still living, was dead to Petra as a father.

Martha was pleased with the outcome of their mother-daughter conversation. Watching the girl, she could see no change in her shy, unresponsive exterior and had no idea that her admission came as a crushing blow. Petra was stunned, hurt beyond repair, but she covered it well. If she was quieter, more timid, seeming to hide in the shadows of their lives, her parents accepted it as a natural part of her personality. Life went on at the sheep station, unchanged.

It was Peter Channing who finally woke to the fact that all was not well with young Petra. As the years passed, she became more and more withdrawn; keeping close to the station, subdued and subservient in the household, her only interests lying in the care of the other Channing children.

"It isn't normal," he told Martha. "A girl her age should be interested in pretty clothes, boys."

"Maybe it's as well," Martha said evasively. "You've got to remember her background. Maybe it's wiser that she keep on as she is. She's happy."

"Good God," the usually agreeable Peter exploded. "I don't give a damn about her ancestry! I've never thought of her as anything but my daughter. She's a girl! And she's growing up to be a woman! She sure as hell deserves a chance! I think she needs a change of scene!"

Martha suggested sending Petra to her half-sister, Cammie, in Melbourne. Peter vetoed that suggestion. There would be much the same atmosphere. Cammie had children of her own. Finally, Martha reluctantly agreed that Petra should visit her grandparents in the States.

Petra arrived feeling lost, rootless; her mind filled with a terrible quaking fear that she'd been sent away because she was an embarrassment to her family; because she was half-Chinese.

Em Courtney unconsciously added to the girl's low self-esteem. Realizing she hardly knew the shy Petra, she bent over backward to be loving and attentive; not knowing that her concern for the girl's appearance and wardrobe was taken as a mark of disapproval, a need to change everything that was Petra. Duke, actually no blood relation—even to Em's daughter, Martha, was awkwardly jovial in Petra's presence. Only Missie had seemed to treat her like an equal.

Petra had liked Missie at first meeting, wishing she could be like her, free, able to meet life head on. She listened to Duke and Em as they talked about her distant cousin, filing away odds and ends of information. Among the miscellany was the address on Polk Street, above the bakery.

The journey to Los Angeles, where Petra and her grandmother were entertained by Duke Courtney's business friends, had been a disaster. Lively and informed conversation frothed around the girl like a stream around an island; touching her, passing her by. She had no knowledge of California politics, of the Civil War, some years past; of mining, commerce, and the like. Neither did she understand polite chitchat pursued on a superficial plane.

Pressed for information about her own country, she was tongue-tied. The sheep station was home, therefore not unique. A socialite could not be interested in shearing sheep, nor her husband enjoy a dissertation on the making of cheese. Once she mentioned settlers and squatters, creating an embarrassing situation in which she was the center of attention.

It seemed that everything was backward here. Here, settlers were considered squatters, and squatters settlers. It was all confusing. She felt foolish trying to explain.

She would leave the great houses and wealthy company to walk along the beach, looking across the vast reach of sea. There, far past the horizon, lay Australia and home.

—Where no one wanted a girl who was unlike the rest of the family—

The return to San Francisco was more pleasant. She had her own room in the mansion, a place she could hide when the house filled with guests. She could not run away from the dinner Em planned in her honor.

Dressed in an ice blue ruffled gown that Em had chosen, Petra was ill at ease as she stood with Em to greet their guests. Her cheeks were hot as she met eyes that were friendly but curious. And finally she felt her grandmother stiffen and followed her gaze. The Wangs, father and son, had arrived.

The elder Wang appeared startled for a space, then his face was impassive as he greeted the granddaughter of his business acquaintance with Asiatic charm. The younger, a boy little older than Petra, had fine, sensitive features that bore an expression of interest.

They know me for what I am, Petra thought miserably. The alien guests Duke forced upon Em had recognized Petra as one of their race—

"Wo shih h'wahn chee'yen nee," the young man said. He smiled at her expression of confusion. "I am delighted to meet you. Do not be concerned, I speak English very well. I was born here."

His name was Lee, and his dark eyes displayed an alert intelligence. His manner put her at her ease, and soon she found herself enjoying a conversation with him. He asked about Australia, and listened—really listened to her description of life on a sheep station. It was evident that he had an inquiring mind.

In turn, she learned that his mother, a traditional Chinese wife, was dead. His father had moved from Chinatown following her death. They "live American-style," since they regarded themselves as Americans.

Petra was suddenly aware they were the object of disapproving glances. Lee's voice trailed off. "I am keeping you from your guests," he said formally. "Forgive me." He moved to stand beside the elder Wang, their presence surrounded by an invisible wall almost as tangible as glass.

At table, the two Chinese were placed near the foot. Petra

was paired with Guilford Linstock; a pop-eyed young man, who could talk of nothing but his studies at Berkeley. Listening to his stories of the academic world—as foreign to her as the coast of China—Petra kept glancing the length of the table, catching an occasional glimpse of Lee's profile, of his father's impassive face.

Maybe, she thought ruefully, if her grandmother knew of her true parentage, she, too, would be seated there. She was glad when the interminable dinner ended and the guests went home.

The next day, a messenger from the House of Wang delivered a mass of perfect blooms to Em. For Petra, there was a small lacquered box. It contained a tiny gold pin in the shape of a dragon; its eyes of inlaid gems. Em gasped.

"That is expensive! I cannot believe those people! The nerve of them! We will have to return it, today!"

Petra looked at the intricate little object. She had never received a gift of jewelry in her life. The dragon struck a chord within her that she didn't know existed. She lifted her head.

"It is a gift. I'm—I'm going to keep it," she said, almost apologetically. Then she turned, her eyes swimming, and ran for the stairs. Em heard the door to Petra's door close with a bang and narrowed her eyes in thought.

"Well, I never!" she whispered to herself, thinking of her granddaughter's timid nature. The girl had never taken a stand on anything before. She'd expressed no interest in gowns or jewelry, and wasn't acquisitive in any way. Then why this interest in a most unsuitable gift? Surely she wasn't attracted to the Wang boy—a Chinese!

A little maid came to announce guests: two women who had attended the dinner party. Em took them into the parlor and ordered tea. When they had gone, she was distracted, at the edge of anger.

"I've never been so embarrassed in my life," she confided to Duke that night. "Myra Jenner commented on Petra's coloring. She said she was confused at first, thinking the girl had come with the Wangs!''

"She does look Oriental."

"I do not see it," Em said icily. "If the Wangs had not come—''

"Their coming to dinner had nothing to do with Petra's appearance," Duke said angrily. "Hell, Em, I remember when Martha and Peter came back from Hong Kong. You wondered about Petra then, and she was just a baby. You said you thought Martha might have—''

"I never thought such a thing! My granddaughter does not have Oriental blood! It's bad enough when my friends make insinuations, but for her grandfather! It—it's unspeakable!''

Neither of them noticed the half-opened door.

Petra had suffered pangs of conscience all afternoon. She'd had no business speaking to Em as she did. Em did not consider the gift appropriate, and she should know more than Petra as to its rightness. Perhaps it should be returned.

She came down earlier to make amends, but her grandmother was entertaining two ladies in the parlor. Not wishing to be caught up in the group, she returned to her room.

Now, she stood outside a door, as her mother had so many years before, hearing something she did not want to hear. And she knew, with a sinking heart, that she would not be acceptable here if the truth were known; that if she stayed, she would be masquerading.

She looked down at the dragon pin. She'd clenched it so tightly that it pricked her palm, drawing blood.

Blood that was not as pure as that of the Courtneys. The blood of a yellow race.

Returning to her room, she wrote a note stating that she was unhappy in this social atmosphere, and was leaving to make her own way in the world. Then she slipped from the house and made her way to an address on Polk Street.

Missie was not at home. Frau Schmitt, upon hearing the drenched, worn girl was a relative of her protégée, unlocked the rooms above the bakery and let her in. Did the woman look at her strangely? Or was it Petra's imagination? Would she ever be able to face anyone without shrinking?

Settling in a soggy heap, she wept until she fell asleep from exhaustion, waking to look into Missie's startled eyes.

Chapter 11

Petra thought she'd cried all the tears she possessed, but she was wrong. Missie sat down beside her, taking her in her arms, and the girl began to sob again. Please, could she stay here—just for a little while until she could get work, find a place of her own? Don't make her go back to the Courtneys. She didn't belong there—

"Nonsense! Your grandmother loves you! They'll be so worried—"

"I won't go back! I won't! Nobody can make me!"

Missie was at a loss. She was concerned at Petra's distress, certain that Duke and Em would be frantic. She was unable to gain a clue from Petra's hysterical sobbing. The girl was making herself sick.

"Of course you can stay," Missie said. "As long as you wish. But I'll have to understand what the problem is. Otherwise," she grinned wryly, "your grandmother will be mad at me. If I'm going to help—"

"Maybe you won't want to," Petra said in a dull voice.

"I can't imagine that. I've needed help a few times myself."

"But there's something you don't know about me," Petra persisted. "You might not want me in your house if you knew."

Was it that bad? Dear God, what had Petra done? Missie was shaken. "Try me," she said.

From somewhere Petra summoned a dignity that made her look even more Oriental.

"I am Chinese."

Missie stared at her, bewildered. "What are you talking about? Petra, have you lost your mind? Cousin Martha's your mother!"

"Yes."

"And Peter Channing is—," Missie stopped, seeing the girl's face whiten, red blotches standing out against her pallor. "He is your father," Missie finished, "—isn't he?"

It was obvious from Petra's expression that he was not.

Petra repeated her mother's story, monotonously, by rote. It wasn't difficult. The words were burned into her mind. She told of Martha's beginnings, that her mother was not the child of Donald Alden as had been believed.

Missie nodded. She knew that. It was in her book. But the remainder of Petra's tale was new to her. She had never heard of Feng Wu. Her first thought was of what an exciting chapter this would have made; the exotic scenes she might have written had she known the truth. Then her heart melted as she looked at the pathetic girl.

"I don't see why you're so upset," she said honestly. "You're a beautiful girl, with an interesting heritage. Your folks love you—"

"Do they? They sent me away, didn't they? And I'm an embarrassment to Grandmother!"

"Aunt Em? Come on, Petra! She's got some stuffy notions, but she would never feel—"

Petra stopped her, reciting the conversation she'd overheard his very night. Missie listened, shaking her head. Her aunt hadn't meant what she said, at least, not the way Petra had taken it.

"Go to your grandmother," Missie urged. "Tell her the truth. I think you'll find she'll take it very well. It will make no difference."

Petra's small fingers clamped on Missie's wrist. "I won't do it," she said fiercely. "It's my mother's secret, anyway, not mine! I won't tell her and I won't go back there, pretending to be something I'm not!"

"All right," Missie sighed, "but we'll have to pay a short visit in the morning, give them some kind of reason, so they won't be hurt."

"I won't do it!" Petra looked like a small, cornered kitten. "I won't."

"Then I will," Missie told her. "Come on, let's get you out of those wet things and fix a place for you to sleep."

Petra finally slept but Missie didn't. Her aunt had been upset enough when Missie moved out. She had a notion that this would be the final straw in their relationship.

Missie rose the next morning and took the cable car to Nob Hill. She would be late for work, but it didn't matter. This was more important. She stood for a long time before the mansion, so impressive, so ornate, befitting the Courtneys' social position. Finally she braced herself and rapped at the door. It was opened by Em, her face serene, her manner unruffled.

Petra had retired early the previous night. Em believed her to still be sleeping, and had given the help orders that she not be disturbed. She heard Missie out, paling, eyes wide with disbelief. Without a word, she left her niece and hurried to her granddaughter's room. She returned with Petra's note crumpled in her hand.

"I don't understand," she whispered. "I just don't understand!"

Missie searched for an explanation. "She doesn't feel she

fits in here, Aunt Em. Remember that she comes from a sheep station in another country. It makes her a sort of—farm girl. She doesn't want to disappoint you, but—"

Em's gentian eyes, so like Missie's, lost their hurt look. It was replaced by a dawning comprehension.

"You!" she breathed. "You've done this to her! You've talked her into this stupid situation with your living alone, your suffragette notions! I—I'm sorry we brought you here from Australia! You've made nothing but trouble—!"

"Em!" Duke Courtney stood in the doorway, his blue eyes wide with disbelief. "Em, what in hell are you saying!"

Em fled into her husband's arms, weeping wildly, and Missie left. She hadn't made things better, she thought ruefully, but worse. But then, hadn't it always been that way? She seemed to spoil everything she touched.

She waited for the cable car, longing for it to appear—and wishing Petra would disappear. She didn't want the responsibility of the younger girl. She hoped she'd decide to return to Australia.

The cable car was coming—and so was Duke Courtney. Missie pretended not to see him. Maybe she could climb aboard before he reached the stop. Duke, his long legs unimpaired by age, won the race.

"Wait, Missie! I've got to talk to you."

Shrugging in defeat, she turned to face him. The cable car rattled on by. Duke was breathing hard, but he was red-faced and obviously upset.

"Now, what the hell is this? I've heard Em's version, but there's something more. Goddamnit, I want the truth!"

Missie looked at him levelly. "It has something to do with a conversation Petra overheard."

Duke was bewildered for a moment, then his jaw dropped. "She was eavesdropping last night?"

"Not eavesdropping, Uncle Duke. The door was open. She couldn't help hearing."

"Goddamn!" He was almost comic in his dismay. "Em didn't mean what she said. The girl can't help her looks—"

"Or what she is," Missie finished for him.

Comprehension struggled with pity in his face. "It's true, then. Does she—know?"

"She knows."

"Will it help if I go talk to her? Tell her it doesn't make any difference?"

"I don't think it will. Why don't you let it rest for a while. She's all mixed up right now. She thinks her folks sent her here to be rid of her, that she'd be an embarrassment to Aunt Em."

"Aw, hell, Missie! You know Em better than that!"

"But Petra doesn't. And she won't believe differently until she's thinking straight. Besides, she's the one to tell Aunt Em, not us."

Duke patted his wife's niece clumsily on the shoulder. "You're right, honey. Let's give it a little time. You headed for work? Let me hitch up the carriage, and—"

"I'd rather catch the next car, but thank you."

Duke looked relieved. "I'll head on back to the house, then, and simmer Em down. May take a heap of doing." He grinned, waved, and headed homeward.

Duke Courtney was a nice man, Missie thought as she waited. He'd been a rough miner when Em married him, and now he ranked among the major business men in San Francisco. He was so different from her own father, Juan Narvaéz. Papa had never lost his royal bearing. Rather somber, darkly handsome, he'd never been close to his children. Then there was Tamsen's husband, soldier of fortune, adventurer, diplomat. The men were totally dissimilar, yet such close friends.

For that matter, the sisters they married were different, too. Gracious Em, prettily selfish Arab. And Tamsen! There were not enough adjectives to describe Tamsen.

She felt a wave of homesickness, of longing for her Aunt

Tamsen—who would know how to handle the present situation involving Petra.

She was late to work as she'd expected. And, true to form, Matthew Blaine glowered at her. When they were alone, he was most gentlemanly and considerate. But on the job, she had to keep proving herself, expecting no favors due to her sex.

She had no idea that he'd been close to panic. Missie was always punctual; her tardiness so unusual that Matthew Blaine had begun to envision all kinds of catastrophes. Missie was ill! He should not have taken her out on such a damp night. There had been an accident; a cable had broken, her car sliding backward to disaster. Or, hell, she had to walk some distance to the line. Maybe some damn man—!

His relief at the sight of her made him unusually brusque. Missie had wanted to confide in him, seek his advice about Petra, but she changed her mind. There was no one to count on in this world except oneself. She intended to handle her own problems.

She went home after a day of exhausting work to find a hot meal waiting, Petra looking at her anxiously to see if it were something she would enjoy. Missie grinned at her. ''I see why working men try to keep women in their place,'' she said. This was certainly a lot more pleasant than returning to an empty room at day's end.

She put her arms around her pretty cousin, giving her an affectionate hug. This was going to work out better than she'd expected.

The feeling lasted until Thursday. That morning, Missie told Matthew she would have to cancel their evening. She had a houseguest, a visiting relative.

Blaine, still searching for a way to break his involvement with a free-thinking girl who was getting under his skin, was surprised at his reluctance to grasp at this straw.

''No, problem. I'll take you both out.'' His dark brows raised. ''It is—a young lady?''

It was. Petra Channing was Missie's exact opposite. She was feminine, quiet, shy, and lovely, too, with that odd Asiatic look; something haunted in the depths of amber eyes. This girl would never be a suffragette. She would be a sweet, submissive wife to some man.

Reading Matthew Blaine's thoughts in his face, Missie's heart plummeted.

This had been a mistake, bringing these two together.

But had it? It certainly made no difference to her. She was unusually quiet all evening, flinching inside at Matthew's deference to Petra; Petra's new-sounding silvery laughter.

Reaching home, she tried to shut her ears to Petra's effusive comments. Matthew Blaine was a wonderful man, so handsome, so intelligent. Petra clasped her hands and sighed. "Oh, Missie, I've never been so happy in my life! I can't thank you enough! It's been such a nice evening—"

It was only the first of such outings. From that Thursday onward, the Matthew Blaine party consisted of three: Matthew, Missie—and Petra. It was Petra for whom doors were opened, Petra who sat at the theater wide-eyed, clapping her small hands in delight; Petra, who was offered the choice of dining spots, glowing with excitement at life in San Francisco while Matthew watched in affectionate amusement.

For the first time in her life, Missie experienced the emotion of jealousy. Seeing the glances the two exchanged, her heart felt like a small, sour green apple in her chest. She told herself valiantly that it was absurd to feel as she did. After all, she and Matthew were only friends; employee and employer. And she knew—had known all along—how Matthew felt about liberated woman. Even if she were interested in him—which she was not!—she could not change.

Yet, she wished he would look at her as he did at Petra, treat her as a woman, just for once. She yearned to smooth back an errant lock that fell across Matthew's forehead in a boyish way; to touch the pulse that throbbed in his temple when he laughed—as he did more often with Petra.

And finally admitting to that yearning, she knew that she wanted something more. She wanted his arms around her, to press her body to his in the act of love; an act she'd experienced once in terror, in the grasp of a brutal man. The only time Matthew Blaine had touched her was in anger. His action had not been in character with the man she knew him to be now. She felt, instinctively, that if he loved a woman, he would be gentle—

What was Petra saying? Missie hadn't heard her remark; only Matthew's answer.

"Your pretty cousin wouldn't agree with you on that," Matthew told Petra, teasingly. "She thinks there shouldn't be any difference between a woman and a man—"

He grinned at Missie, and she blushed. She hadn't been thinking along those lines. Not at all. Somewhere between the salad and dessert, she knew she had fallen hopelessly—and miserably—in love with Matthew Blaine; a man whose basic beliefs were in direct opposition to her own. She could never fit into his life in any way—not like Petra.

She, not Petra, was the intruder here tonight. She wished she had stayed home.

Chapter 12

Petra Channing was happier than she'd ever been in her life. During the day, she could pretend that Missie's little apartment was her own. She cleaned and stitched and cooked like a whirlwind. Occasionally, she sat in the parlor behind the bakery downstairs, exchanging tales of life in Australia with Frau Schmitt, who countered with stories of her girlhood in Germany.

And then there was Missie. She loved Missie so much! Missie was responsible for her blissful life here. And Missie had introduced her to Matthew Blaine!

All week she looked forward to those Thursday evenings.

When Petra lived with her family on the sheep station above Adelaide, she remained at home with the children when the elder Channings went into the city. She had never dined in a large hotel, had never attended the theater, had never known what it was like to do something just for pure enjoyment. And Petra had never been courted by a young man in her life, not that several hadn't tried. She'd managed to turn them away with her reticent manner.

In no way did she wish to become involved, not with her mixed background. For Australians, too, had their prejudices. The few foreigners, Orientals and East Indians who operated small fruit and vegetable markets in town, were not so much looked down on as ignored as a different species.

Matthew Blaine was not like the neighbors at home. He did not share her grandmother's views. He'd mentioned the Wangs, more than once. He knew the family well, and had the utmost respect for them, not only as business people, but as men of excellent character.

Matthew would not reject her friendship because of her parentage. Perhaps, she thought dreamily, one day she would tell him; just let it drop casually. "You do know, don't you, that I am half Chinese?"

The black brows would go up, and he would say, "Really? Then that's another thing I like about you!"

Petra smiled blissfully as she curled on the sofa, weaving fantasies that brought her closer to Matthew Blaine, then closer still—until a coral tint colored her ivory cheeks.

Thursday. She would see him Thursday. But that was tomorrow night. So long to wait—

She looked about at the shining little apartment. There was nothing more to do the long day. She could not visit with Frau Schmitt. The German woman was occupied with an order for a wedding cake. Petra toyed with the idea of dropping by the *Examiner,* catching a glimpse of Matthew Blaine at work—

But Missie said he was all business at the paper. He might not welcome a visit. Would there be anything wrong with going at the end of the day? Just to be company for Missie on the ride home?

She would do just that!

And to fill the interim, she would visit Chinatown. Missie had promised to take her, but somehow they'd never found the time. Petra would go alone—

She dressed, her heart beating a little faster, proud of her new daring self.

It was a bright blue day, the wind off the sea carrying a tang of salt and a hint of chill. Petra was glad she'd worn a high collared gown and padded sacque. She had no idea that it made her look even more Oriental, and that she did not seem out of place as she entered T'ang Yen Gai, the Chinese street.

Only one passerby marked Petra's appearance with a look of surprise. A young man, in Western clothing, paused to stare—then retraced his steps, hurrying to catch her.

"Miss Channing! Wait—"

Petra paused in pretty confusion, then her eyes widened with pleasure. "Lee!"

"I did not expect to see you here," he beamed, pushing back strands of ink black hair that looked like silk.

"Nor I, you," Petra said.

"I'm so glad—" They said it at the same time, in chorus, and began to laugh.

The son of Wang had come to Chinatown on business. It was completed, and he was free. Discovering Petra was sight-seeing, he offered to show her around; an offer she accepted gratefully. Without his escort, she might have missed much of the color of "Little China."

He led her along the Street of the Men of China; here one might purchase winter melons, pork dumplings, dried duck, and exotic spices. Wares were displayed openly on counters, and in woven baskets filled with strange produce; cobblers and chair-menders, vendors of fruits, nuts, and cigars, carried on their trade from doorsills and boxes set along the narrow streets.

Chinatown was actually the old part of San Francisco, Yerba Buena. Most of it lay within an area of nine square blocks: Clay, Washington, Jackson, and Pacific streets, for the two blocks between Kearny and Stockton and the four blocks of Grant Avenue from Sacramento to Pacific. It seemed larger, an alien country that had set its stamp on old Western-style buildings, bedizening them with gaudy Chinese lettering and gilded dragons.

The buildings themselves had been cut into tiny rooms, with shelves a foot and a half wide from floor to ceiling. On these, from twenty to forty men slept—in defiance of a law known as the Cubic Air Act. According to its provisions, sleeping quarters could not be rented unless there were five hundred feet of cubic air per person.

Yet the accommodations above ground were palatial compared to the cellars and underground coops where water dripped from the rooms above, and the air was stagnant, choking from the smoke of oil lamps and open fires for cooking.

"But the women," Petra asked uncertainly, "the children—?"

"There are few in these warrens," Lee said, his jaw hardening. "Families are a luxury only the wealthier can afford." He went on to explain that the exclusionary laws had stopped immigration. Many of the men who came to work in this land of opportunity had left families behind them; wives and children they would never see again. Therefore, women and children were respected here, highly prized. He didn't mention the darker side of "Little China": the poor unadorned Chinese girls indentured to prostitution in fetid cribs—

He led her through the Street of Gamblers, and down dark, narrow, twisting alleys Petra would never have dared enter alone. Here, smoke from cooking fires boiled from doorways. Sometimes they were forced to duck laundry hung to dry across their path. And often, among the odors of too many people in cramped quarters, the mingled smells of spices, smoke, and laundry soap, there was a strange sweetish scent that Petra could not identify. Lee did not seem to notice it, and shy Petra did not ask its origin.

She was greatly interested in the shops, especially the small tunnellike apothecary shops. Here, all the odors of the Orient were blended. Behind the counters, tiny drawers ran to the ceiling. They were filled with dried leaves, barks, and roots, which were measured on hand-held weighing scales and wrapped in squares of paper, later to be mixed and taken in the form of tea. It was fascinating to her, but not to Lee.

"I grew up on that sort of thing," he said, grimacing.

Petra smiled, seeing a small, stubborn dark-haired boy being forced to take some evil-tasting medication. She wanted to reach out, take his hand—

Returning to the wider streets, Lee found a small eating place and ordered tea and *dim sum*. They sat and talked and laughed together until Petra realized it was time to go. Leaving the little establishment, they walked back toward another civilization—until Petra caught sight of an alleyway they had not explored. Was it darker, more narrow than the others? Or was it a trick of the late afternoon sun?

"What is down there?"

Lee looked uncomfortable and shrugged. "It is much the same, I suppose, though less—respectable. Living quarters, markets, an herbalist—"

"I don't want to miss anything," Petra said laughing. "Come on! We can hurry. There's just time—"

She was already almost running, and he grinned wryly then hastened to catch up with her. "Look," she said excitedly, pointing to a garish paper decoration. "And there's the apothecary shop, over there—"

She stopped suddenly, the light of excitement leaving her eyes as she stared blankly at the facade of the establishment. Chinese characters displayed the name of the shop. Below them was a translation, neatly lettered in gold.

"Herbs and teas," the sign read.

"Proprietor, Feng Wu."

Lee almost ran into Petra when she halted so abruptly. Thrown off balance, he caught at her arm in an attempt to keep from bowling her over. He released her quickly, laughing.

"How would this look in the papers! Son of the House of

Wang tramples pretty girl in Chinatown! My apologies. Are you all right?''

She didn't answer and he looked at her more closely. Her eyes were blank with shock. The young Chinese glanced hastily around. There was nothing to have caused her distress. But there was clearly something wrong.

"Miss Channing," he said gently. "Petra—?"

She flinched and seemed to come awake, shivering a little.

"Petra," he said again, "are you ill? Here, take my coat—"

The crisis, whatever it was, had passed. Sanity returned to her eyes, sanity touched with a trace of fear.

"I'm all right," she said. "But let's go, please. I don't want to be late."

Again she was almost running as they left the dark alley— and finally Chinatown, itself, behind them. Petra refused to let him accompany her to her destination. He asked to see her again, and received only a vague answer. It was as if he were already erased from her mind.

Petra entered the *Examiner* building fifteen minutes late. Please God, let Missie be here! And, more important, Matthew Blaine! If she could just see them, hear their voices, she would wake from the nightmare that still clouded her brain.

Let them still be here—please!

Chapter 13

On the morning that Petra decided to visit Chinatown, Duke Courtney entered the offices of the *Examiner*. Though he'd not been there before, he was familiar with the operations of the *Chronicle*. As he'd expected, it was little different; the clattering of machines, smoke-filled rooms, everyone hurrying. He had no difficulty locating Missie. Her bright head was bent over a desk, where she was busily correcting a column.

She looked, he thought with amusement, like a little girl playing school. Conscious of curious eyes turned on him, he made his way to where she sat. A dark-browed man made a move as if to stop him, and he barged on past. Hell, Missie was his niece. He had the right to see her if he wanted to.

"Missie?"

Missie jumped at the sound of Duke's voice, her eyes rounding with pleased surprise that turned to fear.

"There's nothing wrong, is there? Aunt Em—"

"—is as well as could be expected," he finished for her.

"We've got something of a problem, though. Looks like your folks, Dan, Tamsen, and Nell, are coming home—to San Francisco."

Missie leaped to her feet, papers wafting to the floor, her eyes as bright as stars. The staff of the *Examiner* was treated to the sight of their no-nonsense girl reporter throwing her arms around the neck of a tall, distinguished older man. Her words were clearly audible in the hush that followed.

"I love you!" she said.

Suddenly conscious of the attention she'd evoked, Missie blushed. She would take a break, she decided recklessly. If she had to work late tonight, it would be worth it. She took Duke's arm and led him out into the street and to a small eating establishment frequented by reporters. There, they sat and talked over coffee.

Duke had no further details to offer. Em had received a letter from Tamsen saying that such a move was being considered. That was all. In his pocket, he had several letters for Missie. One was from Arab. It might be more explicit. The problem was Em. She was going all to pieces, certain that Arab would blame her for letting her daughter move out on her own. Would Missie—and Petra—consider coming home?

Missie had lost her early euphoria. She'd remembered— *The Book*. If her mother, Arabella, and aunts Tamsen and Em saw it for what it was, a tribute to their strength, all would be well. Otherwise, she would be in the midst of an enemy camp. No, she could not return to the Courtney house. But Petra—!

With the thought of Petra came an image of Matthew Blaine. With Petra out of the picture—!

It was an ugly notion! And Petra was happy now, coming out of her shell.

"I'm sorry, Uncle Duke. Tell Aunt Em not to worry. I'll tell Mama the truth, that I'm only doing what I want to do."

Duke Courtney looked at the watch that fastened to a heavy

chain across his front, frowning. He had an appointment. But should she change her mind—

"I won't," Missie said dully. "I won't."

When he had gone, she opened her mother's letter. It said nothing more than she already knew: that they were talking of coming home—to stay. She missed them, longed to see them—but with *The Book*—

She was torn between wishing they'd arrive soon, and wishing they wouldn't come at all!

Her other letter was addressed to Melissa McLeod. It bore the return address of Brown, Halpert and Brown. Ordinarily, she would have ripped it open in excitement. Now, she was reluctant. It was a symbol of a cloud hanging over her future—a cloud of family disapproval that might destroy everything she loved. How had she dared write such a volume! Suddenly she saw it as a listing of horrors Em, Tamsen, and Arabella would want to forget—just as she would like to erase Arthur Melvin from her memory.

The envelope contained two sheets, one a formal report on the progress of her manuscript. It was to be entitled, *The Survivors,* and would be sent to the binders within the week. Due to its popular content, the firm of Brown, Halpert and Brown, were departing from their usual conservative policies, and pursuing an unprecedented course of advertising through newspapers. They hoped their new policy met with her approval.

They would be New York papers, she thought, trying to still her fluttering heart. Not here! Dear God, not here! New York hardly knew that California existed—

The second sheet of paper was not so formal, though it was hand-scribed on the publisher's letterhead.

My darling Melissa, it read. *Again forgive me for being importune, but I have been through weeks of misery. I relive that last night of bliss constantly, and know I cannot live without you. I am offering you my love and my life, and a*

101

*home for your four fatherless children. I await your answer
impatiently. I love you so!*

It was signed, *Stuyvesant Brown.*

Missie read the letter twice, unable to believe its content.
Another problem! As if she didn't have enough already! She
felt halfway between laughter and tears. Matthew and Petra,
The Book, her family coming home to discover their past was
revealed for all to see—and now this—this amorous idiot!

She finally stood, sighing. She'd have to take care of one
thing at a time. Today, she would answer Stuyvesant Brown's
letter, letting him down as easily as possible. And tonight,
she would tell Matthew Blaine she would not be available for
their usual Thursday outing, but that Petra would accompany
him.

In the meantime, she'd have to figure out some way to
explain that scene in the office. She'd always posed as a
young widow, a girl who must work for a living, carefully
avoiding any connection with the prominent Courtney family.
Surely no one had recognized Duke Courtney, but he was still
an extremely handsome man. There would surely be an
amount of good-natured teasing, questions as to his identity.
She pondered on her answers as she walked back to the
office. An old family friend? Her embrace had been too
impulsive, too warm. A distant relative from Australia?
Duke's very appearance spelled money, influence. Men of his
type felt a responsibility toward penniless female kin. None
of her excuses rang true.

Missie needn't have worried. She walked into an atmosphere where she was treated with embarrassed courtesy. She
couldn't volunteer answers to questions that were not asked.
But it was absolutely clear what everyone was thinking—
even Matthew Blaine, who wore an expression like a
thundercloud.

The attitude of polite avoidance continued through the
afternoon. It was Larry Hiller who finally approached the
subject of her morning visitor. Sitting on the edge of Missie's

desk, he absently moved her pens and inkwell about, seemingly absorbed in them. Finally, he spoke.

"That fellow this morning. Friend of yours?"

"He knew my husband," Missie said quickly. That, at least, was not a lie.

"I was wondering," Larry said carefully, still not looking at her, "if you're tied up this evening. Figured we could grab a bite somewhere, take in a show—"

Missie's nerves were screaming. She had enough problems without having to fend off Larry Hiller all evening! Yet, he had always been kind. She should reciprocate—a little. But, dear God, not tonight! A thought struck her. Why not use one problem to solve another.

"I'm busy tonight," she said. "Perhaps tomorrow?"

Hiller was delighted, and so was she. She would tell Matthew she'd forgotten it was Thursday and committed herself to another engagement. He would probably be vastly relieved.

She finished her work speedily. As it neared quitting time, her desk was clear. She turned to answering Stuyvesant Brown's letter, thanking him for his offer, refusing it sweetly in a way to salve his ego. After the death of her husband, she'd made a vow never to remarry, but to devote herself to her children and career—

Aware that the office had emptied, except for Matthew Blaine, she hastily signed the letter and sealed it into an envelope. Rising, she gathered up the mail Duke brought, the note from her mother, the report from Brown, Halpert and Brown—

"Missie?"

She turned to face Matthew Blaine, feeling as if her heart were beating in her throat. "Yes?"

He stood, his arms folded across his chest, his tie loosened, his shirt opened to show the smooth tan flesh of his throat. An errant lock of hair tumbled over one dark brow. His face was set in serious lines.

"I know it is none of my business, but your visitor this morning—what is he to you?"

"He knew my dead husband," she said defiantly.

Matthew's brows raised. "Duke Courtney?"

She felt her face flame with guilt. "You know him?"

"Let's say I know of him. He's pretty well known around town. It would appear you're—rather well acquainted with him yourself."

"He's been—kind to me," she said stiffly.

"From what I hear, he's a kind man. A good family man." Blaine emphasized the word family. Missie flushed again.

"Yes," she said. Then she sought frantically for a change of subject. "I've been wanting to talk to you. I forgot tomorrow was Thursday, and I've made other arrangements—"

"Courtney?" His face was hard, impassive.

"Of course not! I'm going out with—someone else. But Petra is free—"

Matthew Blaine caught both her wrists in hands as hard as iron bands. "Dammit, Missie, what are you trying to pull?"

"I—I don't understand—"

" 'Understand,' hell! For the last few weeks, we haven't gone out alone! You keep trying to foist your—cousin, or whatever the hell she is—off on me! Now, don't get me wrong, she's a sweet kid, but she's so damned young, and she's not my type. She ought to be going out with somebody of her own kind! Goddamnit—"

Missie was suddenly blind with relief, a tide of joy rising in her veins, making her dizzy as she swayed toward him, only to be closed off at his next words.

"Goddamnit, I don't know what's going on. I don't have any ties on you, I know that! But I'll be damned if I'll settle for a substitute. If there's someone else—this Courtney, for example, tell me, and I'll back off. I don't blame you. Courtney's a rich old bastard. Just—don't get hurt."

Missie drew herself up, gentian blue eyes looking squarely

into angry dark ones. "Thank you for your understanding," she said coolly. "If I decide to have an affair with a rich man, you'll be the first to know. Tomorrow night, I happen to be going out with Larry Hiller. Now, if you will excuse me—"

She was gone before he could stop her. He sank into her chair, running his fingers through his rumpled hair. He'd done it again! What the hell was wrong with him! He recalled now that Duke Courtney once lived in Australia. That part of her story could easily be true. And so could the tale about getting her nights mixed up. As he'd said, he had no ties on her, no right to ask her to hold Thursdays open at his whim. Damn! he'd acted like seventeen different kinds of fool—

A piece of paper on the floor beside the desk caught his attention. He picked it up and smoothed it out. It held the footprint of her small slipper.

Brown, Halpert and Brown, Publishers. A New York address. And the letter, handwritten, began, *My darling Melissa—*

Good God!

Once committed, Blaine read on. *—my love and my life, and a home for your four fatherless children—*

What the hell! He read it again, his face twisting into an agony of disbelief. The missive was signed, *Stuyvesant Brown.*

Just who was Missie Narvaéz, also known as Melissa McLeod? A beautiful widow, trying to survive in a male world? Or an ambitious, conniving, lying little bitch?

At last he stood wearily and straightened his sagging shoulders. He could waste no more time thinking about Missie. He had a responsibility of his own. And now he had to go home to it. Taking his coat from a hook, he slung it over his shoulder and walked, head bowed, out into the darkening twilight world.

Chapter 14

Petra Channing coming late to the *Examiner* office, haunted by the sign she'd seen in Chinatown, arrived at exactly the wrong moment. Her light feet made no sound as she entered the doorway. And she saw Matthew Blaine holding Missie's wrists, heard his explosion of anger.

"You keep trying to foist your—cousin, or whatever the hell she is—off on me!"

Petra stopped, stunned, her heart pounding so hard in her ears that she only heard snatches of what followed.

"—Sweet kid—Not my type—"

Putting her knuckles to her mouth, Petra suppressed a moan as he ended with the most terrible statement of all.

"She ought to be going out with somebody of her own kind!"

Her own kind! Her own kind! Her own kind! The words resounded in her mind as she visualized a dark, twisting alley in Chinatown, a sign that read, Feng Wu.

Her own kind!

Somehow, Petra managed to move, each step like walking in quicksand. Once out on the street, she began to run, narrowly avoiding other pedestrians, who looked at her curiously and stepped out of her way. Finally, her feet slowed as she realized she had no particular destination. Dazed, wounded to her very heart, she wanted only to hide, from Matthew Blaine and Missie, from the world, from herself. She looked around frantically, seeing a narrow path between two buildings. She wedged herself inside, leaning her cheek against cool stone as she tried to decide her next move.

Dear God, what should she do now? She felt sick with guilt and shame. Her folks hadn't wanted her. They'd dumped her on her grandmother. Knowing how Em Courtney felt about—about foreign blood, she couldn't stay there. Instead, she'd intruded on Missie's life, tagging along like a—a bloody fool, basking in the attention she received from Matthew Blaine. He was Missie's friend, not hers! It was Missie he cared for, how could she have been so blind?

And he had recognized her for what she was. A girl who should keep to her own kind—

—Whatever that was!

She could not go back to the little rooms above the bakery still shining from her labors of love; the apartment where the meal she'd prepared earlier awaited Missie even now.

She would not return to the Courtney house. Night had fallen. How long had she stood here, hurt, dazed—hiding. Somehow she had lost several hours. Now she must go somewhere where no one could possibly find her. But where? Matthew would search her out, for Missie's sake, if nothing else. And Duke Courtney's influence spread a long way. Meanwhile, she had no money, nowhere to sleep, no place to go—unless she slept here.

Something scuttled in the rubble behind her and she shuddered. A rat, perhaps—or something worse. If she could only think! Oh, God, if she could only think!

Her cheeks were wet, strands of black hair tear-glued

against them. Somewhere she had lost her bonnet. Pushing her hair back, she reached into her reticule for a handkerchief, gasping as something pricked her hand.

The dragon pin!

She lifted it free. It glowed in her palm, seeming to pulse with life in the fading light. Like an omen.

—Her own kind—

Pinning the dragon to her bosom, she left the tunnel formed by adjacent buildings and began to walk, seeking street signs that were familiar. One by one, they led her back to Chinatown.

Fog had begun to settle in as she reached its perimeter, damping down the glow from streetlamps that were sparse in this section of the city; muffling the sound of footsteps until people were only shadows slipping by in the night. The place seemed more sinister now, in the darkness; the little stores with their bright vegetables, closed, produce taken in for the night. Only the smells remained the same, heavy, rich with alien odors. Occasionally, she caught the murmur of a strange-sounding tongue. The shuttered buildings frowned above her. She sensed them swelling, diminishing, as the multitude of people each housed breathed in—and out—

An alleyway, another. Neither was the one she searched for. It was narrower than most, darker, even in the day. Panic fluttered in her chest. What if she couldn't find the place?

And what if these people—her own kind—turned her away?

Her fingers went to the dragon pin and she whispered a silent prayer, wondering if God, too, thought a frightened girl of mixed blood not worth His time and trouble.

She found the small eating place to which the son of Wang had taken her. It was closed and dark, but she knew it by a gilt paper dragon, suspended from a pole in front. Now it hung dripping with mist, but she recognized its shape against the night sky. It meant only that she had come too far and must retrace her steps.

She started back, hearing a whisper of slippered feet behind her. Someone was following her? She flattened herself against a wall, feeling the wet wood syrupy with damp against her fingers. The stranger passed in the darkness, the fog parting just enough to give her a glimpse of a villainous yellow face stitched by a scar.

For a moment she stayed against the wall, too frightened to move, then forced herself to breathe again. The man had not followed her. There was nothing to fear but her imagination—

She wished she had thought of trying to search out the Wang home, asked Lee to bring her here. But she had no idea where they lived, and she sensed that he wouldn't approve of her errand. Doggedly, she moved along in the mist and the dark.

She found the opening to the alleyway, and here there was no light at all. The fog had settled down, filling its crevice like gravy in a bowl. Petra looked back, reluctant to leave the larger street with its blind light, then she entered the alley's oblivion, cold, wet, senses reeling from the odd sweetish scent she'd noticed earlier in the day.

Approaching the spot where she remembered the herbalist's shop to be, she was relieved to see a faint glow. There was a lamp burning behind an oiled paper window. She had the sudden irrational idea that someone knew she was coming, and put it there to welcome her.

Now that she had reached her destination, she was suddenly, terribly, tired, stumbling the last few feet to the door. Should she knock, or just push it open? She decided on the latter. After all, she had come home.

A round-faced, spectacled Chinese in his early thirties was tidying his stock for the night. He turned in surprise to see a young woman in Western dress teetering on his doorstep.

"I would like to speak to the proprietor," she gasped.

He nodded courteously. "I am Feng Wu."

She stared at him. Her father was an older man when he had—had kidnapped her mother. Well, what had she thought?

That he was resurrected from the dead? The herbalist was looking at her oddly. She must say something—

"I am a daughter of the House of Feng Wu," she said with a desperate dignity. "My father died in Kowloon—a typhoon. I—I need your help—"

Feng Wu's expression did not change. The Feng Wu she spoke of had been his uncle. He had been reared by the woman, Liang, one of the older man's wives, and he had heard the story of his uncle's death many times. The man had been besotted by a young white girl he had taken for himself. And though Liang was sent from him, she returned after the typhoon to find him dead, stabbed to death, the woman gone.

"It will be your duty to avenge him," Liang had hissed as he stood on the docks as a boy with his chest of woven rice straw, preparing to leave for America. She did not know the great expanse of the world outside China. He'd forgotten her admonition.

This girl, clearly of mingled race, would be the child of the murderess. And she had come to him.

He came around the counter with extended hand. "I greet you, cousin. I beg that you partake of my poor hospitality."

He led her to a door at the rear of the shop and into a small room where a brazier burned. Calling to his small Chinese-speaking wife, he instructed her to brew tea, mixing the herbs for it himself.

Petra, warm, secure in the welcome she received, was soon nodding. The wife of Feng Wu led her to a shelflike bed and she fell into a dreamless sleep.

Feng Wu sat on into the night. He was not a bad man or a vengeful one. His uncle was long dead, Kowloon far away. Yet he owed a debt to old Liang—

Just as he owed a debt to the *Hip Shing Tong*, who ran the gambling joints; a debt that threatened him with the loss of this establishment and his livelihood. Perhaps he could accomplish two deeds with a single act.

He rose and put on his padded jacket. He would pay a visit

to a member of the *Kwong Dak Tong,* an organization trafficking in girls. This one was surely a prize, and would bring much money.

He polished his glasses and looked at her one more time. She was small in build, but with long, slender legs. Lying as she did, black hair spread against the pillow, pearllike teeth showing between softly parted lips, she was young and fresh. A pity for such loveliness to be despoiled in the cribs.

He would add a stipulation to the sale. This one would go only to warm the bed of a rich old man, too old to do her much harm.

Shutting the door of his shop with its little ringing bell, he walked out into the fog.

Chapter 15

Missie, following her confrontation with Matthew Blaine, had left the office in a fury. In her own way, she probably attracted as much attention as the fleeing Petra. She was sick of Matthew and his insinuations, upset by Stuyvesant Brown's proposal. After all, she'd known the man only a couple of days! You'd think he'd purchased her along with the book! And Larry Hiller! He was always hanging around, touching her by accident! Did men think of nothing else?

She didn't trust anybody but Papa, and her uncles, Dan and Duke. Come to think of it, she was mad at Duke Courtney, too. He had no business showing up at work like he did, starting gossip at the office.

That was unfair. He'd had his reasons. She was the one who had jumped up to hug him. It was not his fault. She'd been so excited at the thought of seeing her family again. Now she was uneasy at the prospect, along with being upset and—and damned mad!

She rode the cable car, got off, and walked the few blocks

to her apartment, still simmering. The door was locked. Wondering, she searched for her key, letting herself in.

"Petra?"

There was no answer. The rooms, as they had been since Petra joined her, were shining and clean. But the table was not set. There was nothing cooking on the stove. A casserole sat on the shelf above the stove, ready to be popped into the oven. A bowl of lettuce, torn for salad, was on the drainboard, immersed in water to keep it fresh. There was a pie in the cupboard, probably purchased at the bakery downstairs. But no Petra.

Mystified, Missie put the casserole into the oven. Perhaps the girl had gone down to visit Frau Schmitt, and lost track of the time. She set the table herself, and waited. The casserole was done, and it had grown quite dark. Feeling a twinge of alarm, she went down to the bakery.

Frau Schmitt had not seen the little Petra all day. She had been quite busy. Look. She pointed to the cake in pride. It was a towering, three-tier affair, with swags of frosting and a spray of delicate roses.

"Chust like I have made in Chermany," she said nostalgically.

No, she had not seen Petra go out. She had been too intent on her creation. But she was certain the little one was all right. "She is a good girl, that one."

Missie climbed the stairs again, and looked at the food, now growing cold. She tried to make herself eat, but had no appetite. The rigors of her day were fast fading in her worries over Petra Channing. Then the frown lines between her brows faded and she grinned.

Of course! Duke Courtney had given up on her, this morning, and had come here! Petra had gone home with him to make her peace with Em. But it did seem that she would leave a note to that effect. Missie looked at her lapel watch. Eight-thirty, and the streets were heavy with fog. She did not like to go out alone at night, but she couldn't rest until she knew Petra's whereabouts for certain.

Half an hour later, she stood at Em's front door. Duke himself answered, massive and handsome in his velvet smoking jacket. his eyes lit up at her appearance. "Em, guess who's here!"

When Missie left after a brief awkward visit, having given Arab's letter to Em as her excuse, she was even more puzzled. Em had asked after Petra, still stiff and hurt over the girl's leaving. And Missie had lied, saying that she'd left her sleeping.

Maybe it wasn't a lie. Petra had probably returned in her absence. She'd be in her own bed when Missie returned, and she'd have a plausible excuse in the morning.

The minute she unlocked her door, she knew her hopes were false. Her plate was on the table, just as she'd left it, her meal half eaten. There was a cold and empty feeling in the rooms—

Should she go to the police? They would probably laugh at her. Petra was a grown girl, with a right to come and go as she pleased. Besides, Missie remembered her night in jail. She rubbed her arms, recalling the bruising grip with which she'd been hauled into the station. Then, too, she might have to bring the Courtney name into it. No, not the police. Oh, God, where could the girl be at this hour?

She went over the past weeks in her mind, trying to think of any names Petra might have mentioned, any friends she may have had. She could think of none, other than the Courtneys, herself, Frau Schmitt and—Matthew Blaine.

Matthew, she thought, Matthew would help her! She half rose, then sank down again. She would not ask that man for anything! Petra would come home soon. She had to! And, if she did not, she would start searching at first light.

If the girl weren't so darned helpless, so—so vulnerable! She might be wandering somewhere, lost in San Francisco!

Or she might have stepped in front of a carriage. The hospitals! First, she would check the hospitals!

A sound on the stairs brought her to her feet with a sigh of relief.

It was only Frau Schmitt, wondering if the little one had come home. She had brought sweet buns, and she bustled about the kitchen, making coffee. Missie was grateful for her comforting presence. The hours ticked by, and finally she sent the old woman down to her bed. She curled in a corner of the couch, a blanket around her, waiting. At last, she slept.

When she awoke, it was gray dawn. The table was littered with coffee cups and crumbs. The place she'd set for Petra was untouched, mute testimony to her absence.

Missie dressed and left the apartment at five A.M. By seven, she had inquired at the hospitals and reported Petra's absence to a sleepy police sergeant.

"Channing, Petra," the man wrote down. "Height, five feet, weight, about one hundred. Anything else?"

"She's a very pretty girl," Missie said helplessly.

The man leaned back in his chair and grinned. "Know what I think? I'll bet you two girls got into a catfight over some guy. She's probably off pouting somewhere, just to teach you a lesson. If she don't show up in a day or two—"

Missie was already walking out the door.

She would have to go to Duke Courtney. But she would wait until the *Examiner* opened for business. Maybe there would be a report that would throw some light on Petra's disappearance. She hurried to the office, scanning the streets as she went, hoping to see a small, dark-haired girl along the way.

The offices smelling of dust and paper and ink were empty when she arrived. She sat down at her desk and buried her head in her arms. Dear God, she was tired! So tired.

Matthew Blaine, coming in early as usual, found her there. She lifted blurred eyes at his entrance, and he stopped short.

The girl looked like hell, shadows like bruises along her cheekbones. She looked dazed, in shock!

If any of those damned animals who worked here had hurt her, he'd have his hide!

He glanced around the empty room; then strode to Missie's desk lifting her to her feet. She swayed a little, looking as if she'd been drugged.

"What is it, Missie? Dammit, tell me! Missie!" He shook her a little and the dam of her tears broke.

"Petra," she whispered. "Petra. She's gone, disappeared—oh, Matthew, Matthew!"

She clung to him in a paroxysm of grief, sobbing until her words were unintelligible, "—warlord, rape, empty plate, wedding cake, Duke Courtney, hospitals, the police—"

None of it made sense.

There was nothing to do but hold her until she recovered from her hysteria, hold her close, still the panic that had her half out of her mind with his own warmth, kiss those tears away. Whoever she was, whatever she was, didn't matter. For the moment, she was his: a heartbroken, frightened, clinging girl.

Missie gradually felt the tension go out of her body, leaving her limp, helpless, protected by the wall that was Matthew Blaine. His heart beat beneath her cheek, strong, constant, his warmth penetrating the chill she thought would never go away.

She was in a man's arms. And it was sweet, comforting. The ugly memories of Arthur Melvin were exorcised. She looked up at Matthew in wonder and his mouth sought hers. The first kiss was gentle; the second, as she responded, was hot, throbbing, sending a thrill to her toes. It had a taste of honey. Missie pressed closer, wanting more, then suddenly she was pushed away.

"What the hell do you want?" Matthew rasped. It was a moment before she realized his words were aimed at someone else.

Larry Hiller stood in the doorway, his face pale. He looked as if he might be going to cry.

"I work here, remember! The others—I saw Carrington down the street. He'll be here in a minute."

The spell was broken. The thought of Petra had returned, and with it all the night's worries. Missie stood quietly while Matthew settled the day's schedule.

"We have an emergency," he said tersely. "And I'm needed elsewhere. Hiller, take over my desk for today. Tell Carrington—"

Missie stood numbly while the orders went on, still ragged with concern over Petra, confused by her own new feelings. Then Matthew had her by the arm. He took her home.

Once she had had daydreams about Matthew Blaine being in these rooms—not touching—she'd never been able to bring her dreams that far; but sitting across the table from her, or looking across the night-dark gardens of Van Ness.

Instead, it was day. The table was littered with crumbs. She wanted him to hold her, to tell her he loved her—and the ghost of Petra stood between them.

Missie sat huddled on the couch while Matthew paced, asking questions, dwelling on small details. Missie began at the beginning, telling him of Petra's mixed background; explaining why Petra had come here to Polk Street; their relationship with the Courtneys—not seeing the wave of relief that passed over Blaine's face. At least the mystery of Duke Courtney was solved.

There was no time to explore their own feelings. Matthew moved decisively. First, the Courtneys must be told. Duke was an influential man, and he would have detectives combing the city. There were the shipping lines to check, the train stations. Courtney would bring pressure on the police, have them bring in men suspected of crimes against women—

Missie whimpered, her hand over her mouth. Let Petra be safe! Please, God, let Petra be safe!

Matthew Blaine went with Missie to the Courtney house.

Duke Courtney seemed to turn into an old man at their news, but only for a moment. He immediately began to set wheels in motion. Em went into shock and was put to bed, hysterically blaming Missie for her granddaughter's loss.

Blaine took Missie home, leaving her at her door with another tender embrace that set her senses reeling. She tensed and pulled away, and he looked at her oddly, opening his mouth to speak, then deciding against it.

"Sleep, now," he said, finally. "We're doing all we can. Just—rest, and wait."

Missie shut the door and leaned against it for a long time. Rest? Her conscience wouldn't let her! She thought of how often she'd wished Petra away; the jealousy she'd felt when she watched Matthew with the girl. Em was right. Whatever had happened, Missie was at fault.

And she loved Matthew Blaine. She knew it, now. She was beginning to think that love might be returned. But unless Petra was found, safe and well, there could never be anything between them—ever.

LIVERPOOL

Chapter 16

Unaware of the events in California, Arab and Juan Narvaéz, Tamsen and Dan Tallant, and the old ex-madam, Nell, arrived at the most elegant hotel in Liverpool. Here, they would take a ship to New York and cross the continent to San Francisco. Arab, despondent at leaving Luka, her favorite daughter, had sworn she was dying. She entered the hotel, supported at either side by Dan Tallant and her husband Juan, pale-faced, a broken doll.

Tamsen started forward to the desk, and Nell pushed her aside. "Don't never send a youngun t'do a woman's job," she said loftily, bringing a hamlike hand down on the bell.

The young clerk, kneeling to arrange some papers beneath the counter, raised his head to eye level above it and froze there.

He had never seen such an apparition. The woman was of gargantuan proportions, small snapping eyes almost hidden in rolls of fat that were brightly painted. The rest of her, all rolls and billows, was encased in purple velvet. A matching hat with waving feathers crowned the whole.

"Don't just squat there an gawk," Nell said testily. "Hell, man, ain't you never seed a woman afore? We got a sick woman here, an' we got reseyvashuns. Lady Wotherspoon an' party. Gitcher ass in gear!"

The stricken clerk managed to get to his feet. He ran his finger down the roster. "I don't see—"

"You by-God better see! They's other places!"

Tamsen Tallant, behind her, shot a glance at Dan. He was grinning, damn him! And the man behind the desk was terrified. No wonder, the way Nell was glowering!

"It's all right, Nell," she said placatingly. "Don't hurry the man. Give him a chance to—"

"'Chance,' hell," Nell grumbled. "My butt's got callouses from that gawdam train, my dogs is barkin' from standin' here, our Arab-girl's prob'ly gonna puke all over the rug, an' he—"

"I found it!" The clerk shouted as if he'd discovered gold. "Lady Wotherspoon and party! Our three finest suites!" He produced the keys. "The lift is—"

Nell pulled at her lower lip, looking at him suspiciously. "Who says them's good accomydashuns? You? I ain't buyin' a pig in a poke. Gonna look 'em over first, see if ever'thing works. An' yer comin' with me."

He did, though not via the lift. Nell, after a dubious inspection of the ornate little elevator, shook her head. The others could go up if they wanted to. She didn't hold with them new-fangled contrapshuns. She and Sonny, here, would take the stairs.

By the time they reached the fifth floor, Nell was puffing like a steam engine, her complexion almost the shade of her gown. The clerk inserted a key and opened the door to 513, then backed away. Nell grabbed his arm.

"Whoa, Sonny. You're stickin' eround till I have me a look-see."

She grumbled at the size of the tub in the bathroom. "Set in that there thing, you'd have to pry me out with a crowbar—" She pulled the toilet chain, flushing it noisily until she was satisfied of its dependability, then went to the bed, ripping back the sheets.

Horrified, the clerk realized she was searching for vermin. "I assure you, Mrs. Wotherspoon—"

"Lady Wotherspoon," she corrected him. "I got rid of my propitty, but that don't mean I give up my ladyshipness. Bin a lady sence I hitched up with my Dusty, the night he passed on, sweet leetle bastard! Slept with him fer years, an' never knowed he was a lord. Coulda knocked me over with a feather!"

The clerk was backing toward the door, and Nell followed him. Now that she was settled in, she was in a garrulous mood. "Leetle sonofabitch never drew a sober breath in his life," she continued happily. She eyed the clerk with something that resembled affection. "He wuz a goodlookin' leetle devil. Be damned if you don't put me in mind of him! Lissen, why don't you set down, take off yer shoes an' stay awhile?"

Mumbling something about being needed downstairs, the terrified man fled. He spent a few moments regaining his aplomb before calling a bellboy to take the party's luggage to the various suites.

"And I want to give you a word of warning," he whispered confidentially, leaning across the counter. "Watch out for that woman in five-thirteen!"

The other members of the party went first to the Narvaéz suite, where Tamsen helped make Arab comfortable, taking off her slippers, loosening her stays, bringing fresh water. If her sister didn't look so ill, she would feel like shaking her! Arab had complained the whole trip, and poor Juan was at the end of his nerves. Tamsen had hoped Arab's decision to go to the States, leaving Luka, her young husband, and coming baby behind, meant an end to her selfish possessiveness. After all, it had almost broken up her marriage—

Arab was going through with her promises, but apparently she planned to make them all as miserable as she was!

"There." Tamsen said brightly, "You're all comfortable. I'll come back when the luggage arrives—"

The mass of red hair—touched up, now that Arab had reached her fifties—twisted on the pillow. Green swimming eyes sought Tamsen's, pleading.

"Don't go! Oh, Tam, I hurt all over!"

"You'll feel better when you've had some rest."

Tamsen left her, collected Dan, and they went along the hall to their own rooms. Tamsen removed her bonnet and sank down in front of the dressing table, taking her hair down. The trip had been an arduous one. She would pin it up freshly—

"Don't, sweetheart."

She smiled at Dan's mirrored reflection, feeling her heart jolt at the sight of his dark features. It had always been this way, she thought with amusement. And she was nearly sixty years old!

He ran his hands through the silken hair he had always loved. It hung to her waist, black silk shot through with silver, a frame for a small oval face with huge dark eyes.

He bent to kiss the top of her head. "Tamsen—?" His eyes moved suggestively toward the bed and she laughed ruefully, at this easily aroused man of hers.

"Our luggage will be here any minute. Then I must go help Arab into her nightdress—"

"Oh, hell!" Dan growled. "I'm sick of Arab's whining! And Juan's got sense enough to take care of his own wife!" He paused, meditatively. "I never helped a woman into a nightgown—but I guess it isn't any harder than taking one off—"

"You idiot!" Tamsen giggled like a girl. She reached for his hand and held it to her cheek, "Dan, I love you!"

"Of course," he said modestly. Then, "I love you, Tam.

But if I were married to your sister, I'd turn her over my knee!''

"She'll straighten out. She'll be happy, once we get to San Francisco—"

"But will you?"

Tamsen looked up at him, her gaze frank and open. "I think so," she said. "I have to admit, sometimes I get butterflies in my stomach—"

He bent over her, clasping his hands about her middle. "Yep," he said judiciously, "they're there! But—seriously, Tam, you'll find everything has changed. Nobody will even remember things that happened that long ago. Em found that out. But if you're going to let it bother you—"

"I won't," she said firmly, "let it bother me at all!"

The knocking at the door did bother her, however. The luggage had arrived. She left Dan to accept it and tip the boy, going on down the hall to Arab's room. If anything, Arab seemed more distraught. She averted her face from Tamsen and wouldn't speak. No, she wanted nothing to eat. A shiver passed over her small body at the thought of food.

"I'm worried about her, Juan," Tamsen whispered to her brother-in-law. "It isn't natural."

"Is it not?" The handsome Spaniard laughed, mirthlessly. "You recall, this is Arabella, my wife, whom we are discussing. I am well acquainted with her whims. Now, she chooses to be ill. To punish us, I suppose—"

"I don't think it's that, Juan. Maybe we should call a physician. You could ask at the desk—"

He shook his head morosely. "This is not a sickness of the body, Tamsen, but of the spirit. It is not something medicine can help. I know—"

Tamsen was silent, remembering the events of the past year. Arab had fought her daughter's love for the young man she married; fought it with all the fury of a tigress defending her young. Her actions had alienated Juan, who went off to India on a mission with Dan. Juan was grievously injured there, stabbed by an assassin. But something else had happened on his journey; something neither Dan nor he talked about; something that left him with haunted eyes. Tamsen suspected that it had to do with a woman.

He'd decided to leave Arab, to go back to San Francisco. Then Arab, surprisingly, had become her old sweet, loving self. Not until the actual move began did she become petulant—and finally impossible.

"I've been thinking of taking her back," Juan said moodily. "*Dios,* Tamsen! I cannot bear her unhappiness!"

"Don't do it, Juan!" Tamsen's jaw was set, thinking of Arab's attachment to her lovely otherworldly daughter, now Mrs. Alastair Forsythe—and expecting a baby. Arab would interfere in that marriage. She wouldn't be able to help herself! Too much was at stake, Luka's happiness, Juan's—even Arab's own.

"Let her get a good night's rest," Tamsen said firmly. "I'll talk to her in the morning."

That night, lying in her sleeping husband's arms, cheek against his smooth copper brown shoulder, Tamsen reviewed the past years; the hurts they had inflicted on each other. You reach a plateau, she thought, where you look back and wonder why; what was so important that it could drive a wedge between two people in love. And from that plateau, you could look ahead, knowing that it couldn't happen again.

It didn't come from growing old—she felt no older than she did when she married Dan—but from growing up.

She wondered if Arab would ever reach that plateau. She certainly hoped so! Curling close to Dan, she finally slept.

She woke to a pounding on the door, and sat upright. Dan's feet were already on the floor. He searched for his trousers, swearing, as Tamsen slipped into a robe. Dear God, it was still the middle of the night! Her throat contracted as she thought of fire—

Their midnight caller was Juan Narvaéz, eyes like dark

holes in a white face. Arab was worse, much worse, burning with fever—in a delirious state—

Tamsen returned with him to his suite, waking Nell on the way. Dan Tallant went to find a doctor.

Juan had not overstated Arab's plight. Her face was puffed and swollen almost beyond recognition. The hands that clutched at Tamsen's were hot and clawlike. She was babbling of a volcanic eruption, the earth shaking, molten fire pouring in glowing rivers to cover the land—

She had gone back in time to the birth of her strange little daughter, Luka—Luka, who was different.

Nell stumped in, tying her faded pink robe trimmed in bedraggled feathers about her ample middle. She viewed the tossing Arab with alarm.

"Looks like hell," she finally admitted. "Wisht we could get hold of a kahuna—"

She was remembering the old Hawaiian sorcerer who pulled Arab through when the baby was born. If Tamsen hadn't been so desperately worried, she would have smiled.

"I'm afraid," she said, sponging Arab's hot face, "we'll just have to settle for a doctor."

The physician, a Doctor Sedgeley, who arrived with Dan, was short, rotund, a little pompous. He gazed at Nell, fascinated, as though she were some new form of the human species, until Tamsen directed him to the patient. Looking down at the semiconscious woman, he frowned, pursing his lips. Then he instructed Tamsen to remain with him and shooed the others out.

Time seemed to drag, but it was less than fifteen minutes when Tamsen appeared in the doorway. Her eyes were filled with tears, her mouth trembling. Juan leaped to his feet and she looked at him helplessly.

"*Dios,* Tamsen! What is it?"

"Mumps!" she said. And then she collapsed in laughter and a welter of tears brought on by relief. Juan stared at her, foolishly, for a moment, then his own laugh rang out, clear and boyish.

It was the first time he'd laughed, spontaneously, since he returned from India.

A quarantine sign was placed upon the door of the suite. Dan canceled their passage and extended their reservations for at least two weeks. The desk clerk was almost unable to retain his urbane facade.

What had he done to deserve this? The bloody awful woman was bad enough—and now, a flaming plague!

Chapter 17

As it developed, Arab's ailment, though a ludicrous disease for a grown woman, was not to be taken lightly. Her system had been weakened by the arduous move, the train trip—and a night she'd spent wandering through the old cemetery beside Wotherspoon Manor. Hating the place since they'd come here—Juan to help Nell with her affairs in accordance with Dusty's will—she'd been loath to leave it. There in the graveyard with its wet mists and dripping, slanting stones, she felt closer to Luka, the daughter she must leave behind. The cemetery had been Luka's favorite spot. In a way, it was saying good-bye—

But she had been thoroughly chilled by the damp, and possibly already infected by the germ. And she was in her fifties.

In the meantime, she would require around-the-clock nursing. Dr. Sedgeley accepted Tamsen's offer, and frowned as Nell volunteered reluctantly.

"Ain't too good with sick folks," she said. "But, hell, reckon that's better'n nuthin'."

He would have someone sent around from the hospital, a woman trained in nursing. A younger woman—

Nell bridled. "Lissen, I ain't no spring chicken, but I could give you a run fer yer money. You damned old rooster!"

The doctor completed his instructions and fled. The others finally went to their beds, Juan going along with Dan. He must reserve another room tomorrow, and a cot would be brought in for the nurse. With a sorrowing look at his feverish wife, Juan left. Tamsen settled down to her long vigil, wiping Arab's feverish lips with a wet cloth, soothing her as she struggled in the nightmare of delirium.

The nurse arrived late in the afternoon. She was small and quiet, graceful in her dark gown with its high white collar and pleated bosom. She had a foreign look. Tamsen guessed at East Indian in her ancestry. But when she spoke, her voice was harsh and carried the accent of the British slums.

"'Er'll be awraght, won'cher, luv?" she said chattily, her conversation aimed toward Arab's deaf ears. "Ow, this room do be a mess! Not to worry, Peg's 'ere to set it tidy."

She unpacked a small bag, and Tamsen slipped guiltily from the room. She might have unpacked the rest of Arab's luggage while she tended her, mopped up the spills from the basin on the night stand. But she'd been thinking only of Arab and her discomfort.

She was glad to leave her sister to the hands of a professional.

Peg set out her own things neatly on the bureau, then turned to Arab's things, turning them out, hanging them in a cupboard, shaking her head over such finery.

And at last she found a small ornate box, catching her breath as she opened it. "Jools," she breathed. And they were real, or she wasn't Peg Mason! She cast a sly glance at the woman on the bed. Out like a bloomin' baby!

Her gaze returned to the box. "Don't 'ee be greedy, Peg," she whispered to herself. " 'Er won't miss one at a time."

Lifting a little chain with a sparkling diamond pendant, she dropped it into the pocket of her apron. Old Feingold would judge its value. And if it turned out to be worth the taking— there was a lot more where it came from.

She closed the box and placed it carefully in a drawer, then seated herself beside Arab's bed, her hands folded primly in her lap.

It was there Juan found her.

He'd been unable to sleep the rest of the previous night, worrying about his wife. The fact that he'd hesitated calling a doctor, dismissing her illness as a fit of sulks, gnawed at his conscience. He loved her, still seeing her as the pretty dancer he'd met in Spain and wooed in a castle garden. He'd loved her enough to follow her to the ends of the earth. Even this last year when he'd prepared to leave her, he'd known that there could be no happiness without her.

He'd approached the suite several times, talking to Tamsen at the door, straining for a sight of red curls against a pillow. She was doing better, Tam said. Holding her own, though she was most uncomfortable.

Now Tamsen had left the room and Arab was in the care of a stranger. Could a strange woman be trusted to handle his wife as tenderly as she deserved? He approached the door and listened. There was no sound. Finally, he pushed the door open, just a crack. A chair was placed beside the bed. In it sat a slender girl with night black hair falling from beneath her cap; a girl in a terribly familiar pose, hands folded in her lap. He recognized the faint curve of the cheek turned from him, and a hoarse sound burst from his lips.

"Mari! "

The figure turned, dark eyes inspecting him curiously, seeing an elegant older man. A real toff, was her instant impression.

"My name be Peg, sor. Peg Mason. 'Orspital sent me 'ere. Wotcher need?"

The coarse voice brought Juan back to sanity. The fleeting resemblance to Mari, the gentle girl he'd met in India, was gone. He introduced himself to Peg, exchanged a few words in regard to Arab's condition, and fled.

Peg watched him go. 'Andsome devil, that one, and rich enough to live in this posh place. She gazed around the room, appreciatively. He'd seemed proper took with her. And no wonder! She looked at Arab's swollen face and sniffed. Maybe, if she played her cards right, he'd pay off a little, too. It was something to think about.

Arab moaned, and Peg looked cross. The doctor had left some laudanum, but she didn't intend to waste it. She had an idea it might come in handier later on.

Juan left the hotel and walked the streets, his guilt compounded by his recent shock. Mari! *Dios*, how could he have taken that girl for Mari, the delicate little half-caste he'd come to love in Bombay. Love? He had not been unfaithful to his wife in body. But he had, in spirit, until he realized it was a different kind of affection. He'd loved Mari for her purity, her goodness. And for a space, in his wife's sickroom, looking at the half-turned cheek of a small, passive, dark-haired girl, he'd known a sudden ache of need—

He turned into a small open park where he found Nell, her massive bulk occupying a bench. She greeted him loudly.

"Looka who's here! I be damned. I wuz hopin' I'd pick me up a man! Here, plant yer backside!"

Juan glanced, embarrassed, at the amused glances they were collecting. He took the spot she indicated, thinking ruefully that there wasn't much space for anything but Nell.

"Don't skooch aroun' too much," she warned him, "er you'll gitcher rear end full of splinters. But it's a helluva lot better'n settin' in that damn hotel. Jes' bin settin' here, thinkin'—"

Nell looked old, tired. She'd been through a bad experience of her own with Dusty's look-alike cousin trying to step into his shoes, attempting to do a widow out of her inheritance. Maybe the situation had hit her harder than they'd known. Inside her gross frame, Nell had a heart that was as big and soft as a feather pillow.

"I'm wonderin' if I done wrong," she said in a small voice, "ramroddin' ever'body inta goin' back t'Frisco. I figgered it'd git Arab outa Luka's bizness. Hell, she ain't seen Missie fer years! But I didn' count on the girl gittin' sick, dammit. Feel like it's my fault. I delivered that ul-ty-may-tum!"

That she had! Juan suppressed a grin, recalling Nell's surprise statements at a family dinner. She'd announced that she was fed up with being a wet nurse, and that she was heading back to San Francisco with plans to open a little bar and game parlor; maybe a few girls upstairs. The rest of them could do as they wished. She didn't care—

"I ain't mad with nobody! It's like I'm yer maw. An' it's a maw's job t'kick a few tails now an' then. Like I said, anybody what wants t'go along with me is welcome. But when we git to Frisco, yer on yer own. I ain't gonna be yer maw no more, Tamsen, I want a chance at m'own life. You ain't Arab's maw. She's full-growed. An' Arab's gotta rememer Luka's got a husband an' butt out of her life! I figgered it was a damn good idee to start at the top, an' I done it!"

Her grandiose speech, made at great cost to herself, had come a little late. He and Arab had already discussed coming home, but Arab might have changed her mind if it were not for Nell.

He reached for her pudgy, be-ringed hand. "Arab would have been sick in any case, Nell. And we love you, all of us."

"Aw-w, hell," Nell sniffed, blinking rapidly. "Ain't no need to go get sickenin' on me." Her words were followed by a watery smile.

The two of them walked back to the hotel. In deference to

Nell, Juan climbed with her to the fifth floor. For a time, they stood talking before the door to her suite, unaware that they were being observed.

Peg Mason, peeping through a barely cracked door, wondered who the fat old biddy was. She looked like a bloody procuress, damned if she didn't! But she was decked out in enough jools to sink a steamship.

"Lumme!" Peg whispered under her breath. "Lor' lumme!" She was going to come out of this case smelling like a rose.

Chapter 18

Over the next few days, Peg Mason was a busy girl. She ingratiated herself to everyone—except Dan Tallant. He was waiting for Tamsen outside the Narvaéz suite when Peg came hurrying down the hall, a little late. Tamsen introduced them, then went with Dan, leaving her charge in Peg's capable hands.

"I don't trust that girl," he said suddenly. "There's something about her—"

Tamsen looked at him in surprise. "She's been very sweet, dedicated—"

"I know. You've told me. But Tam—" He stopped, unable to put his feeling into words. "She makes me think of the girls in the sleazy bars, back home. Hell, they'd cosy up to a man—and steal the gold out of his teeth while they were at it!"

Tamsen's eyes sparked. "You would know more about that than I," she said.

"Dammit, Tam, I didn't mean that the way it sounded! I only—"

She was walking away from him, head high.

"Tam!" He hurried after her, catching her in a couple of long strides. "Tam, listen to me!" His hands on her shoulders, he turned her to face him. She was sputtering with laughter.

"Damn you!" he said, lifting her into his arms, "I'll teach you!" Reaching their door, he fumbled to open it.

"Wait," Tamsen said. "Open your mouth!"

"What the hell for?"

"So I can check your teeth," she said, dimpling. "For gold!"

Dan got the door opened, entered, and kicked it shut behind them. Then they forgot about Peg Mason, completely.

When Tamsen mentioned his suspicions to Nell, the old woman scoffed at them. "Figger I'm a good judge of hooman nachure," she said smugly. "Hell, the girl's doin' her job. Give 'er a chanct!"

Nell's opinion wasn't exactly unbiased. Peg never forgot to say, "Your Ladyship," and she always remarked on the beauty of Nell's gowns.

"Got a helluva lot of good sense," Nell said. "Say that fer her!"

Juan was appalled at Dan's attitude toward the girl. Like Mari, she was small-boned, with the wistful appeal of a kitten. For a roughhewn man like Dan to criticize her—was almost brutal! Juan went out of the way to be kind to the girl, once bringing her sugar buns from a street stall.

He was startled at the sudden greed in her eyes, at the haste with which she ate them, licking her fingers to get the last crumb. Catching his eye, she ducked her head. "Lor', that wor good! 'Ungry, I was!"

Juan put his hand to her chin, lifting it to see tear-filled eyes. "Are you not paid for your work?"

Peg Mason was, in fact, doing well at the moment. A little

stealing, a little blackmail, helped her keep body and soul together. She spun a yarn that shook Juan to the core. Her pay went to feed her brother's starving children. He was in prison for a crime he did not commit. She also supported her aging mother. Often, there was not enough to go around—

Juan Narváez pressed some money into her hand. She tried to refuse it, and he insisted. Suddenly she was on tiptoes, pressing a chaste kiss on his brown cheek. She would take it, not for herself, but to help pay for her sister-in-law's operation.

She slipped into Arab's room, laughing to herself. He would probably want to look into her brother's case; take on the expense of the operation himself. She knew a mark when she saw one! But before he got around to checking out her story, discovering she'd lied, she'd be long gone!

Arab was fretful and Peg went to her, plumping up the pillows behind the feverish woman. "Don't 'ee worry none, luv," she soothed her. "Peg'll take care of every bloody thing! 'Ee'll see—"

Within the week, Arab was improved enough to hate her appearance. Nobody must see her like this, her face all swollen and blotchy. Tamsen and Peg she had to endure. But no one else! Especially not Juan or Dan. She'd just die! Tamsen sought out foods to please her palate, but she turned her head and wouldn't eat. She wanted the lights out, the shades drawn. And Doctor Sedgeley extended her days of convalescence another week.

The whole setup exasperated Nell. They'd of bin in Frisco by this time, seeing Duke an' Em, and that Missie-girl. Instead, they were settin' on their butts, doin' nothin' whilst Arab squalled like a scalded cat!

She left the hotel and heaved her bulk on a horse-drawn cab, directing the driver to head for the wharf. There, she studied the ships in harbor, longing to be aboard, certain that Dusty's fragile ghost would be there, waiting to welcome her home.

Finally, she walked along the wharf, studying the waterfront taverns with an idea to her future business. One, she especially liked the look of. It was old, two-story, with a swinging sign. A blast of music sounded from it, even at this hour. She shook her head in admiration at the proprietor's expertise, breathing in the scent of sawdust and stale beer. She was of half a mind to go in, have a look-see.

Then she looked down at her gown. It was magenta, with strands of bugle beads that swayed as she walked. She forgot for a minute that she was Lady Wotherspoon. If a lady walked into the tavern, the owner'd bust a gusset! It might discommode his clientele—

She was about to walk away when a sailor sidled up to her. He was new to Liverpool, and he was looking for a woman. Could she steer him to the right place?

Nell gestured toward the tavern she'd admired. He went in and did not come out. She'd guessed right—and so had the sailor. She was flattered. Once a madam, allus a madam! Even dressed like a ladyship, it showed! Happily, she headed back to the hotel.

From that day, Nell varied her schedule: one day at the waterfront, one in the park. She carried a loaf of bread to feed the pigeons, and was gleeful when they clustered at her approach. Often, she felt the eyes of a young man on her, bridling at his attention.

Reddish hair, blue eyes, freckles, he looked like a nice boy. He seemed to share the same schedule Nell did, and she finally began to think of him as a companion. Then one day she noticed that his eyes were not fixed on her, but on the loaf she was shredding.

Goddamn! The kid was hungry!

She hadn't noticed the shadows beneath his eyes, the hollow cheeks, the way he swallowed when a bird made off with a particularly large crumb. But now that she had, what the hell was she to do?

She finally lumbered to her feet and approached his bench. "Brung this to feed them pidgins," she rumbled. "But I gotta leave. You handle it fer me?'' She thrust the loaf at him and waddled away, stopping at the turn in the path to look back. Poor devil, wasn't even stoppin' to chew! Tomorrow, she'd come back and bring her lunch; enough for a army!

She did just that. And bit by bit, she pried the lad's story from him. He was from Ireland, and times were hard there. With him gone, there would be one less mouth to feed. He'd come here to Liverpool, hoping to work on the docks, but he hadn't found anything yet.

"What else kin you do?" Nell asked, conversationally. "Whatchu work at afore?"

His blue eyes, eyes meant to be merry, smiled. "I was afther helpin' me old da in the tavern—"

"I'll be damned!" Nell hitched herself toward him on the bench. "Looks like you an' me is kinda sisters under th' skin! Y'play poker?"

That he did. He'd learned from an American.

"Then fergit all y'learned." Nell reached into her reticule and pulled out a deck, fanning the cards expertly. "Yer gonna git it all straight from th' horse's mouth, so t'speak!" Scooting to the far end of the bench, one huge ham hanging over, she shuffled and dealt.

"Looky there! Three aces an' a pair! Kid, yer a nacheral! Hell, let's do some bettin'."

He ruefully turned his pockets inside out. "I'm havin' nought to wager—"

Nell chuckled. "On'y time I ever got skint was by a High-wayan woman, name of Pua. Took ever' stitch on my back. Give you some odds! This pound, here, agin yer shirt." She cut his protests short. "Me, I'm a real card shark. Uster be my perfession. I'm figgerin' on winnin'."

A short time later, Nell had lost two pounds and a number of shillings. "Reckon I done lost my touch," she said sadly. "I'll practice up afore t'morra."

She grinned all the way back to the hotel. She was still

pretty slick when it come to dealin' from the bottom of the deck.

The next day, he didn't appear. A small boy brought a message. Her friend, Sean Murphy, had a job driving a beer wagon. His day off was Sunday.

How the hell could Nell be glad and sorry at the same time? The park seemed empty without Sean Murphy. Nothing but a bunch of gawdam birds to talk to. She heaved herself up from the bench. Might as well mosey down to the waterfront.

She hailed a horse-drawn cab.

Damn, she wished she could take that boy home with her. But it wouldn't be right, she thought virtuously. Not a handsome lad like that, traveling with a—a matoor woman. Prob'ly cause talk. And she didn't want to embarrass Arab or Tam.

She climbed down, morosely surveying the street. Somehow it had lost its charm. A beer wagon approached and she brightened, hoping to see Sean on its high seat. No, this was an old man. Ugly sonofabitch, too—.

A slight pull on her arm interrupted the thought. She felt her reticule slipping away. Its handle had been cut! A thief!

Nell let out a roar as a slight figure sped away, carrying her handbag. Nell finally got her ponderous bulk in motion and gave chase, blistering the air with invective as the thief widened the gap between them. The girl—for it was a girl—looked back just as the beer wagon was urged into motion. She fell, and went down beneath its wheels—

The driver, thanking God the truck was empty, helped Nell pull the small thief free. She was little more than a child, thin and in rags, dazed from a bump on the head. Her arm was broken. Nell insisted that the old man drive them to the hospital.

"Don't 'ee waste yer time on that," he said scornfully. "Gutter-trash, 'er be!"

"An' you," Nell said, "are a ugly sonofabitch! Figgered that out afore you opened yer damn face! Git movin'!"

Late that evening, a beer truck pulled up at the front entrance of the elegant hotel. Its driver helped a ponderous woman to the ground, and handed her a ragged, spitting little fury with one arm in a splint.

"Wash my hands of it," the driver said. "'Ee be on yer own now, an' good riddance, I says!"

Nell hauled the girl into the foyer. The desk clerk's brows rose to his hairline. "I say, Lady Wotherspoon! You cannot bring—that—into the hotel!"

"The hell you say," Nell interrupted him. "Now, shut yer yap an' lend me a hand!"

She shoved the struggling girl and the protesting clerk into the waiting lift. "See you on the fifth floor," she shouted as it began to rise.

She turned and lumbered toward the stairs.

Chapter 19

When Nell arrived, the desk clerk was trying to remove a wildcat from the lift. His thinning hair stood on end, his collar awry, one sleeve ripped from his shirt. Scratches marred one cheek, and an eye was rapidly blackening from a collision with the girl's flailing splint. He had no idea which would prove more dangerous, the filthy urchin—or the puffing, red-faced woman who steamed toward them.

"My place," she panted. "Here!" Nell thrust the key toward him and he hastened to open the door. Nell shoved the girl inside. "Go git the Tallants, dammit, hurry!" The door closed behind the woman and girl, and there was a sound of breakage.

They were destroying the bloody hotel! The clerk ran for help.

Inside the suite, the little thief stood shivering like a cornered rat. Nell advanced toward her and she spat. Instantly a pudgy hand retaliated, five fingers against the girl's cheek that sent her reeling. The splinted arm came up, grazing

Nell's shoulder as it swung. Then Nell had a good grip on her prey. Dragging her to a chair, Nell sat. The waif's legs were pinned firmly between Nell's knees, her head beneath a ponderous arm. With her free hand, Nell lifted the ragged skirts and proceeded to administer a sound spanking.

The clerk's summons, the screaming that issued from Nell's suite, had brought Tamsen and Dan Tallant running. They opened the door and stopped at the sight of Nell methodically flailing away.

"Got the situashun well in hand," she grinned.

She released the girl, who stood quiet, glaring at her through slitted eyes. Nell glared back.

"Now we got that over with," she said, "what's yer name?"

An ugly retort formed on the girl's lips, then she rubbed her posterior and thought better of it.

"Maggie."

"That all?" It was answered by a surly nod.

"You got folks? No? Well, till that arm's well, I'm yer folks! Yer gonna take a bath, an'—" Nell paused at Maggie's obstinate expression. "Dan, get the hell out. Tell Juan he kin keep keer of his own wife fer awhile. Send that leetle Peg in here. Got a idee I'm gonna need all the help I kin git. You—" she turned to the battered clerk, "don't reckon you got any lye soap? Any goose grease an' turkeltine, case she's lousy? Oh, hell! Send up anything you got!"

Maggie was dumped into the bath water, clothes and all. The water turned murky and was drained and drained again. Maggie kicked and screamed until Peg entered, then she was suddenly quiet. Peg, her face impassive, vigorously scrubbed and rinsed the girl's grimy head.

Clean at last, enveloped in one of Nell's voluminous flannel gowns, Maggie looked quite presentable. "Smells a helluva lot better," Nell sniffed. "Them bruises go way, she might be a hooman bean!"

A cot was brought up. Leaving Peg to check Maggie's

splint and tuck her in bed for the night, Nell stepped out into the hall with Tamsen, briefly explaining the events that led to bringing the girl home.

"But what in the world are you going to do with her!"

"Hell, I dunno," Nell said miserably. "Couldn' leave her layin' in the street—"

"Watch her. She could be dangerous. If there's any trouble—"

"Ain't gonna be no trouble," Nell grinned, blowing on her trusty right hand. "Nuthin' I can't handle."

Inside the room, Peg helped the girl to bed, all softness gone from her smooth features. Green, knowing eyes met her brown ones. Each had recognized the cunning of the other.

"This 'ere's my territory," Peg said menacingly. "Don't want no bloody flummery—"

Maggie's lips curved in an angelic smile. "Looks like there be enough fer two—"

That night Maggie's arm throbbed until she couldn't sleep. She set her lips tightly so that she wouldn't moan. Nell slept in the big bed, her bulk covered by a sheet that rose and fell with her snoring. And while she slept, Maggie had to think, to formulate a plan.

But her thoughts kept getting all scrambled up in her mind. Maggie was an orphan. At eight, she'd been taken from the workhouse to serve as slavey in a religious school. And finally, she ran away. Her life had not been easy. She'd been starved, beaten, kicked around. But nobody had ever spanked her before.

In a way, it had been kind of nice. Kind of like having a mum—

She twisted her head angrily against the pillow, and with movement came the pain. She used the pain to steel her feelings against the woman in the other bed. A flaming monster, she was! A bloody bitch! Maggie intended to even the score.

She'd be good as gold until she had a chance to get away.

And when she left, she'd fill her pockets, Peg or no Peg! She only hoped she didn't have to take another bloody bath!

Peg returned to her patient. Arab had covered her face, refusing to let Juan see her in her present state. After he had gone, Peg administered a dose of laudanum to soothe her nerves. Arab finally slept and the nurse rummaged through the jewelry box once more. She had taken the major items. Any more, and someone might notice they were gone.

The real haul was in the fat woman's room. She'd been wondering how to get at it, and now she knew. If it meant sharing the loot with the little thief—at least half was better than nothing.

Maggie, in the morning, was a different person. Her straw-colored hair contained glints of red and gold that would shine with better care. She was far too thin, her arms and legs all bones, her stomach a little swollen from malnutrition, but dressed in a gown of Tamsen's, basted to fit her wasted body, she was not bad-looking at all.

"She's a sweet child," Tamsen told Dan, "but I don't understand the sudden change. I'm afraid it's all a pose. And I'm worried about Nell! She acts so—so damn doting! Like she did with Winston—"

They were both silent, recalling Nell's infatuation with the little crook who resembled her dead husband. Neither wanted her hurt again.

"Nell's got her head on straight," Dan said. "Maybe she's just proud of what she's wrought! Under all that dirt was a pretty little girl—"

"Who is fifteen years old," Tamsen reminded him, "and a thief!"

"And you're sixty years old, and a temptress," Dan teased.

Tamsen laughed. There was no point in worrying about Nell. She couldn't change the old woman any easier than she could change—Dan.

Not that she wanted to.

Tamsen was right in her concern. Nell, since her famous speech at dinner, had tried to disassociate herself as a mother figure. Her maternal instincts, suppressed, now boiled and bubbled in her massive frame. The Maggie who appeared sweet-faced and docile in the morning was a far cry from the soiled waif she had fought every step of the way.

All she needs is a chanct, Nell thought, recalling her own tough childhood followed by a checkered career. What was going to happen to the child when they left? Her poor little arm still not healed? Nell, who had been counting the days until their departure, now wished she could add a few.

In the meantime, she ceased her visits to the waterfront, taking Maggie downtown, buying her any pretties that struck her fancy, enjoying the gleam in the girl's green eyes. Maggie no longer cowered at a sudden movement and was able to carry on an intelligent conversation. Hell, she was even making friends with Peg.

In spite of her growing affection for Maggie, Nell was still shrewd enough to keep a sharp eye on her. She honestly believed her spanking that first night had done the trick. But it was still possible the girl would cut and run—

At the thought, Nell felt an ache somewhere in her prodigious middle. Maggie was free to go—but not until that arm healed.

On Sunday, Nell turned Maggie over to Tamsen. She had a date, she said, winking lewdly. Tamsen, to Maggie's dismay, took her duties seriously, and stayed by her side throughout the day.

Nell went to the park to meet Sean Murphy, half afraid he'd forgotten his old friend.

He had not. He showed up spick-and-span in a new suit, carrying a basket of cold chicken, fruit—and beer. "It was afther being my turn," he grinned.

Nell ate, patted her stomach, and burped loudly. Then she dealt the cards. This day, they played for ridiculous things. If she won, he must dance a jig. If he won, she must sing a song. The afternoon passed pleasurably, and she didn't know when she'd had so much fun. Not since Dusty—

They parted, agreeing to meet the next Sunday, which would be their last together. Nell found herself hurrying back to the hotel—and Maggie.

That night, Peg and Maggie found a minute to talk together. Peg was tense. She had just learned that she would be dismissed on Thursday of the following week. And she had worked out a plan—

On Wednesday night, Maggie would give the old horror a cup of tea laced with laudanum. Then, when she slept, she would unlock the door to Peg. Together, they would strip the room of valuables, including Nell's rings which she wore at all times. Maggie would disappear, Peg would remain until the end of her stint. With the blame on Maggie, Peg would remain free to fence the stolen articles. Maggie thought of Nell sleeping, of Peg stripping the rings from her fingers. She shivered. Put her in mind of a snake, Peg did. And Maggie felt funny inside, like a bellyache.

"Wot—if 'er wakes as us is at it?"

"Be sorry if 'er do," Peg said with a hard smile. "Yer won't peach on me?"

Maggie shook her head. There was honor among thieves.

For the rest of the evening, she was unusually silent. The chance she'd been waiting for had arrived, why wasn't she happy? These people had been kind to her—as no one in her life had before. Except, Maggie amended, for the baths. Nell had bought her things. This gown she wore was Tamsen's. She fingered the fine material, thinking how she was to disappoint them.

"You awright, kiddo? You ain't eatin' much."

Nell's eyes were soft with affection. Soon, they would be angry, hurt, betrayed. Maggie, hungry all her life, was unable to swallow. She looked around the table in the hotel dining room, at the Tallants who seemed to love each other so, at Juan Narvaéz, handsome and distinguished, at Nell—

" 'Ee all be goin' 'ome ter th' Stytes. I be goin' ter miss yer all."

The girl was lonesome and skeert awready! Nell's heavy face softened. She'd been thinkin' on Maggie's plight all afternoon. And she'd come up with an idea, one so damn nutty she didn' dare mention it, even to Tam. Hell, it was up to the girl. Let her make the decision.

That night, after a reluctant bath, Maggie stood at the window. In the massive, outsized nightgown, she looked more like a waif than ever. She was thinking about the coming week, when all this would be over; when she would be on the run again, dodging through alleys, hunted by the police—

"Maggie-girl."

She turned to see Nell sitting in a chair, her hand outstretched.

"Come here."

A wave of fear went through her. Nell knew what she and Peg were up to! She was going to be punished! A punishment she bloody well deserved—

Nell took her arm, pulling her closer, feeling the tension in the small emaciated body.

"You too big to set on my lap?"

Maggie perched nervously on Nell's knee, still unsure as to what was coming.

"I bin thinkin'," Nell said. "You ain't got nobody. Dusty an' me, we never had kids, though I love them McLeod girls like they wuz my own. I wuz thinkin' mebbe we could kind of git t'gether—" She babbled on, not making much sense. Maggie listened, bewildered. What was she getting at?

She turned, wide-eyed. Nell's face was twisted in a comic mask, tears spurting from her tiny screwed-up eyes. She was crying! Nell was crying—

"Nell?"

Nell snorted and wiped her nose on her sleeve. "Oh, hell! Here I am, bawlin' like a stuck hawg! Didn' go to snargle all over yuh! What I'm tryin' t'say is, do you wanna go to Frisco with us? I prob'ly won't be no great shakes as a maw, but—"

Her words were shut off as Maggie threw her arms around her neck, the splint banging her up one side of her head. They both began to laugh and cry at the same time. Finally Maggie rested against Nell's billows, feeling warm, content and safe as the old woman rocked her like a baby in her arms.

Once abed, Maggie tensed again. There was no sleep for her that night as she searched for a solution to her dilemma. More than anything in the world, she wanted to remain with Nell, the only person in her life who'd ever loved her.

But she couldn't peach on Peg. The robbery was set for Wednesday night and she must find a way to stop it. If they would only dismiss Peg before then—

There had to be a way.

And if she found it, there was still another problem. Nell might not want her if she knew—

Maggie sighed. She would just have to take it one step at a time.

Chapter 20

On Monday, Nell presented her plan to Dan, Tamsen, and Juan, as euphorically as if she were announcing the birth of a child. One massive arm hugged Maggie to her side as she broke the news. Maggie, intuitive and street-wise, studied the listeners for their reactions. She caught the tiny flicker of doubt in each, the haste in which they all immediately offered their congratulations. Nell rushed to tell Arab and left Maggie standing uncertainly behind.

Tamsen stepped forward to hug her. It was a warm hug, smelling of flowers. "I'm happy for you," she whispered, "and especially for Nell. We—we all love Nell so much! More than anything, we don't want her hurt—"

Acceptance—and a warning. Maggie recognized it for what it was. Her smile was strained as she went down the hall where she ran into Peg Mason.

Peg's eyes inspected her face, finding nothing incriminating in the girl's expression. "'Ee a sly one," she complimented her grudgingly. "They'm trust 'ee proper, now. Go off without a 'itch, it will!''

Not if Maggie could help it!

Her opportunity came the next morning. Tamsen had replaced Peg in Arab's room, and Juan happened along as Peg was leaving. He offered to buy the girl's breakfast, and she accepted, sweetly.

"And how is your sister-in-law?" he inquired as they walked away. "And your brother's case—? I still cannot believe a little thing like you can manage to support all those people—"

Maggie, just coming from Nell's room, frowned. People like Peg did not have families. They were loners, fighting and clawing to take from those who were more fortunate. She didn't like the way Peg was smiling up at Juan Narváez. And she remembered that the theft was planned so that she, Maggie, would take the blame. Peg had designs on the handsome, older man. She'd bet on it! And his wife was lying in there, still covering her face in his presence though she was nearly recovered.

Maggie's lips tightened. Maybe she had the key to her problem.

She volunteered to relieve Tamsen for the day. She would remain with the sick woman, leaving the Tallants free to see Liverpool together. Tamsen was delighted, Arab none too enthusiastic. She'd had little opportunity to know the girl who was to become part of their lives—and, considering Maggie's origins, she had her doubts. She still was fretful, insisting on a darkened room, and sat up in protest as Maggie raised the shades.

"I don't—," she began.

Maggie's hoarse little voice overrode her. A proper lucky woman Mrs. Narváez was, with a husband so nice and all. Why she had just seen him taking the nurse, Peg, down to breakfast. Not that Peg could be trusted with a man! A proper home-wrecker, that one was!

Arab was sitting upright, her mouth open. Maggie grinned to herself. She was on the right track! She looked at Arab, admiringly. "'Ee do be a beaut, 'ee do!" Peg didn't have a chance, not with a man who had such a pretty wife. If she, Maggie, was his missus, she'd fix up all pretty and surprise him when he came back—

Arabella Narvaéz ran her fingers over her face. The swelling had gone down. Perhaps a bath—a pretty gown and peignoir. Could Maggie do her hair?

Maggie could.

Within an hour, Arab was bathed and perfumed, dressed in a sea green filmy negligee, her hair freshly brushed and curling around her shoulders. For the first time in weeks, she was smiling.

"Bring my mirror," she told Maggie, "and my jewelry box. There are some small emerald earrings—"

Maggie complied. Arab opened the box and looked at its contents in consternation. Her diamond pendant! The saphires! A gold bracelet inlaid with precious jade—

Where had they gone? A thief had been in her room! A thief!

Arab looked up at Maggie, her eyes hard with suspicion. She would make no accusations now, but would wait for Juan. They would call the family together and have this out. Dear God, poor Nell!

She snapped the box shut and pushed it at Maggie. "Put it back in the drawer," she said grimly. "I've changed my mind. And please leave me. I would like to be alone for a while. When my husband returns, I want to see him."

Maggie obeyed, her hands cold and shaking. She'd seen the way Arab rummaged through the box—as though looking for something that wasn't there. She had also read the look in her eyes.

It was plain that Peg had already struck—and that Maggie was going to be blamed for it.

Juan returned to find his wife beautiful once more—and on

the verge of hysteria. A fortune in jewels was missing. Maggie had taken them.

"You should have seen her," Arab wept, "trying to brazen it out! She just handed me the box, innocent as you please! I suppose she thought I wouldn't notice what was gone!"

"We don't know that she's the guilty party," Juan pointed out. "This is the first time she's been in here alone. And either Tamsen or Peg have been with you in this room, day and night—"

"For Heaven's sakes! I don't know how a thief operates! But she is a thief, we know that!" Her tear-starred eyes lifted to his and she shuddered in his arm. "It isn't just the jewelry, Juan, really it isn't. It—it's Nell! One more heartbreak will kill her!"

Juan held her close. Arab was selfish, spoiled, but when it mattered she came through. She'd meant what she said, honestly and sincerely. It was Nell she was concerned about. *Dios*, so was he!

They were finally able to talk calmly. Maggie's background made her the only possible candidate for the crime. And Nell must never know.

Juan would talk to Maggie. The law would not be called in if she returned anything she still had in her possession. And she must tell Nell she'd changed her mind and decided to stay in Liverpool. Nell would be hurt, but not as hurt as she would be, knowing the truth.

He hated the job he had to do, hated it like hell! The girl was so pathetic, undernourished, looking at him with great green eyes that reminded him of Arab's. Her scrawny form seemed to jerk under the impact of his words as he told her of the missing jewelry and his belief that she had taken it. Worse, she made no denial, offered no defense, just stood there, taking it.

No, she didn't have any of the jewelry in her possession. Yes, she would talk to Nell. No, she wouldn't mention the theft.

"She made me feel like a damned monster," Juan told Arab after the interview. "She looked like she was being flayed alive. Poor pitiful little monkey!"

"But she didn't admit to stealing those things?"

"She didn't say she did—or that she didn't. *Dios*, Arab, I feel like a—a beast! Like I hit somebody who couldn't fight back!"

Maggie went back to Nell's suite. The old woman was napping, a huge mound that heaved up and down with her labored breathing. Nell, her almost-mum; the closest Maggie'd ever come to having a family of her own. And now it was all over. She was aligned with Peg, whether she wished to be, or not.

Tomorrow was Wednesday. Tomorrow night, Maggie would bring Nell a cup of tea, laced with laudanum. And Nell would sleep. Maggie would unlock the door to Peg, and Peg would strip the glittering gems from Nell's pudgy fingers. And if she woke—

"Be sorry if 'er do," Peg had said.

Now, like a preview of things to come, Nell was waking. First a snort, a rumbling like a volcano, then the beady eyes snapped open.

"Hell," she said. "I thought you wuz goin' fer a walk with Juan." She rubbed her eyes. "Musta slep' longer'n I figgered. Bed's too gawdam soft, I reckon."

"Nell," Maggie's green eyes were steady. "Nell, I've got to talk to you—"

Nell fought her bulk to a sitting position, and grinned lovingly at Maggie. "Awright, honey, go ahead. Shoot."

Her beady eyes opened wide as she listened. None of it made sense, but, hell, if the kid wanted to play some kind of game, she'd deal herself in.

On Wednesday night, Maggie carried a silver tray up from the hotel kitchens. It held a teapot, a teacup, and some cakes of which Nell was particularly fond. In Maggie's apron pocket was a small brown bottle Peg had given her. She managed to maneuver her way through the door to Nell's suite, despite her splinted arm, and kicked it shut behind her.

In a less than an hour, she opened it again; a signal to Peg.

The little nurse had sedated her patient, and had been waiting impatiently. She didn't quite trust Maggie. But then, she had never trusted anyone. As the door swung open, she breathed a sigh of satisfaction, flitting along the corridor like a small gray moth. She stepped over the threshold and locked the door behind her.

The room was lit by only a single candle, throwing the bed and its occupant into shadow. Peg could see the giant figure mounded beneath the sheet. Out like a light. This would be even easier than she'd thought.

"'Er ain't 'ardly breathin'," Maggie whispered. "Look over 'ere." She pointed to the bureau top where a number of gems flickered in the candle's flame.

"Lor' lumme," Peg gasped. "A bloody fortune!" She swept the bureau clear, dropping the jewels into a bag, talking as she did so. Maggie was to take the bag direct to a Mr. Feingold. Then she was to hide out. Peg named a waterfront tavern. They would meet there. Maggie would get what was coming to her—

Peg headed for the bed and the sleeping woman, pulling a knife from her bag.

"'Ee ain't be goin' ter kill her!" Maggie swallowed hard.

Peg laughed. It depended on how easily the rings came off. She intended to have them one way or another.

She threw back the bedcovers and froze.

Pillows! Only pillows! Maggie had peached!

She threw herself at the girl, knife upraised, only to change direction as Nell charged from the bathroom. She'd been standing there, as instructed, nose pressed to the barely open door. Her expression had changed from one of doting amusement—to consternation—to anger.

"Put that down, y'thievin' leetle bastard," she roared,

circling the girl, arms spread to catch her in a bear hug. She'd squeeze the life out of the bitch, goddamn her hide! She'd—

The knife flashed back, then forward, aimed for Nell's heart.

But Maggie had gotten there first, thrusting her splinted arm between the two women. The knife struck, glanced, and Nell had hold of Peg Mason.· Maggie whacked the girl over the head with her splint, and ran for help.

It was a solemn group that gathered in the foyer a little later, watching as the police took Peg Mason away. Juan Narvaéz was devasted—not for Peg's sake, but Maggie's. He and Arab had misjudged the girl, accusing her falsely. He said as much, and Maggie turned her big green eyes his way.

From now on, she didn't plan to say a word that wasn't true. It could have happened, she told him honestly. She'd been working along the same lines as Peg—until she changed her mind.

Now that was off her chest, but there was something more, something that might make a lot of difference in her future; something she figured Nell should be the first to know.

Chapter 21

Nell Wotherspoon was more upset by Maggie's confession than any ex-madam had a right to be. She looked at the girl's slat-thin figure in undisguised horror.

"A baby! Whaddaya mean, a baby! Dammit, yer pullin' my leg!" Looking at the girl's steady eyes, she knew it was no joke.

"Migawd," she said feebly, "a bun in th' oven! Who'd a thunk it. Now, what th' blazes we gonna do."

Maggie had no answer for that. She'd felt it only right that Nell should know before paying her fare to the States. Granny Puser on the waterfront sometimes took care of such things. "'Er could rid me of it—"

Nell looked aghast at Maggie's statement. "Not no, but hell, no!" she boomed. "Two wrongs don't never make nuthin' right. But it oughta have a paw." She frowned at Maggie. "You give me that young sonofabitch's name, an' I'll—"

"Dunno," said Maggie. Then her eyes crinkled impishly. "Know 'oo I 'ope it were! Real toff, 'e was!"

Nell wormed the story out of her, finding no clue to help her. Maggie, in her years on the waterfront had lived like a cat, hiding out from males that prowled dark streets at night; sleeping in doorways and trash heaps. Her attempts at concealment weren't always successful. There had been several sailors, dockworkers, and the like. But the one she remembered had been with a trio of fine gentlemen, doing the slums. She had heard them singing from far off as they paraded drunkenly, arm in arm, moving in her direction.

She shrank back in the doorway she occupied, but they had spied her. And one of them had taken her, the others watching.

"Proper elegant, 'e was! Top 'at, an' stick. A luvly man!"

An elegant, lovely man, who had drunkenly raped a child. Maggie evidently regarded it as a high point in her pitiful life. She didn't know his name, and wouldn't recognize him if she saw him again.

"Goddamn," Nell said in dismay, "oh, goddamn!"

There was nothing to do but break the news to the others. A baby was something you couldn't hide. But dammit, she oughta have a father fer that kid! It'd look like Nell hadn' brung her up right!

Nell reddened. Maggie had become her own little daughter in her fantasies; hers—and Dusty's. It was hard to remember that Maggie had been on her own for years that had not included Nell. It ain't what happened afore we met, Nell told herself stoutly, it's what's gonna come.

And what was coming, was a baby.

Nell's eyes suddenly rounded as she considered what it meant. A grandkid! Hot damn!

Maggie was still waiting, with that stoic look of expecting nothing but the worst. Nell threw expansive arms around her and pulled her to her ample bosom.

The trip was still on. And this baby was gonna have one helluva happy life, paw er no paw! No sense in tellin' the

162

others, not just yet. They'd save the news until they reached Frisco, then they'd throw the gawdamdest party anybody ever seed!

The remaining days passed happily. Some, not all, of Arab's jewelry was recovered. Arab took her loss with good grace. What was a diamond pendant, compared to a husband? Young Maggie had been wiser than she, where Juan was concerned. The thought that Peg Mason had flirted with him made Arab especially attentive to her man. Juan had his wife once again, and they would soon be going home—for the first time in years. They would see Em—and Missie. Arab could hardly wait.

Nell watched them all, Tamsen and Dan, Juan and Arab, acting like kids as they talked about returning to the city they once loved. Maggie was as excited as any of them, her face shining, beginning to plump out a little with Nell's tender loving care.

There were only a couple of clouds on Nell's horizon. First, there was Maggie's pregnancy. Nell never figured herself as a gawdam prude, but Maggie's husbandless state continued to bother her. Something ought to be done about it. But what?

Second, they would be sailing on Wednesday, next. Sunday, she'd be saying good-bye to Sean Murphy. Funny how the kid got into her heart so quick! Maybe she was gettin' to be a selfish old biddy. She had a daughter. Now, she wisht she had a son—

On Sunday morning, she dressed in her favorite purple gown, put a fresh deck of cards in her reticule, and headed for the park. She hadn't been there long when Sean arrived, his carrot hair slicked down, a grin on his freckled face. He'd been afraid she was busy packing—that she wouldn't come. But just in case—he produced a basket, similar to the one he brought the Sunday before.

Feeling that time was speeding past them, knowing this was the last time they'd have together, their conversation was awkward. There were long periods of silence, then both would begin to speak at the same time.

"I will be afther missin' yer," Sean said finally.

Nell's old eyes stung, and she blew her nose. "Mebbe y'kin drop over to Frisco sometime," she said.

He nodded, but they each knew it wasn't likely to happen.

Oh, hell, Nell thought, this keeps up, I'll be bellerin' like a steer! She changed the subject. "Good grub," she said, gesturing toward the basket. "Better'n that ho-tel crap. Whereja git it?"

The boy's face burned red. The woman who ran his boarding house cooked it. In return, he washed dishes at night.

"Yer gonna make some lucky girl a good man," Nell said generously. Then her eyes opened wide, her jaw clamped shut like a steel trap. "Never ast you. You got a girl, somewheres?" He shook his head, and she smiled like a wily old crocodile. Her pudgy hand dived into the depths of her reticule, coming out with the deck of cards.

"We're gonna play us a game of five, face up! An' what we're stakin' is favors." At his blank look, she explained, impatiently. "You win, I do any favor you ast, an' viceyversey. Got it?"

He grinned and nodded. It was only a different version of the silly games they played last Sunday.

"I deal," Nell said.

She slapped down an ace in front of Sean Murphy, a deuce for herself.

"Goddamn! Yer off like a herda turkles!"

Another ace for her opponent; a ten for Nell. With a woeful expression, she dealt him a king, herself a deuce; a king to him. "Two pair," she said mournfully, "aces and kings high."

She dealt herself another ten. "Deuces and tens, not much there. An' here's th' clincher! You ready?"

Sean Murphy received a trey. Nell raised her eyes prayerfully to Heaven and put a card down, gingerly, before she dared to look.

"Gawdam," she said comically. "Looky there! Full house. Reckon you lose. Or, hell, mebbe you jus' won! Now, here's the favor I'm astin'—"

Tersely, she stated her demands. She'd adopted this girl who was in a family way. " 'Tweren't no fault of hers," Nell hastened to add. Little Maggie needed a husband, the baby a paw. "Thass where you come in."

Sean Murphy was instantly on his feet, his freckles standing out on his white face.

"Lady Wotherspoon—"

"You bin callin' me Nell," she reminded him. "Now, lissen, you ain't heared me out. The girl's a purty leetle thing, or will be, once I git her fed up. An' with her goes a ticket t'Frisco an' a job in my bar. Hell, you'll be my son-in-law!"

Her voice trailed off, and she reached out blindly for his hand. "Reckon you think I'm a damned idjit. Mebbe I am. Ain't tryin' t'sell yuh no pig in a poke! Girl uster be a thief. Found 'er on th' street. She growed up th' hard way, an' she sure ez hell ain't no virgin."

Nell lifted her raddled face to his, eyes spurting tears. "Thass th' story. You wanna welsh on yer bet, I won't be mad—"

Sean Murphy was in a quandary. He was pretty sure the old woman rigged the deck on him, back when he was jobless and hungry, saving his pride—and his life at the same time. And he had a feeling she'd just done it again; that his answer was almighty important to her.

Well, what did he have to lose? His Kathleen, back in Ireland, had married someone else. His job paid only enough to keep body and soul together. America was a land of promise—and in all of England, Nell had been his only friend.

"I never welshed on a bet in me life," he said.

Nell's huge body sagged in relief. She couldn't seem to stop the tears that streaked her face. Finally, she took out a handkerchief and blew her nose, with a loud honking sound.

"Done?" she asked, extending her hand.

"Done," Sean said gravely. "Now, if I'm to be wed, I should be afther meetin' me wife—"

Nell stood, her brisk self again. "You wait right here. Oughta meet in th' park. More romantick thataway." She charged toward the hotel before he could assent. He looked after her and shook his head to clear it.

He'd come to the park to say good-bye to a nice old woman. And somehow she'd managed to change his whole life in a few deft moves. His first impulse had been to tell her to go to bloody blazes. But something in her face, that hopeless, pleading look, had stopped him.

He sat down, his head in his hands, remembering pretty Kathleen, who had married the miller's son after the Murphy tavern burned. She'd married for security. Wasn't he about to do the same? A ticket to America, a job to his liking—

And a wife?

She was a girl of the streets, Nell had told him. A thief. And a man had put something under her apron before him. In addition, she was probably as homely as a mud fence, hair like a thatched roof. He'd seen the waterfront girls.

And he'd got himself into this mess, he thought wryly, only because he couldn't accuse a lady of cheating at cards! Sean Murphy, he said to himself, sure, an' ye've lost yer mind! Or the auld woman has put a spell on ye!

A puffing Nell escorted Maggie as far as the curve in the path. "Thass him, there," she pointed. She pointed at a young man who sat slumped on a bench, his head in his hands. He didn't look too happy.

Maggie hung back. She'd been stunned when Nell burst into the suite with her proclamation. "Gitcher glad rags on, honey, I done found you a husband—"

The speed with which Nell yanked her out of one gown and

166

into another, then rushed her toward the park, had the girl dazed. There'd been no time to think—

Now, she hung back, wondering how Nell had managed this confrontation. From the boy's disconsolate posture, it was clearly not his idea! Even then, he probably had no idea what he was getting into.

"Do 'e know about this?" Maggie put a hand to her slender midriff.

"I tolt him."

"An' 'e still wants—"

"Oh, hell," Nell roared. "Gitcher butt over there! He won't wait forever!"

Maggie walked along the path, still feeling the little spank Nell added to emphasize her words. She approached the boy on the bench shyly, self-consciously. Sean got to his feet, his eyes with their straw-colored lashes widening.

Sure, and there was some of the Irish in this girl! The way her nose was tip-tilted, with a spattering of freckles to match his own. Eyes as green as the sea on a sunny day, a waist he could span with his two hands—

But the girl Nell mentioned was in a family way. His eyes went to her middle and there was a moment's hesitation before he said her name.

"Maggie?"

Maggie's quick eye had caught his hasty inspection, the brief pause that followed. Her face reddened. What was, was! If he didn't like what he saw, he wasn't bound to take her!

"You are Maggie?"

She nodded, looking at the ground to conceal her simmering resentment at being studied like a—a mare!

Sean rose and went toward her. Gently, he put a finger beneath her chin and lifted her face to meet his. Maggie flinched away with a belligerent expression.

Men had never been kind to her. And Sean's touch had given her a funny feeling, making her go all over weak-like. There was no room for weakness in Maggie's world.

She glared at him. "We ain't wed! Till we be, proper-like, keep 'ee 'ands t'yerself!"

Sean Murphy jerked away, then grinned. He liked a lass with spirit! He had an idea that life with this little wildcat might be fun.

Maybe he'd won, after all, as Nell had said. Sure and begorra, this was Sean Murphy's lucky day.

Chapter 22

Once more the little group of travelers was plunged into turmoil. Only Nell, Sean, and Maggie knew the details of Nell's arrangement. As far as the rest were concerned, the romance had been going on for a long time, coming to a head when young Murphy discovered Maggie was going to the States. Their marriage had been a sudden decision.

"And it's caused a helluva lot of trouble," Dan said grimly. He'd had to use all his influence at court to get the proper papers to take Sean aboard, and get a special order from the church so that they might be married before they left. Nell would settle for nothing less than "a honest-to-Gawd preacher."

While Dan took care of his end of things, Juan Narvaéz took the young groom to a tailor. Nell insisted he be outfitted properly, in spite of his stubborn refusal.

"You got a damn balky mule," she scowled, "you build a fire under 'im! He moves!"

Sean Murphy reluctantly moved.

In the meantime, Tamsen and Maggie secluded themselves in Nell's suite, stitching a wedding gown. Arab made arrangements for a wedding breakfast, and Nell bullied the hotel staff.

On dawn on Wednesday, Tamsen discreetly left Nell to dress the bride. Nell was taking her responsibilities as a mother seriously. She helped the girl into a gown that transformed her into a fairylike creature, carefully fitting a veil over hair that now definitely shone. Maggie was a far cry from the screaming urchin she'd hauled through that door. Nell blinked back tears of pleasure.

"Well," she humphed! "Well! I reckon we better have us a leetle girl-tawk."

Maggie looked at her in awe. Nell was blushing!

"They's two kinds of nachure," Nell said, fumbling for words. "They's hooman nachure—and another kind, which men has got, damn their sweet leetle hides. They spend as much time thinkin' about somethin' else ez they do about—that, they'd be a helluva lot smarter! Point is, they don't git whut they's lookin fer at home, they git it somewhere's elst. Hell, that's whut kep' me an' Tam in bizness, in Frisco—"

Maggie lifted her head, alert. This was a new side of the elegant Tamsen Tallant; a side she'd not suspected.

Encouraged by her sudden attention, Nell droned on, finishing the talk she'd lain awake all night preparing with, "That's how men is."

Maggie knew how they were! And she had something under her apron to prove it. Yet she knew intuitively that Nell considered her little sermon important. She threw her arms around the old woman, clinging to her fiercely. Nell spatted her bottom, blinking back tears. "You be a good wife to Murphy," she ordered, "er I'll paddle yer butt!"

They went down to the hotel dining room, where the hotel clerk, Swithins, stood stiffly at attention, waiting to escort the bride. He had been Nell's choice. Dan and Juan oughta set with their wives, dammit. Besides, the clerk had a look to him that would give the occasion tone.

Leaving the bride, Nell waddled her way to a small group of chairs, settling herself in the front row.

One end of the dining room was a bower of fall colors. Behind the small audience, tables were set up for the wedding breakfast. Not exactly the most ideal arrangement, Nell thought. But it was fine, if you looked straight ahead.

And before her was Sean Murphy, standing a little to one side of an altar with a priest—"a honest-to-Gawd preacher" —behind it. Sean looked like he'd just bet his best britches in a game—and lost. Nell tried to send him a comforting smile, but the blue eyes in his freckled face were blind.

He did look cute, though, she thought fondly; almost as posh as Swithins. Never knowed he had so much class—

Then the hired pianist struck up the wedding march and they all craned to watch the bride enter.

Maggie was almost beautiful. The filmy gown Tamsen had concocted was of palest amber, concealing her too-thin body—and anything else that might show. Her veil was of the same color, only a scrap of material, held in place by a velvet ribbon. Holding to the arm of Swithins, the clerk, whose cheek still bore scars from the nails of a screeching street girl, Maggie moved serenely toward her husband-to-be.

Sean Murphy's knees stopped shaking. His jaw dropped, visibly, as he watched the vision coming toward him. Since that day in the park, she had kept her distance. A dozen times he'd been on the verge of saying, "T'th' divil with 'er," but something had held him back. He watched now, with awe, as she approached him. Then they were kneeling. He gazed distractedly at the top of her small head, deaf to the minister's words.

A small, hard elbow punched him in the ribs, and he realized he was expected to make a response.

Two bruised ribs later, it was over. It hadn't, Sean thought, been so bad after all.

Following the wedding breakfast, the party left the hotel. They were all laughing, bright-eyed with champagne as they boarded the carriages that would take them to the wharf.

The little desk clerk watched them go, his hand going automatically to his scratched cheek. He thought of his first meeting with that bloody awful woman; the red-haired woman's contagious disease; the struggling little thief who tore him to pieces in the elevator—

Nothing had been the same since the group checked into the hotel, completely disrupting the sedate atmosphere he so carefully cultivated. Thefts, an almost murder, the police called in the middle of the night! And now a—a drunken wedding at an ungodly hour of the morning! He hiccupped, covering his mouth with his hand. My word, he was glad they were gone!

But, jove, it was going to be dull without them. Very dull! He wandered disconsolately back to the desk, where the dust of their departure was already settling.

The wedding party was the last aboard *The Hollander*, a Dutch passenger ship with plush accommodations and a gilt-and-mirror salon. Sean Murphy paid no attention to the amenities. He hustled his little bride past the amused eyes of the other passengers, and down to their stateroom, where he locked the door. He faced his bride, his freckled jaw set in determination, his carrot-colored hair standing on end above a stiff, formal collar.

They must get things right between them! Three days of blather and foolishness, and they'd not exchanged a kind word yet. Sure, and they were wed, now! She was to be a good, obedient woman, as his dead mither was! No more elbows t'th' ribs, or he'd smack her one!

He glowered as she put her hand over her mouth. Was she crying, now? Or had that been a muffled giggle?

He ripped the restraining collar from his neck and reached for her, kissing her hard. Then her lips softened under his and his mouth moved on hers, tasting its warmth, its sweetness.

He felt the anger going out of him and pulled away. He hadn't said all his say!

"Yer me wife," he continued. "An' that's," he pointed to her middle, "me child! Mind ye, I'm askin' no questions as t'th' man who give it t'ye! That's behind and done! Th' wee one's a Murphy! If it's a boyo, we're callin' him Paddy, afther me auld da—!"

The sound Sean heard had been a giggle. Maggie no longer felt an urge to laugh. Seeing the wiry boy before her, his rusty hair on end like the comb of a scrappy rooster, his eyes strained and sincere, his mouth trembling a little despite his harsh words, Maggie succumbed to the emotions that had been thrilling through her.

She said nothing, but moved forward quietly, meekly laying her head against his chest. She heard his harsh, indrawn breath, then his arms went around her. He picked her up and carried her to their wedding bed—as the boat rocked, moving away from the wharf.

Maggie and Sean rocked with it. Where a woman would close her eyes, Maggie kept hers open. She didn't want to miss a thing; the absorbed young face above her, pale and stern with his rending passions; the way it seemed to shimmer for a moment and dissolve in a shower of stars that scattered before her own cry of wonder—

Nell had said nothing about this! Nothing to tell her that the act of love could be other than brutality and pain! Maggie had been prepared for it, hoping she could refrain from fighting back as she had done before—but this had been different! An urge to get closer, to take all of him into herself, and then a melting away until the self that was Maggie was gone—

"Lor' lumme!" she said.

On the deck above, the others watched the grimy docks of Liverpool fade into the distance. The rising sun laid a patina over the town, giving it a fleeting beauty. It seemed foreign to them now. Their hearts were already turned toward home—their own shining city.

Dan and Tamsen, Arab and Juan, did not linger long. The late fall air was unusually brisk. They headed toward their own staterooms, leaving Nell behind.

Nell grinned. Chilly? Hell, who did they think they were foolin'? She knew what was on their minds. They were thinkin' of Sean an' Maggie, just startin' married life down there!

And so was she, but there was no sense goin' to her room. There was nobody waitin' for her there. Not even Maggie, now.

Like they allus said, Lose a daughter, gain a son. She'd hit th' jackpot!

If only Dusty wuz here to see their fambly!

She shut her eyes, conjuring up a small man with two missing front teeth, a wispy moustache, white hair standing awry. She imagined him standing beside her and sniffed. There was a smell of whiskey in the air. It was almost like she could reach out and touch him—but not quite.

Someday she would, but not just yet. She had to hang around to meet her grandkid.

Two gulls soared above the ship, dipping and circling. Nell watched them for a long, long time.

CHINATOWN

Chapter 23

At Matthew Blaine's suggestion, Missie was given leave from work. It was conceivable that Petra might show up at any time. The girl could have had a mild loss of memory. Too, she was sensitive. Maybe she'd run away in a fit of pique over something Missie considered umimportant—

Missie shook her head. She'd gone over all those last days, time after time. There was nothing!

Even so, it was wise to have someone at the apartment, in case she should appear; otherwise, she might take off again—

What he said made sense. But it meant that she hardly saw Matthew at all. He'd dropped by after work several times to report on the progress of the search for Petra—but only just long enough to hold her for a moment, to comfort her. Perhaps that's all it was—comfort.

She thought back to the last evening at the office, the night Petra disappeared. Matthew had accused her of—all kinds of things. She'd hoped that, learning Duke Courtney was her uncle, he'd know how wrong he was.

In the meantime, Missie stayed in the small rooms above the bakery—waiting; waiting for Petra, and for Matthew Blaine. If Petra did run away, she thought wryly, it was probably brought on by sheer boredom!

When a knock sounded at her door, she rushed to open it, her eyes starry with expectation. They dulled at the sight of Duke Courtney.

He stepped inside, sniffing appreciatively at the scent of baking bread that drifted from below, and smiled his tired smile. No, there was no word regarding his granddaughter. Every mode of transportation leaving town had been checked out. She hadn't gone by stage, ship, or train. That meant she had to be somewhere in the city. He had detectives checking every block.

As he talked, she watched him, seeing how much he'd aged in just a few days. His graying yellow mane was almost white; his blue eyes red-rimmed with worry. Em was still taking it hard, but she'd probably feel better when Tam and Arab arrived. They'd had word their ship would dock in New York on November fifteenth—

So soon? Missie's hand went to her throat. In the worry over Petra, she'd forgotten the mention of their coming. Before, it had been a hope. Now, it was a reality.

Her mother and father, Aunt Tamsen and Uncle Dan—and Nell! They would be here soon. And they would find their troublesome daughter and relative moved out from under Aunt Em's wing, working—in a man's job—and responsible for the disappearance of Em's granddaughter.

Then, too, there was *The Book*!

Duke was looking at her sympathetically. "Don't take this thing with Petra so hard, honey. You didn't have anything to do with it. It's just that Em thinks—"

"I know what she thinks," Missie said dully. "Dear God, if she'd only come back—!"

"We'll find her," Duke said. But he sounded like he didn't believe it—and neither did she.

He left, and she sat for a long time thinking of the people she'd hurt. She remembered the night she married Arthur Melvin, a love-struck girl in her teens. She'd gone to meet him at night, clad in a pitiful attempt at bridal finery; an old white dress let out at the seams, a cheese-cloth veil fastened with silk flowers from a bonnet.

They'd been married by a walleyed traveling preacher, she and the strapping blond man in white moleskins. He had paid off the preacher and violated her. Then he'd led her to the house, bruised, battered, throwing the fact of their marriage in Aunt Tamsen's face—

He was going to take her away. And Tamsen had shot him, deliberately, in the arm.

Later Missie, still wrong-headed, climbed through the window and went to meet him. He fired Opal Station, burning the whole valley on which the family's livelihood depended. Then Melvin, the man the aborigines called devil-devil, had carried her off to hell.

Because of that fire, because Missie, his favorite, was missing, Dusty had died. He wasn't burned. His heart just stopped beating. No one had ever blamed her, even Nell. But Missie knew—

If Petra was dead, it would be one more mark against her. How she wished she'd bundled the girl up and returned her to Aunt Em! By force, if necessary.

She seemed to hurt or disappoint everybody she loved. Em was shocked she earned her living as she did, working along with male reporters, rubbing shoulders with people who committed sordid crimes. Living on her own was also a sign of immorality to Em Courtney.

Just as it was to Matthew Blaine, who had practically accused her of being a harlot.

Now, with her luck, the book she'd written on the lives of her loved ones would hit the stands about the time her mother and Aunt Em stepped ashore.

Damnation! She hoped she had a chance to explain the

content before they saw a copy. But maybe it couldn't be explained.

She'd stayed faithfully with the facts, just as Dusty had related them to her. Though those facts were sometimes ugly, sordid, she'd tried to portray them with sensitivity. Now, she was shivering, uncertain as she thought back over the book's content.

She'd written of the ruffians who, intending to even the score for a friend, took Aunt Em for Tamsen. They raped her. Martha, Petra's mother, was a child of that rape. Then Em, in the throes of childbirth on the trail to California, managed to stave off an Indian attack.

Would Em's shame at bearing an illegitimate child cancel out the glory of being a heroine? Would her embarrassment at the failure and suicide of her first husband, Donald Alden, take precedence over the wonderful love she'd found in Duke Courtney?

And Tamsen! Dancing in a cantina in Texas to support her sisters; winning that cantina in a poker game; selling it to take pregnant Em to a place she would not be known; using every trick in the trade to purchase a bawdy house—so that Em could live the life of a lady. Would Tamsen see herself as Missie saw her? A beautiful, warmhearted woman who sacrificed herself for her sisters?

Even Arabella, Missie's pretty, selfish mother, had her share of horrors to overcome. Unmanageable in her teens, she'd been put into the hands of a traveling preacher, heading to San Francisco to open a school for girls. A perverted, sadistic man, he'd misused the girl. She'd been purchased from him by the famous Lola Montez, who heard her singing at a street Revival—

Touring with the Montez troupe in Spain, she'd fallen in love with princely Juan Narvaéz, been kidnapped by Spanish gypsies, escaped to arrive home more dead than alive. And Juan had followed her—

Missie put her hands over her eyes. Suddenly, her book

seemed a horrible revelation of family secrets, its pages ripe with lust, rape, murder. She'd been selfishly single-minded in writing it, convincing herself it was a tribute. What had made her think her talents would transform such events to make heroines of those who endured them?

As Aunt Em would say, Missie had displayed the family linen to public view.

She had to stop it!

Missie leaped to her feet and took down her cloak. Perhaps she could make it to the telegraph office in time! She must send a wire—

At the foot of the stairs, she ran into Larry Hiller. He'd been worried about her, knowing she was frantic over her cousin, and had come to see if he could help in any way.

He could. He had a horse and carriage waiting. She had to send an urgent wire. If he could take her—

Frau Schmitt watched as her roomer was lifted into a strange carriage by a strange man. She frowned, wondering at it, and returned to her baking.

When Matthew Blaine arrived a few minutes later, she flatly told him what she'd seen. Hurt and puzzled, he waited a long while, talking with the German woman, until the delay became embarrassing. Then he went home.

Missie had forgotten it was Thursday.

The wire she sent that Thursday night was addressed to Stuyvesant Brown. It did not reach his desk until Monday.

Changed mind, it read. *Arab, Tamsen, Nell, dock N.Y., Nov. 15. Fear disapproval. Stop publication, all costs. Will repay advance!*

It was signed, *Melissa McLeod*.

Stew Brown stared at the yellow page in confusion. The girl had never left his thoughts, and he would do anything to establish himself in her affections. But this was impossible. Copies were already being distributed to reviewers on the larger papers. Pre-advertising, hinting at the book's lurid content, already had the New York readership haunting book stores. His company planned to set up a publicity campaign all over the country.

His hands were tied.

He could not help Melissa, but he could help Brown, Halpert and Brown!

Hastily, he wrote notes to reporters on the more prominent local papers, calling for a messenger to take them around.

Major characters of controversial book soon to be issued by Brown, Halpert and Brown, to arrive in New York November 15. In the party will be the famous ex-madam of one of San Francisco's most notorious brothels, Tamsen Tallant. Her sister, Arab, another chief character in this spicy tale of California's early days, was a former dancer with the troupe of Lola Montez. The book, "The Survivors" describes the lurid details of her affairs in Spain.

The whereabouts of Em Courtney, a third sister, whose escapades make spicy reading, are unknown. Perhaps the newcomers will shed some light on the subject.

Their attitude toward the volume containing their life story is not yet known. It is possible they will be available for interviews.

If that didn't make front page, he'd eat his hat! The senior partners would be highly pleased. And when he got his new office, he'd fire that old bat out there—and try to find a new girl, more like Melissa McLeod.

Chapter 24

Missie was silent on the trip to the telegraph office. Larry Hiller sensed her tension and suited his conversation to her mood.

On the way back to her apartment, the girl seemed to be feeling better. He put himself out to entertain her with happenings at the *Examiner* in her absence.

Miss Elizabeth Anspaugh had been in, upset at not seeing Missie's by-line for several days. Evidently she was using her standing to pull in letters from other suffragette sympathizers. Blaine was so burned up, they were thinking of selling tickets to watch him open the morning mail.

Carrington covered a fire last week. In fact, he did more than cover it. He went in and carried a kid out of the burning building. With the award they gave him—and a nickel—he'd probably be able to buy himself a cup of coffee.

He himself was working on an interview with John R. Haynes, the young doctor formerly from Philadelphia who was launching a campaign against machine politics and corruption—especially where the Southern Pacific Railroad was involved.

"Lots of luck," Missie said with irony.

Hiller grinned at her. "That's what I like about you. Don't know any other woman who'd know what I was talking about. And if they did, they wouldn't give a damn. You're a born reporter!"

Was she? Larry could have no idea of the turmoil going on inside her at the moment! Most writers prayed to get into print. Right now she was praying she wouldn't.

"I miss it all," she said wistfully, "the noise and commotion, the sound of the presses—"

"Then why don't you come to work? It's not the same without you."

"Matthew Blaine thought I should stay home—in case Petra came back—"

Larry filled his pipe, tamped it, held the reins in one hand until he got it going. Then he took his eyes off the street and looked at Missie.

"The girl's been gone a week. Looks like she's not planning on it," he said baldly. "It appears to me old woman's-place-is-in-the-home Blaine has got you right where he wants you!"

Missie felt heat rise in her face. She'd thought the same thing, but she hadn't put it into words. She put a hand on Hiller's.

"You don't have to go, do you? You're not in a hurry?"

He laughed, boyishly. Hell, no! If she wanted, they'd take in dinner and a show. There was a vaudeville act—

When Missie let herself into her apartment, it was very late. She had enjoyed the evening immensely. Larry, with his thinning hair and honest blue eyes, wasn't a—a heartbreaker, like Blaine. But the evening had gone off without a hitch. And she'd agreed to an outing on Sunday.

She intended to go back to work. She had do do something, anything, to escape the cloud of doom she felt hanging over her head.

Now that her wire had been sent off, she'd managed to begin to think straight. The letter she received the day Petra disappeared said the book had gone to the binders. Even if that final job had not been completed, Brown, Halpert and Brown wouldn't stop it at this point. She'd acted like a fool. Her wire had been a fruitless effort, born of desperation. She must be losing her mind!

Larry Hiller was right. She had to get back to her job, if she wanted to keep her senses. Sitting here dwelling on all her mistakes was driving her mad.

She would start again on Monday.

She rather dreaded her outing with Larry Hiller, but Sunday was a pleasurable day with soft blue autumn skies, a faint breeze carrying the sweetness of sun-dry grass. They drove to Golden Gate Park, where trees and shrubs were ripening into mellow color. They walked along its trodden paths, surrounded by young lovers. Here, a quartet bent over a cooing baby on a blanket; parents and grandparents, surely. There, a family spread a picnic lunch on a checked cloth while children ran and shouted in joyous freedom.

The scene only pointed up Missie's loneliness. She did not object when Larry Hiller took her hand. She no longer cringed at a man's touch. At least she owed that much to Matthew Blaine.

Larry had planned to take her to a hotel for Sunday dinner, but they couldn't bring themselves to leave the beautiful setting. They found a vendor and purchased small meat pies and lemonade, sitting beneath a tree to eat their repast.

A single leaf drifted downward, settling in Missie's hair. Larry captured it and put it carefully in his pocket. A keepsake, he said, of one of the happiest days of his life.

That afternoon they listened to music from the bandstand. Missie sat on the grass, Larry lying with his head in her lap.

"Look," he said, pointing skyward. "There are the notes—"

Above them, a flock of birds punctuated the sky, dipping and swirling in time to the soaring melody that emanated from the stand. It was poignantly lovely.

Missie was sorry to see the day end. Larry was imaginative, intelligent, and entertaining. He was kind, gentle, and a wonderful man.

But he was not Matthew Blaine!

Missie's thought made her feel guilty. And perhaps because of that guilt, she was friendlier than she might have been; a friendliness that could have been mistaken for something warmer. When Larry Hiller left her at her door, he kissed her cheek tenderly. It was not unpleasant, but it left her unmoved.

She would have to be careful with Larry, she thought, hurrying to her room. She must avoid getting too involved. His attentions toward her were clear, and she didn't want to hurt him. If she could only feel toward him as she did toward Matthew—

But then, perhaps life with Larry would be pleasant. They enjoyed the same things, he respected her as a woman doing a man's job. He would never attempt to hold her back, or expect her to compromise her principles.

She took off her bonnet and flung it on her bed, scowling at it as if it were a small, intruding animal.

Damn Matthew Blaine! Damn him! If she could only get him off her mind!

Matthew Blaine was both surprised and relieved when she appeared at work on Monday morning. He'd missed the small blond head bent over her desk; the way Missie's pretty face grimaced, childlike, over a knotty phrase. But she'd been so torn over Petra's disappearance, that he'd been concerned.

She'd needed to rest, and he came up with the idea that she keep watch at the rooms on Polk Street. It would give her a chance to relax in familiar surroundings, and at the same time, give her hope.

Now Matthew Blaine was about ready to admit hope was futile. It was likely the girl had been abducted by some madman, her body thrown into the sea, carried by the current to the drifts of kelp that lay offshore.

It was better that Missie begin to face up to her loss, to get back into her normal routine.

Besides that, he had missed her.

Hiding his delight at her return, he gave her a few assignments, noting that Larry Hiller frequently approached her desk.

He frowned. The man had a proprietary air about him that he didn't like. And when Missie brought a charming little article about Golden Gate Park to his desk, describing the vendors in the park, the bandstand, birds circling in the sky above it like grace notes, he knew where she had been yesterday afternoon—and with whom.

Well, she was free to choose her own companions—and he was not. Finding her out on Thursday, he'd played the fool, making arrangements for a few free Sunday hours, rushing like a lovesick kid to call on a girl he couldn't have. And Missie had been gone—

More angry at himself than anyone, he grimly plowed through the pile of copy on his desk, only to come to a sudden halt at an item that caught his eye.

What the hell!

He read the offending article again and leaped to his feet, striding to Missie's desk.

"You will remain a few minutes after work," he scowled down at her. "I have something to discuss with you!"

Turning on his heel, he stamped away. Larry Hiller looked after him.

"What do you suppose is eating him?" he asked. "You want me to stick around?"

Missie shook her head. Whatever it was, she'd handle it, herself.

She was trembling with nerves and excitement when Blaine

approached her desk after the office cleared. It was evident he did not expect their conference to take long. He'd already straightened his tie and donned his jacket for the street. In one hand, he carried a folder with work to go over at home, in the other, a piece of paper. He slapped it down on the desk in front of Missie.

It carried Brown, Halpert and Brown's letterhead. Missie's mind went blank as she tried to focus on its content, reading it twice before she lifted stricken eyes.

Melissa McLeod, reporter on the staff of the *San Francisco Examiner,* was to be congratulated on her upcoming book. *The Survivors,* a daring novel based on fact, was the story of three passionate ladies and their sometimes naughty escapades. Waiting lists were already established at booksellers in New York, and *The Survivors* was already being mentioned as the book of the year.

The publisher was certain the *Examiner* would like to profit from its publicity and aid in assisting their young reporter on the path to fame.

It was signed, Stuyvesant Brown.

Oh, dear God!

"Matthew—"

"We will arrange for photographs," he said, his face implacable, "and an interview. It's the least we can do for an—ambitious woman. And, by the way—I believe this is yours, also."

He put his folder down and reached into an inside pocket, pulling out another crumpled sheet. This, too, bore her publisher's letterhead.

It began with, *My Darling Melissa*—, and ended, *—my love and my life, and a home for your four fatherless children.*

The proposal she'd received from Stuyvesant Brown.

"Matthew, let me explain—"

"No explanations are necessary. Evidently you are most accomplished—at fiction. By the way, you don't need to come in tomorrow. I'm sure you'll want to devote your time to writing. I'll take care of your termination for you."

He turned, leaving Melissa half standing, hand stretched toward him in a silent plea, and strode out of the office.

Melissa sank back into her chair, hands over her eyes. It was beginning. The book that was to be her triumph was already ruining her life. She tried to make herself angry at Matthew Blaine and couldn't. She didn't blame him for feeling as he did. If he had only listened to her—

But he hadn't. And now it was over. She would miss this place with its laughter, confusion and constant hurry. She would miss the sound of it, the smell of it. She would miss Matthew Blaine.

Her eyes fell on his folder. He'd left it, in his anger. In it would be work he should go over for tomorrow. Surely he would come back for it! She waited, fifteen minutes, thirty, her heart beating too fast as she tried to think what she should say to him.

Finally, she went to the file and looked up his address, her chin set in determination. She would take it to him. Meet him on his own ground!

She hailed a horse-drawn cab.

She would have expected Matthew Blaine to live in an urban setting; perhaps an apartment in one of the better hotels. When the cabbie turned into a narrow lane with almond and citrus trees to either side, she looked at the address she'd written down, afraid that she'd made an error.

At the end of the lane was a low, comfortable, rambling house, unlike many of the structures in town with their narrow height topped with cupolas and gingerbread. Missie told the driver to wait and went up the walk to the veranda, suddenly shaken at her temerity. She knocked and waited. Matthew would appear at the door in his shirt sleeves, his hair rumpled and tie awry. He would be caught offguard, and she would say—

Missie stared numbly into the face of the woman who

answered the door: a plain, kind-looking woman, some years older than she, wearing an apron. From somewhere in the house emanated a scent of cooking—

And Missie could see past the woman. On the floor were building blocks—and a little stuffed rabbit with a missing ear, bedraggled from a child's handling.

"Yes?" the woman said, patiently. From her tone it was clear she'd said it before. Missie pulled herself together.

"M—Mr. Blaine will be needing this. He left it at the office."

The woman's smile was sweet, making her almost pretty. "I'll see that he gets it. He's late, tonight, and I've been a little worried—"

"I'm sure he'll be here soon." Missie fled, praying her cab would negotiate that narrow lane without coming face to face with Matthew.

She needn't have worried. Matthew Blaine had done an uncharacteristic thing. He'd left the office and gone directly to a bar. He stared into his glass, moodily, seeing a small pixie face; big blue eyes, shining hair; the face of a girl who was ambitious, conniving, and didn't care who she hurt on the way to the top.

He ordered another drink, another. They didn't help. Finally, he left the place and headed home—to his responsibilities. After supper, he saw the folder on his desk and realized the effect of the drinks he'd had earlier. For the life of him, he could not recall putting it there.

Chapter 25

Missie managed to hold her emotions together until she reached her own address. She paid the driver, tipped him exorbitantly, smiled and said good evening to Frau Schmitt, unlocked the door to her apartment—and burst into tears.

She cried for a long time. Surely no one else had ever made as many mistakes as she, or paid for them as bitterly. The upcoming book hung over her head like an ax about to fall. She had lost the job that had become so important to her. And she'd, once more, fallen in love with the wrong man.

Now, she was acting like a silly female, crying for something that could never be! Dear God, why had she been born a woman!

Swallowing her tears, she bathed and put on an old flannel robe. She was brushing her hair, trying to avoid the sight of her tear-swollen face in the mirror, when a knock sounded at the door.

It would be Frau Schmitt. This was sweet-roll day. She had smelled them baking.

For a minute she thought of being very quiet. Maybe the woman would think she was sleeping and go away. But the thought of being alone was suddenly frightening. Tonight, Missie needed someone—anyone. Frau Schmitt would think she'd been crying over Petra—and hadn't she? Petra was listed among Missie's mistakes.

She went to the door and opened it, shrinking back, her hands to her face at the sight of Larry Hiller standing there. "I can't ask you in—Frau Schmitt would not allow—oh, Larry! I look so awful!"

Then he was inside, closing the door behind him. "I've spoken with Frau Schmitt," he said soberly. "I told her I was concerned about you, that I thought you'd had bad news today."

"Oh, Larry!" His name was a moan as she began to weep again. He gathered her in his arm, holding her blond head against his chest. Then he led her to the divan and sat cradling her like a child.

"Tell me about it," he said gently. "You'll feel better."

Missie drew away and wiped her eyes. "You'd better forget about me, Larry. Stay away from me. I—I'm bad news."

He smiled down at her. Missie was anything but beautiful now, with her pink nose and swollen eyes, her hair disheveled, her flannel robe frayed and faded with many washings. But there was something endearing about her. She seemed more—approachable.

"You could never be bad news, Missie!"

"But I am," she insisted. "I hurt everybody I touch! I—I think you'd better go. Please—"

"Be damned if I do," he said cheerfully. "Not until you tell me what's wrong."

"I was fired."

Her voice was so small that he wasn't certain what she'd said for a moment. Then he began to swear under his breath.

"Blaine! The sonofabitch! Who the hell does he think he is! I'm going to see him in the morning, and—"

"No, Larry," she said wearily. "He was within his rights. He received a letter—"

She told him about the book, her trip to New York to sign the contract; her advance. He whistled under his breath. "You mean I'm courting a rich writer?"

"A fired reporter," she amended. "And Matt—Mr. Blaine was within his rights. He probably figured I wasn't giving my full attention to my job. And—since Petra disappeared, he's probably correct."

"Damn woman-hater!"

Missie thought of Blaine's homelife, so carefully hidden from his co-workers. Larry was one hundred percent wrong, but she didn't intend to tell him what she'd discovered earlier in the evening. Sensing that she was shutting him out, Hiller said, "Tell me about your book—"

She told him about its content, about her intentions in writing it, and how she was afraid now, too late, that it would destroy her family.

She talked of Tamsen, of Em, of Arab; of her own ill-fated marriage, how Arthur Melvin had gone away, leaving her without food or heat. She had borne her dead child alone.

"Missie! Oh, sweetheart!" She was shivering and he held her close as she described Arthur Melvin's death. She had fired at him from far down in the valley, and he fell. The ancient pistol fell far short of its target. He'd died of snake-bite, but she didn't know it then. She had to watch the body there on the cliff, blond hair fluttering in the wind, thinking she had killed him—

Her eyes were blank, unseeing, and he knew she was back in the shack she described, reliving that awful time. He shook her until her eyes focused.

"It's over, Missie! It's all over. I'm going to take care of you now."

Once again, she was crying. Larry Hiller didn't know it

was because she didn't love him, but wanted to. Oh, how she wanted to.

After a pause, she went on, telling him about Dusty's death, how she believed herself to be responsible for his dying. Everyone she loved she'd brought trouble to.

"I can't believe that! Dammit, Missie, you're too hard on yourself!"

"Tell that to my cousin Petra—wherever she is!"

"Missie, you've been a reporter long enough to get a slant on human nature! It's possible the girl took off with some bum! Some girls just naturally fall for bad apples. You can understand that!"

Yes, Missie thought, I can! "Not Petra," she told him. She went on to describe Petra's shy, withdrawn nature. She had no friends, and wasn't the type to take action without consulting Missie.

"But you said she ran away from her grandmother, came here—"

"Larry, Petra had a—a secret. Something that made her what she was."

Missie told him the story of the girl's background. She might as well, she thought ruefully. She'd already spilled almost everything she knew! She was not really betraying the girl's confidence, since it wasn't likely she still lived.

She told of Em's prejudices, her reluctance to invite the Wangs as dinner guests; what Petra overheard the night she ran away.

"I know the Wangs," Larry said quietly. "They're fine people. The boy, Lee, is as American as I am."

"Don't blame Aunt Em," Missie said. "She's a sweet, loving woman. Her past bothers her as much as Petra's does—"

"And it's all in the book?"

Missie nodded, then gripped his arms, fiercely, burying her face against him. "Oh, Larry, what have I done! What have I done!"

He held her close, rocking her, whispering soothing words. "Missie, you say you only wrote the truth. If these people are as nice as you think, they won't fault you for it. And if they do—let me take care of you, let me love you! We'll go away from here if you want, anywhere—just the two of us. Oh, Missie—"

The knocker sounded and they leaped apart. Missie composed herself and Hiller opened the door.

Frau Schmitt stood there with a plate of sweet rolls. She'd decided the gentleman caller had stayed longer than necessary, and had come to the rescue of her young roomer. Her pale blue eyes went to Missie, huddled in her tattered robe, then to Larry Hiller.

"The little one is all right?"

"She got fired today," Hiller said flatly. He made no move to step out of her way, so she leaned around him.

"I have brought *Kuchen*. I vill make coffee." She bustled to the stove, put the pot on, and sat down. It was clear she had no intention of leaving.

Larry Hiller finally went home. There would be other nights, many of them. With that damn Blaine out of the way, he had a chance. He could still feel the sweetness of the small body he'd held in his arms. He wanted to keep her there, always. My God, what a terrible life the girl had endured!

It would be better from now on. He'd see to that!

Frau Schmitt stayed on for a time. "I did not wish to drive your young man avay," she said serenely. "You vill forgive me?"

Forgive her? Missie was grateful. She'd needed comforting, but somehow the situation had slipped beyond that. She knew, instinctively, that Larry Hiller was going to press his suit. But not now! Not when she needed time to think. Her mind was crowded to the bursting point; Matthew, worry over Petra, the book—

She must take care. It would be so easy to use Larry as a leaning post! And it was not fair to him.

Frau Schmitt stirred an alarming amount of sugar into her cup. "So you have lost your chob?" she asked, conversationally.

"Yes, but I have another income. There will be no problem with the rent." Looking at the honest face of the old woman, Missie drew a deep breath.

"That is, if I can stay here. I—I lied to you, Frau Schmitt. I'm a widow, but I'm not a teacher. I'm a reporter for the *Examiner*."

"I know, the little Petra told me. But I pride myself on being a chudge of character."

Missie's eyes filled. Poor Frau Schmitt! What would she think if she really knew her? And what would she have to say when the book came out; a story of the seamy side of life. Would she be fond of her then?

After Frau Schmitt had gone, Missie went to bed. Her unsolved problems buzzed in her mind like a hive of angry bees. She finally rose and stood looking out over the night-dark gardens. In the midst of her confused thoughts, something niggled at her. There was something she needed to remember.

She went back over the afternoon, Matthew's harsh words, her visit to his home; the woman who answered his door, the familiar stuffed rabbit on the floor behind her.

Then there had been Larry Hiller's appearance, the things they'd discussed; her marriage, the book—Petra! It was something about Petra!

"I know the Wangs," Larry had said. "They are fine people. The boy, Lee, is as American as I am—"

Lee Wang! And he was Chinese! Missie felt a sudden wild surge of hope. She and her uncle, Duke, had gone over and over the names of any people Petra might have met, but the Wangs had not been mentioned or considered.

She had a hunch they'd been on the wrong track all this time. And in the morning, she would check out this one new clue to her cousin's disappearance.

Chapter 26

Missie arrived at the House of Wang, Importers, at an early hour. It was not yet open for business, but a pretty young Chinese girl escorted her to the office of Wang's son, making her comfortable as she waited.

Lee Wang had been working since dawn, unloading a new shipment from the Orient. He came in from the rear of the shop, his sleeves rolled up, shirt opened to show a trace of smooth golden flesh. Taking a jacket from a hook, he slipped it on, apologizing for his informal appearance.

Missie couldn't believe her eyes. This boy was Chinese in every respect, even to the odd eye-folds so alien to the Western eye. But he was one of the handsomest men she had ever seen; clean-cut and mannerly. Missie was suddenly uncomfortable, thinking of Em and her prejudices.

"I am Lee, son of Wang," he introduced himself with a small bow. "If I can be of assistance—"

"I am Missie Narvaéz." She watched his eyes as he waited

politely to hear her out. The name evidently meant nothing to him.

"Petra Channing is my cousin."

That brought a reaction. His face tensed, his eyes suddenly intent. "I have been reading about her disappearance. Have they found her?"

Missie shook her head, sick with disappointment. "I came here because I hoped you might know something that would help."

He toyed with a small jade elephant on his desk, seemingly lost in thought as he considered her statement. Then, his face tightening in decision, he looked at Missie again.

"I know only that she was quite happy on the day she disappeared. Then something happened to change her. She seemed in shock, perhaps frightened."

"How do you know this?"

"I was with her," he said simply.

"And you did not come forward? Dear God! We've been looking for any clue! Why didn't you—"

"I discussed this with my father. He said that it did not concern us, and could only bring harm to our people. Our section of the city has been burned for less. Since I could add nothing of importance to the investigation, my information would be of little help. It would only arouse suspicion and cause problems."

"I think this is important," Missie said. "When I left for work, Petra was still sleeping. From that moment on, nobody knows—"

"She went to Chinatown."

Lee's words stopped Missie short. "To Chinatown? Alone?"

"I saw her there. We had met once before at dinner in the Courtney home. I offered my services as escort—guide—what you will. We toured the area until—"

Missie was on her feet. "Mr. Wang—"

"Please, call me Lee."

"Lee, can you get away? I want to retrace every step you took that day! If you can remember—"

"I can never forget," the boy said in a low voice. "If you will excuse me a moment, I will make arrangements with my father."

Missie had visited the area several times in the course of her work for the *Examiner*, but she felt a dim sense of foreboding as they entered the narrow, teeming streets. A few Chinese, like Lee, were clad in Western clothing. The majority wore the baggy trousers and quilted jackets of their homeland. Missie felt she was suddenly in a foreign land.

"Take me exactly where you took Petra," she said grimly. "Try to remember every word you said. Let's duplicate that day as closely as possible."

He led her along the Street of the Men of China. Here, Petra had exclaimed over the colorful display of wares. They had purchased lichee nuts from a vendor. Lee had translated the Chinese symbols that identified the owners of shops and their trade.

Lee described the living conditions of many of the area's inhabitants. Since Missie was frank and open, filled with questions Petra would never dream of asking, he found himself telling her about the wretched women in the cribs, young girls, most of them, sold into slavery. Most of them were pitiful creatures, rarely living to reach the age of twenty.

"Where do they come from?"

They were sometimes smuggled in on ships. Some were daughters of the very poor. A girl fetched a good price, especially if she were attractive, though few of them were.

Missie paled. She clutched at Lee's arm. "Petra did leave this area, Lee?"

His pallor matched hers as he guessed at her thoughts. Then he drew a sigh of relief. "Of course she did. I saw to it myself. And she certainly wouldn't have returned in the dark! Besides, no Chinese would dare to touch a white girl."

Petra, thought Missie, was half-Chinese. But the idea that

she might have been kidnapped within the area could be dismissed. The thought of the poor captive girls, however, appealed to her reporter's instinct. It would be interesting to do an article on their plight. Then she remembered she no longer had a job, and forced her mind back to Petra.

Today she was not Missie Narváez, with Missie's problems. Today, she had to be Petra Channing, see through her eyes, hear through her ears, think with her mind.

Lee took Missie through the Street of Gamblers, then down narrow, twisting alleys. Laundry flew like flags in the brisk autumn breeze. Missie had to laugh as she ducked a pair of swinging longjohns. She sniffed the smells of spices, smoke, soap—and something else; a sweetish scent that hung heavily in the air. Unlike Petra, she inquired about it.

"Opium," was Lee's terse answer.

Somehow, the alleys seemed more sinister than before.

Petra was apparently most interested in the apothecary shops. Missie entered as she had entered, trying to become Petra as she surveyed the tunnellike rooms scented with dried leaves, barks, and roots. She left, feeling their exotic odors would cling to her forever, to her clothing, her flesh, her hair.

They returned to the wider streets. Here, in a small eating place where a dragon swung from a pole, Lee and Petra had entered, partaking of tea and *dim sum*.

"Then we will eat here, now," Missie decided.

As they ate, Missie questioned him. What had they discussed over their meal? Was Petra still enjoying the day? Did any kind of problem arise? Had she seemed to be worried at this point?

She had not. It was later that the change had come. As they walked homeward—

Missie was almost reluctant to leave the little dining room. Only when she relaxed for a moment did she realize how tired she was. The strain of trying to think and feel as Petra would was beginning to tell. She must not miss a single clue to the girl's mood at the time she disappeared.

"She may have had an appointment," Lee said quietly. "I recall she said something about being late—"

"Probably she wanted to get home. She'd left a casserole ready for the oven. Petra—Petra had no place else to go."

Her remark conjured up a picture of a small and lonely girl. The last sip of tea was bitter, the last bite of food tasteless.

The late afternoon sun was slanting downward through murky windows. It was time to go.

"We were talking and laughing," Lee said. "I remember stopping before that shop, watching the owner take his produce in for the night. I translated that character for her." He pointed to a garish symbol splashed in gold on a housefront. "And then, here—"

He paused, looking into a narrow twisting alleyway where shadows had already settled.

"She wanted to go in there. I remember she laughed and said she didn't want to miss anything; that we could hurry; there was just time. She ran ahead of me.

"Not much down here," he continued, as they entered the alley. "Living quarters, small markets, an herbalist. She exclaimed over that," he pointed to a garish decoration, "and then went on. Just about here, she stopped so suddenly I almost ran over her.

"And that was when she seemed to change—"

Missie stood still, trying to think with Petra's mind. The place was dismal, squalid, the air choking with smoke and the sickly opium scent. Maybe, knowing she was descended from this race, it had depressed her. But from the way Lee spoke, it was more than depression.

She ran her eyes along the length of the alleyway, straining to see in the fading light. Whatever caused Petra's disappearance, it sprang from here! She felt it in her bones—

A shabby house, smoke pouring from a small grill that was a basement window; a market, a laundry, another house. An herbalist's shop, a market—her gaze was pulled back to the small Chinese apothecary as something caught her attention.

It had the usual characters splashed above it, with an English translation beneath, lettered in gold.

Herbs and teas.

And there was the name of its owner.

Feng Wu.

Oh, dear God!

Missie whirled to her companion, her expression as stunned as Petra's had been.

"Lee, I'm going in there!"

"This is not a savory part of town. It would not be advisable. If you wish to make a purchase, I will be happy to find—"

"Petra's there, I know it!"

Lee caught at her arm. The young Oriental was frankly alarmed. There seemed to be something in this place that made young ladies lose their senses. "Do not be foolish," he said quietly. "I saw Petra to her own part of the city. Why would she return to this poor place? And I repeat, here she would come to no harm. A white girl—"

"Petra is half-Chinese. Her father was a warlord, a bandit. His name was Feng Wu."

In his shock, he released her arm. Then he gripped it again. "It is possible she is there of her own will. If she is not, we will need help. The police—"

"Forget the police," she said savagely. "I'm going in there, and you're not coming with me! You're to go straight to Duke Courtney! Tell him to come here immediately, and to bring a dozen of the meanest, toughest sonsofbitches he can find!"

"Missie!" Lee was shocked at her language, bewildered at the situation in which he found himself. The charming girl he'd escorted through the day had turned into a white-faced virago. "I think—!"

"It's not your place to think! Just do as I say! Go on, damn you!"

She pulled away and was running through the shadows. He heard a small bell tinkle as she opened the door of the herbalist's shop and disappeared inside.

He could follow her, he thought miserably, and they could both disappear—just as Petra did. If Missie had only allowed him to think! They should have gone for help, together—

It was too late now for alternative plans. An inner sense told him Missie Narvaéz had walked into danger. He began to run.

Reaching Sacramento Street, he caught a horse-drawn cab and leaped inside, giving Duke Courtney's address. Gone was his Chinese blandness and mannerly bearing. He leaned forward and shouted at the driver.

"Hurry, man! This is a matter of life or death! Drive like hell!"

The driver, seeing his expression and certain that every heathen Chinese had a blade up his sleeve, complied.

Chapter 27

Several weeks earlier, the bell on the door of the herbalist's shop had jingled at Petra's entrance. It had admitted a small terrified girl, gown soaked through with San Francisco fog. Her eyes were blank with shock.

Petra was to remember little of that night. She would recall the face of Feng Wu, round, spectacled; the face of a man in his early thirties. He smiled in a welcoming fashion as, discovering her identity, he came around the counter to meet her.

"I greet you, cousin," he said. "I beg that you partake of my poor hospitality."

Her body went limp with relief at his gracious welcome. The flight through the dark streets of "Little China" had been a frightening experience. She'd had no idea what awaited her in the house of Feng Wu.

Petra's lips trembled, tears welling at his acceptance of their relationship. The man led her through a door at the rear of his shop. She found herself in a small room where a brazier burned.

He summoned his wife. The woman brewed a tea, which her cousin himself prepared. Petra drank the warm brew gratefully, and found herself warm and drifting.

Her last memory was of Feng Wu's face. It floated above her like a giant spectacled balloon. She saw her reflection in the glasses that covered his swimming eyes.

Then there was nothing else.

Petra woke to a sumptuous room papered in China silk and filled with what looked like valuable objects of Oriental art. Her head throbbed, and for a time she thought she was dreaming.

"Missie?" she whispered. Then she remembered. She was not in the small apartment above the bakery, but in the house of Feng Wu, her cousin.

She struggled to a sitting position, looking down at dismay at her unfamiliar clothing. Her own wet gown and undergarments had been removed. She wore, instead, a red robe embroidered with golden dragons. A pair of matching slippers had been placed beside the bed on which she lay.

Where was she?

This was not the herbalist's shop! She remembered the poverty of the small room where she'd gone to sleep. Here there was a faint smell of spice and herbs but it was overlaid with incense—and the sick sweet smell of Chinatown's alley-ways was strongest of all. She was still dreaming—

Or she had completely lost her mind!

The room was windowless, with only small barred inserts for ventilation near the ceiling. But there was a door—

Petra rose, feeling the softness of an Oriental carpet beneath her feet and approached the door. There was no knob on the inside, only a monstrous, evil-looking face of gold set into wood.

She was a prisoner!

There was some explanation. There must be! Her father

had been a warlord, wealthy among his people. Perhaps his nephew was also; the shop merely a front for a luxurious way of living. But how did she get here? And why the locked door?

Settling on the piled cushions that had been her bed, she folded her hands in her lap. There was nothing to do but wait —wait until someone, probably Feng Wu, himself, came to fetch her and explain her circumstances.

Perhaps this was the way Chinese ladies of the upper class lived, secluded from the household, in pampered luxury. She would tell Feng Wu she wanted none of this. That she intended to work for her keep. Perhaps she could work in the shop. She knew nothing of herbs, but she learned quickly.

She would also ask for a less elegant room, perhaps with windows. This place, with its silk paper and objects of ivory and jade was beautiful. But she would be more comfortable if it were less—Chinese.

But wasn't that why she'd come here? To deny the part of her that was white? To be with people who would accept her as one of them?

Her own mother had sent her away. She couldn't remain with her grandmother under false pretenses, knowing how Em Courtney felt about the Chinese. She'd practically forced Missie to take her in.

Missie had been kind to her, she thought dully. Then she'd made a fool of herself! She should have guessed it was Missie Matthew Blaine cared for, that she had acted like a child, pushing herself into their lives.

She would never forget his words, etched into her mind as if with acid, knotting her stomach with humiliation even now. "You keep trying to foist your—cousin, or whatever the hell she is—off on me! She ought to be going out with somebody of her own kind!"

She was with her own kind, now.

Missie would be worrying, and she was sorry. She should have gone back to the apartment, left a note, but she'd been so hurt and lost. Maybe she could write her, tell her it was better this way—

No, it was best to just disappear; best for everybody. Petra had begun a new life; a life of her own choosing.

She looked about the room uncomfortably, trying to fit herself into its setting. It was exquisite—if she could become accustomed to its alien smell. She thought of the scent of baking bread rising from the bakery below Missie's apartment. It had reminded her of Mama's kitchen at home.

Tears came, and she wiped them away.

She waited.

When the door finally opened, it was to admit two tiny old ladies in rusty black pajamalike garments. Petra was instantly on her feet.

"Do either of you speak English?" she asked. "I must see Feng Wu!"

The women looked at each other, chattering in birdlike voices. Petra sank back again. There was no help here. But surely someone else would come!

The women had brought pails of steaming water. They moved an ornate screen that concealed a hip-bath of porcelain supported by coiled golden dragons. Petra watched, wondering, as they sprinkled the water with herbs. Then, bowing and nodding, they motioned that Petra should stand. One reached for her sash, attempting to move the dragon-embroidered robe.

Startled, she pulled back. Then she remembered she was in a strange house with strange customs. She was evidently being treated as an honored guest and must respond with good manners. Still, her face was flushed as she felt strange eyes on her body, a body that had been properly concealed since she was an infant. As she stepped, nude, into the scented water, the women twittered, their voices sounding like little bells.

They were obviously discussing her.

Alien hands, like wrinkled yellow claws, washed her with

208

perfumed soap as she tried to disassociate her mind from what they were doing.

Petra's face was hot. She didn't feel like a person—but like a thing! An object to be washed or dusted as the need arose. Dear God, how could she ever live in this fashion? She must learn the language, so that she wouldn't feel she was being talked about behind her back. She must learn to think like her father's people. In the meantime, she would ask Feng Wu to dispense with such services as this!

More birdlike noises and gestures. Now she must step from the tub, be dried with soft towels—rubbed with a perfumed oil. When she was finally dressed in a delicate silk robe, she was sick with embarrassment. Then one of the old women brushed her hair until it was like silk, the other kneeling to lacquer her small toenails. The kneeling woman seemed disgruntled, pointing to Petra's feet in dismay.

Petra, gentle and shy, obedient and subservient, knew a surge of anger. She felt like kicking her!

Then they were through. She watched them gathering up the towels and toilet articles, feeling a twinge of guilt. This was evidently the Chinese way. They had only done what was expected of them. It was she, brought up in the Western way, who must learn.

They approached the door and she observed them closely. Surely there was a way to open it. If she could only find Feng Wu—or anyone who spoke English—to explain her situation—

One of the women tapped in a rhythmic tattoo and the door opened. She could see someone—a man?—outside. Then they were across the threshold. The door shut behind them. A short time later, one of them returned. She carried a tray of beaten copper. It held a teapot and cup of delicate porcelain, a bowl of flavored rice and some tiny cakes.

She wasn't hungry. The sick-sweet smell that permeated the room made her vaguely ill. But, again, she must behave in the manner expected of a guest. She ate what she could, and crumbled some of the sweets to make it appear that she had eaten more.

Hours passed, hours in which no one came, hours in which she tried to blank out her growing fear. Nothing would harm her in her cousin's house. Perhaps he'd thought her ill last night. And she had been! She'd felt sick at heart, betrayed, rejected. He'd known it, and was politely giving her a chance to rest until her nerves were sufficiently recovered—

Still, her eyes kept moving to the door, a door that opened only from the outside. And finally, manners or no, she could stand it no longer. She moved toward it.

"Is anyone out there?" she called in a trembling voice. "Would you tell my cousin I'd like to see him?"

There was no answer.

She lifted her small fist and tried to follow the pattern of the rhythmic tattoo she'd heard earlier. It had sounded like some sort of signal—

Nothing!

She put an ear to the door and listened. There was a whisper of slippered feet, a sound of breathing. Someone was there, standing guard, someone who had no intention of releasing her from this room!

Her heart was hammering in panic, now, her throat contracting with fear until she couldn't swallow. At last, she moved back to her bed of cushions, her knees almost too weak to support her. Sinking into the soft depths, she felt that the cushions were swallowing her up, that soon they would smother her.

An hour passed, another, and the door opened. This time, it revealed a man; a humped dwarfish little creature with a round face and a toothy smile. He surveyed her for a moment, then beckoned.

"You warm-bed-lady," he announced. "Old man wait. You come."

Chapter 28

Warm-bed-lady?

Petra was to learn the grinning little man had meant exactly what he said. He took her wrist and led her to a small room where a trio of men waited. They were all Chinese, all lean and hard-featured, all clad in black Western suits. They did not introduce themselves but looked at her assessingly. Petra shrank before them, conscious that there was nothing but a clinging robe between her body and their eyes.

"She will do," one said crisply. He passed a small pouch to another, who smiled. The smile did not reach his eyes.

"If your honorable father prefers another, I will be glad to make an exchange—"

The first one smiled. The smile did not reach his eyes. "Should that be the case, I shall take this one for myself, and purchase another."

Petra, frightened out of her wits, finally found her tongue. "I don't know what you're talking about," she said. "I don't know who you are, or where I am! I want to see my cousin, Feng Wu. I—I demand to see him!''

"This small one does not know a woman's place, Mr. Chen. I have others more tractable."

The man addressed shook his head. "She will learn. There are methods of persuasion."

"Feng Wu! I want to see him! Now!"

Petra paused. They were paying no attention to her, and the grinning little man who brought her here was plucking at her sleeve, shaking his head in warning.

Dear God, where was she! What was going on?

Two of the gentlemen took their leave. Petra was left with her grotesque little attendant and the frightening man who'd been addressed as Mr. Chen. He looked at her for a moment, then jerked his head in a gesture toward the door. She and the small Chinese servant followed him down a long corridor. Flames flickered from candles set in exquisitely wrought holders. Impassive golden idols watched their passing with jeweled eyes.

They entered a dim room strong with the scent she'd come to associate with this house. Against one wall stood a low bed, piled with cushions. And on that bed lay the emaciated body of an old man, white beard and long, drooping mustaches pointing up his skeletal, yellow features. He looked as though he might be—dead.

The tiny black-clad old women who had served Petra earlier were flitting about the room, obviously preparing it for the night. For a moment Petra had a vision of carrion birds, and the way they'd hovered over dying animals at home in Australia—

She was bewildered, dazed, unable to comprehend her situation, shaking so that she could hardly stand.

"I shall inform you of your duties," her escort said in an impersonal tone. "I am the younger Chen. This, the older Chen, is my father. In his youth, he was a strong and lusty man with many wives and concubines. Now he is as you see him. It is hoped that a young companion to warm his blood at night will restore his strength. Now I shall leave you. Come, Ling.''

He was gone, taking the dwarfish attendant with him. The two black-clad ladies came toward Petra. She cowered against the wall. They took hold of her with small, strong, insistent hands, leading her toward the place where the old man lay, untying the sash that held her robe together, pressing her down beside him.

Petra was too numb to fight back. She could feel the old man's flesh against her own, as cold and lifeless as tallow. A yellow arm twitched, a hand slid along her body. There was a small damp sound of pleasure from a drooling mouth.

Dear God, she was going to be sick!

Then a saucer of burning tarlike substance was placed near the bed. It gave off the sick-sweet smell that was becoming so familiar. She was dizzy with its fumes, so dizzy that she drifted from one nightmare scene to another. She was lying with a dead man, black carrion birds flapping overhead. And then death came, death with a lean ivory face and hard, searching eyes.

''I shall take this one for myself,'' he said. ''There are methods of persuasion.''

And then her mother was there. Martha Channing. Her eyes resigned and sad.

''I tried to keep you from repeating my mistakes. I told you—''

Petra tried to call out. Mama! Missie! Matthew! But there was no one who could help her. Why should they? She was the one who had run away. She'd brought this on herself.

With a small sigh, she ran again, this time from reality. Closing her eyes, she gave herself to the swirling fantasies of an opium dream.

In the morning she was returned to her room still sick and reeling from the night's excesses. At least she thought, through the confusion in her brain, her virtue was still intact.

Old Chen was almost completely paralyzed. Petra had been nothing but—a warm-bed-lady, as the grinning little attendant had said.

If she could only find someone to talk to! Someone who would explain all this; what had happened to Feng Wu, how she came to be in this predicament!

She could not ask the younger Chen. He frightened her with his reptilian eyes, and sinister presence. She shivered, remembering her dream.

But the dwarfish little man with a toothy smile—she was not afraid of him. How could she reach him? She thought back over the previous day.

As they'd left what was to be Petra's chamber of horrors, the younger Chen had spoken to the man. "Come, Ling," he had said.

When the two old crones came to bathe her, attiring her in a fresh robe, Petra tried to communicate with them. She pointed at the door and to herself.

"Ling," she said. "Ling. Ling—come—here."

It was impossible to know if she'd got her message across. When they had gone, she sat, her face in her hands, pondering her predicament. And to her surprise, the toothy little Chinese man arrived.

"Warm-bed-lady wantchee talk-talk?"

She'd never been so glad to see anyone in her life.

"My name is Petra Channing," she began.

Ling nodded, wisely. "Petal," he repeated. "Chang-ying. Petal Chan-ying."

"I want you for my friend."

He nodded again. "Flend."

Did he understand a word she was saying? She burst into tears. "Please help me! Where is Feng Wu? How did I get here? What's going to happen? I'm so afraid!"

The little man answered her, still smiling his toothy grin. Several times he had to reword his comments before she understood them, but she finally had her answers.

Feng Wu had sold her through the *Kwong Dak Tong*, an organization supplying young girls for the pleasure of men.

"He couldn't!" Petra whispered. "He just couldn't! We—he is my cousin! A blood relative!"

"Gleat honor," Ling insisted. "Chen man much wealth! No harm! You still virgin lady! Young Chen likee. When old Chen join honorable ancestors, you go young Chen. Vellee good!"

Her dream returned in force; a dream in which young Chen stood over her. "I shall take this one for myself. There are methods of persuasion."

"If I refuse to go along with this," she said dully, "what will they do to me?"

"Send clibs," the little Chinese said cheerfully. "In clibs, many men—" he made an obscene gesture that completed his statement.

"Ling, would you do something for me?"

He grinned and bobbed. "Yes, Missee Petal."

"If I write a note, would you see that it is delivered?"

"Yes, Missee."

He brought rice paper, ink, and a brush. Awkwardly, she managed to print a few words. *Help me. I am a prisoner at—*, she paused, having no idea where she was. Ling was no help. She inquired about the address, and he looked blank. *—the house of Chen*, she finally wrote.

To whom should she send it. It must be someone who knew Chinatown—and someone her messenger could locate. She addressed it to Lee, son of Wang.

Ling grinned and bowed his way out. Her instinct told her she couldn't trust him. He was probably on his way to the younger Chen at this moment. But he was her only hope.

In her opinion, old Chen wouldn't last the month. If help failed to come before he died, there was only one way out.

She removed the sash from her robe, measuring ∴ A small cabinet holding ivory carvings could be moved. Standing on

215

it, she would be able to reach the grill that served as ventilator near the ceiling.

Petra fashioned the end of her sash into a noose. Yes, it was long enough.

When the spirit of old Chen went to join his ancestors, hers would go with him. But, dear God, she was only nineteen!

She replaced the sash and sat staring dully at her hands until Ling arrived once more with the news that the old man waited.

Had he delivered her message? He didn't volunteer any information, and she was afraid to ask. Mechanically, she allowed the old crones to go through the motions of the previous night, revolted by the old man's touch, the sickening smell of age and opium.

In spite of her revulsion, she prayed. She prayed that the master of the house of Chen would live forever.

Chapter 29

Petra's prayers were not to be answered. As the days passed, the old man appeared to grow weaker. At night she could hear him gasping for breath. The searching hand no longer reached for her in the darkness. She had become accustomed to the small amount of opium burned to ease his passage. Its effects began to fade, and she wondered which was worse, the hallucinations it induced or the reality of her own condition.

Often, now, as she was taken from her room to that of the sick man, the younger Chen waited in the hallway. She knew, from talking to Ling, that respect for one's father was a strong force in the Chinese culture. But it was obvious that the hard-eyed man was only waiting for his father to die, gloating over whatever the man might leave behind.

And that included Petra, herself.

The seriousness of the old man's condition was apparent in the sickroom. The two ancient women busied themselves with spells and charms. Papers were folded in strange shapes, placed beneath his cushions and suspended from the ceiling to swirl in the opium smoke. Petra was never able to ascertain their identity; former wives, concubines, sisters, aunts—or merely servants in this house.

It was clear that they regarded Chen as their master, and were determined to keep him alive. Whoever they were, she was in sympathy with them!

Nights were a time of horror. Days were almost as bad. Petra forced her mind back in time. She was a little girl, tagging along after Peter Channing as he made his rounds of the station.

He had loved her she knew now. Her adoptive father had loved her. And her mother, Martha? She remembered being held on her mother's lap, comforted over the death of a lamb. On a sheep station, there were always lambs, but this one was special. It had been a black lamb. Its mother abandoned it. Four-year-old Petra reared it on a bottle.

Petra had wept. Martha had tried to delineate a lamb Heaven, in vain. Heaven would have white lambs gamboling in verdant meadows, but a black one?

"God doesn't care what color anything is," Martha Channing explained. "He created everything—"

Still, Petra had remembered the black lamb on the day she learned she was not the child of Peter Channing, but of Feng Wu—

Now, she thought of her mother. She had gone through a similar experience: the attentions of a cruel, brutal man resulting in a child. Looking back, she realized there had been no difference in the attention Martha gave her children. Learning that Peter Channing wasn't her father, it was Petra, herself, who made the difference.

And her grandmother, Em Courtney! What would Em have done if she'd gone to her, told her straight from the shoulder that she was a—a bastard, and half-Chinese? Em, with her funny sense of propriety would have tried to convince herself that it was an appropriate thing to be!

In judging herself, she had misjudged them all. Matthew Blaine had regarded her as a sweet child—and a barrier to his courtship of Missie.

Petra had been a fool!

Ling came to fetch her, and she braced herself for what was to come.

At the end of two weeks, the thing she'd feared most came to pass. She woke with a start, feeling the quivering of the body pressed to her own; the body that could no longer move of its own volition. Petra held her breath, listening.

There was a tremor that ran, thrilling, from old Chen's head to his leaden feet. Then a long exhalation, a last sigh.

Petra was petrified. Beyond a candle, the two old women sat in attendance. Their heads were bowed as they slept, sitting upright against the walls.

They had not seen. They had not felt. They had not heard the breath of life leave the body of the Master of the House of Chen, a body that nothing would ever warm again.

Petra lay very still. Perhaps she would reach her own room before they made their discovery in the morning. The thought of the noose, fashioned from her sash, seemed almost welcome.

She lay the rest of the night, a corpse stiffening beside her. Death seemed welcome. Nothing could be worse than this—

Petra spent the dark hours trying to keep from screaming. There was no way of escaping the touch of dead flesh against her own. And her endurance went all for nothing. Old Chen's waxen features were spotted at first light. The women set up a keening that echoed through the house, eating away at the girl's already eroded nerves.

She was not returned to her room, but to a small space that was cell-like. Here, there were no grills, no glass-fronted shelves to shatter for an instrument to cut one's wrists. The younger Chen, now master of the house, had circumvented her most cleverly.

Again, there was nothing to do but wait; the horror of the night almost obliterated by her fear of what was to come.

The small room was all white, possibly a renovated closet. A shelflike bunk occupied one wall. Behind a screen was a pitcher, a washbasin, and the convenience. There was nothing to look at, nothing to do.

Only once did she leave the confines of her new prison. She was led to a small window, the black-clad old women at either side, to look down upon what appeared to be a parade. The street was jammed with Chinese in their native dress. There was a clanging of cymbals and gongs, a caterwauling of strange instruments that sounded like souls in torment. It wasn't until the exotically draped carriage appeared that Petra knew what she was seeing: the funeral procession of the former Master of the House of Chen.

Her one brief glimpse of street and sky, even under such morbid circumstances, only served to point up the freedom she had lost. And one day, the younger Chen would send for her.

She longed for the elegant quarters she'd occupied before Chen's death, thinking of the grillwork near the ceiling, the sash she could fashion into a noose. Only a few moments would put her far beyond the reach of any man.

In this room, there was nothing. The basin and pitcher were of heavy metal. Nowhere was there a sharp edge. Her toilet articles were removed from the room after each use. One of the old women remained with her while she ate, taking any tool she might have used away.

Petra stopped eating, much to the consternation of her ancient keepers. She closed her mouth tightly when they tried to force her, refusing to swallow a morsel.

With luck, she might starve herself to death.

When Ling came to take her to the new master, she was light-headed, weak from hunger, beyond fear. The room she entered was furnished Western-style, a bed, desk, chairs. Only its walls and draperies, of red burnished with gold, betrayed the nationality of its occupant

She saw the table before she saw the man; a small table in

the center of the room, set for two. Silver covers topped serving dishes, but did not keep a delicious aroma from permeating the atmosphere. Petra swallowed.

Then she saw the younger Chen. He was standing at the window, his back to her. Pulling the draperies to close the view, he turned to face Petra.

"You will eat." he said.

Petra clamped her mouth shut and shook her head. He took her arm roughly, and pressed her down into a chair.

"Eat!"

Again she refused, and he fixed her with his reptilian gaze. "Do you know how long it takes to die of starvation? A very long time. I myself do not like emaciated women. But the men who frequent the cribs are not so particular. You should live long enough to please many of them—"

Petra whimpered, her hands going to her face. "No, please—"

"Then you will eat!"

Petra ate, choking down enough food to make her feel as if she would be sick. Chen watched, gauging her reaction to the unaccustomed fare.

"It is enough. At present I am occupied with both business and mourning. You will prepare yourself to please me. You have three days."

"May I—may I return to my former room?"

"I will consider it." He smiled his smile that was not a smile and said, "By the way, I believe this is yours. You are most proficient with our writing tools—"

He handed her a folded rice paper, her message to the son of Wang, her only hope. Then he went to the door.

"Ling?"

The grotesque little Chinese with his toothy grin waited to escort her back to her cell-like room. Her instincts had been right. She should not have trusted him.

Two days later, she was removed to her former quarters. But she was never left alone. The two old crones kept watch

—as they had done over their dying master. A deathwatch, Petra thought, shivering. Propped against the wall, like dry twigs wrapped in black rags, they were ever vigilant. And the hour she must go to Chen drew closer.

She prayed for a miracle that would call them from their posts, an emergency somewhere in the house, a fire!

But the minutes passed, the hours, the days. And no miracle came.

Chapter 30

Missie Narvaéz was not frightened. She was angry. Petra had been a little fool for coming here alone. The Chinese people, between them,. had only a handful of names. The Feng Wu who fathered Martha was dead. If Petra were curious about her background, she, Missie, would have come with her—in the daylight.

She opened the door to the herbalist's shop. It jangled shut behind her and a moon-faced Celestial, in his early thirties, came from behind a beaded curtain to the rear. There was nothing sinister about him. In his spectacles and skullcap, his baggy trousers, padded jacket and slippers, he looked like any Chinese she might have seen on the street.

Then why did she feel a sudden chill? It was the darkness of the shop, its foreign smell, she supposed. And her errand—

"Feng Wu? You are the owner of this shop?"

He bowed in affirmation, and went behind the counter, preparatory to serving her needs.

Missie felt a warning bell of caution. It would be best to

claim no relationship at the moment, and she must go slowly. Petra might be here this minute, living in some rabbit warren behind this tunnellike room. If she were not, if something —worse—had happened to her, it would be wise to stall until help came. She reached into her reticule and drew out her press card.

"I am Missie Narvaéz, a reporter for the *Examiner*. I write under the by-line of Melissa McLeod. Perhaps you have read some of my work—"

Again an impassive bow. "I read only the wall newspapers in Spofford Alley that deal with my people. But my humble shop is honored—"

"I am doing a series of articles on the women of Little China. You are married? I would like to talk with your wife."

"She does not speak your language."

"And you speak it so well!"

She caught a faint flush of pleasure before he replied. "I study and learn in my poor way. Perhaps you wish to talk to the wife of Wing Su—" He began to give directions and Missie noted them as though she might follow his suggestion.

Then, stalling for time, she studied the tiny drawers lining the wall from floor to ceiling. "Are there different herbs in all of those? I cannot believe it! Are they all from China?"

"Some are from China, others from the Indies, others to be found here. I have more than sixty varieties of ginseng." He droned through a list of exotic names and ailments they best suited.

Missie listened, tense, for any sound from the back of the structure as he talked, then jumped as she realized that he'd fallen silent and was looking at her, inquiringly.

"Perhaps I could do a story on your shop. It would be good advertising for you."

"My humble business is small, insignificant, unworthy of your talents. My people know that it is here. Perhaps a larger market, on Sacramento Street?"

It was a tone of dismissal. He was moving to open the door for her.

"There is something else," she said hastily. "Several weeks ago, a young girl disappeared. Her name was Petra Channing. I need to talk to you."

Missie sensed a sudden tension in the man, a tigerish tightening of muscle, though his expression didn't change. He closed the partially opened door and stood before it, blocking it with his body.

"What has this to do with Feng Wu?"

"She entered this establishment the night she disappeared. She was not seen again."

Her statements hung between them in the brief silence that followed. Behind the thick glasses, Feng Wu's eyes darted as if seeking escape, then went flat.

"The police have not honored my poor shop with their presence. If this were true—"

"I am a reporter. I have connections the police do not have."

The minute Missie uttered those words, she sensed she'd made a mistake. Feng Wu smiled with false geniality, slipping into the Pidgen English employed by the majority of the Chinese in the area.

"Velly well, Missee Reporter! Please to see my humble abode. No Petal Chang-ying. You see—!"

He moved to the back of the shop, lifting beaded curtains aside, gesturing for her to follow. She stepped into a tiny cubicle, the living quarters of Feng Wu and his wife. The small Chinese woman knelt above a charcoal brazier that filled the room with smoke. Feng Wu spread his hands as if to say he'd proven his point.

He was lying! Missie knew it. Her years of reporting had taught her to recognize the signs. And if he was lying, there had to be a reason; something more urgent than hiding out a small girl who had come to seek her Chinese relatives. The stories Lee Wang told her earlier were vivid in her mind.

Missie had made a mistake in coming here alone. Now she had alerted the man. If he was guilty of any misdeed, he would disappear into the darkness of Chinatown the minute Missie left the shop.

She must manage to keep him in sight until help arrived.

Missie put a hand to her forehead. "May I sit for a moment? I feel rather faint—"

Feng Wu was all smiles and solicitude. He brought a bamboo stool and seated her, gabbling away at his wife in Chinese, looking sideways at Missie to see if she understood.

Dear God, she wished she did!

The woman heated water, and poured it over the contents of a paper packet Feng Wu brought from the shop. It had a strange, smoky taste. Missie drank, not wishing to offend him.

She had not lied, she thought. She did feel faint! The room seemed to reel around her. She felt so—strange, as if she were spinning through a tunnel that grew smaller as she fell into darkness.

As Missie clung to the edge of consciousness, Lee Wang reached the Courtney house. Em Courtney was already abed, still languishing over the loss of her granddaughter. Duke met Lee at the door, his lips pursing in a soundless whistle as the boy told his story.

Going to his desk, he took a pair of pistols from a drawer handing one to the young Chinese. He thrust the other in his belt.

It would be difficult to round up his men at this hour. It would take too long. They'd have to handle this job themselves. The police? Hell, no!

The two men ran to the waiting cab. Duke pushed the frightened driver from his seat and tossed him a wad of money, slid into the driver's seat and whipped up the horses. The carriage careened down the steep hill and raced through the streets of the city, stopping only once.

Duke yanked at the reins, see-sawing the horses to a stop before a tavern.

One of his man frequented the place. Maybe he could round up some help.

He was gone for only a moment, returning with his man and several others, bullyboys, half-drunk, looking for a scrap. They commandeered another horse-drawn cab. The second paused briefly at another bar, collecting a few more.

Duke massed his troops at the mouth of the dark little alley. Maybe there was no trouble here. Their services might not be needed. Even if they were not, every man-jack of them would be rewarded. First, they would scout out the situation.

Lee was Chinese, therefore not suspect. He would go into the shop, seeking something to ease a toothache. They would know more when he returned.

The men grumbled. One of them, a rough-looking customer with a scowling face and a peg leg, swore ferociously. Hell, he'd been promised a fight! Let him go in! He'd break the damn door down!

He was still waving his fists and growling like a grizzly when Lee returned, his face pale against the shadows.

He'd been given a remedy. Missie wasn't in sight. The proprietor seemed nervous. Boxes were open on the counter. Fresh stock, Feng Wu told him. But it was more plausible that he was packing to leave—

"Let's go," Duke said grimly. He began to run, and with a roar, the others followed, the old man with a peg leg in the lead.

The door had been locked behind Lee. Peg leg shoved Duke aside and, true to his threat, brought the door down with one heave of his mighty shoulders.

Feng Wu cowered behind the counter, his eyes, magnified by his heavy glasses, sliding from one face to another. He licked his lips nervously, too frightened to speak. Duke spoke first.

"The girls, where are they?"

When he received no answer, he grasped the front of Feng Wu's padded jacket, dragging him across the counter and pitching him against the farther wall. The man began to babble.

"No girl here. You wanchee girl, tly clibs. Feng Wu humble shopkeeper, no lun clib—"

"Lemme at the sonofabitch!" Peg leg roared. "Hell, I know how these things is handled in Chiny! He'll talk his goddamn head off afore I'm through! Anybody got a weak stummick better git th' hell out!"

He shoved the sick-looking Feng Wu into the back room. A small, frightened Chinese woman ran out, scuttling through the door. They let her go.

In a moment, they heard screams, a voice babbling for mercy in a foreign tongue. Then the words were translated into English.

"I will show you," Feng Wu said. "Don't—please, no more! I will show you!"

An ashen-faced Chinese led Duke Courtney, Lee Wang, and their group of rowdies to a set of shelves at the back of the room. He touched a certain spot and they slid to one side, revealing an aperature.

A set of rickety wooden steps led steeply down and down into darkness.

Chapter 31

Missie ceased drinking Feng Wu's concoction the minute her suspicions were aroused. She had not been quick enough. The few swallows had sent her spinning into darkness. The darkness was still there when she awoke. She moaned and tried to move, her first thought that she was both blinded and paralyzed. Then she felt the dampness of earth against her cheek and traced the pain she felt to her tightly bound wrists and ankles.

Terror began to hammer at her breast. She was somewhere in the depths of the earth! Buried alive!

Twisting, she managed to hump her body into a sitting position. Water dripped from somewhere overhead. From the impact of the falling drops, she calculated that the space she occupied was as high as a man's head—

The place smelled gravelike; musty. She hitched herself forward a little. There seemed no end to the open space—

She was in a tunnel, one of the labyrinth of mysterious networks that lay beneath the streets of the city. She'd considered them fictional inventions; a story to add to the tales of nefarious activities in Chinatown. But those stories had been true! Dear God—

Her mouth was free. Feng Wu had not bothered to gag her. That meant she was in a place from which she could not be heard; not a main tunnel, but perhaps an old, abandoned branch where no one ever came.

He had brought her here to die!

At the thought, she began to struggle. Her hands were fastened behind her and she tried to break the cord. It was narrow, tightly woven. Her efforts brought nothing but pain. Warm liquid mingled with the tunnel slime. Her wrists were bleeding. This wasn't going to succeed.

She must not panic! Surely Duke and Lee would find her! Unless—unless Feng Wu fled before they arrived. They would have to find the entrance to this place. Even then, they might comb the underground for days. She had no idea how extensively the area was honeycombed—

Missie began to shiver. She was cold. The place was dank and clammy, her hair already wet. Mud streaked her face, feeling slick and nasty. Twisting downward, she tried to wipe her cheek against her shoulder. It, too, was filthy with the tunnel's muck.

Perhaps there were others here! Others left to die, long since buried by seep and ooze, covered over as she would be—

It was a gruesome thought and she fought it away. She must think positively. If the tunnel had been used, there would be refuse here. If she could find a piece of metal, a shard of glass—

She fumbled through the evil-smelling slime around her. Nothing. Hitching herself forward a little, she searched again, finding a pliable sodden object that she turned in her bound hands until she could recognize its shape. A Chinese slipper.

She dropped it, suddenly sick as she recalled her earlier

notion of bodies beneath the muck. Then, grimly, she set herself to search again.

A small sound interrupted her activities, and her heart leaped with sudden hope. It had come from a distance. She strained her eyes into the darkness, praying to see a light appear.

"Is—is someone there?"

Her voice sounded small, lost, hollow. There was no answer.

"Please," she said, her tone rising to a scream, "someone—anyone—!"

Again, all was still. Then she heard a pattering, a squeaking sound. Something was sniffing at her bound feet.

A rat! Dear God, there were rats in the tunnel!

Missie kicked out, and the animal scurried away.

"Uncle Dan," Missie whispered, "Lee! Oh, hurry! Please hurry!"

She could not let herself go to pieces! She didn't dare! It would be easy to lose her mind completely. She must concentrate on something else, force her mind to think rationally.

She was, after all, a reporter, trained to think logically and in sequence. She began to write the story of Petra in her mind, searching for reasons that led to her own present plight.

First, the character: Petra Channing, small, shy, and lonely, inhibited by the knowledge of her mixed blood.

Next, the setting: a small, dark alley in Chinatown; a herbalist's shop, Proprietor, Feng Wu.

The problem: Petra sees the sign on the shop. It bears the name of her dead father.

From this point, Missie could only conjecture. It was understandable that Petra visit Chinatown. Knowing her background, the place would have a fascination for her. It was equally understandable that seeing Feng Wu's name would be a shock. But—

Damn! The rat had returned, it was nosing against her ankle! She could feel its nose twitching!

She drew up her legs and kicked out, viciously. It squealed and retreated. How far it had gone, she had no idea. It was probably sitting on its haunches, just out of reach of her slippers, watching—

Missie shuddered, wondering if the thing might launch a sudden attack. She could imagine its sharp teeth biting into soft flesh, bringing blood that would attract still others—

Blood!

She remembered her bound wrists, bleeding from her struggles with the knotted cord. Bending backward, she dragged her hands and wrists through the filthy, foul-smelling muck, coating them.

It might not help, but it was a positive action. And she must, at all costs, hold on to her senses.

Grimly, she forced her mind back to the problem of Petra.

Petra had told Lee Wang she was afraid of being late. Missie had explained that away with the casserole she'd left prepared for the oven. But what if it was something else? Perhaps she'd had some kind of appointment. But with whom?

Who would hurt Petra so much that she would return to Chinatown at night, seeking out a family she'd never known, denying the other half of her mixed heritage?

Petra did go to the shop. There was no doubt, now. And from that point, she disappeared into thin air. Whatever had happened to her, Feng Wu was frightened! So frightened he'd brought Missie here and left her to die in this hole!

He wouldn't go this far to hide the fact that he'd taken Petra into his home, therefore something terrible had happened to the girl. For some weird reason of his own, he might have deposited her here. Or he could have sold her to the cribs—

In either event, Petra, frail and sensitive, would not have lasted long. Missie's eyes filled with tears, then she laughed aloud. The laugh pealed down the long dark tunnel, ending on a sob.

"What an idiot I am," Missie said to herself, tears making rivers down her mudstreaked cheeks! "What an idiot!"

No one could be in worse case than she was at this moment, and here she was bawling her head off for Petra's sake. Even now, the girl might be perfectly safe and sound, tucked comfortably away in a Chinese household. Feng Wu's actions in bringing Missie herself here, would be incomprehensible if that were true.

But who knew the workings of a Chinese mind?

The poor things were so discriminated against that she probably frightened him out of his wits. A girl had disappeared. He would be blamed. That had probably been his exact reaction to her questioning.

Now, all she could hope for was that Duke and Lee could bring him to his senses. How much time had passed? She had no idea. She had been unconscious for a while—

Something furry brushed her bound hands. She swung them, pendulum-fashion, then scooted until her back was against the wall. She could hear the thing, still hovering near her. It squeaked several times—

And the squeaking was answered. From far down the tunnel, she heard them coming—a horde of them.

"Uncle Duke," she whispered, "Lee—"

Then, mercifully, her senses left her. She slid sideways down the wall, to lie with her cheek pressed to the evil-smelling mud that formed the tunnel floor.

Chapter 32

Duke Courtney, seeing the steps that led down into hellish darkness, demanded lanterns. There were two in the herbalist's shop. One hung in front of a market up the street, another before the laundry. These were scavenged without pausing to ask permission.

Duke gave his orders. Feng Wu was to lead the way, the others to follow. Peg leg, whose real name was Sim Blevins, was not in favor of such action.

"Yaller bastids is faster'n greased lightnin', an sneakier'n hell," he grumped. They settled for making a noose of a length of cord and slipping it around Feng Wu's neck. Blevins carried the other end, unable to resist giving it a yank now and then.

"Sonofabitch," he said. Yank. "Yaller bastid!" Yank! "Oughter string ye up by yer thumbs!" Yank!

"Leave him enough wind to talk," Duke interposed.

"Sure ez hell will. Hangin's too good fer 'im."

The rowdy crew was abnormally silent as they descended

into the depths of the tunnel. They'd come expecting a free-for-all, and would have welcomed it; fists against knives. But this was something out of their experience, like descending into a grave.

"Git outa this," one said gloomily, "gonna stay likkered up fer a month. 'Tain't nacheral."

The others agreed.

The shadows of the tunnel swallowed up the glow of the lanterns. Occasionally, a black patch showed where it branched. The whole of Chinatown looked to be undermined.

"Gonna be keerful where I hit th' bottle arter this," said a seedy-looking man with coarse black whiskers. "Git shanghaied easy in this place! Bet one of them damn holes ends up at th' docks."

"Wouldn' harm ye none," Sim Blevins answered him. "Make a man out of ye. Got hauled in when I was a kid. Wuz a crimp, meself, fer years—"

"You sonofabitch!"

"Look out who yer callin' names!" Sim Blevins dropped Feng Wu's leash, another man caught it, and the two men squared off. Duke stepped between them. "I'll deck the first one that takes a swing," he said harshly. "We're looking for two lost girls, not fighting each other. If you don't want to cooperate, you can head back right now—but we keep the lanterns."

The trouble subsided, and they went on.

Finally Blevins stopped.

"How we know we kin trust this bastid? Hell, we come halfway to Chiny now! Mebbe if I rough 'im up a mite more—"

"Small way," Feng Wu tried to smile, reverting to pidgen English as though ignorance might protect him. "Velly small! Girl all light, you see!"

Grimly, the party stumbled on. Feng Wu paused, pointing to a dark blotch. It proved to be another tunnel, smaller, narrower, its mouth half-choked by debris. "B'long house long-time burn," Feng Wu explained conversationally. His words choked off as Sim Blevins jerked the rope.

They moved ahead, slowly. Here and there, fallen rubble indicated that the roof overhead was not as safe as it appeared. The place was dank and wet, the walls slimy. Duke was sick at the thought of small, blond Missie in this god-awful place.

If the sniveling Chinaman had hurt the kid, he intended to tear him apart with his bare hands. But he'd have to control himself until after he'd led them to Petra.

Feng Wu had confessed, under duress, that he'd sold the girl to a wealthy man. He swore that she was still untouched, treated like a queen.

And that, Duke thought grimly, was a lot of bullshit. He agreed with his new friend, Sim. Killing was too good for the bastard. He slipped in the muck and swore. The place was getting colder, damper, the farther they went.

"There missee," Feng Wu said suddenly. He pointed to a small, mud-covered bundle against the wall ahead.

Duke raised his lantern high. A hundred red eyes caught its glow, reflecting it back. Then, with a scurrying sound, they disappeared.

"My God!"

Duke rushed forward, slipping and sliding, to kneel by the semiconscious body of his wife's niece.

"Missie!"

Missie moaned as he took out his pocketknife and cut the cords that bound her arms behind her back, cutting cruelly into her wrists. Then he released her ankles, lifting her.

Her eyes flew open. She raised a mud-stained hand to his cheek as if to make sure he was really there and not a dream.

"I'm all right," she said clearly. "We've got to find Petra."

"We're on our way, sweetheart." His voice was choked with emotion. She might look like Em, blond hair and blue eyes, but—damned if she didn't make him think of Tamsen.

The party retraced its steps, returning to the main tunnel. A short distance farther, they turned into yet a larger one. Here, the walls were dry. Feng Wu was shaking with fear, the legs of his loose trousers trembling with the knocking of his knees. He dropped his pretense of ignorance, too frightened to maintain it.

"They will kill me," he quavered. "Young Chen is an important man in the tongs. I have betrayed his secrets in disclosing the tunnel. Do not make me go—"

Sim Blevins tugged on the cord that looped around the fellow's neck. He gagged, then closed his lips and moved on.

The door to the tunnel was set in the floor of a cellar. Here, there were boxes, bales of silk and carpets. It was a good place to leave Missie until they returned. She refused. Circulation had returned to her arms and legs. She would be all right—

Setting down their lanterns, the troop climbed cellar stairs leading to another door. Sim Blevins applied his shoulder and it splintered before his weight. Duke and his crew of bullyboys burst into the room to face a screaming woman and a huge man armed with a cleaver.

Duke sidestepped and Sim Blevins cheerily dispatched the man with a hard left, Feng Wu's leash still clutched in his right. The woman's screams brought a number of hard-faced men running. With a blood-curdling war whoop, Duke Courtney leaped forward.

"Hi—ee—yah!"

It was the battle cry of his youth, when he challenged all comers, fighting just for the hell of it. For a moment, he was young again.

His shout unnerved Chen's hatchet men for a brief second. It was enough. The ruffians Duke collected at the tavern surged forward. Sim Blevins gripped two men in powerful hands, knocking their heads together, tossing them aside and taking on another. Duke Courtney, blue eyes blazing, fought like a demon. Hands caught at his shirt, ripping it from his powerful shoulders. He turned from the opponent he'd just flattened and downed the other with a single blow.

Pots and pans flew in the melee. The seedy black-bearded man who'd had words with Blevins fought alongside of him, shouting gleefully. A fallen Chinese crawled toward the cleaver. Sim Blevins brought his peg leg down hard on the man's hand. He doubled in pain, forgetting his errand.

Lee Wang skirted the room, gun in hand, Missie sheltered behind him, and moved out into the living area. A curving staircase, exquisitely carved, led to another floor. They climbed carpeted stairs, to reach a long hallway where candles flickered in ornate holders and golden idols stared with shimmering eyes that seemed alive.

"Dear God, Lee! If Petra isn't here—"

"I think she will be."

There was a tremendous crash from below. Someone had tipped the burning stove. A wave of smoke wafted through the kitchen door and up the stairway.

Lee swore an oath in his native tongue. Pulling Missie after him, he flung open one door, another—

Then two old women burst from a room toward the end, screeching like magpies as they fled, too blind with fear to see the intruders in the House of Chen.

Lee opened another door. The room smelled of herbs used for fumigation. In this room, there had been a recent death. He kept the fact to himself and ran on. Another room furnished in Western style. Another—

They must leave the house. The din below had died away. The smoke was growing thick, and there was a crackle of flames. It was to be hoped that Duke and his people had reached the tunnel—

But above the sound of burning Lee heard something: an odd, scraping noise. And it was on this floor. He listened, then looked at Missie to see if she heard. She, too, was alert. It came again, and from the room the two old crones had quitted.

Lee and Missie hurried toward the sound. Missie reached the door first—and screamed.

Petra Channing stood atop a set of shelves, a silken noose around her neck, the other end of it attached to a grill set near the ceiling. She stared at Lee and Missie in open-mouthed disbelief.

The shelves teetered and began to fall.

Lee Wang threw himself across the room, holding them firm. Petra looked down at him, too numb to release herself. Missie finally clambered up to remove the knotted sash from Petra's throat and lower her gently into Lee Wang's waiting arms. Petra clung to him, weeping. "Lee—Missie! I prayed!"

Petra's miracle had come almost too late.

There was no time for talking. The windowless room was rapidly becoming an oven. The girls followed Lee as he went again from room to room. Here, a porch projected from beneath a window. Situated at the front of the house, it was not yet in flames. He forced the window, lowering Petra to the roof, then Missie. Clinging by his fingers to the sill, he let himself down just as a fiery gust of smoke and fire swept through the upper floor.

A crowd of chattering Chinese had gathered before the house. Two of then ran forward, making a human ladder to help the women down. Lee Wang half leaped, half fell, as the porch roof burned free of the building and leaned away.

He was stunned, but unhurt. The two girls knelt beside him as he gradually regained his breath. Missie sought in vain for Duke, for a white face in the crowd of Chinese who had organized a bucket brigade.

"The others, Lee—?"

"We'll find them. I think I know where they are."

"Ma'am—"

A hand touched Missie's shoulder.

"I'm Carrington, from the *Examiner*, ma'am. I wonder if I might talk to you for a moment? The fire—"

"Good God!"

"Missie?" he asked uncertainly. "What the hell—?"

The face of the mud-coated creature, one of the trio he'd seen escape from the burning building, cracked in a wry smile.

"Sorry, Carrington. This isn't for publication."

Then they were up, melting into the crowd before he could regain his senses. Missie Narvaéz! And the second girl, despite her dragon-embroidered robe, looked hauntingly familiar.

She was the missing Petra Channing, or he'd eat his hat! But what the devil was she doing here? Who was the young man she was clinging to? He was obviously Chinese—

Carrington, veteran reporter, first on the scene at every fire, had one hell of a story—if he only knew what it was.

Chapter 33

Duke and his men retreated. In the melee, a can of coal oil had been overturned. The tipped stove spilled hot embers and ignited the fluid, the ensuing conflagration blocking off entry to the remainder of the house.

They fought their way to the cellar. Their assailants followed, fleeing the fire, only to be clubbed down. Feng Wu had disappeared during the fighting. Sim Blevins, swearing powerfully, sought a replacement. He yanked a groggy little Chinaman to his feet, grabbed a lantern in his other hand, and peg-legged it to the tunnel, the others following.

There, they took stock of their numbers. All were present and accounted for—except Lee Wang, Missie, and Duke Courtney's granddaughter—the girl they'd come to rescue.

Duke turned into a maniac. He was going back in after them! Two men grabbed his arms, trying to calm him. Good God! Did he think he c'd walk through fire? Hell, he'd be tryin' t' walk on water, next! Black-beard had seen Missie and Lee leave the kitchen. They'd make it out, all right—

With a hoarse bellow, Duke Courtney threw his captors from him. Two more tried to halt him, and were scythed down by his swinging fists.

The peg-legged man moved in from the side, throwing a powerful roundhouse punch that landed on Duke's unprotected jaw. He went down, and Blevins surveyed him, glumly.

"I like the sonofabitch. Hope I didn' bust nuthin'. Hell, pick 'im up. Les' go."

Duke Courtney didn't need any assistance. He returned to consciousness, regaining his sense at the same time. The kitchen floor had burned through. The cellar was now an inferno, that end of the tunnel an impenetrable wall of fire.

He stood and nodded curtly to Sim Blevins. They made their way back through the tunnel. Blevin's captive, a small man named Ling, led the way. Duke followed, his hands clenched into fists, his eyes half-crazed with worry. They had not found Petra. He had no idea what had happened to Missie and to Lee. In searching for his granddaughter, he'd lost his beloved niece—and a friend.

They reached the herbalist's shop. From its door, they could see flames illuminating the sky some blocks away. Duke was all for running to the scene. The bearlike Blevins glared at him.

"They ain't nuthin' left of the gawdam place. They git out, they show up here, right? Hell, we could go back an' forth th' whole sonofabitchin' night, passin' each other up."

His words made sense. And Sim Blevins had something to do to fill in the time.

He grilled the Chinese, Ling, in his own inimitable way, and produced some information. Young Chen, the master of the house had not been at home this night, but away on business. The girl? Missee Petal Chang-ying? She was locked in a room on the upper floor.

Duke Courtney froze. The house of Chen was built of wood. The second story would have gone in an instant. At sight of Duke's awful expression, Ling quaked, hastening to ingratiate himself.

"Velly nice loom," Ling said, bobbing and grinning. "Velly nice! Missie Petal Chang-ying old Master Chen warm-bed-lady."

Duke, for the first time in his life, struck a smaller man than he. Ling survived the blow—though his smile would never be regarded as toothy again. Duke sat down, his head in his hands, his shoulders shaking. The tavern toughs regarded him with pity and embarrassment.

"Hell," the black-bearded man said. "I c'd use a drink!"

One of his cronies produced a bottle and passed it to him without a word.

It was Sim Blevins who broke the silence. "Migawd," he roared, "looka who's here!"

Pandemonium broke loose. Duke Courtney reached for Petra with an inarticulate cry, holding her close in an agony of relief. Then he reached for Missie. She wasn't there. Missie Narvaéz, the touch-me-not of the *Examiner*'s office, was busily engaged in hugging every one of the drunken derelicts who had joined Duke in his rescue attempt.

Last was old Sim Blevins. He growled and wiped the cheek she had kissed with a contemptuous hand, muttering something about goddamn silly women. But his eyes showed a hint of pleasure.

Duke Courtney was euphoric. He kept pressing money into the hands of his confederates. They handed it back, Sim Blevins speaking for the group as a whole.

Hell, they'd had the time of their lives an' rescued two purty girls in the bargain. They owed him. They would, however, settle for a round of drinks—

The idea sounded pretty good to Duke Courtney. Tonight, he'd felt like a kid again. Now that the girls were safe, he wasn't sure he wanted it to end. He frowned, looking toward Petra and Missie. They were dead on their feet. He was honor-bound to take them home.

Lee Wang intervened. If Mr. Courtney didn't consider his suggestion inappropriate, he would be happy to escort the ladies.

Duke looked vastly relieved. "Hell, yes. That is, if it's all right with them."

It was. Missie answered for them both. Duke would insist on taking her to the Courtney house. She wanted only to go home, home to her rooms above the bakery. She didn't mention her destination until they commandeered another carriage on Sacramento Street. Duke and the others going on in search of a bar.

Lee obediently dropped her off at her apartment after she'd withstood Petra's objections, then drove Petra to the mansion on Nob Hill.

They both sat quietly in front of the house. Petra seemed reluctant to leave the carriage. She sat pleating the folds of her stained white kimono, looking away from Lee.

"You know about me, don't you? That my father was Chinese?"

He nodded. Missie had told him.

"I've let it—bother me. It's hard, not being one thing or the other. I don't fit in anywhere. I thought if I tried to be like my father's people—"

She began to shiver. "It was—awful! And I caused so much trouble! You might have been killed!"

Lee reached out, taking her small hand in his. "We do not live like the Chens, my father and I. Please do not think less of us."

"I don't," she said, her eyes filling. "It was just—I was so frightened!"

She began to weep, and he took her in his arms, listening as she poured out her story of life in the Chen house. His body against hers was warm, living, breathing, erasing the feel of Chen's dead flesh. And then a spark seemed to ignite between them. Lee's instinct to comfort her had become something more.

Petra lifted wondering eyes and he touched his mouth to hers, at first only a butterfly touch, then deeply, throbbing, pulsing—

"Petra," he whispered, "little sweetheart—"

Her arms went around him and she was clinging, holding to him as they rocked together in an agony of love.

Finally, he put her from him, fighting against his need for her. She was very young. She'd been through a trying time. She must rest, consider his love for her. Lee would speak to his father, telling him of his intentions. And there were her grandparents to consider. They must approve. He must remember that among the virtues of his race was patience—

He led her to her door, cupping her small face between his sensitive fingers, not daring to touch that mouth again. Seeing her into the darkened house where the household slept, ignorant of the night's proceedings, he left her.

Petra moved in a haze of dreaming to the room she had formerly occupied. In the morning, she must face her grandmother. There would have to be honesty between them. But for now, it didn't seem to matter. She was safe, and she had found a place where she belonged.

She loved, and was loved in return.

In the meantime, Duke Courtney was having the time of his life. The round of drinks had turned into two, three, four. The evening's exploits had grown as the drinking continued, their heroics larger than life. A crowd of drunken sailors attempted to intrude on their party. Duke's men pitched the party-crashers into the street, demolishing the bar in the process: The owner promptly shut down for the night.

Duke was excited, expansive. "Hell, why don't we go to my place?"

"Got any likker?" one of them wanted to know.

"Whole gawdam cellar full," Duke boasted.

With a shout, they spilled out of the bar and loaded into the carriages.

Reaching their destination sobered them somewhat. None

of them had ever been in a place like the house on Nob Hill. The group was awed, overcome. Duke was hurt, bewildered. Hell, this was a party—

He woke a servant, and sent him down to bring up a bottle for each men. "Drink it up," he said. "Hell, there's more where that came from!"

Sim Blevins set his bottle down, and spat contemptuously on the floor. "Don't wantcher gawdam likker," he said belligerently.

Duke Courtney glared back, his face close to the old man's glowering one.

"And why the hell not?"

"Didn' figger ye fer one of them Nob Hill snobs! Buncha gawdam pansies!"

"You say that again, I'll punch you in the nose!"

"Buncha gawdam pansies!"

Duke swung, missed. The two giant men circled each other, eyes blazing with delight. Duke connected with a right, shouting his battle cry. It reverberated through the house. A vase crashed to the floor. Black-beard forgot his awe at his surroundings and shouted at the top of his lungs.

"Bettin' on th' Duke? Any takers?"

"Takers, hell! Sim c'd deck him with one hand tied behind his back."

"Yer a iggerant idjit!"

"An' yer a sonofabitch!"

Another pair entered joyously into combat. Soon, Em's lavishly decorated living room was in shambles.

Em Courtney woke to a sound of drunken shouts, of breakage. Reaching automatically for Duke, she encountered his empty pillow. Above the noise of brawling, she heard his battle cry—

"Hi—ee—yah!"

For a moment, she was back in Alaska were she had met him. He'd been like a wild man, then, untamed. Now he was a sober, respected citizen. She shuddered as the sound came again. Duke had been drinking! Who was with him? She must put a stop to this! She could not believe that he would revert to his old rowdy ways—Dear God, what would the neighbors think?—She pulled on a filmy peignoir and went to the head of the stairs, drawing a sharp breath at the scene below.

The scum of San Francisco was collected in her living room! Worse, they were involved in a free-for-all! She flinched as a treasured lamp crashed to the floor, seeking Duke in the melee.

She saw him, shirtless, slugging it out toe-to-toe with a barrel-chested, ugly peg-legged man. As she watched, the stranger kicked out with his wooden leg. Duke sidestepped, then they were straining in a bear hug, attempting to crack each other's ribs.

"Duke!"

Em's voice shrilled above the commotion.

"Duke, stop this!"

The noise died as, one by one, the combatants caught sight of the lady on the stairs.

"What is the meaning of this?" Em asked in a shaking voice. "Out! Out, all of you, or I shall inform the police! Duke Courtney, what in the name of God—"

Duke, the battle halted, was suddenly sobered, feeling a little foolish before his wife's eyes. Now his lips tightened.

He threw an arm around Sim Blevins's shoulders.

"We're celebrating," he said, slurring his words a little. "And goddamnit, Em, these are my friends! Bes' friends I ever had!" Tears filled his eyes as his heart welled with alcoholic affection for his comrades.

"You're drunk!" Em spat. "I'm giving you just five minutes to—"

"Sure as hell am," he agreed. "Remembered tonight I was a man. And I'm giving you five seconds to get your butt back to bed!"

"Duke!" It was a small anguished cry. He moved forward,

his face menacing. Dear God, he'd meant what he said! Em wavered before his set expression—and fled to the safety of her room.

Duke Courtney bowed politely to his friend, Sim, as if extending an invitation to dance. "Shall we take up where we left off?"

Sim Blevins was not to be outdone in the manners department. He bowed, too. "Don't mind if I do."

Duke brought his knee up under the man's chin. Blevins staggered back with a look of pleased surprise, then bored in.

Duke's battle cry rose to the bedroom where Em huddled, furious and humiliated.

"Hi—ee—yah."

All was well with the world. Duke Courtney forgot he was almost seventy years old, and a respected member of the community. He was having the time of his life.

Chapter 34

By morning, Em Courtney had reconciled the situation in her mind. When she married Duke, he was open, uninhibited; a hell-raiser who would rather fight than eat. His companions hadn't been too savory then, she remembered wryly. She'd given herself credit for changing him into the gentleman he was now. But had he changed? Or was it like corking a bottle too tightly? Had he suppressed his basic instincts until now, exploding into action all at once?

And could that bottle ever be corked again?

In spite of her anger at the scene downstairs, the way that Duke had dismissed her like a—a fractious child, the sight of Duke in action had thrilled her. She'd forgotten the way he looked in those early, rougher days, the way he entered so gleefully into battle; his magnificent shoulders bared for combat. She'd seen him again as he was in his youth.

Yet he'd brought those people into her house! Those awful people! Where did they come from, these scrapings of the slums?

And where did she come from, she wondered forlornly. What right did she have to condemn Duke? She'd put her own past behind her so far that it was almost obliterated. Her social position, this house—everything stood between herself and what she was.

She didn't want to remember. Being Em, she convinced herself she must forgive Duke for a temporary aberration. After all, he had no liking for her social functions, enduring them stoically. She would go along with his—his little evening with the boys—and say nothing more about it.

But, oh, her lovely room!

Em rose in the morning, determined to be long-suffering and forgiving. She passed Petra's closed door with a pang of loss, and went downstairs. Duke, though shirtless, was sober now, sweeping up the night's debris.

Em flinched. The peg-legged man was still here, snoring on what was left of her pale green damask sofa. Even in sleep, he was ugly, seeming more bear than man.

She tore her eyes away from the creature, remembering her resolve. Duke looked sick and pale in the morning light.

"I'm sorry, Em. Don't know what got into me."

"It's quite all right, Duke." A pause said it wasn't. "I intended to redecorate, anyway." She looked at the man on the couch with distaste. "Shouldn't you wake your—friend, and show him the door?"

Duke frowned and leaned the broom in a corner. "Sim's working for us, now. I hired him last night."

"Hired him? Duke, I will not have that man—!"

Duke took his wife's arm and led her to the kitchen. "Sit down," he said grimly. "I'm going to talk and you're by-god going to listen!"

Shocked, she sank into a chair and he set coffee before them both.

"In the first place," he said, his features taut, "Petra's home!"

"'Petra'? In her room?" Em was on her feet, her face alight. Duke grasped her wrist and pulled her down again.

"I told you you were going to listen!"

As he'd suspected, he told her, Petra was not the child of Martha's husband, Peter Channing. Her real father was a Chinese warlord named Feng Wu—

It was not true! Em clamped her hands over her ears to shut out the ugly story. Duke pulled them away.

The girl had overheard their conversation about the Wangs, and had gone to Missie. The day she disappeared, she went to Chinatown, seeing the name of Feng Wu on a shop in a dark alleyway. That night she'd gone back, driven by God-knows-what. Feng Wu, a cousin, drugged her, sold her as the bed-companion of a dying man—

"Oh, dear God! That couldn't happen. Duke! Not in this day and time! The—the child made it up, to get attention! I don't believe a word of it!"

"Do you believe me?" His face held the anger of the previous night. "Shut up, Em, and listen! I know what took place! I was there!"

He went on to explain the events of the previous night, how Missie found Petra's trail, and Lee Wang had come to him for help. He described the danger Missie had encountered; the way they'd found her, bound, in a rat-infested tunnel. He told of the battle in the House of Chen; the fire, young Lee aiding in the girls' escape.

The men who had fought beside him were of a certain stamp, but they were his friends. He'd brought them home.

Duke Courtney had never lied in his life. The ring of truth in his words were unmistakable. There was no way to alter the tale to suit her fancy.

"I don't know what to say," Em whispered.

"Then I will tell you! You will apologize to Missie Narvaéz! You will make it clear to Petra that you love her for what she is. You will make Lee Wang welcome in this house! I think there's something going on there—"

"No," Em whimpered. "It—it's not possible!" Her eyes dropped before his hard gaze. "Go on."

"And you will put up with Sim Blevins." Duke set his coffee cup down with a clang. "We didn't manage to clear out that rat's nest last night. Chen, the master of the house, was away on business. It's possible that we'll need a guard, with Petra here—"

Em shrank. In a few short weeks, her life had been disrupted. First Missie in jail, moving out like a—a common woman. Then her doted-upon granddaughter had disappeared. Duke brought home a different girl: part Chinese, like little Liu who did the laundry. She, Em, was expected to receive Lee Wang as a suitor for Petra's hand. Duke had reverted to his old wild habits, and now her home was to become an armed camp.

"I think I'll go up to Petra," she said abruptly.

"You do that. And remember what she's been through."

Petra was sleeping. She still wore the white robe with its embroidered dragons. Her soot black hair spread over the pillow. Her face was smudged with smoke and tears.

Em stood looking down at her. How many times she'd studied Martha in this same way: Martha, her own illegitimate daughter. She'd wondered who the child's father was; the cold-eyed gringo who had hurt her, cruelly, or his young Mexican friend; gentle, almost apologizing for his act.

She'd prayed it was the Mexican boy who impregnated her, and not—not the other. Martha had not been cold-eyed and blond like the first man, but almost the image of Tamsen with her oval face and long dark hair.

Em had tried to see the same Mexican heritage in Petra. Now she realized she'd been a fool. The girl definitely had an Oriental look: the high cheekbones, the odd-shaped eyes—

Poor Petra! Poor Martha! Poor Em—

Petra opened her eyes, surprise giving way to a defensive expression. Em Courtney sat down beside her, taking the girl's frail body in her arms, rocking her in an agony of love and pity.

"It's going to be all right," she kept saying over and over. "Everything's going to be all right!"

The Courtneys had two callers that morning. The first was Lee Wang, clad in a neat dark suit and fresh, glistening linen.

He wished to request permission to pay court to Duke's granddaughter, Petra.

"Hell, yes," was Duke's delighted answer. He couldn't think of a better man! They shook hands, and Lee left. He would return tomorrow when Petra had fully recovered from her ordeal. Perhaps she might wish to take the air.

Duke was certain that she would. He had wanted to tell him to go to the girl's room, grab her up and carry her off. He restrained himself. Things were more civilized these days. And young Lee even more than most.

Duke's second caller was a disheveled newspaperman. Carrington had come into work with a story on last night's fire—and a collection of wild facts he couldn't verify. He swore Missie Narvaéz was present at the scene; that she, a girl he was certain was Petra Channing, and an unidentified Chinese boy escaped from the burning structure.

Missie had been covered with mud, she'd refused to make a statement, and the trio disappeared.

None of the tale made sense.

Blaine had not waited to put on his coat. It was slung over his shoulder when he knocked at the Courtney door. It was answered by an ugly, burly man with a peg leg, who glared at Matthew and looked him up and down before admitting him.

What the hell was going on?

Courtney promptly acquainted him with the story of the previous evening, on condition that it was not to be published. He sketched the details of Missie's visit to Lee Wang, their tour of Chinatown, and Missie's subsequent discovery. Missie had entered the herbalist's shop alone—

Blaine's face, as he continued with the tale of his arrival on the scene, the finding of Missie in such dreadful circumstances, told Duke what he'd already guessed. The man was in love with Em's niece. Again, he approved.

He finally finished the story, telling how the girls had escaped the fire and rejoined them, settling back to wait for Blaine's reaction.

"Of all the damn fool stunts," Matthew exploded, "going into Chinatown at night! Stupid female!"

"Petra?" Duke quirked an eyebrow.

"Well—Petra, too. But Missie needs a firm hand! My God, man!" Blaine saw the amusement in his friend's eyes and his voice trailed off.

He stood and shrugged himself into his coat, made his excuses, and headed back to the office. First, he told the confused Carrington he was mistaken about seeing Petra Channing. The girl had returned to the Courtneys. He was to write a small item for page two, stating that it had been an error in communications. The Channing girl had been visiting friends.

In regard to the bodies found in the charred ruins of the Chinatown fire, play it down. The public was getting sick of reading about tong wars.

And finally, he sent Larry Hiller to Sacramento. He was to spend a couple of days sitting in on the activities of the legislature.

Then he went back to his desk and tried to work; the horror of Duke's story still in his mind. He could see Missie in that dark tunnel, her wrists and feet bound—the vicious tunnel rats surrounding her in the darkness—

The little fool! To deliberately walk into such a predicament! The little fool!

He'd been right in terminating her employment. With her penchant for getting into trouble, she'd go after an assignment and get herself killed!

Dammit if he could only get her off his mind! He couldn't concentrate—

At the end of the day, he frowned at the stack of work in front of him. Again, he must take some of it home with him. Sighing, he slipped his finished notes into one folder, his unread papers into another, and went to get his coat.

He didn't realize what had happened until he reached home. He had picked up the wrong folder.

"What is it, Matt?"

He grinned ruefully at the aproned figure in the kitchen doorway. She seemed to have an uncanny ability to read his mind.

"Just kicking myself for being a damned fool, Cinnie. Left some important papers at the office, something I have to go over tonight. Can you manage—"

The pleasant expression in Cinnie's eyes was replaced by reluctant doubt. "I suppose so—" She brightened as a thought struck her. "Perhaps that nice young woman will bring them by again. Then you won't have to go back."

Young woman? He stared at her. "What are you talking about?"

"The girl who brought your work the night you were late. I'm sure I told you—"

"And I am sure you didn't. Was she small, blond? How the hell did she know where I live! Did she come in? My God, what did she think!"

"Don't raise your voice to me, Matthew! Not after I've given the best years of my life—"

He groaned. "We're not going into all that again. I'm going out, and you'd damned well better be here when I get back!"

He slammed the door behind him.

Chapter 35

Missie, reaching home in the night, scrubbed the filthy residue of the tunnel from her hair and body, and fell into bed. She was still unemployed, still aching over Matthew Blaine. The book loomed on her horizon like a dark cloud containing the elements of wind and storm. But these last hours had drained her. Petra was safe. That one blessing, coupled with fatigue, sent her into sodden, dreamless sleep.

It was after noon when she woke. Her first thought was of Frau Schmitt, who had formed an affectionate attachment to Petra Channing. Unknowingly, Missie gave the old woman a story that paralleled the one that would be published in this day's edition of the *Examiner*.

Petra had gone to visit friends. She'd left a note, which had gotten mislaid. At present, the girl was with her grandmother.

Frau Schmitt was delighted at the news. She'd known nothing was wrong, she said loyally. Petra was a good girl.

Missie hugged the innocent old woman and returned to her

rooms, wondering what she'd think if she knew the true story. It would be beyond her comprehension!

Later in the afternoon, Missie had a visitor. Em Courtney, in a tailored blue street gown, bustled fashionably, appeared at her door.

"I've been wanting to see your apartment," she said as Missie ushered her in. "It—it's quite nice, considering the neighborhood."

"I'm comfortable here. Would you like some tea?"

"That would be very nice." Em settled herself on the sofa, drawing off her gloves, nervously continuing with small talk. Then, as Missie lifted the teapot to pour, Em saw her wounded wrists.

"Missie—," Em reached for her hand and held it to her cheek. "Oh, Missie, I'm sorry! I've been so wrong! I owe you so much! Forgive me!"

Em's blue eyes were filled with tears, her lip quivering.

"It's all right, Aunt Em."

"No, it isn't," the older woman insisted. "Oh, Missie! Please come back to us. Duke and I love you! Petra needs you—"

Missie wavered before the sincerity of her plea.

"And your job at the paper," Em went on, "I won't ever bring that up again, I promise—"

There was no job, Missie thought drearily. But there was a book soon to hit the stands, a book that might destroy any chance of a friendly relationship with her aunt forever.

"I appreciate your offer, Aunt Em, but I'm very happy here." Missie smiled crookedly.

"Modern women," Em sighed. "I suppose I'll never understand them! You won't change your mind?"

Missie remained adamant. When Emmeline Courtney took her leave, she hugged her stubborn, independent niece. "Just remember that we love you, as if you were our own. And that you're always welcome."

Then she was gone, only an exquisite scent of perfume,

like spring flowers, to mark her passing. Missie wished that her final words would remain true; that her book wouldn't raise another barricade between them.

Now, Missie must take stock of her assets. Petra was safe. She must begin to plan ahead for herself. Tomorrow, she would apply at the *Chronicle*, the *Bulletin*, the *Call*. Would Matthew Blaine give her references? It was highly unlikely.

If the book did less well than Brown, Halpert and Brown expected, she would be forced to seek other employment. Teacher? Shopgirl? The still-denigrated nursing profession? None of them suited her.

There were so few opportunities open to women—

Damn Matthew Blaine! She hated him!

When a knock sounded at her door, she opened it to stand in mute surprise. It was if her thoughts had conjured up the man!

Blaine pushed past her, wheeling her to face him, kicking the door shut behind her. He pushed up her sleeve, looking at one small rope-burned wrist, then at the other.

"You damned little fool! You ought to be spanked, pulling a stunt like you did last night!"

Missie jerked her hands away. "At least I did more than you did, with all your contacts! More than Duke Courtney with his detectives! I found her—"

"And Duke might not have found either one of you," he exploded. "Then, what? Of all the goddamn silly females, you—"

"What I do and what I am is none of your business, Matthew Blaine! I no longer work for you—!"

"Maybe you should! At least there'd be some man to keep you out of trouble!"

Missie was livid. "I can take care of myself, thank you. I would suggest you devote your attention to the *Examiner*— and to your family!"

For answer, Matthew Blaine snatched her cloak off its hook and wrapped it around her.

"You're coming with me," he said grimly.

"I'm not!"

Her refusal was ignored. He had hold of her arm and was rushing her down the stairs. She tried to fight free, but he was too strong for her.

And Frau Schmitt was waiting at the foot of the steps, her face rosy with smiles. "It is nice to see you two going out again," she said, playfully shaking a plump finger. "You must not keep our girl up too late."

"I won't," Blaine said, laughing. He handed Missie up into his carriage. She had no choice but to go peaceably in order to avoid a scene.

She closed her lips as he clucked to the horse and the little surrey began to move. She did not intend to speak to him, no matter what he had to say. Evidently he was of the same mind. Neither spoke. They drove for a long way, out to the edge of the city. He turned the vehicle into a narrow, tree-shaded lane, and stopped before the sprawling, comfortable house that was his own.

He came around to her side of the surrey.

"You're getting down!"

"No, I'm not!"

He had her arm, and she must either alight gracefully or be dragged ignominiously to the ground. She chose the former.

With a firm grip, he led her up the path, onto the porch, and into the front door.

"Cinnie, come here!"

The woman Missie had met earlier appeared, vertical lines between her brows. She ignored Missie's presence. "I'm through," she said, tight-lipped. "And don't say I didn't warn you!" She turned a bitter look on Missie. "I suppose she's going to take my place?"

"Could be," Matthew Blaine said mildly.

"No," Missie whispered. "Oh, no! Please—"

"Her name is Cinnie," Blaine said as the woman flounced out the door. "Now, come on. There's something else—"

Missie was shaken to the core, too numb to resist as he forced her, stumbling, to a small room where a shaded lamp burned. He steered her toward a crib set against the opposite wall.

Missie looked down at the face of a small boy, of perhaps three, a bedraggled stuffed bunny in his arms. Dark hair tumbled over a rosy sleeping face that might have been Matthew Blaine's as a child.

"This is Joshua," Blaine said tersely. "My son."

He lifted the bottom of the blanket, very gently. The little one's nightshirt was rucked up, revealing his legs; one chubby and perfect, the other thin, twisted.

The child was lame.

Missie's eyes filled with tears and she turned away. "Matthew, I don't know what you're trying to do. Please—I want to go home."

"Not yet, not until you've heard me out."

He deposited her in a comfortable chair and went to lean on the mantel. "I've never told this to anyone else," he began—

"You don't owe me any explanations, Matthew."

"Oh, but I do."

His eyes were filled with pain. He lowered them, looking away from Missie as he continued, haltingly.

He'd married back east; a pretty girl with some talent in singing and dancing. After the novelty of marriage wore off, she began to mourn her lost career. She hated San Francisco, hated being a wife. Even worse, she'd hated being a mother.

It was clear his recitation was tearing him to pieces. "Please, Matthew! There's no need to go on with this!"

"But there is, dammit! I've been through hell. Maybe if I get it off my chest—"

Missie settled back, and he continued the dreary story. He'd suspected his wife was seeing another man; neglecting the child, but he hadn't known the extent of her ambitions until he arrived home one night to find a note. She had run off with a member of a traveling troupe of entertainers.

"But the baby—?" Missie burst out with the question before she could stop herself.

"I thought she'd taken him with her. I was home for several hours, trying to think of the best course to take. I don't remember much. I suppose I was half-crazy. The house was suffocating me. I went out and walked up and down the lane. Then I heard a whimpering sound—"

"Oh, Matthew!"

"I found my son in the bushes beside the house. He had been beaten, left for dead. Only his leg—"

Missie's heart bled for him. No wonder Matthew was an embittered man! She remembered his face the night of the play, the way he'd stood with murder in his eyes, leaving her to go backstage.

A case of mistaken identity he'd said.

But who was the woman who'd just left the house?

Matthew answered her unspoken question.

"Cinnie is my sister-in-law. She looks after Joshua through the day, and—sometimes on Thursday nights. The rest of the time, I am with him. I—I feel I owe him every minute I can spare. Cinnie's getting tired of the arrangement. She has a family of her own."

"Then, tomorrow—?"

"She'll be back." He grinned, tiredly. "She always is. But I don't know how the hell I'll get you home."

"I could stay," Missie said in a small voice.

"Missie?" He said her name like a question, and read the answer in her eyes.

Taking her two hands in his, he drew her to her feet, holding her against him. She could feel his heart thudding as he kissed her, gently at first, then in a frenzy; kisses that touched her hair, her nose, her throat, and finally returned to her mouth to hold there, throbbing.

"I didn't mean to do this," he whispered. "Oh, God, Missie, stop me."

He was leaning on a frail reed. The love that Missie had dammed up since her ill-fated marriage had broken its bounds, pouring forth in a flood that would not be stayed. The feel of him, trembling with need, thrilled through her, melting her bones. There was a humming in her ears, like a bee-filled garden on a summer afternoon.

"I don't want to stop you, Matthew," she said honestly.

"Missie! Oh, sweetheart!"

He carried her to his bed and she stiffened with the memory of Arthur Melvin—but only for a moment.

Matthew Blaine, that tough and cynical man, was gentle and tender. He kissed her poor, hurt wrists, tasted the sweetness of her mouth, stroking her until all thought was erased. There was nothing but desire, and a need to share body, breath, and soul.

"Now, Matthew, now—"

They moved together into the blinding ecstasy of fulfillment.

Missie lay awake long after Matthew slept, wondering where their relationship would go from this night. Matthew Blaine was a divorced man—who did not believe in divorce. He had said that he needed her, not that he loved her. He did not approve of working women, or women with careers. Having seen the little boy, she could understand his feelings.

But at the moment, she could only be happy; happy that Matthew Blaine was not a married man; that he'd cared enough to bring her here and tell her his story; that the ghost of Arthur Melvin was laid to rest. She was whole again, and for a time she had helped to heal Matthew's hurts. It was enough for now. She drifted into sleep.

They woke at dawn and made love again. Afterward, they walked together in the still-shadowed lane, stopping to hold each other from time to time, unable to get enough of being together.

"Look," Missie said suddenly, pointing over his shoulder. The distant sky held a rosy glow that was not the sun.

Blaine squinted. "Another fire, I guess. Chinatown, or thereabouts. We don't have to worry about it. Carrington will be there."

Missie laughed and he kissed her again. And while they embraced, the House of Wang was burning to the ground.

Chapter 36

Duke Courtney, business associate of the Wang family, was notified of the fire and went immediately to the scene. The smoke hanging heavily over the ruins was scented; smelling of tea, Oriental spices, incense. Among the embers of the establishment were blackened bronzes, woven baskets, and rattan furniture twisted into tortured shapes. Bales of silk and brocade were charred and still burning. Perhaps, somewhere in the hearts of the bales, were vivid traces of Chinese reds, heavenly blues, shot through with threads of gold. It was too late to save them.

Wang had been one of the city's most respected merchants, his stock of fine quality. Courtney found him viewing the ashes of his life's work, head bowed in sorrow. His tall son, Lee, stood beside him. The boy's clothing was scorched, his features streaked with soot; one hand was bandaged. He had aided the fire fighters until there was no hope of saving anything.

267

Duke put his arm around the older Wang. "Damn it, man, this is a helluva note! What started the fire, do you know?"

The two Chinese, father and son, exchanged glances. "It was arson," Lee said quietly.

"'Arson'? Who would—?" Duke read the boy's eyes. "Oh, my God! Feng Wu—?"

Lee shook his head. Feng Wu was but a small man, of little power. And Feng Wu was dead. He had been found before the burning building, his throat cut from ear to ear. A warning that the arm of Chen was long—

"Goddamn," Duke said helplessly, "Goddamn!"

"He will not be missed. And the building was insured," the elder Wang said gently. "Do not feel distress for us. We shall build again. It is only that so much of beauty was destroyed."

"Have you talked to the police?"

The old man shrugged. "They have been here. They believe the fire was set by the hands of enemies. But I cannot name a name. I have no proof. It is only another occasion of Chinese against Chinese, and will soon be forgotten."

"You can't just calmly put up with this—this crap," Duke said angrily. "I'm going to the police, and, dammit, they'll listen! I've been trying to keep this thing with Missie and Petra under wraps, but by God, I'll testify in court—"

"And the honor of your granddaughter will be lessened," Wang reminded him. "There were bodies found in the fire at the House of Chen. You yourself might suffer embarrassment in revealing your knowledge. Please, my friend, dismiss the matter from your thoughts. As I have said, we shall rebuild."

"How do you know the sonofabitch won't burn it again? There's no guarantee—"

"We can only hope his need for revenge is satisfied."

Duke Courtney left the two men standing in the rubble of their lives and hurried back to his home. He was mad! He was so goddamn mad! And he was also frightened. Feng Wu was dead because he had led the rescuers to Petra, betraying the secret of the tunnels. Petra's letter, asking for help, had incriminated the Wangs. How long would it take Chen and his henchmen to tie Petra in with the Courtneys, or with Missie? Would either of them be safe again on the San Francisco streets?

He breathed a sigh of relief when he saw his house still standing, intact. Hell, what had he expected?

Still, something would have to be done; some action taken.

All morning, Em had been thinking along the same lines. The servants' quarters over the carriage house were filled. That horrible man Duke employed had been given one of the guest rooms, temporarily. She would be needing those rooms when the members of her family arrived from England. Duke should recognize that.

That was the best approach. He would never understand her feelings toward the brute! Blevins absolutely terrified her. He wasn't content to remain in his room, but roved over the house as if it belonged to him. He knocked the dottle from his pipe into her potted plants, scowling as if daring her to mention it. Worse, he'd answered the door, his shirt unbuttoned to show his hairy chest. Em had only glimpsed the bustles of two female would-be callers.

"Who were they? What did they want?"

Sim Blevins shrugged. "How the hell do I know? Me an' them rich-bitches don't speak the same langridge. They just th'owed me a coupla tickets. Here—"

He passed over a pair of calling cards. Mrs. Wilson and her daughter! It was probably a longed-for invitation to their musicale, one of the most prestigious events of the season.

"Did they ask to see me?"

"I told 'em you wuz busy, cleanin' up arter the free-fer-all we had t'other night. They took off like a coupla scalded cats."

"Mister Blevins," Em's anger had overcome her fear of the man. "I do not know why my husband employed you, but it was certainly not with my approval! And I want to make one thing perfectly clear! Your duties do not include those of answering the door.''

The old man thrust out a pugnacious jaw, contempt in small frosty blue eyes. ''An' you, ma'am, kin go straight to hell! Duke Courtney tells me to watch over his wimmen, that's damn sure what I'm gonna do!''

He spat on the floor and rubbed a sleeve across his unshaven mouth. ''You tend t'yer bizness, I'll tend to mine.''

Em fled to her demolished living room, blind with fury. ''Either that old—old pirate goes, or I do,'' she told Petra. ''He's a—a low-class, drunken rounder if I ever saw one!''

''But he helped save Missie and me. Grandfather says—''

''I don't give a—a damn what Duke says,'' Em raged. ''He spits on my floor, he talks like a stevedore, he pinches the maids—and look at my carpet! Dents all over from that—damn peg leg! I feel like yanking it off and beating him over the head with it!''

Sim Blevins, listening outside the door, grinned to himself. If there was anything he didn't have any use for, it was them rich sassiety floozies. But, hell, maybe the little lady wasn't as wishy-washy as he thought. Give her a little more rope and she might shape up to a real woman.

Experimentally, he dug his peg into the hall carpet and gave his bulk a little twist.

There! That oughta give 'er somethin' t'cuss about!

Duke arrived shortly, his expression serious and concerned. Em signaled that she would like to speak to him alone, but her signals were either unnoticed or ignored. He wanted to confer with Sim Blevins. With an exasperated sigh, she left them talking in Duke's office and returned to her work.

Duke told Blevins of the fire at the Wang establishment; Feng Wu found dead at the site—

''No loss,'' Sim Blevins said cheerfully. ''Dirty yaller bastid!''

The blaze, Duke continued, had been set, the traitorous

Chinese killed and left as a warning. Wang was certain Chen was responsible; that it was an act of vengeance.

"My concern," Duke said, "is that he isn't finished with us. I'm worried about Petra, Missie—"

"Then, hell, les' go git the sonofabitch."

"My idea, exactly. If we can get the same group of men together, arm ourselves well, move in—"

"Won't work."

Duke stopped short at the interruption, looking at his friend with puzzled eyes. "Why not?"

"No matter where you look, Chen ain't gonna be there. Hell, you c'd go over Chinatown with a fine comb, you ain't gonna find 'im. Even if you called in the whole goddamn army, you ain't gonna find 'im."

"Then you suggest we just wait for him to come to us?" Duke asked dryly.

"Hell, no. Gimme a coupla hours, and I'll try to come up with sump'n. You stick here with the wimmen till I come back?"

Duke gave his assurance and watched him stump down the walk, looking, with his peg leg, like an unwieldy top. Yet, somehow, he had a lot of faith in him. Beneath that grouchy exterior, he was one helluva man.

Sighing, Duke rose to go see what Em wanted. He had an idea he knew.

Sim Blevins made his way from bar to bar that afternoon. He set his limit at one drink in each. He had to be sober enough to think, and drunk enough to do whatever needed to be done. Night was falling, fog insinuating itself into the streets when he entered a waterfront tavern and bellied up to the bar. Drink in hand, he turned, braced his back against it, surveying the smoke-filled room. His lips parted in a rare, humorless grin as he saw the man he was looking for.

Crossing the room, he greeted him with a slap on the back that nearly knocked him into his drink.

"Sam, Sam Ramos! Long time no see."

Ramos, a quiet man with a villainous face and a scar that lifted his lip in a snarl, greeted him courteously. Ramos, who claimed to be half-Chink, half-Portygee, owned Sim Blevins a great deal—including his life on several occasions. They'd done some smuggling in the old days, in the China trade.

Blevins leaned forward. "Lookin' fer somebody, Sam. Need some connections."

Ramos spread his hands. "I got 'em, you got 'em."

"Who you got in Chinatown?"

By eight o'clock that evening, the whereabouts of Chen was known. Now Blevins had to make a decision. He could go back for Duke and let him in on the fun—

Then he remembered the little ladies in Duke's household. There was always a chance something could go wrong, and they oughta have a man around to protect 'em.

Hell, they could handle this little job by themselves, the two of them, him and Sam. They finished their bottle and, singing a bawdy ballad, lurched out of the tavern and into the fog-filled night.

The next morning, early risers passing the ruins of the house of Wang were startled as the face of a Chinaman, at least eight feet tall, appeared to stare at them in the spiraling mist.

Later, they learned the explanation for the apparition. The body of Chen, former power in the Chinese underworld, hanging from a lamppost, lacked several feet of touching the ground.

Chapter 37

Sim Blevins mentioned none of the details of Chen's demise to his employer. Faced with the story, he only grinned.

"Well, I be damned. Must of made somebody mad with 'im, d'ye think?" His air of assumed innocence sat badly on his battered face. "Well, trouble's over, I reckon. You givin' me my walkin' papers?"

"Hell, no," Duke roared. "You got a job with me as long as you live, you old sonofabitch!"

Em, finally giving in to her husband's will, retired their old yardman, moving Blevins into the carriage house. Sim knew nothing of gardening, but allowed he might as well learn. His opinion of Em Courtney went up a notch as she instructed him, actually working beside him for a while. He hadn't figured she ever used those lilywhite hands! After awhile, she left him to it. He moved happily about the lawn, pruning anything that didn't move, poking holes in the carefully tended grass with his peg.

Better the grass, Em thought wryly, than her carpets! And

the fellow wasn't as fierce as he'd seemed. In a way, he reminded her of someone—someone she'd known in the past.

And Duke seemed happy with the old reprobate's company. In the evening, he joined him in the carriage house and didn't come in until nearly midnight. Through her bedroom window, she could hear them laughing, talking, telling rowdy stories that sometimes got so loud that she was sure the neighbors heard.

She missed Duke sitting opposite her while she did fancy work. He would usually read the paper, then fall asleep in his chair. But Blevin's company seemed to rejuvenate him—

Em blushed as she thought of the ardent lover who returned from those visits to the carriage house. Duke was young again, and she wasn't doing too badly for a woman her age!

If she could just keep Blevins out of the house and out of the sight of her friends, there would be no problems. At least, not with him—

There was still the matter of Petra and Lee Wang.

Em loved her granddaughter dearly, and wanted nothing but the best for the child. She'd come to terms with Petra's flawed background. But there was surely no need to flaunt it! Petra's Chinese blood wasn't all that apparent. As pretty as she was, she could marry a man of good family and breeding.

No matter how Westernized the Wang family had become, adopting civilized dress, reversing their surnames with their first in American style, they were still Asiatic. Lee Wang was still Wang Li!

Petra thought she was in love with Lee. Of course she would feel that way. He had aided in her rescue, thus becoming a heroic figure. Em herself felt gratitude toward the boy. Duke had voiced his approval of him. But Duke was blind as a bat when it came to looking at the whole picture!

Em could just imagine the headlines! Petra Channing, granddaughter of the well-known Courtney family, to wed son of Chinese importer.

And the wedding! Em would go through with it, see that it

was a memorable day for Petra, but it would be humiliating. A number of her friends would not attend. Some of those who did would be laughing behind their hands. And how many of the Wang family would appear?

Her living room could be filled with yellow faces. Those people were great ones for ceremonial occasions. They might even stage a parade right before her front door! Em had a wild vision of bride and groom departing on the back of a writhing paper dragon—

She blushed as she answered the door and found Lee Wang on the step. The boy was dressed soberly, conservatively, one hand wrapped in clean gauze. Em felt foolish over her recent thoughts. Taking him into the sitting room, she went to call Petra. The girl's eyes lit up when she heard Lee was waiting.

Lee watched Petra come down the stairs, feeling as if his heart would burst inside him. She was so beautiful, this little ivory figurine. He wanted to go to her, enfold her in his arms, protect her for the rest of his life. Instead, he bowed formally, asking after her health.

He had wished to extend his well-wishes earlier, but circumstances had prevented his attendance upon her. Perhaps she would care to take the air? It was a beautiful, bright day—

Em watched them go, her heart sinking. It was clear they'd forgotten her existence the minute they saw each other. It was going to be harder than she thought. But given time—

What if he proposed today, and Petra accepted him?

Em tried to erase her worries, heading for her living room. It was being freshly papered, palest blue with silver leaves. She had ordered a couch in silver, a carpet in deeper blue; throw pillows to match the carpet. Duke had told her to spare no expense in her refurbishing.

Maybe he and his rowdy crew had done her a favor, after all. The house would be perfect when her sisters arrived. She was anxious for them to see her gracious home at its best.

—Unless she was forced to hold a Chinese wedding—

Lee Wang was silent as he skillfully negotiated his carriage down the treacherous slopes of Nob Hill. He had Duke's permission to court his granddaughter, but he sensed that the aristocratic Mrs. Courtney did not share her husband's opinion in the matter. It was possible Petra didn't, either. That night in the carriage, when he had held her, kissed her, she'd been through a terrible time. Now, he watched her from the corner of an eye, wondering what she was thinking.

Shy Petra was agonizing over Lee Wang's feelings toward her. Since her rescue, her dreams had been filled with him; his gentleness, his caring. Perhaps he had only been trying to comfort her after what she'd experienced. Maybe she'd built something from nothing, as she did with Matthew Blaine. A tinge of pink coral traced her cheekbones as she tried to think of a topic of conversation.

"Your hand. Is it badly burned?"

"A few blisters. It is healing well."

"Grandfather told me about the fire. Was—was there anything left?"

"Nothing." Lee tried to smile, but there was a haunting sadness in his eyes. "We are clearing the site, now. It will soon be open for business again."

"I feel that I am responsible," she whispered. "I've brought so much trouble to everyone. Your father must hate me!"

"On the contrary. He requested that I bring you to tea at our home. My sister is there to serve as chaperone. If you have no objections—"

"I would love it," she burst out. Again there was a delightful stain of coral as she blushed. "It would be—very nice."

The home of the Wangs was large. The central part of the building consisted of two stories. From it, long, low wings extended to either side; jutting bays forming interesting nooks that were carefully landscaped.

The elder Wang met them at the door. Though his welcome

was formal, it was warm and accepting. Lee's sister, Sara, did not stand on formality. A sweet-faced miss of fourteen, she threw her arms impulsively around Petra.

"You are even prettier than Lee said you were!"

It was Lee's turn to blush.

Their tea, Wang explained, was that once reserved only for royal persons. Water-pale in thin porcelain cups, it was delicious. Petra felt at ease in the household. It was almost as if she'd come home.

After an hour of pleasant conversation, young Sara took her to tour the house. It was beautifully appointed, light and airy, none of the gewgaws and gimcracks so popular to the day. The rooms were furnished in Western style, but with the Oriental eye for space. In each, a single statuette, or a porcelain vase, was a focal point.

"This was our mother's room," Sara said, opening a door on the second floor. Here, it might have been a Chinese household. The walls were of silk, brushed with a pattern of chrysanthemums, delicate as mist. Sara opened a closet door to reveal a row of cheongsams, the straight cut, high-necked Chinese gowns of a mandarin lady.

Petra's eyes filled with sudden tears as she realized how Lee's mother must have felt in a new and bewildering country. Lonely and lost—

They returned to the others, and the elder Wang suggested Lee show Petra the gardens, firmly telling Sara to aid in clearing the tea things. Thus the two young people found themselves alone in a small clearing on the rear lawn.

The clearing was masked by trees and shrubs. All flowered in the spring, Lee told Petra, and the air would be sweet as honey. Within the clearing, a small fountain spilled into a pool spanned by a delicately wrought arched bridge. Colorful Chinese carp lurked in the shadows beneath.

"My mother would sit here for hours," Lee said quietly. "It was her special place. My father built it for her with his own hands. And now it is my special place. I would like it to be yours, too—"

Petra stood transfixed, her heart beating too rapidly, not daring to believe what he was saying.

"I have asked your grandfather's permission to speak to you, Petra. Forgive me, if I am too forward, if I presume too much. I—would like to ask you to share my life—"

"To marry you?"

"If you will have me."

"Have you! Oh, Lee! Lee!" Tears were spilling down her cheeks as she reached out to him, blindly. "Lee, I've thought of nothing else since that night! I was afraid you were just being kind—"

Then he was holding her, kissing away the tears that fell like blessed rain, seeking the small trembling mouth that met his so eagerly. Kisses that tasted of salt. If they hadn't, they would have been too sweet to bear.

They finally sank down on the grass, and Petra lay within the circle of his arms as they discussed their future. The business must be rebuilt, for the sake of their sons and their sons' sons. Lee's father was old, tired. Therefore, much of the task of building must be lifted from his shoulders. Their marriage could not take place until the work was under way, perhaps one month, two—

Petra, starry-eyed, did not mind the delay. It would give her time to plan, to dream. She lifted her mouth to his again, feeling the throbbing of his need as he held her close. Life would be all the sweeter for the waiting.

The master of the House of Chen had done more than burn a building for the sake of revenge. He'd given Em Courtney exactly what she wanted.

Time.

Chapter 38

Missie Narvaéz was the first to learn of Petra's engagement. The young couple was waiting for her when she left work, their faces wreathed in smiles. She guessed at their news before they opened their mouths.

She was glad for them, she thought wearily, as she took the cable car home. Someone should be happy—

After their idyllic night together, Missie had gone with Matthew Blaine to the office, helping him do the work he'd left the previous evening. As she blissfully set to the job, she caught him watching her, an odd expression on his face. When the reporters came straggling in, greeting her with expressions of pleasure at her return, she'd accepted their assessment as a matter of course. It had never crossed her mind that Matthew had no intention of rehiring her—

Then Elizabeth Anspaugh sailed into the office, sweeping between the desks until she reached Missie. Her voice was a little too loud, officious, as she demanded space to advertise an upcoming meeting. A noted speaker was coming from the east, to expound upon women's rights.

"I would like you to cover the meeting," Miss Anspaugh said. "We need someone sympathetic to our views."

After she'd gone, Missie took some papers to Blaine's desk, standing close, expecting him to touch her hand behind the cover of her skirts. Instead, he looked up at her, his face blank and expressionless.

"Miss Narvaéz, I'd like to have a word with you after the others are gone."

Missie waited impatiently for the last in the office to leave. When the door closed behind him, she hurried toward Matthew, longing for the feel of his arms around her, his mouth on hers—

Instead, he remained seated, looking at the papers on his desk as he shuffled them.

"Missie, I'm sorry about last night. It won't happen again."

She stood frozen, hearing him out. "It won't work out for us. Dammit, I've been thinking about it all day; the way you stepped right back into your job; your book; this—this damned women's rights business. I've done you a disservice—"

A disservice? He had killed something inside her, that was all!

"Not at all, Matthew," she said in a brittle voice. "You forget, I'm a widow, an emancipated woman. I consider my moral behavior—or lack thereof, my own responsibility. Thank you for a pleasant interlude."

"Missie, you realize this doesn't affect your job. I hope we can continue on a friendly basis—"

"Of course!" Her smile was too hard, too brilliant. "And I shall not even ask for overtime. That would put me in an entirely different category, wouldn't it?"

She left the room, and Matthew watched her go. He felt torn, helpless. She'd taken it better than he'd expected, but there was something different in her behavior, something—hard, that he didn't think was in character.

Maybe he'd hurt her, putting it to her so baldly, but, good God, what else could he do?

He drew a book from his desk drawer. It was an advance copy, sent to the *Examiner* as a courtesy from its publisher. He sat looking at it for a long time, the letters that announced title and author blurring before his eyes.

The Survivors, by Melissa McLeod.

Last night, he'd forgotten everything except that he loved the girl; that he desired her above all. He needed a wife, little Joshua needed a mother. For a few hours, he had dared to dream. The arrival of the book had set his thinking straight.

Missie Narvaéz was an ambitious young woman, independent, and embarked on a career. He had gone that route before. It could only bring unhappiness to all concerned—especially, to the girl he loved.

He took the book home from the office and placed it carefully under a pile of shirts in a drawer. He would read it later, but not while his pain at losing her was still fresh.

Cinnie, a compulsive cleaner, had once disposed of some important papers. She had orders to leave his room untouched. Now, Matthew looked at the unmade bed, the pillow still dented from where Missie's head had rested; remembering that her hair had the scent of summer wheat, that her soft shoulder smelled of flowers—

That night, he slept on a cot in Joshua's room.

Missie left the cable car and walked toward Polk, the heels of her small boots clicking out a tattoo. She had no memory of the journey from the office to her neighborhood. It was already dark, due to the season, the night air chill against her hot face.

Once again, she'd made a fool of herself. She had a penchant for falling in love with men who did not want her. Arthur Melvin had wanted Tamsen, marrying Missie through spite. Matthew Blaine had wanted—

—just exactly what he got! And it had been freely given.

To Matthew, a woman was only good for one thing, to satisfy a—a damn man's physical desires! And she'd gone right along with him!

Her steps slowed as she remembered how willingly she'd gone to him, curving to meet him in the act of love, wanting to become one flesh. She'd given herself sincerely, her heart along with her body, asking nothing in return.

Well, what had she expected. Certainly not this—to be dismissed like a—a paid prostitute!

She reached the steps that led up to her rooms over the bakery, praying that Frau Schmitt wouldn't stop her before she reached the apartment; that the old woman didn't notice her absence the previous night. Perhaps she could say she stayed with Petra—

No, she wasn't going to complicate her life with lies! As she'd told Matthew, she was an emancipated woman, responsible for her own behavior. What she did, where, and with whom, was nobody's business! It wasn't as if she were a virgin!

Missie climbed the stairs and made it to her door without Frau Schmitt's intervention. She washed her hot face in cold water. It did nothing to remove the red splashes of anger and humiliation from her cheeks. She was frowning at herself in the mirror, trying to see an indication of a harlot in her blue-eyed reflection, when there was a knock at the door.

It opened on Larry Hiller. He had just returned from Sacramento and couldn't wait to see her. There'd been no time to explain his leaving. He wanted her to know—

"I have my job back, Larry," she interrupted. "I'll see you tomorrow, at the office. Now, I'm—"

He interrupted with a whistle. "Old hard-nose rehired you? How the hell did you manage that?"

How? She swallowed a hysterical urge to laugh. What would Larry Hiller think if she said, "I slept with him. Now I've got great job security—if only I remember my place!"

"He just changed his mind," she said evenly.

"That's good news! So, why don't we go out and celebrate?"

"I've had a tough day, Larry. I'm sorry. Another time—"

"How about tomorrow night?"

He looked so eager. And, dear God, she had to get rid of him!

"That will be fine."

The door was closing against him. He leaned around it to give her a peck on the cheek. "See you," he said happily. She heard him whistling down the stairs.

Maybe there was something in her makeup that looked like a woman who could be had. Troubled, she locked the door. At least, she thought drearily, this day was almost over. Nothing more could happen—

Missie wasn't hungry, but she knew she should eat. She rummaged through the cupboard. Nothing but a few crackers and some cheese. She would have to do some shopping sometime soon. She'd just taken her first bite and was trying to swallow it when there was another knock.

Larry Hiller had come back! She couldn't face him again! She would probably burst into tears, or send him packing!

"Who is it?" she called.

"Me, Frau Schmitt. Hurry! My arms are full vith things."

Missie opened the door. The German woman had a plate of sweet rolls, a box, and several letters in her arms. A man had come today, an ugly man who looked like a pirate, bringing these things addressed to Missie. The rolls had been Frau Schmitt's own idea. No, no, she couldn't stay. She must put the finishing touches to another wedding cake.

The sweet rolls called for coffee. Suddenly they seemed more palatable than dry crackers and cheese. Missie put the coffeepot on and turned to her mail. A letter from her mother. She opened it. It contained only a brief, ecstatic note saying that they'd all be together soon. The second letter was from Brown, Halpert and Brown. She laid it aside to read later, hoping it wasn't another impassioned plea from young Stuyvesant. She was through with men!

Missie turned her attention to the box. It, too, was from

New York. And with a sinking sensation in the pit of her stomach, she knew what it was!

The package was obstinate. She tore a nail, then went for a kitchen knife to slip between the wrappings. At last, the book lay before her.

The Survivors, by Melissa McLeod.

She surveyed it with mixed emotions. It was her life's work, her dream. And it would probably ruin the rest of her life, so far as her family was concerned.

She had to remember she was an emancipated woman, responsible for her own actions—

Missie opened the letter from Brown, Halpert and Brown. It stated that she would receive a first copy of *The Survivors* under separate cover, and requested that she come to New York for a press conference and book signing on the twentieth of November.

Her family would be docking in New York on the fifteenth. They would already be entrained, on their way home. If she went, they would probably pass somewhere en route to their separate destinations.

She couldn't do that! She must stay and face the music. She would write her publisher to that effect, tomorrow.

That night, she read her own words in print, seeing them with the eyes of Em, Arab, and Tamsen: the survivors who were now aged, respectable, and happy. How could she ever have thought that dredging up the past would do them honor?

She was heavy-eyed and languid the next day at work, avoiding Matthew Blaine's gaze, trying to cope with Larry Hiller's cheerful chatter. That night, she kept her promise to Larry. They took in dinner and a show. He seemed more affectionately attentive as the evening progressed, and she finally pleaded illness so that he would take her home.

She had still not written Brown, Halpert and Brown to deny their request.

Another day at the office, not enjoyed, but endured. Skillful footwork to avoid another date with Larry. Carrington hovering over her desk. She was beginning to think men thought of nothing else—

And then she left the office to find Petra and Lee waiting for her with their news, faces shining with hope and faith in their future. This was what love should be! This!

And it was something she had never known, would never know.

To hell with everyone, she thought savagely. To hell with Matthew Blaine—and any other man! If her family chose to view her book as something scurrilous and ugly rather than as she'd intended it to be, then—to hell with them!

She had a career ahead of her, and she intended to make it a great one! She would show them all!

In the morning, she mailed a letter to Brown, Halpert and Brown, and purchased a round-trip ticket to New York City.

HOMECOMING

Chapter 39

On November fifteenth, *The Hollander,* a glistening top-of-the-line Dutch ship, approached the mouth of New York Harbor. The weather was cold, damp, with a sharp wind. Many of the passengers, seasoned travelers, preferred to remain inside, packing last-minute items in their cabins, fortifying themselves for the landing at the ship's bar, playing cards in a corner of the ship's glittering salon.

Those who were seeing the coast of North America for the first time, and those who were returning after a long absence, lined the rails. Among the latter were Dan and Tamsen Tallant, Juan and Arab Narvaéz, the old ex-madam, Nell, and her two young protégés, Maggie and Sean Murphy. The sea was choppy, the distant land—if it was there—lost in a gray horizon.

Nell, garbed in purple velvet and a voluminous matching cloak she considered fitting garb for a ladyship's homecoming, leaned on the rail. The feathers of her imposing hat whipped in the breeze, her heavy features crimson from the cold.

"Freeze th' balls off a brass monkey," she grumbled. "Hell, dunno what we's standin' out here fer. Won't git us there no faster."

Tamsen hid a smile, knowing Nell wouldn't miss the first sight of her homeland for anything. "You can go below," she suggested. "We'll fetch you—"

"Hell, no! You folks wanna freeze yer butts off, that's awright by me. I'm stayin'." Nell slapped the top of her head to settle her hat, and glared into the mist.

"I believe she's more excited than any of us," Tamsen whispered to Dan.

He smiled down at her, thinking how lovely she was, with her cheeks stained rose, dark eyes sparkling.

"Getting pretty excited yourself, aren't you?"

"I suppose I am. But we've been away so long, I've almost forgotten what it's like. Home is wherever you are, Dan."

"And I haven't always been there," he said softly. "I'm sorry, Tamsen, I'm going to make it up to you."

Tamsen leaned against his shoulder, contented. She'd married a tough, virile soldier of fortune who'd spent his life meeting challenges. It was, in part, his efforts that brought about the acquisition of Alaska for the United States; of Hawaii. He'd played a role in surveying for the railroad in Australia, served as an emissary to Britain on Australia's behalf; had done a brief stint in India at Queen Victoria's request.

Now he was retiring from his profession. They were going home to San Francisco. She sighed, the far-off past weighing heavily on her mind.

But Em was there now. And according to Em, everything had changed. There would be no one to recognize her, no one to remember—

Arab was thinking along the same lines. She'd first seen

the California city under terrible circumstances: as a child who had been molested, battered into submission by a traveling minister, with his wife's connivance. Under the guise of delivering her to a school, of which he would be headmaster, he'd chained her in his wagon.

"Arabella McLeod, you must submit to the will of God, become as a handmaiden to His servant—"

His words, uttered all those years past, burned in her ears. She could feel his loathsome hands on her body, even now! If Lola Montez had not heard her singing hymns at a revival on a muddy street corner; if she hadn't bought her to sing and dance with her troupe; if they hadn't gone to Spain, where she'd met Juan—

She shivered, and Juan's arm circled her waist. She looked up at him, seeing his dark, bearded face, still ravaged from the wound he received in India. "Are you cold?" he asked.

"Just—excited."

"And happy?"

"Happy," she agreed.

She had lied a little. Her thoughts went back to England; to Luka. To Luka, who was—different, the child she had loved to the exclusion of all else; the child who had needed her.

Luka needed her mother no longer. She was happily married and expecting a baby. Now Arab must think of her middle daughter, Missie—oh, how glad she would be to see her!—and Juan. She had neglected him, thinking only of herself when he had needed her—

Tears welled briefly in her eyes and she blinked them away. Juan, turning to her, touched a finger to the tip of her small nose.

"You look like a bunny-rabbit," he teased.

"Juan!" she bridled.

He grinned, knowing his vain, wrong-headed little wife. "A very delightful bunny-rabbit," he said tenderly. "With slanty green eyes," he touched her hair, "and fur like sunshine. But I'm afraid you are cold. Do you wish to go in out of the weather?"

"No, Juan. I don't want to miss—anything."

As the older members of the group looked inward, remembering the past, young Maggie and Sean Murphy were facing their future. They'd scarcely left their cabin during the voyage, taking their delight in each other. The small, abused street thief and an impoverished Irish lad were looking forward to a land of opportunity. Hand in hand, they gazed raptly into the distance.

Nell watched them from the corner of her eye, remembering Dusty, the frail little man she'd loved and lived with for years, finally marrying him on his deathbed. She tried to recall how long she'd been a widow. Ten-twelve years, she reckoned, since they buried Dusty on the grounds of the station on the Billabong.

For a time, she'd felt he was close by. If she just looked fast enough, she'd see the leetle bastard standin' there, a silly grin on his face at bein' caught out. That notion had kept her going. Now, he had become a faded picture in her mind. Nell felt old, lonely. She shook her massive head.

Hell, she'd find him again in Frisco. Wait'll she opened up her bar. Dusty'd be the first in line—

"Look!" It was Maggie shrilling and dancing with excitement. "Lor' lumme! 'Oo's 'er?"

A giant figure had appeared in the mist, holding a lamp high, the figure of a woman. Her light, blurring into the gray day, seemed to be guiding them in.

Dan broke the awed hush that enveloped them. "It's a monument, a statue. I've read about it. They call it, 'Liberty Enlightening the World.' It was given to America by France, to celebrate the centenary of our independence in 1886. It marks the entrance to the harbor. Good, God, what a magnificent piece of work!"

"It's like an omen," Tamsen said mistily. "As if we're being welcomed home."

"Damn fine figger of a woman," Nell put in. "Hell, I coulda posed fer that myself!"

She looked complacently down at her billows of purple velvet, and her companions laughed affectionately.

A little tug came out to meet the ship, a pilot coming aboard. It was still a long time before the buildings of New York appeared through the mist, and *The Hollander* docked. Now, aboard the white ship, there was pandemonium. Steamer trunks and luggage appeared on deck. Passengers lined the rail to wave at acquaintances below. The gray skies seemed to brighten, rays of a wavery sun peeping through. The faces on the dock were clearly visible.

"Wisht there was somebody to meet us," Nell said wistfully.

"Just wait until we get off the train in San Francisco," Tamsen comforted her. "Em, Duke, and Missie—"

"Looky there!" Nell interrupted her, pointing a pudgy finger directly below, where the gangplank was being lowered. "Lookut all them cameras set up. Must be some big cheese aboard, mebbe one o' them Royal Hineys—"

She stopped, perplexed. A man had approached the purser, who was pointing directly at them. Then there seemed to be a number staring in their direction.

Nell looked behind her, to either side. It was clearly their group which had been singled out. "Whaddaya think?" she asked Dan, "what th' hell's goin' on?"

"I haven't the slightest idea," Dan confessed. "Not unless one of us has been taken for someone else. There must be at least ten cameras. And I'm certain those gentlemen are reporters." He pointed to a group of men with press cards in their hatbands, talking vociferously to each other.

Nell's face cleared. "Hell," she said archly, "I know what th' hooraw's about! They's waitin' fer me. Don't git many ladyships in these parts! I look awright fer a innerview?" Her hands went to her hat.

Dan looked doubtful as he picked up the luggage. "Sean,

can you handle Nell's trunk? Juan, I believe these are yours. Tamsen, Arab, why don't you go on ahead. We'll follow."

Tamsen was disappointed. She wanted to be beside Dan when they stepped foot on American soil again. But she could see his point. It would be wise to go ahead of the cumbersome luggage. And Arab was already on her way.

Tamsen joined her sister, taking her hand, smiling at her, sharing her anticipation.

Then, midway of the gangplank, Tamsen heard her name.

"Tamsen! Hey, Tamsen, over here!"

She peered into the crowd. No one was meeting them. It was not a voice she recognized—

It was followed by a series of bright flashes, full in her eyes, blinding her, a strange whooshing sound, a smell of gunpowder. Smoke rose above a number of black boxes set on tripods, the photographers behind those boxes holding bulbs in one hand, flash-bars high in the other.

Oh, dear God!

"Smile, Arab, honey! Give us a big smile—"

Tamsen and Arab turned as one, trying to fight their way back through the descending passengers, their only thought to reach Dan and Juan. A hand caught at Tamsen's shoulder. She turned to see a grinning young man with a card in his hatband.

"Just what is the meaning of this?" she raged, "let me go!"

"Hey, don't get sore at me! Just trying to do my job. What say you girls give me an exclusive. Then I'll try to keep the others off your necks—"

Tamsen stared at him. He made no more sense than if he'd been speaking in a strange language. Perhaps he was a madman—but if he was, a number of men who were similarly afflicted waited below.

"I do not have the slightest idea what you are talking about!"

"You are Tamsen Tallant?" A departing passenger bumped

against him, and he clung to the rail with one hand, her shoulder with the other.

"I am."

"What's your opinion of the book? Does it tell it like it was? Are you going to make personal appearances while you are in New York? What are your plans for—?"

"Book?" Tamsen was genuinely startled. 'What book?"

The reporter's grin widened. "You don't know? Hot damn! It's called *The Survivors*, written by some relative of yours. First edition sold out, lines at the bookstores a mile long. Hell, you ladies are the hottest thing to hit New York in a long time. Take my advice, you can write your own ticket! Talks, appearances—you can make a bundle, especially you! Don't get many ex-madams on the podium—"

The Survivors—written by some relative—hottest thing in town—ex-madams on the podium—

Tamsen listened, dazed, remembering the letter Arab received from Em, concerned over Missie's suffragette activities.

I have heard she is writing a scandalous book, based on Tamsen's life, Em had written. *At least, we can have the satisfaction of knowing it will never reach the public. I myself prefer male authors and do not believe women's minds are suited to the art—*

Evidently they were!

Anger blazed through Tamsen's small body. Anger at Missie, at this man who kept his hand on her in such a familiar manner, looking at her with knowing, worldly eyes.

She moved quickly, shoving him hard in the stomach. Caught off balance, he rolled down the gangway, taking a number of people with him. Gathering her skirts, Tamsen ran upward, back to the deck to find Dan.

The flash-bars exploded from below, catching a shot of extremely nice ankles. The photograph would be viewed over breakfast by the readers of each paper the next morning.

Chapter 40

Tamsen and Dan, Arab and Juan, Nell and her protégés, were the last to leave the ship. They waited, hoping the reporters below would leave. Still, they clustered there, passing a bottle between them to keep warm.

The entire family was in a state of shock, Arab weeping softly and steadily. They had come home with such hopes, thinking to live out their lives happily, respectably, and now this! Their shameful pasts would be revealed to all eyes. And it was Arab's daughter, Missie, who had brought about this state of affairs.

"How could she," Arab moaned. "Oh, how could she do this to us! Our lives will be ruined!"

"Oh, hell," Nell growled. "This here's New York we're talkin' about, buncha sissy-britches! Californy's clear on t'other side of the country. Them books ain't gonna show up out there. If they did, who'd read 'em? Them folks out there works. They ain't got no time fer literachoor!"

Dan, having been in communication with Duke, learning of

the vast changes that had taken place, disagreed with her, but he kept his thoughts to himself.

The important thing right now was to get off the ship, bypassing the waiting reporters. There was no point in giving interviews until they'd seen the book. Right now, Dan Tallant would like to punch a few noses. But that would only result in worse publicity. They must try to handle this in a way to draw as little attention as possible.

"Hell," Nell said, "jes' foller me!"

Linking arms with Maggie on one side and Sean Murphy on the other, she charged down the gangplank, scattering the reporters clustered directly before it. Then she disposed her troops like a general. "Sean, you an' Maggie take that side, I'll han'le this'n. Keep 'em back—now, let 'er r-r-rip!"

Nell smashed one massive shoulder into a persistent reporter, sending him rolling. Switching her heavy rear, she caught another below the belt. "Who-o-f!" The breath went out of him as Nell turned her attention to a third. He backed away from the purple-clad old woman, the feathers on her hat shaking ominously.

A flash-bar went off, another. Nell went for the photographers, who grabbed their precious cameras and ran for their lives.

At the other side, Maggie and Sean had given a good account of themselves. Maggie hadn't grown up on the streets of Liverpool without learning the art of attack. "Bloody barstids," she screeched, kicking the gentlemen of the press in what she considered appropriate spots. Sean, fists flailing, also gave a good account of himself.

Dan and Juan had rushed their ladies through the lane the others cleared. Seeing them safely away, Nell and her protégés fell in behind them, walking backward, presenting a united front that no reporter was dedicated enough to breach.

When they finally reached their hotel, they learned that

inquiries had been made. Some enterprising newsman had called every hotel, asking if the party had reservations. The manager, not wishing any notoriety, had outsmarted him. The party was registered under the names of Smith, Brown, Miller, and Jones. Their meals would be sent to their rooms in order to protect their anonymity.

Dan Tallant's first act was to employ a bellboy. He was to go to a bookstore—every bookstore in town, if necessary and return with a copy of *The Survivors*.

His next step was to comfort his bewildered wife.

"I can't understand it," she kept saying. "This isn't like Missie."

"If she did it," Dan said angrily, "and if the book is—is scandalous, as Em suggested, she needs her bottom paddled. Good God! To put us through a thing like that—"

"I have an idea it isn't over," Tamsen said in a small voice. "Dan, we don't have to go to San Francisco. We could go back to England—"

"And run away? That isn't like you, Tam. Besides, if the book's popular enough to cause the ruckus it did today, it'd follow us. There's Em to think of—"

"It's supposed to be about me," Tamsen said slowly, "maybe they won't connect me with Em at all. If it's the story of my life—"

"It's so tied up with Arab and Em that sometimes I've felt like I had three wives," Dan reminded her. "The cameramen were photographing Arab, too. And what did the reporter say?"

"'You ladies are the hottest thing to hit New York in a long time,'" Tamsen repeated, reluctantly. "Dana, Missie couldn't have gone that far back into the past! Most of the—the bad times, took place before she was born."

"Don't you remember how Missie and Dusty always had their heads together when she was little? Missie scribbling notes? I would imagine it begins with Dusty's advent into your lives."

"Oh, dear God," Tamsen whispered, "poor Arab! Poor Em!"

"As soon as I get a look at that book," Dan said decisively, "I'm going to wire the Courtneys. If it's as bad as I'm afraid it is, judging from our reception, I'm going to sue the hell out of the publisher."

"You can't do that! It would ruin Missie!"

"And just what the devil has the girl done to you? To her mother? To Em?"

"The past is like a ghost, isn't it? It keeps coming back to haunt you. I don't mind so much for myself, Dan. It's what it will do to you. We were going to San Francisco to retire, to live peacefully, to make a quiet life for ourselves—"

"We still can. This will blow over."

Tamsen raised tear-filled eyes to his. "And whenever you go down the street, someone will say, 'There goes Dan Tallant, a man who has worked directly under presidential order. Did you know his wife was an entertainer in a bawdy house? An ex-madam?' And God only knows what else has been raked up! The way I blackmailed you—"

"Which you couldn't have done if I hadn't been blackmailable! Hey, remember me? I'm the roughneck who'd tackle any job, even if it took being on the wrong side of the law to handle it. There's so much blood on my hands that—"

"And that just might be in the book, too," Tamsen reminded him.

"We haven't seen it. Let's read it before we go making mountains out of molehills. Take it slow. Right now, let's try out that bed. Those bunks on the ship left a lot to be desired. And now that I'm alone with my wife—"

"A most un-respectable wife," Tamsen said, trying to smile.

"That's what makes it exciting," Dan grinned. "Adds a little spice. Never was one for respectable women myself. They're so damned dull!"

"And I am not?"

"Never," he said, huskily. "Whoever she is, whatever she's been, that's one thing I can truthfully say about my love. She's never been dull. She's a wonderful, enchanting mystery that I have to solve over and over again. And, with your permission, I'd like to give it another try."

"Dan, you fool!" She went into his arms, and for a time, they forgot the world outside that seemed to be battering on their walls, wanting into their private lives.

The bellboy returned much later, his face dark with disappointment. There was not a single copy of *The Survivors* to be found. At each shop, there was a waiting list. Supposedly, a second edition was expected within the next several weeks.

That night, they all met in the Tallant suite for a family conference. The contents of the book were still an unknown quantity. It was impossible to wait until it appeared on the stands again. Their train compartments had already been reserved. They were to leave on the morrow. But with the enterprising newsmen, it was possible that they'd face the same scene when they boarded the train.

The bellboy was sent to the station to check connections. He managed to change their accommodations to a train leaving in the small hours of the morning. That suited them all.

They slipped out of a rear entrance and into waiting carriages under cover of darkness, boarding the train with no problems. Their first visit to New York City had lasted less than a day. They left like thieves in the night.

Only after they entrained did Dan remember he hadn't sent a wire to Em Courtney. It was probably just as well. Maybe the flap over the book, as Nell had said, was restricted to the East Coast.

He hoped to God it was, and that there was no reason to have upset Em.

Em Courtney had already received the shock of her life.

Her living room was now complete, the painting and

papering done, the carpet laid. She was supervising the placement of the furniture when a knock sounded at her door. Thinking it to be a lamp she'd ordered delivered, she left Petra and the maids at work and hurried to the door, not bothering to remove her coverall.

The young man on the step smiled at her engagingly. He liked what he saw: a pretty woman, whose looks certainly belied her years. Soft blond hair, faintly touched with silver, escaped to frame a gentle face of aristocratic beauty. Hal Milledge stepped to one side, motioning to the photographer who had set up his equipment on the walk. The man pressed a bulb, a light flashed, smoke spiraled into the air.

Em took a step backward. "Whatever in the world!"

Her caller touched his hat. "Hal Milledge, ma'am. *New York Journal.*"

Em wiped her hands uncertainly on her apron. "I don't understand—"

"I want to talk to you—about *The Survivors.*"

The woman's face was suddenly panicked. " 'Survivors'! Dear God! An accident? The ship?"

"No, ma'am, the book. Since you figure in it prominently, I'd like to ask a few questions. How do you feel about this being made public? It's well written, of course! Especially, the rape scene. Then, when you stand up to the Indians on the trail—"

"Oh, my God!"

The woman seemed to wither before his eyes, the door slammed against him. Milledge was not too disappointed. He already had a dossier on Duke Courtney, prominent San Francisco businessman. Now, he had a photograph of the third sister, the woman nobody had been able to find. Hearst, still in New York, had read the book—and recognized his old friend, Duke Courtney. He passed his knowledge on to Milledge, who hot-footed it here. He regretted not meeting the boat, but this was a real scoop. It made a damn good story.

It would have made a better one had he known the woman on the other side of the door had leaned against it for a moment, then slumped to the floor in a dead faint.

Chapter 41

Petra found Em lying crumpled against the door. She sent one of the maids screaming for Sim Blevins. He carried the frail little woman to her bed, where Petra tried to revive her with smelling salts.

"Hell, try some whiskey!"

Em woke, sputtering, then put her hand over her mouth.

"Go away," she whispered. "Just leave me alone." Tears seeped from beneath her blue-veined lids.

"We'd better get a doctor," Petra said in a low voice.

"No," Em said. "No! Just get Duke! I want Duke."

Blevins went to the office to fetch him. "Don't know what th' hell happened," he explained on the way home. Em had answered the door. They had heard her talking to a man. The door closed and she didn't return. Petra found her on the floor. She was awake, now, but she wasn't talking.

Duke had left a pretty, girlish wife behind him that morning. Em was pleased with the progress of her redecoration, filled with anticipation over her family's imminent arrival. He returned to find an aging, feeble woman, eyes sunken, plucking at her quilt with nervous fingers.

Shooing Petra from the room with one gesture, Duke sank down beside the bed, his blue eyes filled with alarm.

"What is it, Em? Damn it, what's wrong?"

"It's over, Duke. Our life is over!"

He grasped her shoulders, giving her a little shake. "Em, what are you talking about? Goddamnit! Try to make some sense!"

In a low, dreary whisper, she told him of her caller; the reporter all the way from New York, the questions he'd asked. Missie's book had been published—

Duke Courtney sagged in relief. "Is that all?"

Em sat up, showing signs of life for the first time. " 'All'! Duke Courtney, do you realize what this will do to us? We'll be notorious! Our friends—"

"Will still be our friends, sweetheart. If they're not, then they weren't worth a damn anyway."

"Your business—"

"Won't be harmed at all. If it is, hell, I'll retire. Been wanting to, anyway."

Em dissolved into tears. "You don't understand. I've tried so hard to—to be somebody. Now it will all come out; everything I've tried to hide. Duke, we're going to have to sell our home, move away—"

"Em, do you remember when you practically proposed to a mean, hot-tempered, hard-drinking two-fisted young heller? How you took off with him, on foot, going into the wilds— and dragging little Martha along? We were dirt poor, then. You ashamed of that?"

"Those were the happiest days of my life."

"Then it's Donald Alden you're ashamed of?"

"He was an honorable man, caught in a trap of someone else's making. No," Em's head came up. "He was a good man."

"Then it's Martha. You're ashamed of Martha."

"No, never!"

"If you hadn't been raped, you wouldn't have Martha. And rape isn't all that unusual. It's happened to other women."

Em's face was red, now. "Please, Duke—"

He went on, inexorably. "You're embarrassed about Tamsen's profession, is that it? Because she entertained in a cantina to put food on your table? Because she ran a bawdy house to set you up in style, so you could marry a senator?"

Em put her hands to her ears. "You make me sound so terrible!"

He pulled her against him, groaning. "You're not terrible, sweetheart. It's just that you put so much emphasis on the wrong values. Because of all your problems in the past, I suppose. Now, put this out of your mind, and let me handle it. Remember, we haven't even read the damn book."

Duke left his wife's room and took a deep, shuddering breath. He'd managed to stay cool and reasonable, but he was so damn mad he felt like putting his fist through a wall. Em was sweet, gentle, flowerlike, with a yearning for the finer things in life. He didn't give a damn about them for himself, but it had been a pleasure to provide them for her.

And with a few strokes of a pen, young Missie Narvaéz had destroyed the image Em had created for herself. Em would survive. Beneath her tender exterior, there was a core of iron. But she would be hurt. And it was all so unnecessary.

He had to get his hands on a copy of that goddamn book!

That proved to be impossible. The first edition, he was told, had already sold out on the East Coast. It was, however, on order—

He did manage to get the name of the publisher, *Brown, Halpert and Brown*. Duke went immediately to the telegraph office, and sent a wire.

"Second one to New York in the last hour," the clerk said, conversationally. "Reporter in here from one of their papers. Wired his whole story. It was a doozie!"

He looked at the signature on Duke's copy and reddened.

Duke turned on his heel, his face black with fury. It was already beginning.

Now, he intended to see Missie. He slipped his watch from its pocket. Too late to reach her at the *Examiner.* It was just as well! What he had to say to her should be handled in private. He went to her rooms on Polk Street. She did not answer her door.

Frau Schmitt volunteered the information that Missie had gone to New York. The old woman's eyes were shining with excitement. "Something to do with her chob," she said proudly. "She is such a good girl!"

At the moment, Duke did not feel inclined to agree with her.

He went home, mulling over the situation. The important thing now, was to protect Em; give her a chance to get her head on straight. He had a notion that the *Journal* reporter was only the first of many. He did not intend for his family to be harrassed!

Duke thought of his children, thanking God that Victoria and her family were visiting Cammie, in Australia. That left only Scott, at Berkeley. He could handle himself.

But Em and Petra were his responsibility. And he would watch over them.

Reaching home, he had a talk with Sim Blevins. The talk resulted in the hiring of Sam Ramos, a villainous-looking man with a scar that lifted one corner of his mouth in a sneer. Sam was to guard the house from the front, Blevins from the rear. No one was to be admitted. No one.

The elegant Courtney home on Nob Hill had become an armed camp.

On a train, just beginning the first leg of a cumbersome journey to the West Coast, Dan Tallant ushered Tamsen into their compartment, closed the door, and slipped a still-folded newspaper from inside his coat. He'd purchased it, surreptitiously, at the station. Now, he spread it out, Tamsen reading over his shoulder, both of them paling.

There were three photographs: one of Arab, looking lost and frightened; another of Tamsen, fleeing, skirt lifted to show her ankles; the third of Nell, using her massive, velvet-clad rear to send a reporter flying.

The Hollander, arriving in New York Harbor today, became a warship, as a trio of notorious ladies, formerly from San Francisco, did battle with the press. Those who have managed to get hold of a copy of The Survivors, *will recognize Tamsen Tallant, former entertainer and madam, who has the starring role in this true account of the lusty days of the early west. The racy novel portrays her life and loves, ranging from commoners to kings.*

Present also, is a second McLeod sister, Arabella Narvaéz, whom you will remember as the hoydenish redhead, child-victim of an unscrupulous minister; daring entertainer with the troupe of Lola Montez. The story of her affair with a princely gentleman of Spain, her kidnapping by Gypsies, keeps the reader agog.

The third sister, Emmeline, with a heartbreaking story of violation, resulting in the murders of her attackers, was not present; her whereabouts as yet unknown.

In the melee between reporters and the new arrivals, Tamsen Tallant proved she still retained her old fire, despite advancing age, sending a reporter tumbling down the gangplank with a single shove.

Another prominent character, Nell, known now as Lady Wotherspoon, spearheaded their escape with the aid of two unidentified confederates.

We were unable to ascertain the group's reaction to their life story, The Survivors, *written by a relative, Melissa McLeod.*

The article went on to state that the book, considered one of the most controversial of the era, was sold out but would soon be reissued in a mammoth printing.

Dan and Tamsen looked at each other for a moment, then

Dan rose wearily. "I suppose I'll have to show it to the others," he said.

"I will go with you."

Juan read the paper in tight-lipped silence. Arab became hysterical.

Missie had always been a prickly child. "It's because she thought I neglected her," Arab wept. "I didn't! It was just—Luka needed me more! Now she's getting even!"

"I don't think it's that," Juan said quietly. "Remember these people are selling papers. They naturally would make the book look more—more lurid than it is. Give Missie a chance—"

"I'll never forgive her," Arab wept. "Never!"

Only Nell took the article philosophically—even with a faint tinge of pleasure. "Hell, it all happened, didn' it? What's did is did, I allus say." She squinted at the photographs. "Arab looks like a spanked kid. Tam, yer legs is still purty damn good-lookin'!" Turning her own picture to view it from all directions, her face reddened.

"Action's fine," she said modestly, "kind of a boomps-a-daisy. But they didn' git my best side."

Tamsen began to laugh and the others joined in. But their laughter was close to tears.

Chapter 42

Nell was not as unconcerned as she seemed. She, personally, saw nothing wrong with the book. In fact, she was secretly proud of young Missie. Life had been purty damn inneresting! Mebbe, seein' what real people lived through would give some of these younguns a boot in th' butt. Hell, in them days, folks had character!

But it was hurting her beloved Tamsen and Arab. Em was prob'ly havin' a shit-fit! People wuz funny. Nell shook her old head in bewilderment as she went to confer with Maggie and Sean.

"Lor' lumme," Maggie breathed. " 'Er writ a book on 'em? A 'ole bloody book! Wisht I could get me hands on one!"

Nell stared at her in amazement. "You kin read?"

Some, Maggie confessed. There'd been this girl at the school where she cleaned, a real nob. She'd taught Maggie her letters.

"Damn nice of her," Nell boomed.

Maggie shook her head, putting a finger beneath her nose and tilting it upward to indicate snobbishness. The girl had been a high-class bitch. Her services had been offered in trade.

" 'Er learned me," Maggie grinned, "an' I learned 'er wot I knowed."

To illustrate, she opened her hand to reveal Sean's watch that she had lifted during the conversation.

"Ye little divil," he said, shaking her, "sure, an' ye said there'd be no more of it!"

"Leave 'er alone." Nell was looking at Maggie with admiration. "It's awright ez long ez it's in th' fambly." She hitched closer. "Kin you learn me ter do it?"

Time passed more quickly for Nell and her companions than it did for the others. As they worried their way across the country, Nell took lessons in picking pockets. When that grew stale, she played poker with Sean Murphy. He had learned enough tricks of his own to almost keep up with her. Sometimes they varied their games by "playing honest" for a change.

Dan and Tamsen, Juan and Arab, kept to their rooms in fear of being recognized. They tipped a porter to bring their meals. After the first dainty tray he brought, Nell would have none of it.

She was a lot of woman by God! And all of it needed filling up. She and her two charges went to the dining room for meals. If anybody reckanized her, to hell with it. She'd throw him off the train.

It was Maggie who spotted the book. She'd seen the lone diner who always read during his meals, absorbed in the book propped before him. But it wasn't until evening of the third day out that she noted its title. She said nothing to the others. When they rose to go, she lagged behind, waiting until a Negro waiter came down the swaying aisle, a tray in one hand. Then she moved, somehow catching the waiter's foot

312

with one of her own, tripping him. They both went down, Maggie pulling a tablecloth with her.

The contents of the tray spilled over the reading diner, his plate went into his lap. The apologetic waiter was still sponging him off when Maggie escaped from the dining car.

Nell and Sean had been waiting for her. She by-passed them, hurrying on through the train to Nell's compartment. Inside, she pulled a book from the folds of her skirt.

"Little coffee didn' 'urt it none," she said modestly.

Nell's eyes bulged. "That there ain't—?"

"The Sur—vi—vors," Maggie read happily from the cover.

"I be damned!"

Nell's first impulse was to rush to Dan and Tamsen with it. Then she had second thoughts. There'd been enough of a tizzy over that newspaper article. Might ez well see what Missie had to say before th' fat hit th' fire.

Nell crossed her massive arms and glowered at Maggie.

"Start readin'," she growled. "An' don't leave out a goddamn word!"

Maggie spelled out the title page, the dedication, painfully forming each word with her lips before she uttered it.

"For the Sur-vi-vors, the daughters of Scott McLeod, women of strength and char-ac-ter, who fought for their hap-pin-ess, and won. For Nell, and especially for Dusty, who made this book pose—poss—possible."

"I be double-damned," Nell said, her small beady eyes filling with tears. "Dusty, an' me! Hell, don't stop now, girl! Git goin'!"

"St. Louis, at the confluence of the Missouri and Mississippi rivers, known as the Gateway to the West, was booming in that summer of 1848. For years, the city had served as a marketplace, a supply depot for the frontier. Now, the first ranks of gold-seekers had arrived, heading toward California."

"Thass where they met my Dusty," Nell interjected. "Hurry up an' git t' th' facks!"

The girl read on, mispronouncing some words, but managing to convey the sense of Missie's book, describing the early comers, the covered wagons blooming like a vast sea of mushrooms in the wagonyards, a new train leaving each day, moving west.

"It was here that the McLeod family was stranded. They had left their home in Pennsylvania with two wagons, each drawn by a span of fine oxen. They carried a cargo of agricultural implements they planned to sell in the new state of Texas. Scott McLeod, former farmer, father of three motherless daughters, now fancied himself a business man. His first mistake lay in selling his oxen, planning to take a flatboat downriver. With word of gold drifting east, all boats had been secured by ambitious drifters. Now three lonely girls waited for Scott to find replacements for their team."

"That's them," Nell interjected, "Tamsen, Arab, an' Em."

The reading continued until nearly morning. By that time, they had covered Dusty's meeting with the McLeods, the terrible trek west, Scott McLeod's death along the trail. The story of Tamsen and Dan had begun. Forever at odds with him, Tamsen had stolen Dan's horses to replace her team, which were sick and dying. Dusty escorted the girls to Magoffinville, and Tamsen to a meeting with Nell.

Maggie was worn out. For a time, fascinated with the story, her reading speed increased. Then, exhausted with her efforts, she began to stumble over every word. Nell closed the book, reluctantly, and sent Sean and Maggie off to bed.

She, however, was unable to sleep. Missie's words had brought Dusty to life in her mind; the way he looked, scraggly little moustache, wispy hair, two missing front teeth—but so elegant! He had been such an elegant man! She could see him now, bringing the small frightened dark-haired Tamsen into the cantina she operated near the Rio. The girl had been desperate with worry over supporting her sisters, and she'd given her a job.

Nell grinned, remembering how Tam brought the house down with a few wiggles and a naughty song—

So far, every word had been true. Nell had an idea there wouldn't be much left out. How Tam, Arab, and Em were going to take it, she didn't know. But Nell figured it made them look pretty damn good.

They said when you wuz dyin', you saw your whole life pass afore you. Nell, through Missie's book, was beginning to do it now, while she was still alive. Good thing, too, she thought happily. She might of left something out.

She looked mournfully at the stained volume. At the rate they were going, she hoped she'd live long enough to reach the end.

The lessons in purse-snatching and card-sharping were tabled for now. Each day was given over to reading, punctuated with exclamations by Maggie—"Lor' lumme, lissen 'ere!"—and by Nell, "I remember that, damned ef I don't."

They were still not halfway through the massive book when they, unknowingly, crossed the California line.

Tamsen had been acutely aware of each stage of the trip. It was so long ago that she'd traversed the country in a covered wagon. Scott McLeod had been dead for more than forty years; yet she remembered standing beside his snow-covered grave as if it were today.

The trip had taken months. Now she was making much the same journey in comparative luxury. The years had changed everything. She was not prepared for it.

She leaned against Dan's chest, enjoying the feel of his arms around her. "Dan," she said, "I feel suddenly—very old."

"Some things," he whispered, "improve with age. And you are one of them."

"We're almost there, aren't we?"

"Soon," he said, nuzzling her hair.

"I'm not sure I want to be. I'm not ready to face up to—what's happened. I just wish we could go on and on like this, the two of us, and never have to get off the train."

"We'd go right off into the Pacific," he said in mock alarm.

"But we'd be together."

"With my luck, they'd put me to surveying some damn tracks—under water."

"All the way to Hawaii."

They were quiet for a time, each remembering the same thing; Dan recalling a golden shaft of morning light gilding a creamy body, Tamsen, hip-deep in a shallow pool beneath a waterfall. Her hair hanging almost to the water, a yellow hau flower tucked into its dark cascade.

Tamsen was thinking of the man who came toward her, his dark skin warm amber against the hau forest behind him, dappled with the sun—

She put a hand to his dark cheek, thinking how little he had changed. Only his hair, winged with silver, was different.

He pulled her to him. "I agree with you," he said huskily. "We'll just stay on the train, all the way to forever!"

Chapter 43

Warm winter sunshine greeted the travelers when they wearily detrained in San Francisco. Tamsen stumbled. "Don't have my landlegs yet," she said, holding onto Dan's arm. It seemed they had been in constant motion since they left Liverpool; first the ship, then a few brief hours in the hotel before they boarded the train.

It wasn't exactly the homecoming they'd planned on. The Courtneys had no idea when they would arrive. After debating wiring from a stop, they had decided against it, wishing to arrive as inconspicuously as possible.

They hired two carriages, making arrangements for their luggage to be delivered later, and set out for their final destination, lost in wonder at their surroundings.

Tamsen remembered her first sight of San Francisco in 1851. Then it had been a sprawling octopus, reaching tentacles into the hills in the form of mud-slick roads; a city drenched in fog, doused with sunshine, perfume, and whiskey, ripe with chicanery; a place of sleazy bars, casinos.

"I cannot believe this," she said. "Look!" She gestured toward the pleasant thoroughfares, the cable cars that passed, laughing passengers holding to the rails. "I think we got off in the wrong place! I see nothing familiar."

Arab, silent until now, grinned rather crookedly. "Do you remember the sign at Clay and Kearney? 'This street is impassable; Not even jackassable.'?"

Arab certainly remembered it. It was on that corner that she was singing when she was discovered by Lola Montez. It was part of the life she wanted to forget, which had now been brought home to her with a vengeance.

They made the steep pull up Nob Hill, exclaiming over the beautiful homes that had risen in their absence. And finally reached the address that would be Em's.

"Damn," Dan whispered as he saw what waited there. A bevy of reporters lounged against the front fence, several cameras set up and at the ready. It looked as if the place were under siege.

He drove on past; Sean, in the carriage behind, following.

"Now what in the hell do we do?" Dan wondered aloud.

He drove farther and turned into a narrow lane. It opened into another that ran behind the Courtneys. The house in which Duke and Em lived was backed by a high wall, a heavy wooden gate set in the middle of it.

Dan stopped the carriage and got out. The gate was bolted from the inside, immobile.

He returned to the others with a wry grin. They had two choices. They could yell themselves blue in the face, hoping somebody in the house would hear them and let them in—or they could go to a hotel.

"Sure, and I c'd climb th' wall," Sean offered, "then be afther lettin' ye in."

He grinned at Dan's approving nod and went up and over like a monkey.

Sim Blevins had been spoiling for a fight. To his way of thinking, Duke should turn him and Sam loose on those sonsofbitches out front. Man's home was his castle, wasn't it? By god, he'd clear 'em out if he had the say-so.

At present he was venting his spleen on a rhododendron. It had already been pruned, but he figured it could use a little more. He whacked away, cursing reporters with every whack, and was almost down to its roots when he saw a figure leap down from the rear wall. His eyes narrowed, and he grinned gleefully as he started pegging it toward the newcomer.

Sean Murphy jolted from his leap drew a breath and extended his hand. "Th' rest o' thim's just outside th' gate. If ye'll be kind enough to lend a hand—"

Sim's fist swung, but the boy had quick reflexes. The blow grazed him up one side of his head, and Murphy let out a startled yell. Then Sim swung again.

Sean's shout was heard outside the gate. It was followed by a crashing and thumping as the two men rolled in combat. Dan leaped from the carriage, but Nell was ahead of him, slamming a mighty shoulder into the gate. It splintered and she hit it again, the bolt ripping away from the old wood.

Sean Murphy lay on the grass, Blevins just getting to his feet. His jaw dropped at the apparition in purple velvet storming toward him, the feathers on her hat trembling in righteous anger.

"You sonofabitch!" she exploded. A hamlike hand drew back and she cracked him in the jaw. Sim Blevins teetered for a moment on his wooden leg, then sat down.

"Be damned," he said, staring at Nell in pleased surprise.

She reached down and heaved him to his feet. "Dunno who th' hell you are," she said haughtily, "but I figger you work fer Duke. Gitcher ass in gear an' tell 'im Lady Wotherspoon an' party has arrived. Less'n," she glowered at him menacingly, "you want some more of the same."

She made a fist and spat on it, then did a little shadowboxing. Blevins hastily retreated to the house to shout for Duke.

The others had poured in through the gate, Maggie rushing to cradle Sean's head to her breast. He was groggy and bruised, but otherwise in one piece when Duke, Em, and Petra ran from the house; Em sobbing with joy at seeing her sisters again.

She kissed Tamsen, clinging to her as if she'd never let her go. Tamsen was shedding tears, too. She'd always loved her delicate older sister. Her heart ached at the way she looked now, dark shadows under her eyes, so thin and frail. Duke was worried, too. Tamsen could tell from the way he watched her.

Em moved on to Arab. Arab clutched at her and burst into noisy tears. "What Missie's done! Oh, it's so awful! I'm sick over it! Is she here?"

Duke intervened. "Missie's in New York, Arab."

"She can stay there as far as I'm concerned," Arab said defiantly.

Duke sighed. "We can discuss that later. In the meantime, you probably don't recognize Petra, our granddaughter, Martha's girl—"

Tamsen smiled at the exotic little creature and moved to embrace her. Dan looked at the child-woman his wife was hugging, recognizing her definitely Asiatic features. He looked quickly at Duke and saw that he, too, knew.

"Hell," Duke said with forced heartiness, "here we are, together again. We've got a lot to celebrate! And who are these young folks? I don't think we've met—"

Nell introduced them proudly. This was her new daughter, Maggie, and this here—was Maggie's husband, Sean Murphy.

Duke looked at the battered lad, raising his brows in question.

Nell had the answer. "Yer man," she gestured toward Blevins, "beat th' hell outen the kid. I hadda whop 'im one."

Duke's startled eyes moved to his employee. Sim was looking at Nell with awed admiration. His jaw was definitely swollen.

Leaving Blevins to fix the gate, they trooped into the house. Tea was served in Em's refurbished living room. The women were all talking at once. Tamsen steered the conversation to Ramona's children, her new baby, redheaded Denise who looked so like Arab; Luka's wedding, so different, but suiting Luka; Arab's mumps, which had delayed their journey. Anything but what was uppermost in their minds at the moment! This should be a happy occasion. It should not be spoiled.

Duke shook his head at the chatter, inviting Juan, Dan, and Sean into his study, pouring them each a healthy slug of brandy.

"Now," he said, "how the hell are we going to handle this mess we're in?"

Dan described their arrival in New York Harbor, and handed him the clipping from the paper he'd picked up at the time of their departure. Duke read it and whistled.

"It's worse than I thought. I don't want Em to see this."

"She won't," Dan said grimly. "And Tamsen won't mention it."

"Arab won't, either," Juan added. "I told her to keep her damned mouth shut."

Duke jumped a little at his words. Juan had always been the most doting of husbands, spoiling his pretty red-haired wife beyond belief. He was obsessed with the woman. Duke had secretly considered it weakness. But this was a new Juan, almost a stranger. His face had matured into hard, masculine planes set off by a black trimmed beard that was most becoming.

"How long has this been going on?" Duke's attention was brought back to Dan.

"The reporters? About a week. And it looks like they're here to stay."

"I've got an idea," Dan said slowly. "I don't especially like it, but it might get them off our backs. Let me think about it awhile."

"Sure," Duke said. "And in the meantime, let's drop the whole damn thing and have another drink."

Somehow they managed to steer clear of Missie's book. Dinner that night was a feast in honor of their homecoming. Nell took it upon herself to announce that Maggie had a bun in the oven, and that she was going to be a grandmaw. Toasts were raised in honor of the blushing young couple, and Sean Murphy's chest expanded fit to burst his buttons.

If Em looked frail and old, if Tamsen had a worry line between her brows, if Arab burst into unexpected tears, it was tactfully ignored.

That night, they retired gratefully to their beds, all except Nell, Maggie, and Sean. They retreated to Nell's room and she handed Maggie the book.

"Now," Nell said, "were wuz we?"

Chapter 44

Two days later, Tamsen dressed carefully in a slim-waisted street dress. Of russet faille with touches of cream, it was fashionably bustled. A small, tilted hat with a sheer veil added to its elegance. She surveyed herself in the mirror and turned to face Dan.

"Will I do?"

"If you did any better, we wouldn't be going," he grinned. "Come to think of it—"

Pretending to ignore him, she picked up a number of packets she'd prepared. They left the house by the back gate and drove downtown, stopping before the *Chronicle*.

"You sure you don't want me with you?" Dan wore a concerned expression as he helped Tamsen down from the carriage.

"No, this concerns me and my sisters. It's better this way."

She entered the building head high, and returned with a smile.

"I think it's going to work, Dan!"

The packets she carried each contained photos of herself, Arab, and Em. They were studio portraits, showing them to their best advantage. In addition, there were signed statements prepared for the press.

"We, the undersigned, are unable to comment upon the book, *The Survivors*, at this time, since we have not been privileged to see the book and discover its content. This is all we can offer for publication."

Attached was another letter, drafted by Duke Courtney's attorney, stating that his clients had complied, willingly, with the press by presenting said photographs and statement, and that the sustained presence of reporters at the Courtney home would constitute a suit claiming harrassment.

One by one, Tamsen visited the various newspaper offices, obtaining the desired results. The last was the *Examiner*. Missie had worked here, Tamsen thought, as she entered the doors. But they probably knew nothing more than she, since the girl had used a pseudonym. She asked to speak to the managing editor, only to be told he wasn't in. There was, of course, Mr. Blaine, at present at his desk.

"Then I will see him."

Matthew Blaine looked up from his work in annoyance. Another female, probably with a cause.

Then the woman he faced brought him to his feet. She was one of the loveliest creatures he'd ever seen; no longer young, of indeterminate age, but obviously a lady.

"I am Tamsen Tallant," she said in a low, husky voice that had an odd, endearing little break in it.

"Missie's aunt!"

"Then you know. You have read her book?"

"No, I haven't."

It was true, the thing was still stashed away, under his shirts—though the temptation to take it out had been great.

He knew some of its content, of course, through the news releases that had crossed his desk briefly on the way to his wastebasket. But if this woman were an ex-madam, he was no newspaper man!

"Then we are even," she said with a smile that made his heart turn over. "I haven't read it, either. We've been unable to obtain a copy, my sisters and I. Therefore I am distributing these in order to avoid further embarrassment. There is nothing more we can add, at this time."

She stood as Blaine read the statement and accompanying document. He raised his eyes, finally, to meet hers.

"I can assure you none of the reporters you mention are from this paper. I know. I give out the assignments."

"And you are Missie's friend," she guessed intuitively.

Was he? He thought of the night Missie had spent in his arms, warm, tender, giving.

"Yes," he said, quietly. "I am Missie's friend."

"I'm glad. I—I have an idea she's going to be needing her friends. Do you suppose you could get word to me when she returns. I need to talk to her before—before anyone else, if possible."

"I certainly will."

He escorted her to the door. She smiled up at him, liking the strong lines of his face, his rumpled masculine appearance. And then she was gone.

Matthew Blaine went back to his desk and lit his pipe, staring moodily through the smoke. Tamsen Tallant would be the last woman he'd select for a harlot's role. He had met Em Courtney, and she was sweet, retiring. The other—he thumbed through the photographs, finding the third sister, Arabella. Curls, dimples, a touch of selfishness about a slightly pouting mouth, but—nothing evil.

Was it possible that Missie, in her ambition, had exploited these people? The thought was too awful to consider.

Dammit, he'd have to read the book.

Carrington was looking over his shoulder. Blaine hastily

slid the photographs into a drawer. "You have a question?" he asked, rather acidly.

Carrington shrugged. "Just wondering who the lady was. Good-looking dame—"

"If you attended to your business as much as you do to mine, we might get a paper out."

Carrington went back to his article on the condition of city streets. It was dull as hell. He almost wished there was a fire!

Matthew Blaine left early that night. This time, he didn't take his work home with him. He dawdled over the dinner Cinnie had left, did up the dishes, and played with his son. Much of the play consisted of exercising the boy's injured leg as the doctor had prescribed.

"Does that hurt, son?"

"No." It was a satisfactory answer. At first, there had been so much pain. Blaine moved a few steps away.

"Walk to me."

Giggling, the boy limped forward to fall laughing into his father's arms. Matthew held him close, his cheek against the crisp curls of his son. He loved him more than anything in the world—and he was improving, every day. Nothing should happen to jeopardize that!

Finally, the child's eyes were closing from sheer fatigue. Matthew bathed him and tucked him into bed. The night was cool, and there was a fire in the fireplace. Taking the book from its resting place, Blaine sat in a big chair, a shaded lamp beside him, and began to read.

Matthew Blaine, unlike poor illiterate Maggie, read speedily and well. After all, reading was his profession. He began the book with a swelling anger at Missie for revealing secrets which, if true, she had no business to reveal. Then he became enthralled with the unfolding tale, unable to view it objectively. He was about halfway through when he realized what the girl had done.

It was not merely a lurid fantasy. This book, through its characters, depicted the strengths of women. And she had done it more thoroughly than Miss Elizabeth Anspaugh with all her marching and meetings could ever do! These women had gone through hell—and come out on the other side, still strong, surviving. Missie had depicted them with love—and with humor. Em's primness had come across, Arab's slight selfishness. They were so—damn human!

He sped through the pages, moving from the States to Alaska, to Hawaii, to Australia.

And toward the book's end, he found Missie—

A Missie who was sixteen years old, a middle child, relegated to the background due to a frail younger sister, Luka. Missie, who had a secret place, a fairy ring of salt cedar near the banks of the Billabong; who went there to write and to dream of the book she would one day publish— the story of her beloved family, as it had been related to her by Dusty, her only friend.

"Missie will be needing her friends," Tamsen Tallant had said.

Matthew rubbed his eyes and read on.

He read about the aborigine family Missie befriended, about Arthur Melvin, the handsome foreman who wooed young Missie with soft words and poetry.

He read of their marriage, how Melvin fired the family station. And how he'd degraded the girl before his father, finally leaving her to bear and bury a dead child.

He suffered with her through those last agonizing days after Melvin's death as she watched the man's decaying body on the bluff above the duffing yard, thinking she had killed. Then her wild and terrible fantasies that Arthur Melvin wasn't dead at all; that he crawled down the hill and loomed over her, his face menacing.

Blaine drew a shuddering breath and forced his hands to unclench. If the man weren't dead, he'd go looking for him! But this explained so much! The way she'd stiffened at first when he touched her, the wonder in her eyes when their love was consummated—

Damn the man! Oh, damn him! Missie was still so fragile—
and at sixteen—!

He forced himself to return to the book, reading through
Missie's rescue, Tamsen's trek across vast deserts to Dan,
sun-blind and ill, Ramona's romance with her redheaded
Scotsman. And finally, the separation of the sisters, Em
coming to the States, the others heading for England.

> Missie stood on the deck of the ship, looking toward
> the shore. She ached for those she was leaving behind,
> Aunt Tamsen, small, almost nunlike, so beautiful, cling-
> ing to Uncle Dan's arm; Mama, her red curls catching
> the sun, Papa, tall and distinguished, Luka, Nell . . .
> But not Dusty. Dusty lay buried in the hot red center
> of Australia. The mallee scrub would cover his grave,
> goannas seek shelter there, lorikeets wheel above it. A
> small blond girl would not sit at his feet, raptly listening
> to his tales again.
> But she would not forget him. She would find a way to
> help him be remembered.
> Nor would she forget those others, disappearing now
> into the distance. Perhaps she had never been an inte-
> gral part of their lives as they had been to her, but the
> memory of their strength would help her heal her own
> wounds.
> They, and Em, who still stood beside her, were the
> survivors.

"My God," Matthew Blaine whispered. "Oh, my God!"
He rubbed his eyes again, but this time it was more than
fatigue. Missie, too, was a survivor, and he'd accused her of
being shallow, ambitious, self-seeking. He'd been a damn
fool!

He closed the book and sat staring at it for a long time. The
sun, slanting through a window, touched its title with letters
of fire.

The night had ended, and it was morning.

Chapter 45

Tamsen's errand to the papers was successful. The crowd of reporters hanging around the Courtneys' fence dispersed. Now that they were gone, she felt free to do what she'd intended to do earlier; look for a home for herself and Dan. She loved her sister, but at present their visit was more like a wake. Her patience with Em and Arab was wearing thin.

They were like small children, imagining something outside in the dark. Each reinforced the other's ideas until they had created a monster, sinister and frightening.

"Dan and I are going to look at houses," she coaxed, "why don't the rest of you come with us."

"They might not sell to you in the nicer areas," Em said. "Not with a reputation—" she put her hand to trembling lips, her blue eyes welling with tears. Tamsen said a rude word.

"Bullshit!"

She stormed off in search of Dan, thinking how many of the names Em dropped as socially desirable were familiar to her. The wealth of many old San Francisco families was based on sharp dealing, conniving, chicanery.

One thing about having been a madam, Tamsen knew where a lot of bodies were buried—both literally and figuratively!

Nell found herself alone with two grieving women. Duke had gone to the office, Juan accompanying him. Maggie and Sean, uncomfortable in Em's delicate house, remained in their room. Hell, she didn' blame them. Em was Nell's girl and she loved her dearly, but she felt like a bull in a chiny shop.

She wandered out into the rear yard where Sim was staunchly hacking at a rose bush, swearing as he pricked his fingers. Nell eyed the rapidly diminishing plant with concern.

"Hell, whyn'cha cut its throat an' put it out of its misery?"

Blevins glared at her balefully and continued his task. Nell watched the ripple of his shoulder muscles admiringly. He was a fine figger of a man. Not elegant, of course, like her Dusty. Mean-tempered sonofabitch, though.

"Like t' ast you somethin', ef you ain't too overworked an' underpaid t' lissen."

He acknowledged her statement with a jerk of his head and went on with his job.

"I'm looking fer a certain kinda place." She went on to explain that she'd lived in San Francisco a lot of years ago. Now it had grown until she didn't know where anything was. She was wanting to set herself up in a little bar or casino, somewhere around the waterfront where the action was. "Problem is," she said candidly, "when it comes to Frisco like it is now, I dunno my butt from a hole in th' ground—"

Blevins grinned fleetingly, then returned to his customary scowl.

"Reckon I kin lend you a hand. That's purty much my stompin' ground."

"I figgered it wuz."

He looked at her, wondering if she were being sarcastic. She wasn't.

One helluva woman, he thought to himself.

Em, learning of their plans, was only too glad to be rid of Blevins for the day. The sight of her suffering garden had become a sore point. In fact, he and Nell must take the surrey.

She watched them go, two burly figures in the tiny vehicle, wondering if the springs would survive.

Nell was having the time of her life. She was Lady Wotherspoon out with a man. She smoothed her skirts, simpering coyly at passersby, the feathers on her hat bobbing as she bowed.

"Y'got a itch?"

Blevins's question settled her squarely. "Hell, no. That's what ladyship's do, bow like that."

"How the hell'd y'git t'be a ladyship?"

Nell found herself telling him about Dusty.

Sim's craggy face softened as he listened to her love-embroidered tales of the little man's heroics. He had never married, never found a woman who could stand up to him. He rubbed his jaw, reflectively, finding himself almost jealous of a dead man.

He countered with tales of his own life in the early days of San Francisco. First, he'd been shanghaied, spent a lot of time in China. Then, returning at the time of the gold rush, he'd become a crimp; helping to fill the crews of ships deserted by men rushing to find their fortunes. "Gold, hell! I went where th' money wuz!"

Nell's eyes admired him as he went into the details of impressing unwary men into seafaring careers. Drugged drinks, smokes—but this was the way he liked best. He lifted a heavy fist and grinned.

"Don't sound none too legal-like t'me," Nell said dubiously.

"Teach 'em a damn good lesson. Don't git shanghaied no more."

The carriage turned a corner and Nell swayed, bumping against him. She righted herself, settled her hat more firmly, and returned to the conversation.

"Then, I reckin stealin' could be put in th' same cattygorry. A lesson, like?"

"Damn right."

Nell grinned and extended her hand. Sim Blevin's pocket watch lay in her pudgy palm. He looked at it, startled, and felt in his pocket.

"How th' hell d'you do that?"

Nell shrugged, airily. "Jes' figgered yer needed a lesson."

Sim Blevins laughed, a harsh rusty bark from a throat unaccustomed to mirth. He slapped Nell on the back with a hearty hand. "You'll do," he said, gleefully. "You'll do!"

Nell returned his slap with equal heartiness, numbing his shoulder.

"You do purty good, y'self," she rumbled.

Two kindred spirits, at peace with themselves and each other, they rolled along a waterfront street, to the sound of the surrey's complaining springs.

They looked over a few places listed for sale. Blevins kept shaking his head. This was not what Nell wanted. Finally, he stopped the surrey in front of a narrow building almost intruding into the street. Its unpainted wooden frame was weathered to a soft gray. Upstairs, shades hung crookedly at dirty windows. A sign, proclaiming it to be *Pete's Place*, dangled by one chain.

Nell clasped her hands and looked at it, prayerfully. It looked like—home.

"It don't say it's fer sale."

"It will be."

Blevins climbed down from the surrey. Relieved of his weight, it tipped dangerously to Nell's side. For the first time in his life, Sim Blevins felt a gentlemanly urge. He peg-legged around the vehicle, took Nell's hand, and helped her to alight.

Inside, the place was everything it should be. An old mahogany bar with clouded mirrors backing it stood along one wall. A brass rail ran the length of its front; its taps were old and ornate, thickly coated with verdigris, but they would shine when cleaned and polished.

There were two rickety tables before the bar, three or four in the ell formed in one corner of the room. Nell liked what she saw. Pete, a small bald-headed nervous man, was not too enthusiastic about selling. Blevins, one hand twisted in the man's shirtfront, convinced him.

The deal closed to Nell's satisfaction, they tramped upstairs. Here, there were four rooms, two to either side of a narrow hall. They opened the doors on several startled young women, resting from their night's labors. Nell jerked a thumb toward the street.

"Out!"

"I uster have a operation like that," she told Blevins, nostalgically. "Was kinda figgerin' on it this time, but now that I've got a fambly, 'tain't right. Did I tell you I'm gonna be a grammaw?"

She had, but he listened again, feeling that strange pang of jealousy once more.

They surveyed the rooms, small, shabby, each furnished with a single metal bedstead, a sagging mattress, pitcher, and washstand.

"This here'll be my room, up front. Put the kids across th' hall. Nexta them, we'll fix up a nurs'ry. Leaves one." She looked at Sim Blevins doubtfully. "You could have that'n, if yer thinkin' on changin' jobs—"

At first she took his expression to be a ferocious scowl, then realized that this, for Sim, was his pleased look. He was beaming.

They left the building and returned to the Courtney home. Nell was in seventh heaven. Tomorrow, they would return and clean the place up. Sean Murphy could refinish the bar, Maggie clean the floors. Upstairs, Nell intended to repaper every room. "Sorta partial to cabbage roses," she said wistfully. "Brightens up things." The woodwork would be painted, new tables purchased for downstairs—round ones so's to give plenty elbowroom.

The place would have class—and be homey at the same time. She would call it—she screwed up her face in concentration, then glowed with inspiration—

"*Nell's Place!*"

Young Missie didn' have all the cree-yative talent in this fambly!

As they neared the Courtney home on Nob Hill, Nell looked up at its imposing, gingerbread facade. Em and Arab wouldn't think much of the deal she'd made today. It would be strictly between herself, Sim, Maggie, and Sean until she got it gussied up.

Again, Sim hurried around to help her down. She simpered. It was almost like being courted. The old girl still had what it took to attrac' a good-lookin' man!

Chapter 46

Sean and Maggie had also left the house. Arab and Em, alone for the first time, had an opportunity to discuss the problem uppermost in their minds: Missie's book.

"Duke thinks I'm terrible," Em said wistfully. "But a man's reputation isn't as important as a woman's. He doesn't know what this is doing to me."

"Juan's the same. And it's our daughter who's done this. I think that's what hurts the most! It looks like she's set out to destroy the family! I—I suppose everybody's blaming me!"

"Blame you?" Em reached her hand to her sister. "How could anybody blame you?"

Arab's cheeks were hot. "I know what everybody thinks: that I was a—a rotten mother! But, Em, I had Luka to think of. And I couldn't get close to Missie. But I never dreamed she would turn on us so—viciously."

"Tamsen says we should give her the benefit of the doubt, wait until we see the book." Em's blue eyes were troubled.

"Tamsen! If anybody's at fault, it's her! She was the one

who spoiled Missie, always buying her paper and pencil
when she was little, leading her to think she was some kind
of—genius! She probably filled her full of those—those damn
filthy stories, too!''

"I doubt that, Arab. Tamsen's no prouder of the past than
we are. Perhaps Nell—''

"Nell and Tam are two of a kind,'' Arab said scornfully.
"Nell's got the morals of an alleycat! If Tam hadn't got
involved with her, our lives would have been different! Oh,
Em, this all just makes me sick!''

Bent over their embroidery frames, the women failed to
note their conversation had an audience. Maggie and Sean
had come in the back way, Maggie coming in search of Nell.
The girl paled as she heard Arab put down her beloved
benefactor, her small hands clenching into fists. She swallowed
her first impulse—to enter and tell Mrs. Narvaéz off in
inimitable gutter language; slipped quietly back in the direction from which she'd come, and went to tell Sean.

In the sitting room, Arab and Em continued commiserating
with each other.

"Nell's been good to us,'' Em said loyally. "And Tamsen's
heart's in the right place. I'm sure she wouldn't have encouraged Missie if she'd known—''

"But she did! Oh, Em, I can't stay here, not with tongues
wagging all over town. I'm going to try to talk Juan into
going back to England.''

To Arab, that was the only sensible solution. The queen
would never countenance the publishing of such a book! They
could all go. London was a wonderfully exciting place! Arab
recounted their presentation to the queen, ignoring the
embarrassing circumstances that occurred. Luka had forgotten
to curtsy, going off into one of her strange moods, mentioning
Victoria's dead Albert as though he were alive. Then Tamsen
had stood straight as a board and offered her hand to the old
woman.

Arab almost died of humiliation.

"I can't leave here," Em said drearily. "This is my home, mine and Duke's. Duke's almost seventy, Arab, and I'm not far behind him. Our friends are here—"

"I hardly think so," Arab said sharply, "not a single soul has come to that door since we've been here!"

As if to refute her words, the knocker sounded. Em froze. "You go, Arab. I—can't."

Arab opened the door to an extremely handsome young Chinese boy, his arms filled with packages. He smiled, engagingly.

"I am Lee Wang. Is Miss Petra Channing—"

Arab looked at him haughtily. "Deliveries are to be taken to the rear," she said stiffly. She closed the door in his face and returned to Em.

"The Chinese are certainly getting uppity, these days," she said. "But he was a good-looking young man, I'll say that for him. He had something for Petra. I sent him to the back."

Em's thread suddenly knotted. She dropped her needle. "Dear God! Petra's in the kitchen—"

She hurried to the rear of the house, her confused sister following. They arrived just in time to see Petra open the door to the service porch, uttering a cry of delight.

"Lee!"

Arab's mouth fell open in shock. Em's granddaughter had thrown her arms around the neck of—an Oriental delivery boy! And Em was tugging at Arab's arm, drawing her out of sight. Em led her into the living room and looked at her defiantly.

"There's something I have to tell you."

"Well, I should hope so!" Arab tried to laugh. But from her sister's face, this was no laughing matter.

"Petra is half-Chinese."

Arab's eyes widened. "Em, what are you saying!"

Em Courtney sighed. "I had hoped to break it to you gently—if I had to mention it at all."

Em Courtney had carefully briefed Petra for the arrival of

her sisters. Missie had written a most shocking book, she'd explained, one that might be damaging to their reputations. They must have nothing more to worry about at the moment, therefore nothing should be said about Petra's background, her recent—adventure, or her engagement to Lee Wang.

It could be discussed later, when things were settled.

In the meantime, Petra should remain in the house so that she wouldn't be interrogated by reporters. She must write a note to the Wang boy, suggesting he not call for an appropriate period of time. He would probably welcome it, busy as he was, rebuilding the burned factory.

Petra obediently complied with Em's wishes. She'd been disobedient once, and look at the trouble it caused. But it had been a lonely time, despite a house filled with people. She'd missed Lee until she ached, physically. Keeping quietly to herself, she'd relived that day at his home, over and over—

And now he was here!

It was cook's day off, and the girl had been making small tea cookies. Her arms were covered with flour, but it didn't matter! She ran and hugged him, packages and all. He stiffened in her arms. The sensitive mouth she had stood on tiptoe to reach did not respond. Finally, she backed from him.

"Lee, what is it?"

"I have brought gifts for your relations. I was told to deliver them at the rear door."

"Not by—Grandmother?"

"A red-haired woman in green—"

Petra laughed. "Aunt Arab! Don't look so hurt, Lee! She doesn't know about us!" She reached to remove a dab of flour she'd left on his cheek. He pushed her hand away.

"And you have not seen fit to tell her?"

"I couldn't, Lee! Grandmother asked me to wait. She wanted to break it to them gently. Please, Lee, don't look like that!"

"Perhaps we have made a mistake, Petra. An engagement

to marry is a happy thing, to be proud of." He flushed. "I have wished to shout it to the world."

"I have, too!"

"But you have kept it hidden, like something ugly. Perhaps I was too presumptuous in asking for your hand." He gave a stiff, jerky little bow. "I release you from all promises."

"Lee!"

"I want only your happiness. There is nothing more to say."

Before she could reach out to him, he was gone, rounding the house, his back stiff; his gifts still clutched to his chest.

Petra stood stock-still for a moment, too stunned to move. Then she ran out and followed him. When she reached the front gate, his carriage was disappearing down the hill. Pressing her hand to her quivering lips, she went inside and up the rear stairs to her room. There, she lay for a long time, looking at the ceiling with wide, tearless eyes. She was beyond crying.

Downstairs, Em concluded her story. She had described Martha's background, adding only that Petra had recently been involved in an unpleasant situation, giving Lee credit for saving her life.

Petra's affection for the boy was understandable. But when her gratitude faded, it would be a different story. It was Em's plan to prolong their engagement until the relationship died of its own accord. Petra was a pretty girl. She could have any man she chose. In another generation—

Arab, still rocked back on her heels by the story, agreed. The idea that Em's daughter, Martha, had been romantically involved in China was a shocker. As far as Petra was concerned, dear God, all the McLeod sisters needed now was some more scandal! Imagine the talk a Courtney-Chinese wedding would cause!

"I think you're handling this the right way, Em. But I wish I'd known. I hope I didn't complicate the problem."

Em reached for her embroidery. "Nonsense," she said

briskly. "Probably the best thing that could have happened. If the boy has any pride, he'll realize he isn't too welcome in this house."

Again, Arab agreed. They spent the remainder of the afternoon reinforcing each other's feelings of bitterness toward Missie, toward Juan, Dan, and Duke who couldn't seem to understand the impact the book had on all their lives; toward Tamsen, who'd encouraged the girl in earlier days; toward Nell, surely the source of the unsavory stories Missie had collected.

Nell arrived. Leaving Blevins to put up the horse and surrey, she entered the back door. Someone had started to make cookies, and left the mess; dough rolled out, partially cut, flour on the floor. Mebbe she oughta finish it up.

Dammit, it wasn't no skin off her backside!

She stumped up the back stairs, going to Sean and Maggie's room. Wait'll they heard about the deal she pulled off today! They were in for one helluva surprise!

The edge was taken from her enjoyment as Maggie recounted the ugly words she'd overheard. Nell suddenly looked old and tired.

"Mebbe they got a point," she admitted. "I dunno. Gotta remember, them girls is upset right now. I reckon Arab ain't thinkin' straight."

"'Er's a bleedin' liar," Maggie raged. "Wanna tear 'er bloomin' 'air out!"

"Fergit it," Nell said firmly. "Gawdammit, simmer down! Them girls is like my own, an' don't you never fergit it! Any trouble comes up, I han'le it! Besides, here comes th' clincher!" She paused, impressively. "We ain't gonna be stayin here long! Me an' Sim jes' shot th' works! Bought us a home! Needs some fixin' up, but—"

She was choked off as Maggie threw thin arms about her neck, overcome with delight.

"Hell," Nell said, her face ruddy with pleasure, "you don't have t' git so all-fired het-up over it. Lemme breathe!"

Tamsen and Dan hadn't been so lucky in their search for a house to purchase. Nothing they'd looked at suited them. When they returned, Em went to the kitchen. The meal, prepared earlier needed only warming and setting out. She stopped, seeing the littered table. Petra had been making cookies when Lee came.

The forgotten work told its own story. It was clear that the boy was upset, and that they'd had words. Possibly their engagement was at an end. Em's emotions were mixed. She would be glad to see it over, but her heart ached for Petra. The child probably thought this was the end of the world, but there were other men, men who were much more suitable. She would get over Lee Wang. It was better this way.

Subduing an urge to go to Petra and comfort her, Em set to cleaning up the mess. She was unusually quiet when they finally sat down to eat, flinching when Duke noticed Petra's empty place.

"Where's Petra?"

Petra wasn't feeling well. She'd been making cookies and had to leave them. Some kind of upset, Em imagined.

Em's words were plausible, and she certainly had no reason to invent an excuse for Petra's absence. But why did Em and Arab look so suddenly guilty?

Duke's mystification disappeared as Juan began to talk about the small shop he'd found. It was suited to his dream of marketing imported goods from India; sari cloth, and temple bells. He intended to become a respected merchant.

"We cannot remain in San Francisco," Arab said positively. "Not after Missie's book—"

Juan rose, crumpled his napkin and threw it down. "Damn Missie's book! *Dios*! I'm sick of all this furor over nothing!"

Before Arab could open her mouth, he was gone, up to their room.

The spirit had gone out of the evening. Nell, Maggie, and Sean congregated in Nell's room, not to read, this night, but to gloat over Nell's purchase, their first real home.

Tamsen helped Em do up the dishes, and was heading toward bed when a messenger arrived. He carried a note for Tamsen.

Matthew Blaine asked her to meet him for lunch, on the morrow, at the Palace Hotel. There was something he wished to discuss.

Missie, Tamsen thought, with a mingling of anticipation and concern. Missie had come home!

Chapter 47

Missie Narvaéz had not returned to San Francisco. Some-where in the east, the travelers passed each other. Missie had watched the yellow squares of other trains flicker by at night, wondering if Tamsen might be behind one of those windows, or her mother. The thought gave her a sinking sensation in the pit of her stomach, a heaviness of guilt as she remembered what they were coming home to.

They would be angry, possibly hate her for what she'd done. They were, after all, only people, human beings, not the characters she idealized in her book. She had to make herself remember that. The characters she'd written about were her family, probably all the family she'd have left when this was over.

She stepped from the train, weary from a long journey alone with her thoughts, to find a bevy of reporters waiting.

Her first impulse was to retreat. Then she lifted her head. She was an independent woman. She had written a book, and she intended to do it justice! She was Melissa McLeod, female author who had broken through into a man's world! She owed it to her own sex to stand by what she'd done. She would show Matthew Blaine—!

She posed for a delighted press, her smiling face revealing no indication of the turmoil inside her. Yes, she was pleased that it was selling well. No, she wasn't working on another at present. Perhaps later. No, she had not learned of her family's reaction to the story.

Shown a clipping that described the fracas ensuing when the passengers left *The Hollander*, Missie blanched but maintained her poise, deftly changing the subject to her autograph signing. It was to take place at a leading bookstore, at two o'clock, the following afternoon. Please, only one more photograph. She must go. She was expected at the offices of her publisher, Brown, Halpert and Brown.

Whisked to her hotel in a cabriolet, Missie buried her face in her hands. It was even worse than she'd thought! How awful it must have been for all of them, arriving home, unsuspecting, to face a—a riot. Oh, dear God!

Her hands were like ice as she dressed to go to her publisher's office.

There, Stuyvesant Brown waited once more for a female writer, adjusting his cravat, squaring his shoulders in a natty dark suit. He'd wanted to be at the train when Melissa McLeod arrived, but decided against it. He'd make a better appearance behind the desk in his plush new surroundings.

He looked approvingly at the walls, done tastefully in a soft blue stripe with a rose accent. The charcoal carpet was echoed in frames surrounding the faces of earlier Browns, founders of the company. It didn't hurt to show that one had breeding.

He had straightened his nameplate for the tenth time when a secretary, new to match the office, announced his expected guest. Despite his resolve to receive her with cool dignity, he rose too hastily, his chair catching on the carpet, leaving him bent in an awkward position.

"M—Melissa!" he stammered.

The girl, tastefully attired in a rose gown, charcoal cape lined to match its color, might have dressed to suit the office decor. There was something different about her. She'd lost the look of child-like innocence he'd remembered. It was replaced by a look of purpose that was not unattractive—

Managing to disentangle himself from his offending chair, he came around the desk to take her hand. Missie forced a smile and gestured at her surroundings.

"So nice," she said.

"I hoped you'd think so."

"Oh, I do! It suits you." Her words made him redden with pleasure.

"I'm going to be made a senior partner, Missie. Halpert's due to retire—"

"I'm happy for you."

He'd thought he'd recovered from her spell, but he was drowning in a wave of desire. "Missie," he gulped, "the wire I sent you—I hope you've reconsidered—"

"Mr. Brown." His secretary appeared. "The gentlemen from our advertising staff are here."

Stew Brown cursed the urge that led him to fill the entire day with appointments for Melissa McLeod. It had been a way of showing off his new importance. Advertising, a press conference, the sales department, a sherry party to introduce his writer to other writers and editors; a banquet for a small select group following—

He must have been out of his mind! They wouldn't have a moment alone!

As the afternoon progressed, Stew Brown was exultant. It was clear that Brown, Halpert and Brown had that rare combination, a top-notch book and an author to match. The girl handled herself with grace and dignity. His advertising people were bowled over immediately. He grinned as she proceeded to charm the pants off tough George Fisher of the press.

Flash-bars exploded, filling the room with a sulphurous

stench and drifting smoke as Missie posed with her book; holding it before her so its title might be seen; handing a copy to Brown's secretary, who posed as a fan; seated at Stew's desk, pen in hand, paper before her, looking thoughtful as if waiting for inspiration.

She was a natural! Stuyvesant Brown's heart swelled with pride.

How did she feel about her book? Happy, of course! And she felt she owed so much to her publisher.

The scene that occurred when *The Hollander* docked was referred to again. This time, Missie was ready for it.

"It was my fault," she said quietly. "They knew nothing about the book. I was keeping it for a surprise. Can you imagine being met with this?" She gestured at the smoke-filled room. "And not having the slightest idea what it was all about?"

She painted a humorous picture of a group of people who had lived for years in the staid English countryside, their shock at being met by a mob of avid American newsmen, completely in the dark as to the reason.

"And they still may not know why," she said, smiling with forced amusement. "They left New York immediately, and we missed connections. I came here to meet with you."

Every man in the room felt as though she'd singled him out personally.

Including Stuyvesant Brown.

"I understand you're a widow," one gentleman interposed. "Is there a man in your life at present?"

"I try to keep my life as private as possible. But, no, there is no one."

There was a mass sigh of relief.

The day moved onward; the meeting with the sales department, in which Missie offered some constructive ideas; the sherry party, where she was surrounded by a throng; the banquet, where she spoke briefly and delightfully.

Then it was over.

Stew Brown brought her cloak, forcing the way through the crowd around her. Melissa McLeod had just completed a long and tiring journey. She had a busy schedule set up for the next day. They must excuse her—

They fought their way outside and to Brown's waiting carriage. He helped her into it, and she sank back, instantly exhausted. Melissa McLeod had faded. She was only Missie Narvaéz, too tired to speak, to think.

Stuyvesant Brown drove Missie to her hotel and went with her to the door of her room, his heart hammering. Now was the time to press his suit—

He put his arms around her, kissing her. She offered no opposition, but leaned against him, wondering wearily if this, too, was part of an author's life.

"Missie," he said hoarsely, "we've got to talk. I—"

Good God, her eyes were closing! She blinked and lifted a hand to stifle a yawn.

"Forgive me, Stew. It's been a long day. And you said we have a busy schedule tomorrow. Thanks for everything. Good night—"

He cleared his throat. "We'll talk tomorrow. But I'll leave this with you. I haven't acted on it yet, and I thought you might know the best position to take—"

He handed her a slip of yellow paper, and she closed the door against him.

Missie placed the paper on the dresser and sat down immediately to pull off her slippers. After the long train ride, her slender feet were swollen. She ached all over for that matter!

Numbly, she headed for the bathroom, where she drew a bath, undressed, and slid into the water with a sigh. All day, she'd pretended to be someone else. The role of Melissa McLeod, writer, had exhausted her. Dear God, would she be able to cope with another day of this?

Reluctantly leaving the tub, she dried herself and slipped into a warm, fluffy robe. She was heading for bed, praying she would be able to shut home, Matthew, her family from her mind. She glanced at the note Stew Brown had given her. It was probably another protestation of his affections. She would leave it until morning.

But it looked like a telegram—

Sighing, she limped to the dresser and picked it up. She read it, her eyes widening, then read it again.

It was from Duke Courtney, in San Francisco, and addressed to her publisher. He requested that a copy of *The Survivors* be sent to him immediately, for his perusal and that of his attorney.

There was no need to guess at her family's reaction to her book anymore.

Now, she knew.

The next day, she became Melissa McLeod once more, lunching with the firm's senior partners, signing the limited number of books reserved for this special occasion in the afternoon. That evening, she had dinner at the Brown home, meeting Stew's mother, a vague, fluttery, rather silly woman. Missie longed for the dinner to end, wanting only to get back to the hotel, to be alone with her troubled thoughts.

She was silent on the way home. Stuyvesant Brown was concerned. "You're worried about that wire? Do you expect him to take legal action?"

Missie shook her head. A suit would only promote more publicity. None of their family would want that. She smiled painfully. She wasn't looking forward to going home.

"You don't have to," he said passionately. "You belong here! We can send for your children—"

"There are no children, Stew. I—I lied. I didn't want any emotional entanglements."

For a moment, he looked immensely relieved. Then he asked, "Have you changed your mind? Oh, Missie!"

"I don't know." She looked up at him with troubled eyes. "Give me time—"

"But you will stay in New York," he begged. "Tell me you will stay. Give me a chance!"

"Perhaps for a little while."

He hugged her close, kissing her forehead, her lips, in a frenzy of love.

She felt nothing.

He deposited her at her hotel with a proprietary air. When he had gone, she moved disconsolately about her room. The place was comfortable, well-appointed, but it wasn't home. Home consisted of a couple of small rooms above a bakery on Polk Street. She wanted to sleep in her own bed, to rise in the morning to go to the *Examiner*, to see Matthew Blaine—

She must convince herself that part of her life was over. She couldn't return to face a man who didn't love her every day. And she had cut herself off from her family, irrevocably. Missie Narvaéz was dead, and Melissa McLeod was born. It had been hard, being someone else, but she would learn to handle it. She must begin all over again.

And why not make that beginning here, in New York? Here, she was a success. At home, there would be Matthew's indifference, the censure of her own family. Here, nothing could hurt her.

She would never love anyone too much again.

Chapter 48

Tamsen sent Dan off with Duke and Juan on the morning of her meeting with Matthew Blaine. If Missie were with him, she needed to talk to her alone, try to make some sense out of the thing she'd done. If Blaine had news of her, she would keep that, too, to herself. She arrived at the dining room of the Palace early and scanned the room. Matthew had not yet arrived.

She stood for a moment, uncertainly, conscious that a woman was staring at her. The woman whispered to her companion, and there were two pairs of eyes.

Tamsen flushed. Several of the newspapers had published the photographs she'd taken them, along with her carefully worded statement. But they'd also mentioned the content of the book, using terms such as lusty, lurid, passionate, stating that waiting lists were on file at local stores.

She could not blame Em and Arab for the way they felt. Her own past had haunted her for many years, and Missie'd been cruel in raking it up. At times like this, sensing she was being discussed, Tamsen would like to wring the girl's neck herself!

But she didn't have all the facts, she thought wearily. She mustn't jump to conclusions, judging Missie until the facts were all in.

"Mrs. Tallant?"

She jumped a little, then turned to face Matthew Blaine. He looked tired, rumpled, as if he hadn't slept. His eyes were dark and troubled. Her heart went out to him as he led her to a small table for two in a far corner.

"I've already been recognized," she said softly as he seated her. "I hope I'm not compromising your reputation."

Her words brought a spark of a smile. "Does an editor have one?"

They gave their order, asking that coffee be brought while they waited. It was placed before them, and Blaine was silent, as if he were searching for words. Tamsen led him into the subject.

"You have word about Missie? She's come back?"

He shook his head. "I've been thinking about something you said; that she needed friends. I've met Mrs. Courtney. I suppose your family is upset about all the recent publicity—"

Tamsen smiled wryly. "That's putting it mildly. It's upsetting to have one's dirty linen aired publicly. I can't see why Missie—"

"I can. I've read the book."

"Then it's everything they say—"

"And more."

"Oh, dear God!"

Blaine pleated his napkin, avoiding her eyes. "It's the —the 'more,' I mentioned—that I want you to look for when you read it. I want to know if you see the story as I did, and I don't want to influence you in your judgment. I've brought you my copy."

He handed her the book, wrapped in newsprint. "Don't

show it to the rest of the family until you've read it to the end and formed an opinion."

Tamsen stared at him with sudden insight. "You're trying to protect Missie, aren't you?"

Blaine shrugged. "What are friends for?"

"But it's more than friendship, isn't it? You're in love with her, and it's not working out!"

"You're a discerning lady."

"I'm an old lady, and I've been around for a long time as you obviously know, if you've read this." Tamsen looked at the package beside her with a grimace of amusement. "If there's any way I can help, if you need to talk to someone who—who loves the little scamp, too, I'll be glad to listen."

Old lady? There was no one less suited to that category than the attractive woman who sat across the table from Matthew Blaine. But there was something in her dark eyes, sympathy, understanding, that made him want to unburden his soul.

He told of his unfortunate marriage, his crippled son, his bitterness toward women who sought careers outside the home. Then Missie had come along disrupting his emotions, Missie, ambitious, talented, sweet, funny, brave.

Tamsen had known nothing of Petra's background, her disappearance, or the part Missie played in her rescue, almost losing her life in the process. She went white.

"Missie's life hasn't been easy. This isn't the first time—"

"I know." Matthew gestured toward the book. "It's in there. And I haven't made it easier." In a low, stumbling voice, he explained that he'd led Missie to think he had serious intentions, then got cold feet.

"I've been a damned fool!"

He looked so anguished that Tamsen leaned to touch his hand. "It isn't a thing that hasn't happened before. If you love her—"

"I guess," he said dully, "I wasn't thinking of anyone but myself. I remembered that she was a newspaper woman, and she loved her job; that I was on the verge of getting caught in the same trap. Then the damn book came—"

He paused, and Tamsen said, "Go on."

"I apologized, saying that I'd done her a disservice, and that nothing could come of it. I suggested that she forget what happened, that we return to our employer-employee relationship. I suppose I—rejected her."

Tamsen flinched. Poor Missie!

"I guess I thought I was doing us both a favor. I didn't realize how—vulnerable she was, until I read the book. I love her, dammit!"

"Then tell her so!"

Blaine pulled a telegram from his pocket. "This came yesterday."

The wire was from Missie, sent to the *Examiner*, giving Blaine the option of extending her leave or terminating her position, since she was undecided as to whether she would return.

"I figure she's either hurt as hell, or afraid to face her folks," Blaine said somberly.

"I think it's both. Mr. Blaine—Matthew—wire her back, if you love her! Ask her to come home."

He clasped his hands on the table, thumbs together, and studied them as if he might find an answer there. "I don't know. I've got to think about it. She's a success, now. I want her to be happy."

"You think about it, and I'll read the book. Fair enough?"

He forced a rueful grin. "Fair enough."

He had to hurry back to the office. Tamsen left him and did a little shopping to account for her absence at home. Her first purchase was a large shopping bag. She dropped the book into the bottom of it. Even wrapped in newsprint, it looked like what it was—a book. Smiling to herself, she purchased a warm flannel gown and a quilted robe, along with a pair of furry slippers. She might as well do this in style!

If she was unusually quiet that evening, no one noticed.

Another out-of-town newsman had called during the day. Em
and Arab were devastated. Dan, Juan, and Duke discussed
Juan's new venture. Nell was kittenish and coy, fairly bursting with her secret. She had changed her gown, but her pudgy
hands were covered with spots of bright pink paint. She,
Maggie, and Sean kept exchanging what were supposed to be
covert glances. The others were too involved in their own
conversations to notice, but Tamsen was amused.

She wondered what Nell was up to.

Petra was at the table this night, her pallor bearing out
Em's statement that she'd been ill. Tamsen studied her,
seeing the Oriental cast of her features, thinking of the
horrors the girl had undergone in Chinatown. Strange that
she'd had to get the story from Matthew Blaine. Em hadn't
mentioned it. Did Em think that ignoring Petra's background
would make it go away?

It would seem that Petra, like Missie, might need a friend.

Tamsen resolved to talk to her in the morning.

Following the evening meal, Tamsen excused herself and
went up to the room she shared with Dan. There was a small
dressing room attached to it, with a lounge. And here was
where she intended to spend the night.

She dressed in the warm gown and robe, and waited for
Dan to join her.

He grinned at her attire. She looked like Mother Hubbard,
he told her. Then his jaw dropped when he informed he
was sleeping alone. She was catching cold, she lied. She was
feverish and ached all over. She just wanted to be by herself.

He was none too happy, certain she was either sicker than
she pretended, or mad at him about something. Tamsen had
to reassure him, then soothe his feelings. Finally, he gave in
and retired. She went to the dressing room, settled herself on
the lounge, and began to read.

The dedication to the McLeod daughters and to Dusty
caught at her throat. She read on, the scene at the wagonyard
in St. Louis bringing memories of her father vividly to mind.

It was incredible that Missie could have reproduced a past, long before her birth, so vividly.

Here was Dusty come to life! And Dan, mocking and sardonic; her feelings as she fought her attraction toward him.

The girl was a witch!

Cheeks hot, she read on, seeing her father die again on the trail, snow sifting over his grave. Missie's words brought back the pain she thought she'd buried with him.

There had been pain, then terror, as Tamsen wondered what would become of them. Her terror was followed by determination. That determination took them to Magoffinville, Nell, the cantina Tamsen won, using herself as collateral. Tamsen's face darkened as she relived the day she sent Arab off to San Francisco with Reverend Smythe, the worst mistake she'd made in her life. She cringed as she reached the section where Em, sweet, flowerlike Em, was violated by Tamsen's enemies.

So much of it was her fault! She had so much to account for! She fought back a growing anger at her niece.

Missie had no right to do this! Yet she could not put the book down. It was all here, all that had taken place, the feelings of each of them. Tamsen watched them grow in character as they moved ahead. Alaska, Hawaii, Australia—

The End.

They, and Em, who still stood beside her, were the survivors.

Dear God, what a story! Tamsen's eyes were raining tears, soaking the cushion beneath her head. Through the book, she had alternately raged, laughed, cried—and remembered.

This was not the scandalous thing they'd believed it to be, but a tribute! A tribute written by a small, lonely girl, a prickly child no one could get close to, but who had loved them from afar.

Matthew recognized what Missie'd done. But would Arab? Em?

Tamsen slid the book beneath the lounge and wiped her eyes. It was almost dawn and Dan was still sleeping. Her love for the young Dan and the person he was now had come together in her mind.

She needed him.

Slipping into bed beside him, she teased him awake, informing him she'd just made a miraculous recovery.

Chapter 49

Tamsen woke long after Dan had risen. Exhausted after her night of reading, she'd fallen into such a sound sleep that she didn't hear him get out of bed. She looked at the clock on the bedside stand and gasped. It was nearly ten! The household would be awake, have breakfasted, the dishes would be done.

What would Em think of her!

Still, she lay quiet for a time. Missie's book had had a terrific impact on her mind. She must try to lay a little groundwork before she gave it to the others. They might see only the shame of their bared secrets and not look beyond to the message of the book.

And she had also promised herself a talk with Petra. The girl looked so miserable, there must be something on her mind.

Tamsen dressed and went downstairs to discover Dan had made her excuses for her. Her sisters were worried, solicitous. Em forced her to drink a cup of chamomile tea that she

359

neither wanted nor needed, and insisted that she return to bed.

Tamsen didn't protest too much. Petra was probably in her room. This would give her a chance to talk to the girl in private. And Missie's book drew her back like a magnet. There were some chapters she wanted to read again before approaching Arab and Em.

She went up the back stairs, stopping at Petra's room. There was no answer. Probably she had used the other stairs, and they'd missed each other—

They had missed each other by several hours. Petra had dressed for the street, slipping out while the family was at breakfast. She took the cable car to a spot where a large area had been burned. It was cleared now, industrious Chinese workmen already beginning to raise the new structure that would be the House of Wang, Importers.

Standing across the street, Petra looked for Lee among the workmen. Her search was in vain.

With dragging feet, she moved to take the cable car back to the Courtney home. She'd been praying that Lee would have second thoughts and return. Since he hadn't, she'd come to him.

And he wasn't here.

The car she'd planned to board was arriving. But up the block was a horse-drawn cab for hire. Ignoring the cable car, she began to run, her heart palpitating as she gave the driver the Wang's home address.

She was trembling when she alighted and walked up the curving path to the house with its intriguing wings. Behind it, surrounded by shrubs that would flower in the spring, was Lee's special place; her place, that he offered to share with her along with his heart.

Tears stung her eyes as she remembered. But she mustn't cry! She must keep her senses and talk rationally, make him understand—

The door was opened by a houseboy who ushered her into

sitting room where Sara sat painting at a delicate watercolor. The girl showed a fleeting expression of delight that changed quickly to one of caution. "This is a surprise," she said lamely.

"Is Lee here? I must see him."

Sara shook her head, her face closed and wary. Lee and her father had taken the steamer to Sacramento the previous day. They would not be home until quite late.

Petra faltered, searching for words, then burst into the tears she'd been trying to suppress. Sara got quickly to her feet, putting her arms around her guest, hearing her out.

Yes, Sara knew what had taken place at the Courtney home. They had discussed it, as a family. She had pleaded with Lee to return to Petra, but he was a proud man. The elder Wang, recalling the unhappiness of his dead wife in a strange country far from her own people, had agreed with Lee.

Such a marriage would only bring unhappiness to Petra, and therefore to Lee.

"I am half-Chinese," Petra whispered.

"But only half. You could find a husband of whom the Courtneys would approve, and live as they do."

Petra shook her head. "I don't want anyone else." Her soft mouth set in determination. "If my grandmother doesn't approve of Lee, she doesn't approve of me. I've come to—to ask Lee to marry me. I'll get down on my knees if I have to! Sara—help me!"

"I don't know," the younger girl said uncertainly. She studied Petra, the picture of a pampered young lady in her smartly bustled gown, all frills and lace. "If you only looked more—"

She paused and Petra raised her eyes, questioningly.

"More Chinese," she finished. Her eyes widened and she giggled. "Come with me! I have the most wonderful idea!"

She led Petra up the stairs to her mother's room, sliding back the closet door that revealed a row of shimmering

cheongsams. She took down one of green, then hesitated, p
it in place again and took another from the closet. It was
rich, vibrant red.

"Try this! Let me see—"

Petra had lost all modesty in the House of Chen. Sh
hastily removed her cumbersome garments, gown, petticoat
chemise, and stays, slipping into the long-dead woman
Chinese gown.

It might have been fashioned for her.

"Your hair! Let it down! Oh, can we cut it?" Sara pulle
Petra into her own room, seating her before the mirror. Sh
brushed Petra's hair until it hung straight and silky, then c
the front straight across above her brows.

"Look at you," she breathed. "Look at you!"

The face reflected in the mirror was not that of Pet
Channing. The black fringe covering her forehead had altere
the planes of her face. The cheekbones were higher, mor
Asiatic in contour, the eyes those of a lovely Oriental girl.

"You think, perhaps if Lee sees me like this—that h
will—?"

"He won't be able to resist you! My father, either. Do yo
know what you are wearing? That is my mother's weddir
gown! Red, to our people, is the color of happiness!"

"I can't—"

"You can!" Petra said firmly. "Now sit still, I am n
through!"

She brought a little enameled box. It contained face paint
Carefully, she made up Petra's face, outlining the eyes
kohl.

"Now you look very like my mother, as I remember her.

Petra caught at her hands. "I can't be your mother, Sar
but I—I hope I can be your sister."

Sara giggled again. "I have another idea—if you have th
courage!"

"If it will make Lee love me again, I have the courage
do anything."

362

Sara outlined her plan, and Petra's face paled. It was a desperate gamble, but it was worth trying. Lee would remain adamant unless she took the initiative.

"Wait here," Sara said decisively.

She went downstairs and spoke to the houseboy in her native tongue. He was to go to the temple and find Ah Sing, the Taoist priest, asking him to appear just prior to sundown.

"Tell him the daughter of Wang has much trouble and is in need of him," she added extravagantly.

The boy, Hing, looked confused. If Missee was troubled, perhaps it was best that he remain here—

"Go," Sara said. "And remember, just before sundown!" She hurried upstairs. Petra could change to the green cheongsam until evening. They would have tea, and Sara would instruct her in exactly what she must do.

It was Sara's plan to set the stage and have everything ready. Once more, Petra dressed in the red cheongsam. They waited nervously for Ah Sing to arrive. Sara was certain she could convince the old priest. After all, had he not performed the marriage of her mother and father?

Unfortunately, two carriages drove into the drive at the same time, one following the other. Ah Sing occupied the small trap driven by Hing; Lee and his father the other. They had completed their business and returned sooner than expected.

Sara was suddenly terrified, her heart beating like that of a hummingbird. She seized Petra's arm. "Go to the pool. Just stand there. I'll send Lee to you. I will talk to my father—"

Petra obeyed.

Sara faced the newcomers, suddenly feeling very small and frightened. The Wangs were clearly surprised at finding the priest in their home, the old man a little bewildered.

He understood there was need of his services?

"Lee," Sara interrupted nervously, "please go out to the garden. There is a problem. The—the fish are dying!"

"But, Sara—"

She stamped her foot. "Please, Lee! Go! Hurry!"

He shrugged wryly, and left the room. The elder Wang's face wore a look of censure.

"You have summoned the honorable Ah Sing for this?"

"No, Father. Father, please listen."

She began to speak.

Lee Wang walked toward the little glade, wondering whatever in the world had gotten into his small sister. He hadn't believed that tale about the fish for a minute. If it were not for the presence of Ah Sing, he would think she'd concocted some kind of prank. Sara, reared in Western fashion, was totally unlike their shy little mother. The girl had been pampered and indulged. Just as he was indulging her whims now—

He followed the little twisting path, entered the glade, and froze in his tracks.

On the bridge stood a lovely Chinese girl, outlined by the glow of a setting sun. Black silken bangs framed a delicate face, cheeks rouged, eyes rimmed with kohl in the Oriental style. Even in the dimness, her red cheongsam—red, the color of weddings; the wedding gown of Lee's mother—was visible.

For a moment, Lee Wang was certain he was seeing a ghost. Then the girl spoke.

"Lee—"

It was only a single word, but it brought a choked cry from his lips. "Petra! What are you doing here?"

"I have a right to be here. You said you would share this place with me."

Lee looked as if he'd been struck. He braced his shoulders. "You know there can be nothing between us," he said quietly. "I discussed our situation with my father—"

"But not with me." Petra was trembling, but she faced him, head high.

"I want only your happiness," he said on a helpless note.

"And you are a better judge of that than I am? Lee, you

364

asked me to marry you. I'm holding you to it. But only if you want me—"

"Want you! Petra—"

There was no mistaking the anguish in his face, the yearning in his voice. Petra left the bridge where she had waited for him and moved toward him. He took her in his arms, holding her as if she were made of porcelain, tracing the lines of her face with a tender finger.

"Petra! My dearest—"

He kissed her, and they were in a world of their own, oblivious to the approach of those who would intrude on their love.

The senior Wang had heard his daughter out. He was tight-lipped and angry. Perhaps he had made a mistake with this girl, allowing her too much freedom of thought. A child should reverence her elders, have respect for a father's decisions. Not only was she attempting to reverse the decision he'd made after long and careful deliberation, but he must also suffer humiliation before a Taoist priest.

He left the house and walked toward the glade, Sara and the ancient Ah Sing following. He sincerely hoped young Lee had kept his senses. Much of Wang's business was with Duke Courtney. An unwanted liaison between their houses would be an embarrassment. But more important, he loved his son, wishing for him all the happiness—

He stopped short, stunned at the scene before him. Lee was holding a Chinese girl in his arms; a girl who might have been his own lost Mei. Wang felt a pain in his chest and pressed his hand against his heart.

The young couple, with the background of the arched bridge against the sunset, presented a picture of rare beauty. They belonged here, in this special place he had constructed for his beloved wife. He shuddered with an ache of memory, feeling Mei's hand on his arm.

He looked down into Sara's amber-colored eyes. They pleaded with him, and he nodded, almost imperceptibly.

Sara was gone, running toward the house. She returned with a red robe over her arm. Wang motioned to a stone, and Ah Sing moved toward it, to sit cross-legged in his proper place.

Wang stepped forward, clearing his throat, and the young couple leaped apart.

"The priest awaits you," Wang said quietly. "I give you my blessing."

The blaze of happiness in two faces assured him he was right in doing as he did. Silently, he slipped the red robe over Lee's shoulders, then gripped his son's hand for a moment before he released him.

Wang folded his arms across his chest and watched as Lee and the lovely girl, so like his own dead wife, walked forward to prostrate themselves before the priest. Just so they had done, he and his Mei, who had come to him from their homeland.

The priest spoke a few words over them. In the Chinese way, they had now become man and wife. They rose, moving backward from the glade and the priest's presence, then ran hand in hand, toward the house.

The others followed more slowly. Wang saw his old priestly friend into the carriage, then returned to find Sara alone in the living room. Lee and Petra had disappeared. He had an idea where they were. They had returned to the glade, now that Ah Sing had gone.

He rubbed his face meditatively. There would certainly be repercussions to follow. He had listened to his heart speaking rather than his head. What was done was done. He had no regrets. Unless it might be that he had reared a disobedient child!

"Sara," he said sternly, "I am humiliated at your behavior."

"Yes, Father."

"From this time forward, my wishes will be respected in this house!"

"Yes, Father."

He looked at her suspiciously. She was a model of decorum, but her eyes were dancing with mischief. He groaned. ara had always been able to twist him around her little nger. He put an arm around her, and hugged her close.

In the glade, Lee and Petra were lost in the wonder of each ther. The sun had set, and the moon hung like a golden antern in the sky, gilding them with magic.

Petra Wang, née Channing, timorous, subservient, had run way from life for the last time. Now, she had come home.

Chapter 50

Petra was not missed by the Courtneys until evening. Tamsen, engrossed in Missie's book, did go to her room several times, but the girl was apparently downstairs. Em assumed she was still depressed over Lee Wang, and ignored her absence. When they sat down at the evening meal, Duke was concerned about Petra. The child had to eat!

Em said she would take her a tray when they were done, and the conversation turned to topics of the day.

It was almost eight when a messenger appeared on the porch. Duke took the envelope he carried, recognizing Wang's seal. He opened it, read it, and handed it to Em.

It stated that Petra Channing and Lee Wang had been married in a Taoist ceremony this day, taking this course in order to avoid further embarrassment for Petra's family.

"'Embarrassment'! What the hell's Wang saying here? The kids were engaged!"

Em's shocked expression had turned to one of guilt, Arab's matched.

"Em," Duke's voice was deceptively soft, growing louder with each word, "what have you done!"

"I've done nothing! I admit I've discouraged them from seeing each other, hoping Petra would come to her senses. I did not consider Lee Wang a suitable—"

"You 'did not consider'! My God, woman!" Duke looked as if he might strike her. "I suppose you told Lee that he wasn't up to your social standards?"

"I didn't," Em insisted.

"Em, I'm going over there! If I find out you're lying, I may not come back!" He started toward the door and Em gave a little cry of pain. Arab leaped to her feet.

"Wait, Duke! What happened was my fault! The boy called with some packages, and I sent him to the back door. I had no idea, until Em told me—"

"And then what did you do? Did either of you go after him? Apologize?"

"We thought it was for the best," Em whispered. "And I still do! Go after her, Duke. Bring her home. This wedding isn't legal—"

"I'll be damned if I will!"

"Then she's no longer a member of my family! I will not countenance her living with a—a heathen! I blame Missie for a lot of this! Filling her head with a lot of wild ideas, turning her against us!"

Em wept, and Arab put her arms around her. Tamsen, her face flaming, rose and left the table. She hurried upstairs and came down with a book, slamming it on the table.

"You're going to listen to me, all of you! This is Missie's book! And she's just done me the biggest favor I've had in my whole damn life! She's reminded me who I was! And I like the person I was! If I keep on remembering how I got here, and don't try to pretend I'm better than anyone else, I might even like the person I am now! I suggest you try a big dose of Missie's medicine!

"As for me, I've had it! I'm sick of hearing Missie blamed

for things we did ourselves! I've tired of trying to whitewash the past. You've made a helluva lot of mistakes yourself, Em! You, too, Arab! They're all down on paper, especially mine! And I'm glad! I've had enough of wanting to hide my faults and lick my wounds in private. From now on, I'm Tamsen Tallant and proud of it!

"Dan, help me pack our things. I'm not respectable enough for this crowd! We're going to a hotel until we can find a house!"

Dan rose. He and Tamsen went upstairs. Em and Arab looked at each other in shock. And finally, Nell hoisted her bulk to her feet.

"Reckon we might ez well pack, too. Bought me a place, t'other day. Spec' th' paint's dry enuf t' move in."

Em and Arab, unable to bear the eyes of their husbands, stood and began to clear the table. They made an effort to stay in the kitchen after it was done.

Duke and Juan helped the Tallants with their luggage. Sim Blevins was called to drive them to their hotel, and then to return as speedily as possible for others who would be leaving. Nell and her protégés were waiting on the porch when he returned.

When they were finally gone, Duke went into the kitchen, took his wife by one arm, Arab by the other, and dragged them back to the table. Juan sat waiting, Missie's book open before him.

"Start reading, Juan," Duke said harshly. "Ladies, make yourselves comfortable. You're not leaving this spot until this is all out in the open."

"I don't want to hear it," Em wept.

Arab clapped her hands over her ears. "I won't listen!"

Juan's voice overrode her. "The dedication," he began.

"*For the Survivors, the daughters of Scott McLeod, women of strength and character, who fought for their happiness, and won. For Nell,*" Juan paused, choking up a little, "*and especially for Dusty, who made this book possible.*"

371

He paused again, looking over his reading glasses at the two silent women, and read on.

"Page one."

Tamsen and Dan had reached their hotel. Tamsen, now that she'd spoken her mind, was subdued. It wasn't until they had reached their room, the door closed behind them, that she spoke to Dan.

"Dan, I'm sorry."

"You only said what you thought. They had it coming."

"The funny thing is," Tamsen said, reflectively, "I'm not really mad. I just wanted to give them a jolt. Dammit, they've been sitting there, reinforcing each other, twisting things out of proportion! I can understand it—"

Dan, shaking out some hastily packed shirts, cocked a questioning eye at her. "You can? Em's prim and self-righteous, Arab's turned into a selfish bitch—"

"But not inside, Dan. Em's basically gentle and sweet. The things that happened to her in the past were terrible, alien to her nature. She's fought hard to attain respectability, a social position, trying to erase all the rest."

"I liked her better the other way," Dan grinned. "All right, now find some excuse for Arab!

"Arab was never a real mother to Missie, you know that. She couldn't see any of the girls but Luka. It killed her, leaving Luka in England. Now, she's trying to justify her feelings by insisting Missie let us down. I imagine she feels guilty as hell."

"And you, Mrs. Solomon! How do you feel?"

"I felt the same way they did," Tamsen said candidly, "hurt, frightened, humiliated. But I wasn't about to hate my niece until I read what she wrote."

"And now that you have?"

"Now that I have, I feel like a whole person. I did what I thought was necessary at the time. I don't think I'd change if I had it to do over again, except," she smiled up at him, "I might have married you a little sooner."

Dan put his arms around her, remembering the small dark-haired girl he'd first seen bending over a cookfire in a St. Louis wagonyard. He'd loved her then, his Tamsen. He would love her all his life. Beautiful, brave, scrappy—even a little bit naughty.

There was nothing he would change about her, either, unless it was her strong sense of responsibility toward her sisters. Tonight had hurt her—

"Tomorrow," he said softly, "I've agreed to meet with Duke and Juan. Something to do with the business Juan's buying. But then we're going to start looking for that house again. The Tallants need a home of their own."

Leaving Tamsen and Dan at their hotel, Sim Blevins had returned for his next set of passengers. He didn't have a clue as to what precipitated the sudden departures. There must have been some kind of family argument to send the Courtney guests off at this hour. He supposed the second group would consist of Juan and Arab Narvaéz.

He almost fell off the carriage seat to see Nell waiting on the porch, arms akimbo, hat slammed flat on her head, its feathers dangling over her nose. Behind her, Maggie and Sean sat on her steamer trunk.

Sim climbed down. Together, he and Sean loaded the trunk and the group clambered aboard.

"What th' hell y'doin'?" Sim asked.

"Movin'," Nell answered shortly. "Over t' th' bar. Git goin'."

"They throw you outa th' joint?"

"No, dammit!" Nell turned a ravaged face toward him. Tears streaked her heavily rouged cheeks and she blew her nose noisily.

"Hadda git out afore I smacked them two prissy-pants! That pore leetle Petra-girl!"

Bit by bit he drew the story of what had happened from her; Em's efforts to keep Lee and Petra apart, the way they tore into Missie.

"Tam tolt 'em off," Nell said proudly. "Duke an' Juan ain't too happy with 'em. Reckon all hell busted loose after we got gone."

"Mebbe y'shoulda smacked 'em! Damn rich-bitches!"

"Now wait a minnit!" Nell turned on him. "Watch who th' hell yer callin' names! Thass Em an' Arab yer talkin' about! Don't go critter-sizin' yer betters!"

She burst into noisy sobs. For a moment he stared at her in perplexed anger, then his hand stole out to pat her pudgy one.

"Aw, Nell, I didn' mean nuthin'." Clumsily, he drew her head against his shoulder, chin high to avoid the feathers that made him want to sneeze.

They reached the tavern. Cans of paint still sat about. Ladders leaned against walls. The beds, left behind by the previous owner had been stacked in a back room to haul off. There was nothing to do but drag them out and set them up again.

Nell looked at hers dubiously. The frame was frail, the slats thin, the mattress sagging and lumpy. She wasn't too sure it would hold her bulk.

"Oh, well," she sighed, "after what that thing's been through, it oughta be able to hold jes' one!"

Sim finally left them to bed down for the night. Driving home, he pondered his situation. He liked Duke all right; and Juan, though he looked stuck-up, was a decent feller. But them wimmen! He'd like to smack 'em himself for upsetting his Nell. The place wouldn't be the same without her.

Shifting his peg leg to a more comfortable position, he whipped up the horses. Tonight, he would pack his sea chest. Tomorrow, he would tender his resignation. By nightfall, he would be living with Nell and the kids. He'd begun to think of himself as part of their family.

Around the Courtney table, the reading went on; vocalizing words a much longer process than scanning with the eye. The women were stiff and resentful at first, Arab softening a little as Juan read of the madcap young girl she had been in her early teens. Duke chuckled at a description of an interlude in which Tamsen rescued Arab from a young ruffian. She thought she had killed him. It had been Em's idea to bury him, and hide the evidence.

The boy wasn't dead at all, but dead drunk, waking as they tried to roll him into a shallow grave, frightening them out of their wits.

"You never told me that," he grinned. Em, her face pink, looked down at her hands.

Juan, growing hoarse, passed the book to Duke. The sisters wept at the death of Scott McLeod. Duke read on with a growing wonder at Tamsen's strength as she stole Dan Tallant's horses and broke from the train, making the trek to Magoffinville. He had heard some of the old stories from Dusty and Nell, but Missie painted a vivid picture of hunger, privation, dogged perseverance.

Tamsen's job at the cantina; Arab's ill-fated trip with the spurious Reverend; Em's travail, her heroic actions along the trail to California; facing down hostile Indians while in labor with Martha.

Duke closed the book. Em's face was white, and she was reeling in her chair. It was already morning.

"We will read again tonight," he said. "I suggest you girls get some sleep during the day. Juan and I are meeting Dan, signing the final papers on Juan's building."

Arab reached for the book and he held it away from her. "No, this is to be read when we're all together! Otherwise, you'll dwell on certain passages and overlook others. Personally, I think this is one helluva book! And I want Missie to have a fair shake."

The women went upstairs. Em lay sleepless until long after the men had left the house. Her door opened, and Arab came stealing into the room. Her face was blotchy from crying.

"Am I disturbing you, Em?"

"No, I can't sleep."

"I couldn't, either," Arab confessed. She burst into a storm of weeping. "Oh, Em, I'd forgotten so much! Were we ever that young?"

THE SURVIVORS

Chapter 51

After Dan left for his meeting with Duke and Juan, Tamsen paced the hotel room nervously. The past, aroused by Missie's book, filled the room, suffocating her with memories. Finally, she donned a cloak and left the hotel, walking the streets, trying to clear her aching head.

A great deal of the book pertained to Madam Franklin's Parlor for Gentlemen; the plush bawdy house Tamsen had owned and operated on Stockton Street. Since her arrival in San Francisco, Tamsen had stayed clear of the place with its bitter recollections.

But were they so bitter, after all?

Memories tugged at her heart and her feet followed. She was suddenly drawn to her old haunts, pulled as if by some invisible cord. She turned a familiar corner, trembling a little, her eyes to the ground. Then she made herself look up, afraid of what she might see—

It was still there, though many of the tall old buildings, twin to it, were gone. And it looked much as it had when she first saw it, gray and gaunt, unwelcoming. Again, she went back in time. A disastrous fire had struck the city, burning the small sewing shop that was their livelihood: hers, Em's, and little Martha's. They'd been rescued by Sam Larrabee, a happy-go-lucky man who'd wanted Tamsen to marry him and go to Hawaii.

She couldn't. She loved Dan, even then. But she had slept with Sam, and he'd left a bag of gold behind.

Gold, to be invested in a business venture; in this weathered building that now had a For Sale sign on its tiny square of dead lawn.

Tamsen made herself approach the building. She'd had the hand-hewn shingles stained to a charcoal. The color had faded away, and some of the shingles were missing. The passing of years had eroded the gleaming white exterior she designed; the oak door was pitted; the pink shutters designed to enhance the too-small windows were long gone. The door hung slightly open, and she forced herself to enter.

The long bar had been here, the piano, there. The chandelier was missing, though the eight-foot round mirror above it was still in place; clouded now, with age. Scraping the floor with the toe of her slipper, she could see that it was still the same parquet she'd had polished, scattered with Oriental rugs.

There was the private dining room, now filled with someone else's castoffs. Gone was all the luxury, the opulence that she had created with Sam's money—

And Dan's, she thought, a little wickedly. She'd let him think she was the mother of little Martha, and that the child was his. It had been a case of blackmail, pure and simple!

Had it been so wrong?

She had loved Sam Larrabee in a way that didn't detract from her love for Dan. He had been kind to her, she knew that her refusal to marry him hurt him. He had been going away, to a land that seemed so far at that time. That night in his arms had been a gesture of gratitude and affection. She'd found the money on the table in the morning—

And Dan had long since forgiven her for blackmailing him. He deserved it, he said. He had taken her one night in anger, rather than in love. There could have been a child of that union.

There hadn't been, not then, or since. After her marriage, Tamsen had devoted her life to Dan, to Em and Arab; Arab's children—

And especially to Missie, Missie who had shown her that her past was not as shameful as she'd thought. This business had helped Em to live in a style becoming to a lady; to marry a wealthy senator. For a while, Em had known happiness with Donald Alden, a happiness she'd forgotten at his tragic death.

Sighing, Tamsen left the building. At the corner, she turned to look back. If she looked hard enough, she could see a charcoal roof, a facade of glistening white, pink shutters—

The place could look like that again!

The thought struck her like a lightning bolt!

She'd had no roots, no place that was home to return to. The Courtney mansion with its pastel rooms suited Em, but never Tamsen! She needed color, velvets, rich textures, warmth—

Dear God! Home was Madam Franklin's Parlor for Gentlemen, situated on a shabby, rundown street! It could be restored to its former elegance! She could imagine coming down that curving stair, seeing the glimmer of lights from the chandelier reflected in gold-framed mirrors along with a dozen Tamsens, all young again—

It was only a conceit. But yet—why not? What would Dan think! Would he consider a former bawdy house a home? Her hand went to her lips as she thought of Em's opinion, Arab's!

And finally, she threw back her head and laughed, a silvery, infectious laugh that rang along the silent street like bells.

This was her life she was considering! Not Em's, not

Arab's! Tamsen McLeod of the trail, Poppy Franklin of the Magoffinville cantina, Madam Franklin of the bawdy house, Tamsen Tallant—they were all there, inside her, and it was nobody's business but her own—and Dan's! Except where he was concerned, she didn't give a damn!

Dan had returned to the hotel. Tamsen burst into the room, her dark eyes luminous, her cheeks painted with excitement. Her words tripped over each other as she delineated her plan.

Dan listened, a grin beginning to form on his lips. "If that's what you want, sweetheart—"

"Not unless you want it, too!"

He took her hands. "Remember me? Gunslinger, horse-trader, surveyor? I've been out of my league with this ambassador crap. Hell, I spent a lot of years hanging around places like that! Might as well spend my best ones the same way—unless, you're planning to put the house back in operation—"

"No, Dan, but I want it exactly like it was. And it looks so awful, now."

He waved her worries away. "I'll look at it. If it's structurally sound, we'll get a crew right on it. We've got to get out of this damned hotel."

"Dan—don't say anything to Duke or Juan about this."

He quirked an eyebrow. "Ashamed of it already?"

"No. I just want to wait until it's done, when we move in. Promise?"

"I promise."

"Dan, I love you."

He cupped her face in his hands, looking down into her enormous dark eyes, windows to her heart.

"I love you too," he whispered. "And I can't wait to go—home."

Nell was already ensconced in her tavern. The previous night, the slats gave way beneath her bed. Maggie, having been told of the San Francisco quakes, came screaming into the hall, Sean following in his nightshirt. Today, new beds

had been installed, along with a wood stove, screened in front
to reveal its fire. The temperature had dropped, a cold wind
moving from the sea. But the big downstairs room was clean
and warm.

"This is purty damn cozy, I'd say," Nell beamed. "Here
we's all set, snug ez bedbugs! Nuthin' like home an' fambly."

As yet, the beds were their only furniture. They sat flat on
the floor around the stove, preparing to return to their reading
now that the day's work was done. Nell was giving a
synopsis of what had gone before to the incredulous Sim
Blevins.

"That ain't Missus Tallant yer talkin' about? I be damned!
An' the Em in th' book's Missus Courtney? Hell, I thought
they wuz ladies!"

"Wuz, an' is," Nell reminded him with a frown. "Now,
go on readin', Maggie. I reckin we's about where we left off.
I'm anxious t'git t'Rooshian Alaska, an' when I run inta His
Royal Hiney."

Sim Blevin's adventures in China, his experiences as a
crimp, paled before the story that unfolded before him. Nell
took on a new dimension, the glamour of a character in a
book. He felt a reverent awe in her august presence.

"You're a lotta woman, Nell," he said sincerely.

"That's what my Dusty allus said. Hell, what we all settin'
so fur apart fer? Ever'body ooch a leetle closer, friendly like.
Awright, Maggie, git goin'."

At the same time, the quartet at the Courtney table took up
where they'd left off reading the previous night. Em relived
the horror of the San Francisco fire; gasped at Tamsen's
shocking affair with Sam Larrabee, her blackmailing of Dan.
Then she wept as Missie went into Tamsen's mind; establishing
her notorious enterprise so that her family would never know
poverty again.

Donald Alden appeared on the scene. And Em remembered
that she'd loved the gentle, silver-haired senator, loved him in
a way that took nothing from her love for Duke. After he died

by his own hand, she'd thought he failed her. Now, she came to terms with it for the first time.

She wept silently, and Juan read on.

Then it was Arab's turn. Her romance with Juan, a passionate affair begun in a castle garden; her kidnapping, her return to San Francisco after months of degradation. Juan following, giving up his life and ambitions for her sake.

She had forgotten. In these last years, she had demanded more and more, thinking only of her own best interests.

They listened, seeing themselves in the mirror of time. And it was Missie who held the mirror before their eyes.

Chapter 52

Three days later, Em Courtney lifted the dragon's head that
served as knocker on the door of the Wang home; a gracious-
appearing building with its wings and ells, its exquisitely
ended lawn. She and Arab were nervous at their errand, but
determined.

The door was opened by a very pretty, very young Chinese
girl. Em extended her card.

"I am Mrs. Courtney. This is Mrs. Narvaéz. I would like
to speak with my granddaughter."

The girl's eyes, topaz-colored, widened. Then she said, "I
am her sister-in-law, Sara Wang. Please come in. I will
inform her that you are here."

She led the guests into a spacious room, sparsely furnished
but attractive, and seated them. Then she left, her graciousness
forgotten as she hurried down the hall. They could hear a note
of panic in her voice as she called for Petra.

"I suppose she thinks we're ogres," Em said wryly. "And
perhaps we are."

385

"We were," Arab reminded her. Her gloved hand went to clasp her sister's as they waited. "Em, I don't know what to say!"

"I don't either," Em confessed.

The situation took care of itself. Petra appeared in the doorway, a slim girl in a cheongsam, her hair cut in Chinese style. Even her wary, defensive expression didn't conceal the fact that she was happy. She fairly glowed with it.

Em rose. "Petra," she said uncertainly, then she held out her arms.

"Grandmother!" The girl threw herself into Em's embrace, weeping. "Pease don't be mad! I had to do it this way—"

"If I'm mad at anybody, it's at myself," Em told her. "We're here to apologize, Arab and I. Both to you and to your—your husband."

Lee wasn't home. But, oh, Grandmother, he was wonderful! They must see the wing they occupied! He was letting her decorate it as she wished.

Tea! They must have tea! And while it was being prepared she must show them her special place; where she and Lee had been married. It was the most beautiful spot in the world.

She led them to the lawn at the rear, along a little crooked path to the hidden glade, where water sang as it spilled silver into a pool with an arched bridge. Everything miniature, as if to suit Petra's small stature. Everything perfectly planned, perfectly proportioned, the setting might have been lifted from the Orient.

Arab was quiet, remembering a pool in Spain. She had been able to see it from the window of Juan's home; a Roman-style pool with white pillars. Beyond had been terraced gardens, dropping to white sands—and then, the blue Mediterranean.

She thought of herself as she had been then, a white-skinned girl with flaming hair; of Juan, his brown body dark and smooth to the touch as they played like children in the

386

waters at night. The moon transformed them into silver and amber creatures, otherworldly, unreal—

Petra noted that Arab was ashen, and they returned to the house. Over pale tea in delicate porcelain cups, Em broached the subject uppermost in her mind.

First and foremost, she loved Petra—and Lee. She wished him to take his place as part of her family. Secondly, she wished to give Petra a proper wedding.

"Wait," she said, lifting a hand as she saw the girl's face close against her, "it isn't that I don't consider you married, now." She faltered for a moment, then set her lips in determination. "Listen, I want to tell you a story—"

She told of walking with Duke Courtney, along an old Indian trail in Alaska; that she had been the one to do the proposing; that they'd sat together on a sun-warm rock, butterflies opening and closing their wings above them, holding each other—

"We were married then," Em said quietly. "I would have gone with him like that. But the ceremony that followed was—special, because it included the other people I loved. It was a way of telling the world we belonged to each other.

"I would like to show the world that I'm proud of you and Lee. That you're my grandchildren. Please, Petra, I want to do this!"

Em's face was contorted with emotion, her blue eyes welling with tears, her plea agonized and sincere. Petra ached for her.

"I will talk to Lee."

That night, Lee Wang and his young wife, Petra, arrived at the Courtney mansion. Lee's doubts were dispelled at the warmth with which they were welcomed. It was he who had considered repeating their vows in Western fashion, Petra who rebelled until her talk with her grandmother. He wanted only for his wife to be happy. Strongly conscious of family, he had no desire to separate her from those she loved.

The wedding was set for December tenth. The young

couple took their leave and went home to sleep in each other's arms.

The thought of romance was contagious. Duke kissed his wife.

"I'm so proud of you!"

"I'm proud of me, too," Em smiled. "I haven't really liked myself for a long time. This is going to be the biggest wedding of the year! I'm going to inform the papers tomorrow, ask for reporters and photographers! And I'm going to invite all my—my former friends."

"They probably won't show up."

She clenched her fists. "I don't care! But, dammit, Duke! I won't have them look down on Petra! I just won't!"

"Have you talked to Tamsen, told her what's up?"

She shook her head forlornly. "Duke, I—I'm still trying to get my thoughts together. Arab, too. It—it's like I've been asleep for a long time, forgetting a lot of things that were important. I'm beginning to face up to who I am and where I've been wrong. But I can't face Tamsen, yet. I suppose I'm too—ashamed. I'm just going to send her an invitation to the wedding and let her see for herself—"

"I'll take it to her myself. Sending one to Nell?"

"Nell, Maggie, Sean, Sim Blevins, all of them."

Sim Blevins? Duke pursed his lips in a soundless whistle. Somewhere, the socially minded Em Courtney had fallen by the wayside. He had his own girl back again.

By morning he'd lost her to a flurry of preparation. The newspapers were notified. Mr. and Mrs. Duke Courtney were pleased to announce the coming marriage of their granddaughter, Petra Channing, to Lee Wang, scion of the House of Wang. The wedding, to be held in the Courtney home, was to be one of the largest of the season. It would take place—

"Do you really want to go this far, Em?" Duke asked.

"I do. If nobody comes, they—just don't come!"

The invitations, hastily printed, were ready for delivery within a day. Duke hand-carried the Tallants' to the hotel, hoping to lay a little groundwork for Em. He knew Tamsen well enough to know she'd come more than halfway in patching up the quarrel between herself and her sisters.

The Tallants were not in, and the clerk didn't know when to expect them. Duke left the invitation at the desk and went on to Nell's Place, grinning as he saw the rather seedy little bar. Nell had plenty of money, yet she had chosen this. It was a replica of all the taverns he'd seen throughout the world. It suited her.

He entered, seeing the long bar across the room, spittoons beside it polished to match its brass rail. He could almost imagine Dusty standing behind it—

Then Nell appeared, a cloth in her hand. She'd been shining up the new tables that had just arrived.

"I'll be damned," she boomed. "Sim, look who's here! Duke, yer a sight fer sore eyes. Well," she waved the dustcloth, beaming, "waddaya think?"

"I think it's a helluva good setup."

"Wisht we wuz in operation. Give y' drinks on th' house. How's things t'home?"

She had lost her early gladness and looked old, concerned. Duke grinned at her.

"Couldn't be better."

Missie's book had accomplished miracles. They'd read it through to the end. The news brought Nell back to her ebullient self.

"Howja like the part where I ooched acrost that log over th' river, carryin' the sammy-var I got off them Rooshians? Still got splinters in my butt. Still got th' sammy-var. Wuz gonna set it in here, jes' fer dekky-rashun, but I wuz afeared some bastid'd spit in it!"

Sim came down the stairs, covered with wallpaper paste, Maggie and Sean behind him. Duke presented Em's invitations, telling them of the wedding plans.

Nell was pleased. It looked like Em and Arab had cleaned up their act.

"Who all's comin'?"

Duke grimaced. "I know who she's asking." He named a number of socially prominent people. "But I doubt there'll be many more than just family."

When he had finally gone, Nell leaned her bulk against the bar. "It's a damn shame," she told Sim. "All them high-falutin' sonsofbitches are goin' t' stay away in droves! By God, somebuddy oughta drag 'em to that there weddin' an' make 'em crawl! I'd give ever' cent my Dusty lef' me, if on'y—"

"You mean that?" Sim Blevins asked, grinning his ferocious grin.

"Yer damn tootin'!"

"Well, why th' hell we standin' around? Les' git goin'!"

Chapter 53

That afternoon, Nell Wotherspoon and Sim Blevins were on their way to the bank. Nell wore her favorite ladyship costume of purple velvet, her largest hat festooned with feathers. Sim Blevins had resurrected a rusty black suit and top hat from his sea chest. Maggie brushed it and touched it up with a sadiron. Its sleeves strained over his muscled arms and shoulders, but Nell insisted that he was "th' spittin' image of a gennulman."

When he stopped the carriage and aided her down, she simpered. Ever'body was lookin' at them. And why not? Prob'ly ez much class ez they'd laid eyes on before.

Placing a hand in the crook of Sim's arm, she swept into the bank. The clerk, having encountered Lady Wotherspoon before, went immediately for his superior. And finally, Nell and Sim were seated in the vice president's office.

"You han'le it, Sim," Nell said coquettishly. "Yer th' man of th' fambly."

Sim Blevins had a photographic memory. He reeled off

names of a number of San Francisco's prominent citizens. These folks were Lady Wotherspoon's friends. He knew the bank held notes for some of them. She'd like to buy those notes up, as a favor to them—and the bank.

The banker ran his finger down the list. Many were his creditors. "This would amount to quite a sum—"

"No skin off my butt," Lady Wotherspoon said modestly. "I got piles."

They left the bank, exulting, having procured a number of notes. "Now," Sim Blevins said. "We go to my bank."

Here, the number of creditors mounted. Nell paled a little. "I dunno how much I got left," she said doubtfully.

"I'll take care of it," Sim said. "Jes' put the papers in this here lady's name."

"Sim, you ain't got that kinda money!"

"Hell I don't," he grinned. "I own th' damn bank."

Nell subsided. Evidently crimping had been a lucrative profession. She filed the occupation away in her memory—just in case she ever needed it.

Their last stop was at a printing office. Nell wanted to have some calling cards made. "They got to have class," she informed the clerk who took her order.

He suggested that they contain only her name, "*Lady Eleanor Wotherspoon*," spelled out in delicate script, showing her an example. Nell considered it a little too plain.

Hell, she thought, this was costing her a bundle, so why not kill two birds with one stone. She tapped the card with a pudgy beringed finger.

"Right there, under where it says it's me, write in '*Owner and Proprietor of Nell's Place*.' And make it fancy."

The cards were printed by the next afternoon. Nell was as enthralled with them as a child with a new toy. She and Sim immediately set out on their rounds.

"Reckon we'll take this Wilson bitch, first," Nell boomed. "She's the one didn' invite Em to her—whatever th' hell it wuz."

Sim waited in the carriage while Nell plodded to the front door, presenting her card to a startled maid who fled before her scowl.

Edna Wharton Wilson was breakfasting in bed when the maid burst in with the news that a caller was waiting. She frowned. It was far too early for respectable people to be abroad.

"Lady Wotherspoon, did you say?"

The maid nodded. Edna Wilson did not intend to let a Lady escape, no matter what the hour. She rose reluctantly, dressed, and went downstairs to stop, openmouthed, in the doorway.

Someone was playing a dreadful joke! This raddled old horror had gotten in through false pretenses! She took another look at the card. *Owner and Proprietor of Nell's Place.*

"What is the meaning of this?" she asked icily. "If you're trying to sell something—"

"Ain't sellin'," Nell grinned. "Tradin'. An' I'm givin' you a damn good deal. You go to a weddin', an' I don't foreclose."

The wedding announcements had been marked R.S.V.P. Em was amazed when acceptances began arriving; even more so when she received one from the Wilsons. Certain of a refusal, she hadn't sent their invitation, yet.

Also among the acceptances were a number of names from the Chinese community, an almost illiterate note penned by Maggie on behalf of Nell and her party, a formal acknowledgment from Tamsen and Dan, and one from Matthew Blaine.

Em had puzzled over his name on the list. Petra had insisted that he be included, a surprising demand from a girl who knew so few people—

Petra had not forgotten Matthew Blaine. In a way, she would always love him—just a little. Now she had managed to come to terms with the conversation she'd overheard, the sentences that sent her flying into Chinatown, searching for her own kind.

She had been attracted to Matthew, basking in his kind

attentions. She hadn't realized it was Missie he cared for, and that she was an intruder in their relationship. His explosive words hadn't been directed at her, at Petra Channing, but at a situation he could find no way to remedy: a third party always present, standing between him and the girl he loved.

Missie was in New York, something to do with her book. But Petra knew, intuitively, that she and Matthew must be estranged. She could never have left Lee, for any reason.

Maybe when Missie returned, and they got together, alone, it would be different. She wanted Matthew at the wedding, to show him that she was no longer an obstacle; that she had a man of her own.

"Write down Matthew Blaine," Em told Arab, "and Tamsen and Dan. Oh, Arab, I wonder if Tam's still mad! What she's thinking!"

Tamsen had never been happier. The invitation to Petra' wedding, to be held at the Courtney home, was proof that Em and Arab had come around. The brief announcement of the coming event in the papers settled her mind completely.

The knowledge of Petra's background had been difficult for Em. Her marriage to Lee Wang would be a bitter pill for her to swallow. Yet she was handling it with good grace.

"I hope Em's bitchy friends don't tear her to pieces," Tamsen told Dan. "After the publicity about Missie's book not a damn one showed up. This big wedding the paper mentions will probably be a flop."

"I don't think Petra and Lee will notice."

"But Em will. Oh, Dan, I wanted her to get her value straight, but I don't want her hurt."

"There'll be some high society types there," Dan said grinning. "The Tallants, from their mansion on Stockton Street!"

"It's beginning to look like home, isn't it? The red carpet on the stairs—and that bar you found is exactly like the one that was there when—"

"Every home should have a forty-foot bar with a brass rail!"

"You don't mind, Dan?"

"Hell, no. When they set it up, I could almost see Dusty behind it."

They were both quiet for a moment. The old house was slowly regaining its original splendor, but there were some things that could never be replaced.

"I ordered a piano, today," Tamsen said in a subdued voice. Then, "Dan, do you think we can move in by Christmas?"

"I don't see why not."

"I'd like to have a housewarming, invite Arab and Em."

"Whoa, let's take one thing at a time. We don't know what the atmosphere's like over there. After the way you walked out on them, it could be pretty damn cool!"

Dan was right. There had been only the one message since that night, a wedding invitation. And it was probably sent as a courtesy. She intended to attend, welcome or not. If no one else came, Em would need her family to stand behind her.

There would be others there. Nell left the home of the last name on their list, chortling. Missus Beaseley had been taken with a fit of vapors. The maid called her husband, and Nell put it to him straight. "Seems his finances is in bad shape, on accounta some more folks owes him. Tolt 'im, hell, put th' crews t' 'em, make 'em come along. Hit th' gawdam jackpot!"

She put her pudgy hand on Sim's. "This is gonna be one helluva weddin', Sim, thanks t' you."

He blushed with pleasure. "Hell, I didn' do nuthin'. Jes' knowed where a few bodies wuz buried."

"Thass important. Minds me of Dusty, th' sweet leetle sonofabitch. Mebbe—mebbe it's th' moon an' all that brung im t'mind. Allus makes me feel romantick."

Sim ran a finger inside his collar. "Sorta like a bellyache," he said in a rasping whisper.

"You sure hit th' nail on th' head. You feel like that, too?"

"Sure ez hell do," he growled.

Nell looked up at the sky in wonder, seeing the stars, th sliver of a California moon. It wasn't cold, but she felt a shivery—

"Nell!"

She turned to face Sim Blevins. The eyes in his battere face were soft and searching, then commanding. He reache out, yanking her toward him, knocking the hat off her head a he planted a resounding kiss on her cheek.

"Well, I be damned," Nell said in girlish awe. "Look like I done hit th' jackpot agin!"

The next morning, Emmeline Courtney went in search c her husband. "I can't believe what's happening," she sai distractedly. "Look here! Here are some more acceptances, lot of them! And, Duke, I've never heard of some of thes people in my life!"

Chapter 54

The weather held. The morning of the much-publicized Courtney-Wang nuptials was soft and warm. Sliding doors had been opened, the living room, a sitting room, and the dining room to be utilized for the occasion. Due to the expected crowd, there would be standing room only. Perhaps some of the guests would have to crane their necks to see the bride, but it couldn't be helped.

Em wished, forlornly, that she'd hired a hall.

On the rear lawn, the caterers had set up tables beneath canopies, should the weather change. Em prayed that it would hold.

In the living room, an altar had been set, an arched trellis twined with pink roses and silver ribbon. The decor had been carried throughout the remainder of the house. For a time, it seemed that nothing would be done in time, but the chaos seemed to resolve itself a few moments before the guests were to arrive. Em hurried upstairs to view the bridal party.

Petra wore a simple, traditional gown and veil of palest

ivory, a concession to her Chinese relations since white was color for funereal occasions. It transformed her into a slender fairylike creature. Em's breath caught in her throat as she saw the radiant girl who was her granddaughter.

There were to be only two attendants, Arab in soft rose a matron of honor; and small Sara, an elfin child wearing a deeper shade of the same color. Even in Western dress, the girl was unmistakably Chinese.

Em felt a wave of misgiving, then, angry at herself, put he arms around Lee's young sister.

"You look beautiful," she said.

Below, the guests had begun to arrive, ushered in by butler employed for the occasion. Nell and her group were among the first on the scene. She looked around with possessive eye, recognizing some of her creditors and nodding

"Glad y'made it," she boomed heartily to one. She slapped a red-faced gentleman on the back, nearly flattening him "Good t'see yuh—agin."

She approached the pallid Mrs. Wilson and looked her over with a judging eye. The woman was dressed in a subdued gray dress, an uninspired hat. Hell, y'd think she was goin' t a gawdam funeral! But Nell was bound to show her manners.

"Yer purty ez a speckled pup," she said jovially.

Mrs. Wilson gasped, bearing a strong resemblance to a fish out of water. "That is a—a very charming gown," she finally managed.

Nell looked down at herself complacently. She'd wangled the colors Em planned to use out of Duke, and had thi special-made for the occasion. Her elephantine bulk wa encased in shocking pink satin; her hat a gigantic platter swathed in the same material. Atop it rested a pink bird in nest of egret feathers.

Dusty would have loved it. And Sim, dressed in hi go-to-the-bank suit, couldn't take his eyes off her.

Nell surveyed her family with loving eyes. She'd decided on green satin for Maggie, a replica of her own outfit. The girl was a knockout, except for the bulge in front now beginning to show. Sean had a brand-new suit, its visible green checks complementing Maggie's outfit.

They made the rest of this lot look like a buncha goddamn crows.

She'd never felt so proud in her life.

As the guests infiltrated, she returned to checking them off her mental list. There were the Beaseleys. Good. Then she noticed that members of the Wang family stood alone.

This joint needed a soshul direcktor!

Nell gripped Mrs. Wilson's arm. "We's gonna do us some minglin'," she growled. "Git over there an' innerduce yerself!"

The cream of San Francisco society was treated to the sight of one of its most exclusive members moving toward a group of Chinese merchants, nodding stiffly, touching hands—

"Awright, Beaseley," Nell hissed into that astonished man's ear. "Your turn!"

Tamsen and Dan, arriving late, were astounded at the carriages lining the street before the Courtney house. They entered to find a mixture of high society and Chinese apparently on the best of terms, Nell directing the show.

"I be damned," she shouted, "looka what th' cat dragged in! Folks, this here's th' Tallants, Tamsen an' Dan. You bin readin' about Tam in th' papers! Tam, Dan, git in here, make yerselfs t'home!"

Tamsen moved about the room, suffering Nell's flowery introductions, embarrassed at first at meeting red faces and averted eyes. Then her mouth began to tremble with amusement. Somehow, Nell had managed to fill these crowded rooms for Em's sake. How she'd bullied these people into it, Tamsen had no idea. But she'd done it!

Tamsen met Dan's eyes across the room, and saw that he, too, had guessed.

Matthew Blaine was the last to arrive, entering just as Em descended the stairs to take her place at the piano. As the soft strains of music began, Nell made loud hushing sounds, and the crowd settled into silence.

Arab came down the steps, beautiful in her rose gown, followed by little Sara—so definitely Chinese.

"You would think—," someone said in a whisper. Further comment was cut off by a glare from Nell. Then all attention was directed to the descending bride.

She stood for a moment, a picture in her ivory gown, an arm bouquet of pink roses spilling to the floor, their color echoed in her cheeks as she put a small hand in the crook of Duke's arm. Walking gracefully down the steps, her eyes did not leave Lee's upturned face.

He was already her husband. They were one. This was only a further step in their relationship. They would be doubly bound to each other—for eternity.

They repeated their vows in reverent hushed tones, then moved as man and wife to accept the congratulations of the guests. They left in order to make the steamer that was to carry them to Sacramento for a brief honeymoon, and finally the crowd spilled on to the back lawn to partake of refreshments. Em remained behind, catching at Tamsen's arm.

"Wait, Tam. Arab and I need to talk to you."

While the guests outside converged upon tables laden with tidbits and champagne, the three sisters stood in an echoing room, heavy with the scent of dying roses.

"I want to thank you, Tam," Em said quietly, "for waking me up, letting me see what I—I'd become." Her eyes filled with tears, and she couldn't continue.

"What she's trying to say," Arab chimed in, "is that we—" Her own voice stopped, and she burst into noisy sobs. "Dammit," she said savagely, "I never could cry like a lady, Tamsen—I—I wish Missie would come home!"

Tamsen Tallant hugged them both, shedding a few tears of her own. Once again, they were gentle flowerlike Emmeline, hoydenish Arabella, daughters of Scott and Martha McLeod, the sisters she'd loved and cared for all these years.

It was all right. She understood. She still loved them. And for a while, she had been as much at fault as they.

"I suppose we must join the guests," Em said finally. "But do you know something, Tam, I—I don't look at most of them the way I used to. They're pretentious, stuffy, dull—"

"Dull as hell," Tamsen offered, smiling.

Reluctantly they made their way outside. If their eyes looked as if they'd been crying, if the tip of Arab's nose was pink, no one noticed. Nell's captive audience had hit the champagne with a vengeance. Mrs. Wilson was definitely three sheets to the wind, her uninspired hat askew as she carried on a maudlin conversation with a courteous Chinese gentleman. Nell dug her elbow in Em's side with a chuckle.

"This here's one helluva party, kiddo. You done yerself proud!"

Tamsen left her sisters and went in search of Matthew Blaine. He stood against the rear wall, a glass of champagne in his hand. Even dressed for a wedding, he managed to retain his slightly rumpled look. His cravat was a bit askew, his hair falling over his forehead. And he looked even more worn and haggard than he did at their last meeting.

"Did you enjoy the wedding?"

His eyes lit at sight of her. "Of course, especially since I'm fond of the bride." His eyes returned to the milling crowd. "The Courtneys have a rather—er—varied group of people here, do they not?"

"I'm not too sure how she managed to gather them," Tamsen confessed. "I have an idea that Nell's involved in some way."

"And that is Nell?" Matthew pointed unerringly at the woman in shocking pink satin.

"I forgot you hadn't met. And there," she pointed, "is my sister, Arab."

"I would have known any of you, anywhere, from Missie's description."

Tamsen's heart went out to him. She understood why he

401

had been standing here where he could view the guests one by one. He'd been expecting—hoping—to see Missie.

"Missie isn't here, Matthew. We haven't heard from her."

"Nor have I. I do know, through newspaper contacts, that she seems to be taking the East Coast by storm. I imagine she will stay there—"

"And you're going to let her?"

He shrugged, gloomily, as if his actions could have no bearing on Missie's future plans. Tamsen felt a wave of irritation at his passiveness. If he didn't take the bull by the horns, she damn well was going to!

"I did as you asked, Matthew. I read Missie's book. And I saw what you read into it. The others, Juan and Arab, Duke and Em, are in agreement with me. Do you remember the deal we made? I suggested you wire Missie to come home; you asked me to read the book and said you'd think about it?

"I'm calling you on the deal! I'm giving you exactly twenty-four hours. You will wire her this afternoon, telling her you love her and need her, in your own name—or I wire, tomorrow, with the same message. Except it will be in the name of myself and my family.

"I have a notion she'll be happier if the request comes from you. Now, suppose you—you get the lead out, and tell me what you plan to do!"

She glared at him. He looked surprised, then began to grin. "You're a bossy wench! You know that?"

"And so is Missie," Tamsen said stoutly. "That's something to consider before you make up your mind!"

He handed her his glass of champagne. "Haven't touched it," he chuckled. "Don't let it go to waste. Right now, I must make my excuses to our hostess. I have some pressing business—"

Tamsen watched him go, gladness growing in her like a bubble. Petra had her love, the wedding had gone off without a hitch, Tamsen and Dan would soon be moving into their new home—

And Missie would return to her own love, and to the bosom of her family.

All was well with Tamsen's world. She looked at Blaine's glass, and lifted it in a silent salute. "To the McLeod daughters, and all their descendants," she said aloud. Then she drank it down.

Chapter 55

As Petra's outdoor reception progressed, Missie stood at a window of her New York hotel room, watching the miracle of softly falling snow. There had been nothing to match it in her memory.

She wondered how she'd dared to write of her family's adventures in Alaska without having seen the awesomeness of drifting white flakes—like feathers, blanketing a landscape. The streets below were decorated for the coming holiday. Everything was a blur of red, of gold, of green. Sleigh bells sounded, muffled and distant in a beautiful white world.

Missie had just come in from shopping, and her hair still sparkled with damp. Brushing it back, she turned to look at the parcels laid out on her bed.

What a fool she had been!

Freed for a few hours from personal appearances, free of Stuyvesant Brown's constant presence, she'd joined the holiday crowds; enjoying the sight of bright-faced shoppers spangled with snow as they searched for gifts to give their loved ones. Then, she, too, was carried away with the holiday spirit.

First, she had seen a delicate pale green shawl—just right for Mama. There was also one of blue—for Em. Aunt Tamsen would look elegant in the black, shot through with gold—

Before she could stop herself, she had bought them. Then she'd purchased pipes, a straight-stemmed rugged one for Duke, in light wood; the same style for Dan Tallant in darker finish; a slender, aristocratic pipe for her father; and finally, an ebony bulldog type, made to be clenched in the teeth of a man with frowning brows, an untidy lock falling over them—

Why had she bought a gift for Matthew! Indeed, why had she bought any of these things? She understood her actions a little better now. There had been that terrible feeling of aloneness among the happy throngs of shoppers. She'd been like a child on the outer fringes of happiness, wanting to join in. So, for a time, she'd pretended she was going home; that she would arrive to a warm welcome, laden with Christmas. She'd pretended that Matthew would be waiting.

She had lied to herself. There was nothing for her in San Francisco. And tonight, she planned to cut all ties.

Perhaps she could return her purchases tomorrow. Or she might give them to someone else. Stew might like the slender pipe, his father, the rugged ones; his mother and sisters the pastel shawls—

But the Gypsy shawl was appropriate for no one but Tamsen. And the bulldog pipe suited only one man she knew.

She turned it over in her hands, remembering Matthew's face. Then, setting her lips, she began to gather her purchases and put them away. Finished, she changed to a gown of soft blue wool, trimmed with bands of white fur. It had been an extravagant purchase, but it seemed to suit the holiday.

It made her look like a princess, she thought, viewing herself in the mirror. For a moment she wished that Matthew could see her dressed like this, then she pushed the thought away.

Stew Brown would like it. And she had purchased it for him, for this night which would probably be a turning point in her life.

She wandered into the sitting room of her small suite. It contained a fireplace with gas logs, giving a spurious home-like touch to her temporary quarters. She looked at her watch, realizing Stew was a little late. It didn't matter. She needed these moments to compose her mind.

At his request, they were dining in tonight. He wished to discuss something of importance to both of them. And she knew that she would be forced to make a decision.

Life with Stew would be pleasant. He had courted her assiduously. They had taken long drives, crossing ancient covered bridges, seeing a countryside of scarlet and gold. He had shown her the city, his city, that could now be hers. He had stood beside her at personal appearances and receptions, glowing with pride in her achievement.

With Stew, she could continue her career, and have the things she wanted most: a home and family.

Missie looked at the fireplace, pretending this was not a hotel room, but a house. In the corner would be a tree, blazing with candles. There would be a smell of greenery, and from the kitchen would come a scent of roasting turkey, spices.

She tried to visualize the children. They did not have Stew's features in her imagination, but those of Matthew Blaine—

A tap at the door brought her out of her reverie, and she panicked. She needed time—

She breathed a sigh of relief to discover it was only the meal she'd ordered. Two employees of the hotel kitchen wheeled in a small table, setting it with covered hot dishes; a silver bucket containing a chilled bottle of wine.

She tipped them and they went on their way.

Missie looked at the table and frowned. Stew was more than forty-five minutes late, and now she began to worry. Was she already thinking like a wife? Or was it her conscience. She'd dreaded the evening so. If he'd had an accident—

Again, there was someone at the door. She opened it to reveal a smiling Stew Brown. His hat and overcoat, his stubby lashes, glistened with snow. He'd never looked so appealing. His cheeks were red with the weather, his eyes bright, and he brought with him a sound of music.

It emanated from an object he held out to her, a small ceramic tree, studded with gemlike decorations, strung with fine gold wire for tinsel. Twisted on its base, it became a music box, chiming out an ancient English carol.

"I saw this in a window," he said boyishly, "and stopped to buy it. I don't know why, but it made me think of you. I thought you'd like it."

Missie's eyes brimmed with tears of pleasure. It was a thoughtful gift. Endearing—

She placed the little tree in the middle of the table, then took his coat and hat to the bathroom, shaking the snow from them so that they might drip dry. When she returned to the sitting room, he was standing by the fire.

"I don't think I've ever seen you look so beautiful," he said softly. "That gown suits you. Missie—"

"The food's getting cold," she said hastily. "Won't you sit down? Perhaps you'll open the wine—"

He performed that duty with expertise, noting the label with pleasure as he half filled their glasses. Then he set the little tree to playing before he raised his glass to hers.

"Here's to us," he said, "and to Christmas."

"It isn't Christmas yet, Stew."

"It looks and sounds like it," he persisted, "with the snow, the bells. And you look like the angel on a tree. Missie, I'd like to make every day Christmas for you—"

"Speaking of Christmas, how's the second edition of my book coming along? Will it be on the stands in time for—"

He grinned proudly. "Back from the binders this morning. We sent massive shipments to California immediately. Tomorrow, we'll ship to all the larger cities where we have the most demand. In the meantime, we're already working on local distribution."

He continued on with the plans of Brown, Halpert and Brown, while Missie toyed with her food. She thought of the family she loved, disaster hurtling toward them on a train, and couldn't swallow.

"Enough of business," Stew said firmly. He pushed his plate away and poured another glass of wine for each of them. "I want to talk about us, our relationship—and I don't mean that of author and publisher! I've been a patient man. Missie—"

He took a small velvet box from his pocket and placed it on the table, then set the small tree to chiming out its carol before he came around to kneel before her.

"I'm sure you see me as a businessman. I suppose I am, Missie. But inside, I guess I'm as romantic as the next fellow." He took her hands, looking up into her eyes with a pleading expression. "I've loved you since I first saw you. I'm asking you to become my wife."

A knock sounded at the door, and his face reddened. For a moment, he lost his aplomb, scrambling awkwardly to his feet. Good God, did nothing ever work out as he had planned?

Missie opened the door to a messenger, signing for a telegram with trembling fingers. She'd received many congratulatory notes, but she still feared one might carry bad news. Closing the door against the boy, she ignored Stew's presence as she tore the message open, reading it and then reading it again.

It contained a message consisting of five words.

Come home. I need you. It was signed, Matthew Blaine.

Stuyvesant Brown cleared his throat. "Missie?"

She jumped a little, looking at him with dazed eyes. For a moment, she'd forgotten he was there.

"It—it's not bad news, I trust?"

"No." She folded the message carefully, and slid it into a drawer.

"Then shall we get on from where we were interrupted?" Passion came back into his voice. "I've waited a long time—"

Missie put a hand to her forehead. "Forgive me, Stew. This isn't a time to discuss anything of importance. I—I have a blinding headache. Perhaps another time—"

Somehow, she managed to get his coat and hat, and shove him, protesting, out the door. She was to call him if her headache didn't improve. He would send his own physician. Poor darling, why hadn't she told him in the first place—

Then he was gone, and she stood alone in the ruins of her carefully planned evening. The little music box, a gesture of tenderness, sat mute, the velvet box beside it.

Missie opened the box. An enormous diamond winked back at her. She closed it again, and went to the drawer, taking out the wire that had shaken her to the core.

She hadn't lied to Stew. Her head did ache. It hurt so that she could hardly bear it. She went to the window and leaned her forehead against the cold pane, seeing the gentle snow still drifting down against a black sky.

It had all seemed so simple earlier. When Stew appeared, snow-covered, smiling, she'd even felt a wave of affection toward him. His mention of her books thundering toward California had been a reminder, setting her decision. She was prepared to marry Stuyvesant Brown.

And then the telegram had come; a wire consisting of five words. "Come home, I need you."

Come home to what? To a friendly employer-employee relationship? To a family who probably wished they'd never laid eyes on her?

Damn Matthew Blaine! He had no right to do this to her!

She crumpled the yellow paper in her hand. She was a free and independent woman. The choice of returning to California or staying here was strictly her own! Matthew Blaine's wishes had no bearing on her present life!

She smoothed it out, and read it again. He needed her. If he'd only said he loved her—

She looked out of the window, as if she might find an answer in the softly falling snow, the festive decorations that blurred before her eyes in a kaleidoscope of color.

Dear God, what was she going to do?

Chapter 56

In San Francisco, the weeks following Petra's wedding were not quiet, by any means. Though Em begged Tamsen and Dan to return to the Courtney home until they found permanent housing, they put her off with vague excuses.

They were sure to find something soon. There was no sense in making a move just to pack again. The hotel was comfortable. They were enjoying the sights of the city.

They were only too happy to get back to their project, that of renovating the old house on Stockton Street. How and when they were going to break the news of it to Em and Arab, they hadn't quite decided.

Tamsen intended it to be a surprise. It would be a shock, too, she told Dan, smiling. She couldn't wait to see their faces.

On the day after the wedding, they returned from the old house to find Matthew Blaine pacing the corridor in front of their door. His hair was tousled, his coat hung over one shoulder, and he looked as if he hadn't slept for a week.

"Where the hell have you been," he asked. "Dammit, I've been walking the floor for hours—"

Dan's face hardened. He stepped in front of Tamsen, his fists doubled.

"I don't know who the devil you are, but you are not going to shout at my wife!"

Tamsen tugged at his sleeve, laughing.

"Dan, this is Matthew Blaine, Missie's friend. I think he might have some news for us."

Blaine's face was scarlet. "I'm sorry," he said sheepishly. "I guess I lost my head. I—I sent that wire we discussed. And Missie's coming home. She'll be in at midnight on the twenty-third."

"Matthew! How wonderful!" She threw her arms around him, hugging him until Dan cleared his throat.

"I'm still not sure whether I should punch him or shake his hand. At the moment, it appears my first impulse is in order."

Tamsen blushed and backed from Blaine, laughing. "I think this is going to take some tall explaining! Dan, open the door. Matthew—won't you come in?"

He could not. He must hurry home to his son. He just wanted Tamsen to hear the good news.

"We're going to dinner at Em's, tonight," Dan put in. "The rest of the family will be delighted to hear—"

"No, Dan!" Tamsen's eyes were dancing. "I have a better idea. Matthew, can this be a secret, just between us for a while?"

"I wasn't planning on telling anyone else," he confessed. "I planned on meeting that train alone—if you don't mind."

"Can you keep Missie occupied until the evening of the twenty-fourth?"

He flushed, then smiled. "I think I can."

"Good! I—I have an idea. I'll contact you with the rest of the details later. And—Matthew, I'm so glad!"

"No gladder than I am. And, Mrs. Tallant—Tamsen—thank

you!'' He put his arms around her, kissed her, then turned to Dan as an afterthought.

"It's been nice meeting you, sir."

He was gone.

Dan opened the door to their suite and propelled Tamsen inside. "Still think I should have socked him one," he said gloomily. "Dammit, woman, you shouldn't go around hugging strange men!"

"That man," Tamsen smiled, "is going to be my nephew. You'll just have to get used to it."

"All right, I'll buy that story. Now for the next one. You mentioned some kind of idea. What in the hell are you up to?"

Tamsen sketched the details of her plan, and he began to grin. Once in show business, always in show business. Tamsen hadn't changed a bit in all these years. What's more, he wouldn't change her if he could.

He wanted to hold her, and tell her so. But they had to dress hastily and rush to dinner at Em's.

Nell and Sim Blevins were already there when they arrived. Sean and Maggie had stayed home, due to Maggie's indisposition which Nell proceeded to describe in detail.

"Minds me of that fool elley-vaytor in Liverpool," she said chattily, loading her plate. "Ever'thing what goes down comes right back up. Em, wouldja pass me that there plate of horse's ovaries?"

The purpose of the dinner, that of rehashing the wedding and finishing up the leftovers, faltered for a time. Then someone mentioned Missie's book. Nell was delighted to find they'd read it to the end, the rest surprised that she'd read it at all.

Nell told the story of how they'd obtained the book, chortling over the plight of the passenger on the train. Maggie had read it aloud to her and to Sean, Sim getting in on the tail end—

"Woulda read it myself," Nell explained, "but I figgered

it'd help Maggie out. Hell, now she talks English almost ez good ez me!'' She shot a defiant glare at Em and Arab. ''Well, wotcha think of it? I figger she made us look purty goddamn good. You girls still pissed off?''

Em smiled painfully. ''Only at myself. And I've been surprised to find it doesn't bother anyone else. I've had invitations to three different functions, today.''

Nell suppressed a grin. ''You don't look too het up about it.''

''I'm not, really,'' Em confessed. ''I guess I discovered that my—my present company is what really matters to me.''

''I wish Missie were here,'' Arab said forlornly. ''I feel so—so damn guilty! I haven't seen her for so many years, I guess I—I forgot! Then, when I read the book, I remembered—''

''I think we all did, Arab,'' Tamsen said. ''And not just Missie. We remembered ourselves, each other, Dusty—''

''Th' sweet leetle sonofabitch,'' Nell put in, tears spurting and streaking her rouge. Sim stroked her pudgy hand. He was not jealous of the dead man, but rather proud of wooing the widow of a man of such heroic proportions.

''Member the time Buck Farnum kicked up a ruckus?'' Nell continued. ''He wuz goin' t'drag you off upstairs, an' drawed down on me? Member how Dusty got in fronta me, and give you time to jab a gun in his backside?'' She whispered loudly in an aside to Sim, ''That there's a part of the book you ain't heared, yet. Reckin we's goin' to have to start over at th' beginnin'.''

The story set off a chain of reminiscing. Em rose and brought the book to the table, refreshing their memories from time to time.

''I like that last part, special,'' Nell said. ''Wouldja run that past us agin?''

Em read the last pages, of a young girl on shipboard, watching those she loved fade into the distance as she sailed with Em for the States—

''But not Dusty. Dusty lay buried in the hot red center of

416

*ustralia. The mallee scrub would cover his grave, goannas
eek shelter there, lorikeets wheel above it. A small blond girl
'ould not sit at his feet, raptly listening to his tales again."*

Nell snorted, trying to control a flood of weeping. "God-
amn," she kept bawling, wiping her nose on her sleeve,
'didn' mean t' snargle all over yer! But that there story
rung it all back—"

"Hell, ever'body unnerstands," Sim put in gruffly. His
ell was a woman of tender sensibilities, and he respected
er for it.

Finally she got her massive grief under control, and Em
ontinued.

*"Nor would she forget those others, disappearing now into
he distance. Perhaps she had never been an integral part of
heir lives as they had been to her, but the memory of their
trength would help her heal her own wounds."*

Now, it was Arab's turn to fall apart. She remembered the
orrors of Missie's marriage, the day she and Duke found her
ear death, to take her home. Perhaps that was the only time
he'd really been a mother to her child. Missie had always
ved on the fringes of their lives, and she knew—

*"They, and Em, who still stood beside her, were the
urvivors."*

Em's voice trailed off to die on a sob.

Duke stood, inviting the men to join him for brandy in the
en; otherwise they might all drown in a flood of tears.

On their way home, Dan brought up Missie's homecoming
nce more. Em and Arab were suffering. Perhaps it would be
inder to tell them.

Tamsen shook her head. Her sisters had come a long way
rom the girls they had once been. It was an equally long way
ack. The delay would give them more time to come to terms
vith their feelings: Em with her social pretensions, Arab's
elfishness. It would do them good.

Besides, the family must remain secondary. Matthew should
ome first.

He had to agree.

417

Nell and Sim Blevins, their carriage pointed toward Nell'
Place, were also discussing the evening. "Didn' mean t' go
pieces like that," Nell explained. "But I reckin a good cry
like a dose a epsim salts. Cleans out th' system."

"You sure got a talent fer describin' things," Sim sai
admiringly. "Bet you coulda bin a writer, y'self."

Nell flounced coyly. "Mebbe."

There was a long silence, then Sim slowed the horse
"Way you talk about Dusty, he wuz one helluva man."

"He wuz, th' sweet leetle bastard!"

"Reckin it'd be hard t' fill his shoes."

Nell's heart began to pound, her massive bosom quivering
"Reckin it would," she said cautiously.

"Man hadn' oughta try." Sim looked at her with h
grimace that passed for a smile. "But I don't s'pose he'
mind ef there wuz somebuddy, sorta hangin' around, not
take 'is place, mind, but t' sorta look arter yuh. Purty woma
needs perteckshun—"

"Sim!"

"Nell!"

They spoke at the same time, and both began to laugl
Then the big man put his apelike arms around Nell as far a
he could reach—She was all woman, he told her, and a yar
wide!—

He had dropped the reins and the horses stood stock-stil
uncaring that Sim Blevins, tough and tender, had just locate
an empty corner of Nell's heart; that he'd made a bid for i
and had been accepted.

Chapter 57

The reading and rereading of Missie's book brought more than a reevaluation of the lives of the McLeod sisters. To Em, it brought a haunting.

That night she lay awake beside her husband, overcome by memories of another man. For years, she'd nursed a resentment toward her first husband, Donald Alden, considering his suicide a form of desertion. Now his face appeared before her out of the darkness, prematurely white hair shining like silver, blue honest eyes in a tanned face; a handsome, gentle, distinguished man.

She shivered, remembering the day he had proposed marriage. She'd told him it was impossible, that she had been violated, that Martha, the child he thought to be Tamsen's, was a result of the brutal act.

His eyes became as cold as winter, not because of his feelings toward her, but on her behalf. If he could have reached the men who used her, he would have done murder.

On that day, he'd held her close. She remembered the feel

of his strong heart beating against her own. Over his shoulder she saw the rippling of the sun on blue waters, the blurred image of a gull in a gliding turn, and knew the touch of his firm mouth on hers.

The days she had tried to forget came back in full color. She remembered the soft sound of the surf, the scent of salt, his smooth-shaven cheek against her own—

In a panic, she reached for Duke's hand in the darkness, holding to it tightly, willing herself back to the present.

Duke stirred. "Something wrong?" he asked drowsily.

"Nothing. Nothing at all. Go back to sleep."

"Love you," he mumbled, drifting back again.

"And I love you."

It was true. She loved him. And she had loved Donald Alden in a different way. He had been older, a father figure catering to her every whim, giving her a beautiful home, social position, everything.

Then, when the banks failed, his name was linked with his worthless stepbrother, Adam, and with Harry Meiggs, who absconded with more than a hundred thousand dollars belonging to the people of San Francisco. He'd sold all they owned to repay what he considered his debts, sent her and Martha off to Alaska to join Tamsen.

And then he had killed himself.

"Oh, Donald!" She put her hand to her lips to cover the sound of his name, uttered on a sob.

He had killed himself, and she'd made certain he stayed dead. People are not dead as long as they are remembered. And only Missie, who had never known him, had tried to keep his memory alive.

She rose the next morning and dressed carefully, wearing a gown of soft blue. It had been Donald's favorite color.

"I am going to the cemetery today," she informed Duke quietly.

For a moment, Duke was taken aback. To his knowledge, Em had never been there, even refusing to attend the funeral.

of friends. He opened his mouth to question her, then closed it again. Suddenly he knew.

"I will drive you," he said quietly.

She shook her head. "I think I should go alone."

"I will drive you!"

His insistence on accompanying her meant only that. Reaching the cemetery, he found someone to guide her to Alden's grave, and returned to the carriage. It was a fog-filled morning. He filled his pipe and watched with troubled eyes as her frail figure disappeared into the crying mists.

He knew her errand, without being told. Missie's book had brought the past back vividly. This was a kind of pilgrimage. Em had to do this, to make her peace with a dead man—and herself.

His only concern was for her well-being. If the experience proved too difficult for her, then he would be here, waiting.

Donald Alden's grave was in an old part of the cemetery. Giant stones reared around Em, black with age and damp, some leaning and untidy, most with ornate inscriptions. She knew she would have recognized Donald's without identification. It was of gray marble, rectangular, set on a firm base, his name, the dates of his birth and death firmly incised in plain letters.

She shut her eyes, remembering the letter he'd given Juan to hand her when they were at sea. Every word of it was etched into her brain.

My Dearest wife, I have failed you once more, choosing a coward's way to deliver my last words to you. Before you read on, I must assure you this is not a whim. I am not an impulsive man. My plans have been made for a long time. I have merely awaited a moment that would be less painful and embarrassing for you and for Martha.

I cannot live with failure, or with the knowledge that my honor has been weighed and found wanting. Pray forgive me for what I am about to do.

When you read this letter, you will be free, no longer tied to a dull, old and broken man. Free to begin anew in a new country.

I have instructed Lin as to the disposition of my body. All expenses incurred by my death have been paid; all arrangements are made.

Bless you for those happiest of years.

It was not surprising that she would recognize his monument among the others. He had chosen it himself.

"Please leave me," she whispered to her guide.

An old man in boots and a waterproof, he hesitated. "Can you find your way back in this fog, ma'am?"

"I can find my way back."

Em knelt beside the grave in the wet winter grass, the mists closing in around her, leaving her alone with her dead. And she remembered him; not as the aging, defeated man, overweight, white hair like a lion's mane, who had said good-bye with a chaste kiss on her cheek; but as the man she'd married, strong, handsome, with a dignified bearing.

Too numb to cry, she placed her hand on the sunken grave. She had not helped him in his silent agony. She'd accused him of putting his honor above his home when he sold their house. Since he wasn't at fault, he didn't owe his depositors anything—

And then, not understanding what she was doing to him, she'd insisted he sell his offices, behind which they were reduced to living. They would go to Tamsen and Dan, who would find him work, take care of them—

He had gone out, and hadn't come back until nearly morning. Now she could see that her solution was the final blow to his pride.

"Donald," she whispered. "I remember you, now, and I—I love you. Please forgive me! Oh, God, please forgive me!"

There was no answer from the grave, only the sound of

water dripping from nearby stones to penetrate the muffled gray world.

Finally, soaked through, she stood, lifting her eyes to get her bearings.

And suddenly, the fog parted above her. For just a space, there was a glimpse of blue sky, as blue as the sea—the blurred image of a gull in a gliding turn before the fog closed in again.

Now, Em could cry.

When she finally joined Duke in the carriage, her blue gown was sodden, covered with bits of grass; her eyes were red and swollen, but her face was serene.

"I see you found your way back," Duke said quietly.

"Yes."

Em had found her way back to the past, and had returned again.

Duke drove home in silence. He did not want to know what had occurred in her mind, there in the fog-blanketed home of the dead. It was enough that he had his Em again, and that her errand had brought her peace.

Arab, too, had a pilgrimage to make. But being Arab, she waited until the skies cleared and the sun came out. She went to the site of Donald Alden's former offices. Once a thriving place of business, the building had been purchased by Lin, Donald's Chinese houseboy, and turned into a laundry. Now, even that was gone. The structure had been torn down, a new one rose in its place.

Arab stood across the street, remembering that last year of trouble and privation. Juan, arriving penniless, trained only for a career in the politics of Spain, had been employed by Em's husband. When Alden went under, he took Juan with him, both tarred by the same brush. Em, Donald, and Martha were forced to move into tiny rooms behind Donald's office, and they had taken Juan and Arab in, sharing what they had.

Then, Arab thought, her face burning, was when she had become a—a bitch!

It had been difficult, living on someone else's charity. Juan's reputation had been soiled, he had no skills, and he was a "furriner." He'd been unable to find work. It was she who insisted they go to join Tamsen, certain they would find a place with the Russian court at Sitka, dreaming dreams of luxury—

There was nothing for Juan there. He had left her, seeking gold along the Fraser River. And she'd received a false report that he was dead.

It might not have been false, she thought now. But the experience had taught her nothing. Throughout their married life, she'd goaded him onward, perhaps taking a secret satisfaction in her ability to manipulate the man she loved.

In Australia, through her desire to move to Sydney, she'd almost lost Missie. In England, she'd insisted upon moving to London. There, she'd nearly lost Luka. Juan, in an uncharacteristic rebellion against her demands, accompanied Dan to Bombay. There, he nearly died from a stab wound—

And, more terrifying, she suspected that there might have been another woman—

Standing in a San Francisco street, her faults all seemed to be delineated by the bright sun, just as it picked out the weeds in the cracked paving of this once respectable neighborhood.

Weeds could be removed, pulled up by the roots! The paving could be repaired, the cracks smoothed out! Just so, the roots of her selfishness could be extracted, the cracks in her marriage repaired!

She thought of Juan, a dark-eyed prince, far from his homeland, living at the edges of his wife's dissatisfaction. For days, they'd been searching for a house that would suit her. Now, she intended to let Juan choose their home.

Her cheeks were wet as she left the site of Donald Alden's former offices, erased now, praying that she, too, could change.

Tamsen had already come to terms with the past. The

pieces of it came together as she watched the old building, once known as Madam Franklin's Parlor for Gentlemen, resurrected to its former splendor; opulent, even gaudy with its mirrors, velvets, crimson and gold, it suited her.

But then, she thought wryly, she had never been a lady.

Chapter 58

Missie Narvaéz, the cause of such upheaval within her family, finished her last commitments in New York City; several autographing sessions, a dinner, some interviews that had already been scheduled. Then she boarded a train for San Francisco.

Stuyvesant Brown drove her to the station, himself.

Missie had faced him honestly. She did not love him, but someone else. She had no idea that anything would come of it, but it was not fair to Stew to marry him under those circumstances.

He tried to tell her that it didn't matter, that she could come to care for him in time. But she remembered the dream children she'd visualized before the hotel fireplace, children who wore the face of Matthew Blaine.

"No, Stew. I—I'm too fond of you to let you take second place."

At last he'd given in. He was silent as they drove through streets that were no longer white. Snow lay in heaps along the streets, yellowed, smoke-blackened now. The landscape was gray and dreary, despite the city's festive decorations.

Reaching the station, he handed Missie into her car, then stood on the platform watching her small square of window. Finally, the train began to move. Stuyvesant Brown did not. He remained until it was out of sight, another engine nosing in to take its place.

Then he went to his jewelers, returning the ring he'd purchased with such high hopes. There might be another girl one day, but there would be another ring. This had been selected for a very special one, one he would remember all his life.

Morosely, his hands shoved in his pockets, he wandered around the store, too depressed to return to the office. His eye caught sight of a crystal paperweight, a delicate pink rose embedded in its center.

It made him think of Missie.

He purchased it and went to his office, immeasurably cheered. Always, near him, would be a little reminder of his love.

Missie did not look back as the train left the station. She had taken a worn bit of yellow paper from her reticule, smoothing it out on her lap.

"Come home," it read. *"I need you."*

She shut her eyes, seeing a disheveled young man glaring at a form, running his fingers through his rumpled hair as he decided how to phrase his wire.

And the words he chose could mean anything.

They could mean that he had a series of articles he wanted her to do. She smiled wryly. Perhaps Miss Elizabeth Anspaugh had been breathing down his neck again, along with some of her cohorts from the Women's Suffrage group. She could imagine Matthew growing redder under their barrage, slamming his hand on the desk and shouting, "You want her? Dammit, I'll send for her!"

And then again, this wire could mean something—more

Matthew was wary of women, wary of love. Could the words, *I need you,* mean that he'd had second thoughts?

Or there could even be something wrong at the Courtney house. He knew Duke—

If her book had driven Aunt Em into a heart attack or stroke, she'd never forgive herself! And there were the others—

Why hadn't she wired Blaine asking for the particulars! Even just the one word, "Why," would have sufficed. Instead, she was doomed to a long journey, forming all kinds of wild hypotheses—

Just let nothing be wrong at home!

Just let the words "I need you" mean, "I love you!"

Just—

She forced herself to stop thinking, taking up a book to read. Within minutes, the unending circles of her worries had started all over again.

When a young man sat down beside her, she wished she'd reserved a compartment. She'd thought of it and ruled against it, knowing it would be a long trip to be alone with her thoughts. Now, however, she resented the man's intrusion.

He did not attempt to strike up a conversation, but immediately opened a book, reading with such absorption that she slanted a glance toward its title.

The Survivors!

"Are you enjoying your book?" She could not help interrupting him. He lifted eyes that were glazed, far away.

"I beg your pardon?"

"The book," she said impatiently, "I—I've heard of it. Is it good?"

"Absolutely fascinating. I recommend it." He gave her a brief, unseeing smile and returned to its pages. She had a feeling that if she interfered with his reading, he would move on farther down the aisle.

She was to discover, as she went from her seat to the sleeping and dining cars, that there were more copies of *The*

Survivors in evidence. She was tempted to converse with the readers, get their various reactions, but decided against it.

Her photographs had been very much in the papers of late. Someone might recognize her. She had dressed plainly, deliberately choosing a course that would bring her into San Francisco at night, hoping to avoid publicity.

If her mother and aunts were angry, there was no point in adding fuel to the fire.

The stained slush of New York City was behind, giving way to white-clad rolling hills; then the train ran through snowy valleys, running along rushing streams that cut their way through a frosted landscape.

At one point, she saw a deer, frozen at the waterside as the train, a monstrous intruder in a pristine land, rumbled past.

Mountains, cities, deserts. Missie forced herself to memorize the scenery.

She did not plan to pass this way again.

As the weather warmed, coats and cloaks were removed. Windows were opened, relieving the stuffiness of the coach but allowing the smoke and cinders of the engine to enter the cars. Missie's seatmate finished his book and discovered with interest that he had a pretty girl at his side.

"I'm Dick Carter," he said, "and you?"

"M—Margaret Norris," she stammered.

He recalled that she'd noted his book and proceeded to review its contents, pleased that she seemed to be hanging on his words with fascinated interest. His chest expanded at her rapt attention.

"Then it's not really as shocking as they say?"

"I don't know if I'd recommend it to a young lady like yourself. Men are out in the world to a greater extent. They are more aware that—that certain things go on."

"I see," Missie said, demurely. "The heroines of the story, did you like them?"

"I think I fell in love with Tamsen," he confessed.

Maybe, Missie thought, Tamsen wouldn't hate her.

Missie did not go to the sleeping car at the end of her last day. There would be no point in it. She was too nervous to sleep. The closer the train came to its destination, the more tense she became. Her fists clenched tightly in her lap. More than once, she remembered to loosen them, deliberately. Then they curled again.

It was ridiculous to be so apprehensive, she told herself. She would merely arrive in the middle of the night, get a horse-drawn cab, and go to her lodgings above the bakery. No one would even know she was here until Frau Schmitt learned of her presence in the morning.

But what if Matthew had told Uncle Dan? Would they come to the station?

No, it was more likely they would pretend that she didn't exist.

The train was slowing. Missie's heart was in her throat as she searched for her cloak in the overhead rack. She knew that her face was smudged, her gown soiled, but there was no help for it. Her seatmate woke, also preparing to alight.

"We ought to keep in touch, Margaret. Perhaps dinner, some night?"

"I'm afraid I don't have an address, as yet."

"We could meet at the Palace, on New Year's Day."

"I will have to see."

The train had come to full stop, the conductor calling for disembarkation. Dick Carter went ahead of her, assisting her down.

It was a typical misty night, light rain falling. Missie cast a swift glance over the few who had braved the weather to meet incoming passengers.

There was no one to meet her. She was both glad and disappointed at the same time. Moving to pick up her luggage, she was stunned as a man stepped out of the shadows, blocking her path.

"Matthew!" She was unable to suppress a glad cry.

He took her in his arms and kissed her. She trembled

431

against the wonderful familiar feel of him, pressing her body closer, needing him, wanting him, gasping out little love words as he sought her mouth again.

Behind her, Dick Carter looked on morosely. He should have known better than to trust a woman on a train. Better to stick to those in books—

Like Tamsen.

Chapter 59

Conscious of staring eyes and the steady drizzle of rain, Matthew and Missie finally moved apart. Matthew collected Missie's luggage, loading it into his carriage, then took her arm—

The gesture reminded her of another time; the evening he'd taken her to his house; the night that ended with her sleeping in his embrace.

"You can drive me to the apartment on Polk Street," she said quietly. "I've still kept it."

"We're going to my place. Then if you insist, I'll take you home later."

"I prefer to go now."

He cocked an eyebrow at her. "Do you plan on coming back to the *Examiner*?"

"I—I suppose so," she faltered.

"Then I'm your boss. Get in and shut up."

She sat far from him, wondering what tack to take. This was a different Matthew. His eyes were sparkling. He seemed full of repressed glee. Was he laughing at her because she'd come running when he called?

"Matthew, you wired me. I—I was coming home anyway. But now that I'm here, what did you have in mind?"

He answered with a mock leer that set her heart thumping.

"Matthew Blaine, turn this carriage around, this minute! I—can't—"

"Oh, but you can!" he said suggestively. "And very well, I might say! Who should know better than I?"

Not only had he rejected her, now he was taunting her with her moment of weakness. Her face fiery, she made a move to leap from the carriage. He grasped her arm.

"Wait, Missie. I was only teasing. I want to talk to you. It doesn't have to go any farther than that, unless you wish it to. Just promise to hear me out."

His expression was so tender that she settled back, trembling inside, waiting—

They approached the narrow lane. Ahead of them, Matthew's comfortable rambling house glowed with light. Matthew Blaine helped her down, led her to his front door and left her as he went to put the carriage away.

Missie stood uncertainly in the living room. It was warm, bright. A fire burned in the fireplace, the logs licked with flame. In one corner stood a Christmas tree, glittering with tinsel.

It was the room of her dreams. She could visualize stockings hung on the mantel, children before the fire, children with Matthew's unruly dark hair and eyes—

Joshua! She remembered Matthew's little lame son. Cinnie had not been here when they arrived. Surely he hadn't left the little one here alone—

She went to the boy's room, opening the door quietly. The light from behind her showed the crib to be empty. Her heart jolted.

Was it possible something had happened to the child? Dear God, she hoped not!

"Joshua's not here."

Missie whirled to face Matthew, who had come up behind er. "He's at Cinnie's. I asked her to keep him overnight."

"Why, Matthew?"

"Because we have to get something settled between us." le looked determined, almost grim.

"I thought we'd settled everything before I left."

"Missie, come here!"

She stood rooted to the spot, and he repeated his command. Timorously, she walked toward him. He guided her own the hall and back into the living room, pushing her head of him, his hand on her shoulder burning through her own. When they reached the fire, he took her hands, holding er at a distance, looking down into her eyes.

"What did my wire say?"

"That—that I should come home. You—needed me."

"Now, I want to tell you what it didn't say. It didn't go any urther, because I wanted to tell you myself, face to face, like is—

"Missie, I'm asking you to marry me."

The room seemed to spin around her in a blur of tinsel, leaming ornaments, and Christmas green. She closed her yes against the sudden swirl of color, vertigo pulling her way from his clinging hands.

"I haven't got much to offer." The lines of pain around his ensitive mouth deepened. "You're a successful writer. I'm ust a poor hack of an editor, a divorced man with a crippled id. I'm no damned bargain—you could do a helluva lot etter!—"

Missie found her voice. "Matthew, I—"

"I'm not finished yet," he said, doggedly, "I've been wrong about this career bit, Missie. I've been wrong about a ot of things. I don't expect to saddle you with being a ousewife. We'll hire a cook—"

"Listen, you bloody stupid bloke!" Missie's odd choice of words silenced him for a moment. "When it comes to bully eef and dampers, I'm fair dinkum! I can boil a billy with the

best of 'em! If you want kangaroo, it's stringy! But I ca
roast an emu—''

He looked so ridiculous, his mouth open in shock, tha
Missie began to laugh.

"Oh, Matthew! Matthew!—"

Her laughter turned into tears.

He pulled her gently to him, his dear, funny, mixed-up girl
kissing her blond curls, her finely arched brows, the tip of he
small nose, still smudged from the train, then sought he
mouth.

Sweetness of honey. Scent of flowers. Passion thuddin
through their veins, pulses beating as one. Tenderness, emo
tion, passion. And finally a wanting that could not be denied

He carried her to his bed, unbuttoning her gown, running
finger along her collarbone, marveling at its fragility. His lip
touched her throat with a burning she felt to the soles of he
feet.

And then everything was forgotten as she gave herself t
him with abandon, reveling in the fire that destroyed her, jus
as the flames had swept along the valley of the Billabong s
long ago. Out of the devastation had come a new gree
world, fresh and bright, more beautiful than ever before—

"I love you, Matthew," she whispered.

"And I love you."

There! It had been said. "If you're going to change you
mind tomorrow," she told him, "I hope I die, tonight."

He assured her that she was going to live for a long, lon
time.

Throughout the remainder of the night, they turned to eac
other again and again, napping intermittently; Missie's golde
head nestled against his dark shoulder. When morning came
Missie woke to find Matthew up, her breakfast waiting.

"We still have to talk," he said quietly. "It's going to be
hard to change my way of thinking. I'll have to become
accustomed to a working wife."

"Must I work?"

The question stopped his cup halfway to his mouth. He set down, spilling a little coffee into his saucer.

"I thought that's what you had in mind. Back to the paper, nother book—"

"I'm not sure there's another book in me," Missie said onestly. "*The Survivors*—the people in it are real."

"It's one helluva story, Missie."

"You've read it?" She looked at him with startled eyes. He odded, and she looked down at her plate. "Then you know bout my first marriage."

"I think that's what straightened me out, Missie. That's vhy I want to make sure we both enter into this thing with ur eyes open; try to compromise enough so we'll both be appy. I don't want to let you down, sweetheart."

Missie gave him a gamin grin. "I've already worked out vhat I'm going to do. I plan to do some research at home and rite a series of articles on the rights of wives and nothers—!"

He scowled at her ferociously. "I have something better to esearch. And if you dare write one word about it, young dy, I'll strangle you!"

He picked her up and carried her back to the bedroom. The offee sat on the breakfast table and grew cold.

"When are you going to tell your folks," he asked later as ney lazed, sated with love. "I understand they're in town."

He could feel her stiffen against him. "I don't know. Later, guess."

He wanted to tell her he knew what was worrying her and hat it was going to be all right. But he'd promised Tamsen—

"I made arrangements to take the whole day off," he said, "so let's make the best of it. Tomorrow's Christmas. Do you vant to go downtown and look around? Or shall we stay right ere?"

"Here," she said promptly, cuddling close to him. Here vas safe, here was a haven; here Missie Narváez was loved.

There was only one problem, he told her. Tonight, he'd

been invited to a small party. He'd asked if he could bring friend.

Missie sat up. "You were pretty sure of me, weren't you?"

"Never, Missie. I'll never understand a woman as long as live. But I intend to do my damndest to try. You can title that 'The life's work of Matthew Blaine'."

Missie was a little hurt that he would want to share the first day together with strangers. Tonight was Christmas Eve She'd had visions of bringing Joshua home, spending th evening by the fire as the family they would become. But sh would go if it made Matthew happy.

It evidently did, from the way he lay grinning at th ceiling. She tugged at his hair and turned him toward her, t kiss the smile away.

MADAM FRANKLIN'S PARLOR FOR GENTLEMEN

Chapter 60

That evening, a number of carriages moved through the
treets of San Francisco on their way to spend Christmas Eve
t the new Tallant home.

Nell, all gussied up in her purple velvet, deeming it more
ppropriate to the occasion, was talking a mile a minute.

"Where th' hell we goin' Sim? Sure you know th' address?
Vatch them bumps, dammit. Don't wanna bring on nuthin'
reemachure. You all right back there, Maggie? Hang onta
er, Sean?"

She turned again to Sim. "I figgered about where we are.
Iell, ef y' turned that there corner—"

Sim turned, and Nell choked, her face purpling.

There it wuz, jes' like it uster be! White paint, pink
hutters an' all! She rubbed her eyes and looked again. It
adn't gone away.

"I be damned," she said worriedly. Then, "I be damned!
Ih' leetle devil!"

With a bray of laughter, she slapped Sim Blevins on the

back with such a blow that it knocked his pipe out of his
mouth. He scrabbled for it as Nell adjusted her hat and
squared herself. "Don't set that peg leg on fire," she cautioned
him. "I got a idee this's gonna be one helluva party!" She
began to crow with glee. "Wait'll Em an' Arab set their
peepers on this! Goddamn!"

Em and Arab were equally disturbed about the route they
were taking. The area they'd entered was definitely rundown.
And something about it was disturbingly familiar. Em looked
at Arab, and saw they were sharing the same memories.
When the banks failed, all those years ago, they'd come to
this part of town, seeking Nell, hoping to obtain a loan. And
Nell, managing Tamsen's parlor in her absence, was having
financial problems herself—unable to help them.

The sisters reached out and clasped hands with a growing
uneasiness as the carriage bumped over the uneven streets.

The carriage turned a corner and there it was, the tall white
house to which they'd come, practically on their knees, just
as it had been in the past. Nell's carriage stood before it, and
Sim was helping her down.

The thought flashed simultaneously through Arab's and
Em's minds.

Tamsen had gone into business again!

"Em," Arab gasped, "you don't think—!"

"I don't intend to think," Em said. "I'm going to wait and
see!"

They all converged on the house at the same time. Dan, his
face relaxed and happy, opened the door to them. They
walked into a fairyland of glittering crystal, scarlet velvet, and
gilt-framed mirrors. A Christmas tree stood near a polished
grand piano, its starry spire touching a fourteen-foot ceiling,
shimmering with baubles and tinsel.

"Welcome to the Tallant residence," Dan said smiling.
"Tamsen will be down in a minute."

Residence! Tamsen had bought this place, restored it not as

—a house, but as a home! It was exactly what Tamsen would do!

"It's lovely, Dan," Em said graciously. Then she and Arab both began to laugh, sincere laughter, pealing through the room.

Nell didn't see what was funny. She stood misty-eyed, seeing the place just as it was in the old days. Cep'n Dusty oughta be there, behind the bar. She reached for Sim's hand and squinched her eyes to clear them.

Dusty wasn't there. The only man who'd really ever loved her—until now—was dead and buried at Opal Station in Australia, clean on t'other side of the world.

She'd tried to keep in touch, somehow, hoping she'd find some remnant of him in England, where he was born. Then she was sure he'd be waiting here, that if she just turned quick enough, she'd see him stepping around a corner with his jaunty walk.

It hadn't happened. She had to face the fact that he was nowhere on this earth, unless—

Unless he had got inside her mind, brung her all this way to meet another man, who'd love an' unnerstand her. It'd be jes' like th' sweet leetle bastard!

Her face lit with wonder and a glow that made her heavy features almost beautiful for a moment. Leaning toward Sim, she whispered to him coyly.

"Hell, Tam don't need to think she's got the on'y s'prise! Whatchu say we spring our news on 'em t'night?"

As Tamsen's guests waited for her descent, a third carriage drew near. Missie and Matthew had been delayed. Blaine, refusing to be separated from little Joshua on this magic eve, had picked him up at his sister-in-law's and brought him along. This night would be special for the child. Fearing he would be conspicuous because of his lameness, Matthew had kept him from public view. Now, he realized how wrong he had been. Joshua was cuddled in Missie's lap, his face turned trustingly to hers.

They looked, Matthew thought with a lump in his throat like a picture of the Madonna and Child.

Missie was so intent on the little boy in her arms, she didn't notice their route. When the carriage stopped, Blaine helped her down. It was still misting rain. Matthew took his son, and they ran, laughing, toward the house. Matthew knocked.

And Dan Tallant opened the door.

Missie froze.

Dan reached out and drew her inside. For a moment she was blinded by color and glitter after the darkness. Then she heard a small strangled cry.

Arab had recognized the small stylish stranger in the doorway. She had Missie's hair, Missie's blue eyes! This was the same little girl she had neglected so shamefully, whom she'd almost lost! Her Missie—

She took one halting step toward her daughter, another then began to run—

"Missie! Missie! Oh, dear God!"

She held her tightly, sobbing, almost unable to relinquish her to Juan. Em and Duke stood back, watching the reunion. Em frankly crying.

"I was afraid you'd be mad at me," Missie whispered, wiping her own streaming eyes. "The book—"

"The book is the best thing that ever happened to the McLeod daughters," Em said stepping forward. "And Arab will bear me out, when she can talk!"

Arab was still weeping, clinging to the daughter she'd loved the least; the daughter who had given her more than the others ever had.

Joshua had discovered the tree. He limped toward it, looking at its height in awe. Then he found the piano.

Dan watched him, admiring the lame child's courage.

"Em," he said, "why don't you play something for him? Maybe we can liven up the party, get rid of these tears."

Em crossed to the piano and thought for a moment, remembering back to her father's favorite.

"Black is the color of my true love's hair—"

Arab moved to her side and began to sing.

Missie's eyes widened. She knew where she was, now! This place was set down in her book, true to Dusty's description! *Madam Franklin's Parlor for Gentlemen!*

Fascinated, her eyes were drawn to the stair. There, in a crimson gown, stood Tamsen, smiling, young again—

It was her song. For Tamsen, the room shimmered. And suddenly the room was filled with awed gentlemen, all eyes drawn to the small figure on the stair. Tamsen felt the old, familiar surge of power at knowing she had them in the palm of her hand. She took one step, another—

The picture righted itself, and she saw only the faces of those she loved: Em and Duke, Arab and Juan, Nell and her charges—Missie!

Missie who had brought the family to its senses, and together, who had helped them to remember—

Then there was only Dan.

He stood at the foot of the stairs, looking upward, a world of love in his eyes, as his beloved, who had chosen him out of all the men in the world, came down to meet him.

ROMANCE...ADVENTURE...DANGER

DAUGHTERS OF THE SOUTHWIND
by Aola Vandergriff   *(D30-561, $3.50)*

The three McCleod sisters were beautiful, virtuous and bound to a dream —the dream of finding a new life in the untamed promise of the West. Their adventures in search of that dream provide the dimensions for this action-packed romantic bestseller.

DAUGHTERS OF THE WILD COUNTRY
by Aola Vandergriff   *(D30-562, $3.50)*

High in the North Country, three beautiful women begin new lives in a world where nature is raw, men are rough...and love, when it comes, shines like a gold nugget. Tamsen, Arab and Em McCleod now find themselves in Russian Alaska, where power, money and human life are the playthings of a displaced, decadent aristocracy in this lusty novel ripe with love, passion, spirit and adventure.

DAUGHTERS OF THE FAR ISLANDS
by Aola Vandergriff   *(D30-563, $3.50)*

Hawaii seems like Paradise to Tamsen and Arab—but it is not. Beneath the beauty, like the hot lava bubbling in the volcano's crater, trouble seethes in Paradise. The daughters are destined to be caught in the turmoil between Americans who want annexation of the islands and native Hawaiians who want to keep their country. And in their own family, danger looms...and threatens to erupt and engulf them all.

DAUGHTERS OF THE OPAL SKIES
by Aola Vandergriff   *(D30-564, $3.50)*

Tamsen Tallant, most beautiful of the McCleod sisters, is alone in the Australian outback. Alone with a ranch to run, two rebellious teenage nieces to care for, and Opal Station's new head stockman to reckon with —a man whose very look holds a challenge. But Tamsen is prepared for danger—for she has seen the face of the Devil and he looks like a man.